# Duty and Defiance

by

## John Selby

*Zanchee Chronicles, Book 1*

**Duty and Defiance**

Cover Art by *Debbie Taylor*

The Wild Rose Press, Inc.
PO Box 708
Adams Basin, NY 14410-0708
Visit us at www.thewildrosepress.com

Publishing History
First Mainstream Sci-Fi Rose Edition, 2020
Trade Paperback ISBN 978-1-5092-3217-8
Digital ISBN 978-1-5092-3218-5

*Zanchee Chronicles, Book 1*
Published in the United States of America

# Dedication

This book is dedicated to my family,
especially my wife, Holly,
my son Matt and my daughter Elizabeth.
Their encouragement and support
were essential to the completion of this book.

~

This book is also dedicated to
traditional science fiction fans everywhere—
especially those who grew up with Star Trek like I did.

~

In addition to the above, I dedicate this book
to those who refuse to let their dreams die
but instead put in the effort, hours,
and sacrifice necessary to make them a reality.

## Acknowledgments

First, I thank my wife, Holly, without whom this book would not be possible. She gave me the love, strength, support and motivation I needed during my fight with terminal cancer. Then she supported me when I decided to pursue my dream of writing, even though the average author makes about $1,000/year. She's also a pretty good editor.

My two children, Matthew and Elizabeth, were indispensable in the writing of this book. Not only did they provide good models, but their love, support, help and inspiration helped me through many tough times. Simply put, this book would not have happened without them. I love them, and my wife, dearly.

I also thank Alexandra Christle, whose editing advice has greatly shaped my writing, as well as the Southeast Writers Association and Florida Writers Association, both of whose conventions provided both badly needed training and inspiration. And I especially thank Dianne Rich, who took the chance on me and has been a wonderful editor and a pleasure to work with.

I want to thank the authors whose works entertained, consoled and inspired me in my youth and whose influence will be seen within. They include Gene Rodenberry, Robert Heinlein, Frank Herbert, George Lucas, E.E. "Doc" Smith, Madeleine L'Engle, Isaac Asimov, and many more.

Most of all, I dedicate this to you, the reader. May your love of reading never die.

# Chapter 1

*September 6th, D Minus 245.24 Hours*
*Dallas*

The saucer-shaped alien craft silently floated over the still city, like a hawk seeking its powerless prey. Allison's heart pounded against her chest as twin beams of death suddenly emanated from underneath the craft, destroying whatever they touched in a crimson blaze of glory. Buildings, cars, and people instantly disintegrated in the intense heat generated by the beam's Satanic touch. Blackened remains charred beyond recognition littered the streets in their wake. The beams' loud eerie hum provided background to the din of explosions, buildings collapsing, and people screaming. Relentless, the red beams of Hell continued their rain of destruction as the craft glided on, unimpeded and unperturbed. Death followed.

She desperately searched for an escape. The roads were clogged with vehicles frantically trying to flee but failing. People poured from the burning buildings, some with their clothes on fire, as panic and chaos reigned supreme. Some of the condemned cried with overwhelming grief, while others simply stood and gazed up at their airborne executioner. Gunshots echoed, firing fruitlessly at the giant invaders hovering so seemingly serenely over the city.

Spotting a subway entrance, Allison ran toward it, only to be caught in the surging crowd. The blazing beams crept closer…

"Jeff, will you *please* turn that racket off!"

Ignoring the plea from his intruding mother, Jeff continued watching, transfixed by the chaos emanating from the screen a few feet in front of him.

"Jeff, do you *hear* me?" Sue Miller took a few steps toward the family room, threatening an immediate end to his viewing. "*JEFF*!" she said in a voice better not ignored.

"Ah, Mom, it's just getting to the good part," he pleaded. "The aliens are destroying New York!" Jeff exclaimed, eyes still glued to the screen. Another skyscraper disappeared.

"You know I don't like you watching all that crap on TV—it's rotting what's left of your mind."

"Yeah, but it's New York! That doesn't really count, does it? I thought you hated New York." Not getting any indication of sympathy, he continued. "Don't you want to see it get melted into a gigantic parking lot?" His main attention didn't waver from the flickering scenes of alien devastation in front of him.

"Some other time, perhaps. Right now, I need you to go pick up your sister from soccer practice. Besides, I know you've probably seen this movie at least a dozen times." Her voice changed its pitch. She was getting serious. "Of course, since it is Labor Day, the other alternative will be for us to find some actual labor for you to do around the house…like bulldozing your room."

"Oh, all right." Further protests would be in vain.

He clicked the TV off in a dramatic show of surrender, but not before hitting "record." He then tossed the remote onto the couch, where it would no doubt disappear.

Jeff scanned the room for his shoes. When Mom was in one of *those* moods, which she appeared to be in now, there was no point arguing—even though he often did. One of his tennis shoes peeked out from under the couch. The other was not to be seen. The main reason against arguing this time was to keep his mom from coming farther into the family room. If she did, no doubt cleaning it would be added to his chores. A slight smile creased his lips. However, he still had to find the other shoe.

"Can I go to the mall after dropping her off? I told Greg I would meet him there," Jeff called out as he searched. The fact Tess would also be at the mall was only a happy coincidence.

"All right, as long as you're back by six. I have a nice dinner for us tonight…Why don't you see if Becca wants to go with you?"

"Uh, yeah, right, Mom. Get real."

"Jeff…she is your sister."

"Don't remind me." Jeff sighed. Truthfully, he didn't mind taking Becca to the mall, not that he would ever admit it. She was finally past the age where she clung to her older brother like an unwanted zit. Now she hung out with her own friends who were also loitering around the mall. Besides, it gave him an opportunity to watch out for her. He cared a great deal for his sister and felt protective of her.

"All right…I'll, uh, we'll be back by six."

He pushed his ever-sliding glasses back up his

nose. The thick glasses only added to his nerdy reputation, yet he couldn't stand putting things in his eyes, ruling out contacts.

"Thanks."

Pushing aside a collection of clothes and unopened schoolbooks, he finally found the missing mischievous shoe hiding underneath the overturned Monopoly game, victim of his sister's sportsmanship at this morning's battle. Monopoly had been a family ritual ever since Jeff was old enough to count, although now the battles were usually only between Jeff and his sister—often with the rules augmented with their own innovations. He quickly slipped the shoes on over his bare feet. He didn't bother with socks—after all, it really was a beautiful day.

On his way outside, Jeff paused in the kitchen long enough to lighten the cupboard of a half-dozen cookies. Two were popped directly in his mouth. The other four went crumbling into one of the oversized pockets on his shorts. The cookies would not hold his appetite off for long, but he didn't feel like carrying the refrigerator around. Besides, he could grab something at the food court when he got there. With the cookies, he could survive at least thirty minutes without more food.

Jeff glanced at his watch. It was only 1:05. His friends said they would meet at the Oak Park Mall around 2:00, so he had plenty of time to get Becca. The mall was strictly a social gathering spot as he never bought anything other than food and an occasional gift for his girlfriend, Tess. He had to pinch pennies. Every cent Jeff earned while working at Aberfinches during the summer went to supporting four wheels, his cellphone—and his meager social life. And now, his parents would not allow him to work during the school year to earn extra money. It wasn't fair. He could handle a part-time job and school at the same time.

Jeff scoured the kitchen countertop for his car keys. He threw them up there somewhere when he came home last night after his date with Tess. He pushed aside the piles of his mom's papers, magazines, and whatnot stacked haphazardly about the countertop. Evidence he wasn't the only organizationally challenged person in the family brought a smile to his lips. Finally, a tinkling sound indicated he was getting close. After a little more digging, he uncovered his keys.

He headed out through the garage. His car was parked down the driveway, far enough back so his mother and father could get around it when driving into or out from the garage.

That was another thing bothering him. Everyone else at school had nice cars their parents bought for them. Not him. His parents said they couldn't afford it. So, he had to buy his own—a now twelve-year-old Ford Escort, two-tone—sort of blue, sort of rust colored—as in real rust—complete with plush ripped-cloth stained interior. It had enough miles on it to make it to the moon. But it still ran, and his parents helped with the insurance—which was a good thing, because that wasn't cheap.

Even though they couldn't afford to buy him a new car, his parents were happy when he got his driver's license. Now he knew why…so he could do all sorts of errands—like picking up his fourteen-year-old sister from soccer practice.

\*\*\*\*

Becca's soccer practice was at Dirkson High School, which both he and his sister attended. Jeff was now a senior and Becca a lowly freshman. Despite his teasing to the contrary, it was nice having Becca there. She said it meant a lot having him show her the ropes.

Unlike him, Becca had tons of friends. She was popular at school and easily made friends with her bubbly outgoing personality. Everyone liked her. In contrast, he had a few close friends and never really fit in with the crowd. But that's okay. He wasn't fond of groups anyway.

Speaking of crowds, there wasn't one on the soccer field when he arrived. In fact, there wasn't anyone on it at all. Strange. The dashboard clock read 1:20. Practice was supposed to run till 1:30. Could they have ended this early? Now that he thought of it, why were they practicing on Labor Day, anyway? Had Becca gotten confused? Or had she lied about the practice? If so, why?

He texted her. Getting no response, he dialed her phone, but there was no answer. Frustrated, he parked the car and got out to scan the area. There was no one to be seen anywhere. Weird. The best option now was to drive around the block to see if she might be at some local hangouts.

As he turned the corner onto Waco Boulevard, the Stop In convenience store, a local hangout for students, came into view. A small group of teens were clustered off to the side of the store. One of them was shorter than the rest, with blonde hair and wearing a soccer uniform and backpack. Two of the kids, both boys, towered over everyone. One, in fact, looked big enough to be an offensive lineman in the NFL.

Jeff continued to stare at the two taller boys as he approached. Something was familiar about the smaller of the two. He peered through his thick glasses trying to make out who it was and what they and his sister were doing.

"Oh my God!" Jeff exclaimed aloud as both recognition of the boy and realization of what was happening hit him. He was none other than Steve Michaels, a kid about his age who dropped out of school last year. The new cherry-red Miata parked near them was probably his, as Michaels was rumored to be a dealer who preyed particularly hard on freshmen at Dirkson.

And that appeared to be what he was doing now. Michaels held what looked to be a baggie filled with a fine white powder. It wasn't likely flour in the bag. What's worse, Becca was reaching around for her backpack and the money probably hidden within.

"No!" Jeff screamed at his sister through the windshield as he stepped on the gas, turning left in front of an onrushing car in the other lane. Tires screeched and horns blared, but he managed to swerve and avoid being hit as he squealed into the parking lot.

Jeff had to get Becca out of there. That was his only thought as his Escort headed toward the group…going a bit too fast. He slammed on the brakes, causing even louder screeching. The kids jumped out of the way of the oncoming murderous machine. Becca's eyes grew wide as she leaped back then recognized whose car was hurtling recklessly toward her.

Jeff's car had lost most of its speed when it hit the curb…most, but not all. The vehicle continued moving forward, ramming a trashcan overflowing with garbage in the process.

The rest of the scene played out in slow motion. The trashcan flew into the air, with the lid coming off and trash spewing forth...all making a direct line for Michaels, who reacted in even slower motion.

As the trash made its majestic way toward the too slow-moving Michaels, Jeff reached over to the passenger's door handle. Yanking it, he flung the door open shouting, "Becca, get in here *now*!"

Ok, so this wasn't exactly the best plan, but you make do with what you're dealt. "BECCA! NOW!"

Likely reacting more reflexively than with thought, Becca headed toward the open door. Her shocked expression showed her surprise not only from his sudden appearance but also from the grandiosity of his entrance.

Jeff's eyes focused on his sister as he emphatically implored her to get into his car with both his voice and his waving arms. However, he couldn't help smiling as the contents of the trashcan impacted on Michaels and his mammoth friend, who were now coated with remnants of old newspapers, paper cups—some with soft drinks still in them—cans, coffee, gum, half-eaten candy bars, crumbs, and the wrappings the above came in, plus a hodge-podge of other gooey stuff. As the junk hit him, Michaels instinctively jerked his hands up to cover his face. That caused the white powdery substance neatly contained within the plastic baggie to also exit the scene. Said powder had an affinity for Michaels as it too sought him out, adding a fine white coat on top of the now moist dealer.

The grin spread across Jeff's face as he took in the sight. It was quickly replaced with apprehension as he considered what Michaels' reaction was likely to be. Thankfully, both Michaels and his friend were slow to respond. They were still recovering from the shock and soak when Becca reached the car. Jeff, realizing the pair wouldn't stay frozen forever, slammed the car in reverse and hit the gas as soon as Becca began closing her door. Fortunately, she hung on—barely—and quickly buckled her seat belt.

Laying an additional coat of rubber on top of what he recently deposited on the asphalt, Jeff peeled out of the parking lot. As he did so, Michaels, whose reddened face spoke of unabashed anger and embarrassment, rushed after the escaping Escort, yelling obscenities and threats as he did so.

Jeff did not wait for Michaels to catch up. Instead, he forced his way into the traffic to the din of horns blasting at his abrupt entry. Trying to keep one eye on the road, Jeff risked a quick glance in the rearview mirror. He saw Michaels scramble into his Miata convertible, scattering kids as he went. Jeff stepped on the gas.

Becca, who sat in shocked silence, stared at her brother. However, any questions she might have never escaped her throat. No doubt her greatest current concern had become simply surviving the ride home.

Like most every teenager, Jeff had visions of exciting car chases, squealing tires, and racing through town in a life-or-death situation. But now that it was happening, it didn't seem so lit. Any excitement he might have felt was tempered by terror. Adrenaline surged through his system, heightening his awareness and quickening his reflexes.

Knowing Michaels was not far behind and had a

far faster, more maneuverable car, his best course of action was to elude rather than race. So, he took the first right-hand turn possible, tires yelling their protest at the sudden change of direction, followed quickly by his sister's similar sounding squeal.

As soon as the car completed its 90-degree change of direction, Jeff began looking for his next turn. There was an alleyway about 100 yards ahead.

Fortunately, there was no oncoming traffic, so he swerved to the left before turning right, allowing him to make the turn a bit faster, as the alleyway was narrow. Again, tires and sister protested noisily.

Jeff's hope for a clean getaway was dashed as Michaels' Miata made the turn onto the street as he and Becca started down the alleyway. His sister's *"watch out"* shout returned his attention immediately to the alleyway ahead.

Jeff barely had time to slam the brakes, sending both him and Becca ramming into the seat belt straps, likely earning them a sore souvenir of the day's adventure.

Even though Jeff stomped on the brakes, they still hit the rather large speed bump moving too fast, jarring the car and its occupants more. As the seat belt dug into his lap, the top of his head banged into the low-hanging roof, an impact which would leave another rather painful reminder of the day's events. Hopefully his car would survive as it rattled and protested loudly.

Michaels was gaining, so Jeff pressed his foot down on the accelerator as soon as his head stopped bobbing. However, the alleyway turned sharply to the left up ahead, so he once again had to step on the brakes and brace for the turn. Before turning, he chanced a glance back. What he saw almost made the whole episode worthwhile.

Apparently, Michaels had not seen the speed bump either, at least not in time. When the tiny car hit the bump, it briefly became Air-Miata. Michaels, however, wasn't wearing a seat belt, so he failed to return to the ground at the same time as the car. He flew out of his seat with a look of terror, shock, and anger etched on his face. Michaels managed to stay connected to the Miata only because of his death grip on the steering wheel. However, he was unable to keep the wheels straight. So, when the front tires of the car once again hit the pavement, they took off on a slightly different course than before.

Michaels, while still airborne, tried to adjust the car's direction by turning the wheel sharply…too sharply. So instead of plowing into the fence on the left side of the alleyway, the Miata, whose speed fortunately had slowed considerably, now careened into a bank of trashcans on the right side of the alleyway. Because of the Miata's low profile, one of the trashcans was sent rolling over on top of the hood of the car, making its way up the windshield and into the open passenger compartment, where it proceeded to disgorge itself of its contents on the interior of the car and the hapless driver inside.

Prudence dictated not hanging around to see if Michaels was okay. Michaels hadn't hit anything hard enough to sustain a serious injury to anything other than his pride. Jeff also didn't want to learn how long it might take Michaels to recover enough to regain pursuit. So, taking advantage of Michaels' momentary incapacity, he turned the corner and disappeared.

\*\*\*\*

After making enough turns to get them dizzy, Jeff was satisfied they eluded their tormentor, for now. However, Michaels likely knew whom he was chasing. Thankfully, he was not known to carry any weapon other than the "missing link" that always seemed to accompany him. But it did mean Jeff probably hadn't seen the last of him.

As his heart rate slowed to mere racing, Jeff pulled over to the side of the road and turned to face his still silent sister.

"What the hell were you thinking?" Jeff angrily asked.

"Why the hell did you do that!" Becca retorted in a mix of sobs and screeches.

"Because I didn't want you to do anything *stupid*. That's why."

"Yeah, as though driving around like a drunken renegade cowboy, riling Michaels and his goon in the process, was an act of sheer genius." Jeff flinched at that one. "Besides, what I do is my own business."

"Not when it involves drugs, it isn't," Jeff replied, matching her agitated voice and trying to regain the upper hand.

"I can take care of myself." Becca's blue eyes blazed in indignation.

"I saw how you were taking care of yourself."

"I don't need you to tell me what to do, thank you very much," Becca responded tersely. She started to open the car door.

Jeff reached over and grabbed her arm, preventing her escape. "You don't want to do that," he said sternly.

"What do you know about what I want? Let go of

me," Becca demanded.

Her eyes blazed with the fury burning within. His own eyes were equally ablaze. He wanted to scream at her. But he didn't. That would only make her more defiant and less likely to ever listen to him again. He could not afford for that to happen.

Jeff recalled his own ambivalence toward drugs. The yearning to experiment—to try something different—something forbidden—something exciting. But he refrained. It wasn't easy as so many of his classmates took drugs of varying sorts and touted the attributes of the latest and greatest to anyone who listened and to many who didn't. His refusal to submit helped further ostracize him from a lot of his classmates.

But then David died. David had been one of Jeff's best friends since grade school. Accidental overdose was what they called it. Whatever. His death cemented Jeff's mind forever. Happily, most of his close friends felt the same way. But now his sister…

The thought made him almost physically sick. But he couldn't take it out on her. Nor could he control her or watch over her shoulder every minute.

Jeff looked back at Becca, this time with compassion and understanding. He loosened his grip.

"We'll talk about it later."

Becca stared back at her brother for a long time. His eyes never wavered. Slowly the fire in her eyes dimmed.

"Becca, just promise me this. You'll stay away from Michaels."

Slowly, she nodded.

Chapter 2

The *Druize,* massive flagship of the Zanchee alliance fleet, orbited unobserved 10,000 miles above the beautiful ball called Earth. The ship harbored thousands of adult crewmembers, representing some thirty-odd different species…and one teenager—son of the Fleet commander, Axelasome.

Axel, short for Axelarone, anxiously paced back and forth around the anteroom to his father's office, awaiting word his father was finally free and would see him. His cat-like mentiot companion, Chermal, rubbed up against his legs, trying to reassure him and silently reminding him to keep cool and calm. It wasn't working.

Speaking to his father was never easy. Part of it was his age. Most nescreets, or preadults, his age had difficulty "talking" with their parents, as conversations with his friends confirmed. But it was especially difficult talking to *his* father. After all, he was Thermax of the entire Zanchee Alliance fleet in this sector. Virtually everyone had difficulty talking to him, let alone his son.

His father was very demanding. He had high

14

expectations for his son and was not shy about showing it. That was why Axel was on the *Druize* in the first place. His father wanted an active role in shaping his Nemseck, the Delion ritual test of adulthood determining Axel's future path.

The knot in Axel's stomach tightened more. He was used to his belly complaining, but usually due to a lack of food—despite an almost constant ingestion of foodstuff. But this time it responded to the anxiety over the inevitable paternal confrontation.

It was so simple, so reasonable. He just wanted to know exactly when his Nemseck was going to be and at least a hint as to what he would have to do for it. Was that too much to ask? Or maybe he would be allowed to go home for a short vacation to visit his mom, sister, and friends. He needed a break, having gone non-stop now on board the ship for six months.

His father seemed oblivious to the fact not one of the forty-odd thousand Alliance members in the fleet were his age—not counting the Branglee, who only lived to be twenty-two—let alone any on the *Druize*. In fact, there probably wasn't anyone within four years of his age, especially among the Delions. He certainly was the only nescreet. He longed for someone his age to talk to—to hang with. After all, he was still a nescreet, at least until his Nemseck, and wanted to take advantage of his remaining childhood—before it slipped away forever.

Axel imagined the scene to come. His father would look at him thoughtfully, the ridges on his forehead moving closer together. Then he would move nearer, possibly put his hands on Axel's shoulders and state, "Axel you know why you're here, don't you? You are special." He would take a dramatic pause, then no doubt mention the Nescian, his master teacher of both the physical and spiritual worlds.

"Your Nescian agrees. Thus, your Nemseck must be special." Translation—'more arduous and painful than anyone else's.' Why couldn't he be normal? Why couldn't his father be an ordinary dad and not the Thermax?

Axel's eyes narrowed as he chanced a glance at the door leading to his father's inner office. Soon it would open. His father was meeting with his second in command, Centasome. *They had been in there for over an hour, which was highly unusual.* Curiosity now overcame impatience. *What could they possibly be discussing for so long? Although I wouldn't put it past my father to make me cool my heels, no way would Father keep Centasome so long unless it was something extremely important.*

Axel looked down at Chermal, who still rubbed up against his legs. The faux feline, his soft brown-and-blue fur covering him head to toe, looked up at him with his round aqua eyes that radiated both intelligence and compassion. Obviously, he didn't have a clue as to what the meeting was about, either. That said something. Not many things could be kept secret from his mentiot.

Finally, the door slid open and Centasome stormed out, his furrowed brows and quickened gait betraying agitation. Axel's father stood at the doorway, shaking his head slowly, then gradually raising his eyes to meet Axel's pensive stare. There was something in his father's eyes he had rarely seen before. They were...sad. Something clearly and profoundly had upset him…which was doubly not good. Whatever bothered his father must be very serious. This was definitely *not* the time to be approaching him for favors.

Axel stood quietly for a second or two, trying to come up with something to say, since the original reason for his requested meeting now suddenly was unimportant. Fortunately, his father saved him the embarrassment.

"Axel, I'm sorry. Something urgent has come up requiring my immediate attention. I can't meet with you today." His father came over to him and gazed deeply into his eyes. "You know this must be important for me to cancel our meeting at the last minute. Trust me, it is. Unfortunately, the nature of the emergency is such I cannot tell you about it.

"I will see you as soon as I can. In the meantime, I'm sure your Nescian can see to your needs." And with that, his father strode purposefully into the hallway, leaving Axel alone and confused…and very curious. Axel's father had uncharacteristically left the inner door to his office open, providing him an unheard-of opportunity. Maybe he could discover what this "emergency" was all about. Perhaps things wouldn't be so boring after all.

Axel sent a mental command to Chermal to be ultra-alert and let him know if anyone approached. Such a command was not necessary, as Chermal likely anticipated the need. The coast was clear. Axel glanced down again at his furry friend, expecting to be reprimanded for what he planned to do. But, surprisingly, none was forthcoming. Axel took that as a tacit approval and headed toward the inner door.

Cautiously, as though fearing a trap, Axel crept

into his father's office. "Office," though, was an inadequate term. It was more a cross between a control room, workplace, and sanctuary. The Thermax, his father, could control the entire fleet from this room, should the need arise. An unrestricted QUAIC terminal provided his father with unfettered access to the ship's powerful quantum computers, as well as those on Delios. Control pads were on his desk and at several stations around the office. A 3-D holographic viewport adjoined the desk. Axel studied the image and recognized the area being shown as "California" in human terms. In fact, the image was of the southern part of the state over the city of Los Angeles from a perspective of 500 miles in the air.

Axel's father loved his work. But more than that, he was really enamored with the humans they studied.

Whatever upset his father most likely involved Earth—and probably humans. Perhaps they learned of some new plague that would kill several thousand people…a plague the Zanchee could cure with little more than a snap of the fingers. Axel imagined the pain his father would bear watching tragedy befall a sentient race knowing the Zanchee could prevent it but were forbidden to do so. It also impacted Axel, but he was not nearly as invested in the humans. For him, they were something he studied…a curiosity perhaps, a lesson definitely.

Axel moved over to the QUAIC terminal. Could he be so lucky? Was it possible his father hadn't cleared the terminal? There was one way to find out.

He sat in the contoured seat of the terminal. To Axel's amazement, his mind was instantly flooded with images. His father had not cleared it.

Not daring to breathe, lest they fade away, Axel sorted through the massive amount of information flowing into his brain. Whatever upset his father would be here.

His attention was drawn to a report from the forecasting department. They were extrapolating on various events occurring on earth below. Skimming the report, he hurried to the conclusions.

"NOOOO!" Axel shouted. The terminal went blank.

Chapter 3

*September 7th, D Minus 215.48 Hours*
*Monterrey, Mexico*

Special Agent Doug Stanton unwrapped his last piece of gum and stuffed it in his mouth as he wiped the newly formed sweat off his brow. It was unbelievably hot, although it was to be expected since he was in Monterrey, Mexico, and it was still summer. He should be used to the heat, having followed his "suspect" from Tehran, as well as living in Dallas, but he wasn't. It didn't matter how "dry" it was, 105 degrees Fahrenheit was just plain hot. Doug suspected FBI Deputy Director Stinson, head of the anti-terrorist task force, had a dark sense of humor. Why else station someone from Minneapolis to Dallas then assign him duty in the desert—in the summer?

Doug briefly ran his hands through his sandy-brown hair, trying in vain to smooth it down. His hair naturally tended to go every which way, as though each strand had its own mind. He rarely paid it much attention, which only contributed to the problem. His lack of vanity may have contributed to his being assigned desert duty, rather than some nice air-conditioned undercover work in some high-tech wall street business. He certainly didn't fit the James Bond stereotype of a spy. Heck, he didn't even like martinis.

Doug looked down at his tablet, which had been specially programmed by the agency. On the display was a detailed map of the block he was on. A blue dot indicated his current location, in his rental car on some nondescript side street. A red dot indicated his target, suspected terrorist Abdul Raheim, in the hotel across the street.

Doug smiled slyly. What would Abdul think if he knew he had the Bureau's latest hi-tech tracking device surgically implanted within his belly? How convenient Abdul had acute appendicitis while supposedly secretly visiting New York. The little powder surreptitiously slipped into his bottled water may have had something to do with his urgent visit to the hospital. Serendipitously, an ambulance "happened" to be nearby when Abdul had his "attack."

It was fortunate Raheim had no idea the US government knew he was in the country, as he went to great lengths to sneak in. However, one of Doug's colleagues got lucky and spotted him. Even in this world of high technology, luck still played an important role.

Doug checked for the tenth time to make sure the camera on his lap was completely charged. The camera, which looked like an ordinary tourist-type Nikon, was anything but. It took high-res digital photos and transmitted them instantly via satellite to the FBI lab in DC. There, the photos could be immediately enhanced and analyzed by the top experts in the field. Copies of the images were also stored in the camera so Doug could review them at his leisure.

Yes, technology made his job easier. Yet it still

hadn't answered the million-dollar question—what was Abdul Raheim, head of one of the most violent Arab terrorist groups, The United Arab Freedom Front, doing in Monterrey? It certainly wasn't to get out of the hot sun. And it was highly unlikely he was here on vacation, either. Whatever it was, no doubt it wasn't good for the United States. The UAFF had picked the US as public enemy number one. But this was more than simple political expediency. Abdul acted like he had a pure hatred for the US and everything American.

Stanton stared at the tablet. The red dot had started to move. He traced Abdul's route as he made his way from his room, down the hall to the elevator, and from there to the front lobby. Doug started his car, in case Abdul had a vehicle waiting for him. He didn't. Instead, Stanton watched as Raheim exited the hotel and came into view. He looked around casually before heading down the street on foot. Abdul was dressed in a business suit, rather than as a tourist. Interesting. He raised his camera and took a couple quick shots.

Doug had to make a quick decision. He could follow in the car, but it might attract undue attention, given how slowly he would be moving. Or he could go on foot, risking instead Raheim getting into a car around the corner. He sighed. That was the downside of all the new high-tech equipment. To pay for the equipment, or perhaps justify its expense, the department felt it necessary to reduce manpower. So, while there used to be at least three men assigned to a job like this, Doug was forced to go it alone.

He remained in the car, at least for the time being. Raheim rounded the corner, so Doug followed his progress on the screen. When he had gone about a block, Doug eased the car around the corner and looked for a place to park. The dot continued moving down the street. He was not visible from where Doug was, but he was not concerned. The dot was moving at walking pace and the signal was strong.

After proceeding for three blocks, the dot stopped. Doug quickly shifted into gear and drove past the spot. Apparently, Abdul was hungry, as he had stepped inside a *restaurante*. Doug quickly found a nearby parking spot, grabbed the camera, and headed there. He put away the tablet and put on his "coolest" shades, with the camera slung casually over his shoulder. He looked, he hoped, like any other tourist. He certainly couldn't pass for a native. But, then again, neither could Raheim.

The *restaurante* Raheim chose was a typical, touristy type of place, which was fortunate for Doug. However, it was also apparently a hangout for area businessmen, as there were quite a few sprinkled about. It figured Abdul would adopt a business motif as there were not likely many Arab tourists in Monterrey. But what "business" could the terrorist be transacting?

One of the advantages of the sunglasses Doug wore was he could move his eyes around and scan the restaurant without moving his head much and drawing attention. As he casually glanced around, he spotted his target out of the corner of his eye being seated at a table in the back. He was, for the moment, alone.

The lounge area fortunately provided him with a view of Raheim's table. If he chanced being seated at a table in the main dining area, it might be in a completely wrong location for spying on the terrorist and asking for a different table could attract undue attention. Doug casually strolled to an empty booth in the lounge. Once seated, he was almost immediately greeted by an attentive server. This was not too surprising as locals were eager to assist American tourists, who were known to be good tippers. Once seated, he surreptitiously hit a button on his camera, setting it to automatically take a picture every five seconds. It did so silently. Then Doug set it on his table aimed in the general direction of Abdul's table, but not directly at it. Its wide-angle lens would take in Abdul's table just fine, and its high resolution would allow the analysts to count the hairs on his beard, if needed.

Although Doug spoke fluent Spanish, he often found it convenient to play the ignorant tourist. So, he ordered in English—slowing his speech to a ridiculous pace, as though thinking if someone couldn't understand English, somehow speaking louder and slower would magically allow that person to know what he was saying. He also intentionally mispronounced several menu items. While it was likely all the servers spoke English, he noted with amusement some chose not to show that fact. His server, though, politely responded in perfect English.

Doug was also lucky to have an attractive server, who was very friendly—almost flirtatious. This made his job easier, if not more enjoyable. Doug quickly drained his Mexican lager and was promptly given another. Raheim still sat alone but was fidgeting. Obviously, he was not a man used to being kept waiting.

Doug continued his boorish behavior—talking loudly and drunkenly to the waitress and anyone who came close to his table. The more obnoxious he was, the more likely he would be ignored by Raheim. It worked, as the terrorist never gave him a glance.

Raheim's wait was not long. While Doug pontificated the virtues of the Vikings to another American tourist that happened to walk by, Raheim was joined by four other men. Three were obviously bodyguards. Interestingly, none looked Mexican, but rather Central American. The fourth and obvious leader dripped with jewelry and expensive custom-tailored clothes. He looked very familiar, but Doug could not place him.

Okay, showtime.

Doug picked up his camera, setting it back to manual, and started shooting pictures of his American "friend". The first shot was toward the bar. But then his waitress came by, and he grabbed her, imploring, loudly, he wanted her picture as well. This time, he positioned her so Raheim's table was in the background. As he suspected, they totally ignored the boorish American tourist, and he happily snapped away.

It was hard for Doug to maintain his act when he focused in on Abdul's "guest." As he got a clearer view of him, Doug easily identified him as Rico Bivardo, the leader of the Bogotá drug cartel. No wonder he had not initially recognized him. It never crossed his mind an Arab terrorist would meet with a drug cartel leader.

Doug put his camera down, leaving it indirectly pointing at the terrorist's table, set it to record every ten seconds, then bought his tourist "friend" a beer. He toasted American football and its superiority over Mexican "football," or soccer as it was known in the States. But his mind raced. What on earth was an Arab terrorist leader doing meeting with the leader of the Bogotá Drug Cartel? And why in Monterrey? Whatever they were meeting about could not be good. He only wished the "bug" planted in Raheim contained a microphone as well as a tracking device. No doubt, future generation "bugs" would be so equipped.

He had a powerful microphone built into his camera. However, to use it required pointing the camera directly at the group, a risky move. And because it wasn't aimed directly at him, the background noise made it difficult to hear Abdul clearly. While the boys in the lab would be able to do so eventually, it would not help him now.

Not wanting to risk staring at the table, Doug used quick glances out of the corner of his eye to keep track of Raheim while he chatted with his fellow American tourist and dined on the meal that had materialized before him. During one glance, he saw Bivardo nod briefly, then pull a cellphone out of his pocket. Bivardo put the phone back in his pocket before any trace was possible. Apparently Raheim told Bivardo what he wanted to hear, causing him to give a quick command via the cellphone.

Doug did not have long to think about it though, as Raheim and his three "guests" quickly got up and left the *restaurante*. As he could follow them on his tablet, thanks to Abdul's bug, Doug waited a couple minutes before he flagged down his server to settle his tab. He was glad he waited. He almost missed it.

Someone else had been seated near Raheim's table. His back had been to Doug, so he had not recognized him. But, shortly after the terrorist left, the tall blond gentleman also rose. After glancing around the room, he followed Abdul and his three companions out the door. Doug only caught a glimpse of him. But it was enough to immediately recognize the man. Victor Krenchenko, formerly a Russian spy for the KGB, was one of the last people he expected to see in Monterrey. His face was well known to him, though, as he had been assigned to investigate the Russian mafia before being abruptly pulled off the case to be put on this one. How ironic both cases suddenly came together. He hoped the former KGB Associate Director had not recognized him.

The mystery deepened. The FBI believed Krenchenko was currently very high in the Russian mafia. Was the organization more interested in Raheim or in Bivardo? Or both? Was Krenchenko following them, simply spying on them, or meeting with them? The latter thought was the scariest. It was bad enough the UAFF leader met with a Colombian drug cartel, but what did the Russian mob have to do with either of them? Then again, back in his KGB days, Krenchenko was supposedly buddy buddy with the Russian President. Was this a government sanctioned visit?

Even without Russian government involvement, the thought of these three already formidable organizations teaming up...an involuntary shudder shook his spine. Something was up. Something big. And his instincts were rarely wrong.

All this flashed through his mind as he paid his tab. Doug forced himself to remain calm and professional. He smiled at the cashier as he casually put his wallet away. His instinct was to run after them, but they were long gone. Yet they were not lost, thanks to the "bug".

Doug snapped a few pictures of the outside of the

*restaurante*, to maintain his cover as he nonchalantly made his way to his car. Given Krenchenko was involved, Doug had to be especially careful. His former adversary was no slouch.

As soon as he climbed into his rental car, Doug pulled out his tablet. The red dot was already about two miles away and moving quickly. Since Raheim's rental car was back at the hotel, he was either with Bivardo or Krenchenko—or both. Doug turned the key and started his own car, an older model Toyota Camry.

Before pulling away in pursuit, he quickly accessed the SatLink file on Rico Bivardo. When the file came up Doug let out a long, low whistle. Bivardo's organization had been recently stung severely by the DEA. LXA, Inc., one of the major money-laundering companies used by Bivardo, was seized, and all its American assets frozen. Because of these actions, it was estimated Bivardo lost over $400 million. The DEA also attempted to seize another one of Bivardo's companies, Transdigital, but Bivardo's attorneys were so far able to block the action, due to the complexity of ownership and Bivardo's seeming indirect involvement.

Another cold shiver went down his spine. That meant all three of these very powerful men had a deep hatred for the US, or at least the US government. That they were now possibly getting together was not good. Not good at all. His dread ratcheted up.

Doug shifted the car into gear and headed out in pursuit. He couldn't afford to let them get too far away.

Raheim headed toward the main business section of Monterrey. Doug kept one eye on the tablet while negotiating the busy streets. It was not an easy task watching both the blip and the road at the same time.

Due to erratic traffic, with taxis weaving in and out, he had to pay close attention to the road, unless his mission, along with him, be prematurely terminated. Unfortunately, he had no idea what kind of vehicle Raheim was in, knowing only the red dot was moving about 50 kph through the city streets.

After avoiding what seemed like a certain accident, he glanced at the tablet screen only to discover the absence of the telltale red blip. He was so shaken by its disappearance he nearly had a wreck as he stared at the screen. He pulled over to the closest parking lot where he examined the screen in detail.

Doug first did a diagnostic check, which revealed everything was still working properly. This meant, for whatever reason, the tablet no longer received a signal from Raheim. Since the tracker's signal was relayed via satellite, it was highly unlikely to be out of range. It was possible Raheim went underground, or inside a shielded building, which could block the signal. This was the most logical conclusion. So, he replayed the past ten minutes of tracking. The program highlighted the route Raheim took, allowing Doug to retrace his steps.

He watched as the blip stopped and started again and again, apparently in conjunction with the city's traffic lights. Finally, it stopped, only this time when it started, it was at a slow pace—a walking pace. It proceeded for about fifty feet, and then abruptly disappeared.

Doug zoomed in on the address, and then accessed a sat photo, discovering the location was home to a rather unremarkable warehouse. But unless it had a tunnel underneath, or was built of lead, a warehouse should not shield Abdul's signal from him.

Doug put the car back into gear. With a little more urgency than previously, he made his way back into the heavy traffic. He had to get to that warehouse quickly. He needed to know what had happened.

\*\*\*\*

Stanton looked around with utter dismay. The warehouse was absolutely deserted. There was no sign anyone had been here in the past several months, let alone in the past hour. Where could they have gone?

It also did not make sense the warehouse lock was so easy to pick. If this was a secret base, there should have been more security. Yet there was not so much as a camera. He checked his tablet and noted it had a clear link to the satellite, meaning the building wasn't shielded. So, if there were no secret hiding places or underground passages, and the building wasn't shielded, what happened to the signal? More importantly, what happened to Raheim?

As Doug headed toward the loading dock, he stopped and sniffed. There was a faint odor. He took a few steps closer to the bay door and sniffed again. Now he could identify the smell. Diesel fuel. There had been a truck here. That must have been what happened to Raheim—he got on the truck. But why did Doug lose his signal?

Could Raheim have found the device? No, removing it required surgery, which could not possibly have been accomplished in the time it took Doug to get here.

Doug continued to search the building for clues. It appeared they only used this building for a quick rendezvous, or whoever was here did a thorough job of cleaning up. Other than the faint smell of diesel fuel he detected, there was no evidence anyone was here recently.

He was about to leave when he spotted a cigarette butt on the floor by the bay door. He bent over to pick it up and examine it. Barely noticeable on the butt was a word written in Cyrillic. The cigarette was Russian. That meant, in all probability, Krenchenko was meeting with Raheim, not just following him.

It was at that moment luck intervened. The tablet beeped, indicating it regained the signal from Raheim. He quickly accessed the microcomputer to see where his target was now. He determined Raheim was at a small airstrip outside of town, before the dot disappeared again.

Cursing the dot's disappearance, Doug hustled back to his car and headed to the airstrip as quickly as possible. While driving, he racked his brain trying to deduce why Raheim's dot disappeared, and then reappeared only to disappear again.

The dot moving from the warehouse to the airstrip confirmed Raheim was not underground. It also meant he had not been surrounded by five feet of concrete for the past hour. But why had the signal disappeared, then suddenly reappeared? Was the device malfunctioning? Or was there something in the truck blocking the signal? That required either thick walls, or sophisticated electromagnetic meshing, or lead lining. But why? What were they hiding? Doug had no answer. The feeling of dread increased.

****

Doug arrived at the airstrip some fifteen minutes later. Accessing the tablet, he zeroed in on where the dot last appeared. As it turned out, it was a bathroom in the back of one of the hangars. Thank goodness for urges of nature, or he might have disappeared without any clue. As it was, Doug had no idea whether Raheim was still at the airport or even on the ground. While the hangar was now deserted of both people and planes, there likely was a plane here when Raheim was. Whether he got on the plane or not, Doug could not be sure—at least until nature called him again. Either way, it was imperative to learn where that plane, assuming there was one, was headed.

The airstrip was large enough to have a control tower. Doug headed for it. If no planes had left recently, there was a good chance Raheim was still around.

He found a lone controller manning the tower. He was idly reading a paper and munching on a sandwich when Doug entered the small room. In fluent Spanish, Doug asked if any planes left recently. Getting no response, Doug reached into his wallet and pulled out two twenty-dollar bills, knowing American money spoke loudly. He was correct. Instantly, the controller became Doug's best friend, allowing him to see the control sheet.

In the past thirty minutes, there were three departures. Notably, they left one after the other and were identical Beechcraft 560 dual-engine planes.

For another forty dollars, he got a copy of the flight plans of each of the three aircraft. He also learned all three arrived yesterday, from three different airports. They were all parked at the south end of the airport, either in or near the hangar where Raheim had been.

Doug thanked the controller and went back to the

car. He headed back to do a more thorough search of the hangar itself but knew he would find nothing there. Raheim was on one of those planes. Both his instinct and deductive reasoning said so.

He immediately activated the SatLink to report to headquarters. They would check out each of the three flight plans, although it was likely all three would be bogus. The three planes would probably be making illegal landings in the US. But he feared they were heading to different locations, to further confuse the American authorities, should they track them from here. This was not good, not good at all.

Chapter 4

Jeff wasn't feeling much better the next day as he and Becca sat on the bus together. Not only was he worried about his sister, but he may have made a dangerous enemy out of Michaels, who was not the type of person to be pacified easily. No telling what he might do.

Riding the bus was demeaning, but his car had not run right since its encounter with the speed bump in the alleyway. In fact, it got worse and worse. On their way to the mall, the wheel kept pulling hard to the right and it rode extremely rough—more so than usual. Plus, the car's engine sounded like it had a two-pack-a-day habit, coughing and wheezing as it plugged along.

So he dropped it off at Joe's Garage instead of heading straight to the mall. Fortunately, they were open on Labor Day. His little adventure earlier in the afternoon took its toll on the aging car. Greg was good enough to pick them up at the garage and take them home—after spending several hours at the mall.

His parents weren't too happy about his car being in the garage, especially as the mechanic called while Jeff was at the mall, reporting the car had not only been knocked out of alignment, but whatever he hit had jarred something loose in the engine, requiring a new part. It would take a week to get and cost $600 to fix.

Naturally, his parents were upset—not only because they would have to foot most of the bill on the repairs, but he had not told them about the incident before getting home. Of course, if he had told them, his mom would have insisted on picking them up, and that meant no mall and no Tess. It was lucky they bought Jeff's explanation about hitting a pothole on the highway. But as a result of his serious miscalculation, he lost not only the ability to drive his own car but the privilege of borrowing his parents' car for the week.

So, Jeff and Becca were forced to ride the bus to school, something he hadn't done since his sophomore year. The bus hadn't changed much. He swore the same bubble gum still coated the undersides of the seats, the same dysfunctional driver was behind the wheel, with the same unruly kids terrorizing the interior, and the same foul order of stale food mixed with teen sweat still lingered.

Jeff and Becca shared a seat by mutual agreement. He wasn't exactly friends with the other riders on the bus, who were mostly freshmen and sophomores. And it certainly wasn't "cool" for a senior to be riding a bus to school. Becca wasn't used to riding either as she normally rode in with her brother. By sitting next to her, he could at least feel protective and save himself the horrible embarrassment of having some gum-popping freshman sit next to him.

It was great that they went to the same school, but it was only for a year. Next year he would be off to college, while she would start her sophomore year. But this year, they could enjoy being together—at least on the way to and from school. They rarely saw each other in the halls, and their lunch periods were at different times.

Becca and he were very close and always had been. They shared—and fought over—just about everything and were each other's best friends. Which was why it hurt so badly to see her doing something so stupid yesterday—especially because she did not talk to him first. But it was also why she listened to him. That thought brought a slight smile to his face as the bus turned into the school drive.

Becca was quiet all the way to school, which was unusual considering her great gift of gab. By mutual unspoken agreement, neither of them talked about yesterday's episode. She told Jeff to have a good day as they started to get off the bus, but that was about it. He probably wouldn't see her again until nearly four, as he had choir practice after school while Becca would ride the bus. Mom would pick him up. At least Becca didn't have soccer practice, nor did she claim to. Becca had explained to their folks that yesterday was a "try-out," but the actual practices would start in two weeks. The last part was true at least. He didn't bother correcting her.

Jeff almost let it go, but he just couldn't. As they headed toward the school entrance, he put his hand on Becca's shoulder. "Remember your promise."

"I will," Becca said solemnly. Then she turned and gave him a smile. Relieved, Jeff headed off to class, glancing around to make sure no one he knew saw him getting off the bus.

The bell was still ringing when he not so quietly

flopped into his seat. Jeff rarely was late for a class—but then again, he was seldom early, either. He always managed to make it to class as the bell rang, although maybe not to his seat. It wasn't that he deliberately waited until the last moment to arrive. And he certainly wasn't trying to make an "entrance." It's just there were always things coming up to delay him. Not the least of which was the sadistic moron who scheduled his classes so he was constantly traipsing from one end of the school to the other every class.

Mr. Maxwell, Jeff's twelfth grade AP US History teacher, shot him an "it's a good thing you're a good student" glance. Jeff was used to them. He managed a weak smile back as he fumbled through his backpack, attempting to retrieve his textbook, which he hoped was still there. He had been so worried about Becca, he just threw things in his backpack that morning, hoping most of it was right. To be truthful, that was not much different than his normal morning routine.

Finding it, he propped the book so it rested on his stomach and leaned against the desktop. He assumed his normal semi-slouched sitting position.

Jeff liked Mr. Maxwell. He had a good sense of humor and put a lot of enthusiasm into his teaching. He wasn't too ancient either—maybe thirty-five or thirty-six. However, he was a good five inches shorter than Jeff, who reached six foot one and a half inches over the summer. Jeff couldn't get over how he now towered over most of his teachers. He grew nearly three inches the past summer…but, unfortunately, added weight wasn't included. Now he looked even more like a geek. Given the absence of social graces, his love of science and technology, lack of participating in any school sports, and his academic proficiency, not to mention thick glasses, it was a label he found hard to shake. Not that he cared.

Mr. Maxwell was pretty cool. He never read from the textbook and often engaged the class in wonderful discussions that usually ventured considerably from the topic. One thing he didn't like about Mr. Maxwell, though, was he had a nasty habit...

"Since you like to make such a grand entrance, Mr. Miller, perhaps you can enlighten us by telling us what year President Washington first took office."

...of calling on him when he wasn't prepared. Like now. While Jeff took the book home, it never left his bookbag. It was as though senioritis had already set in, despite school being in session only a couple weeks. But instead of admitting he didn't know the answer, he blurted out "1789," the first date popping into his brain.

Mr. Maxwell, looking somewhat surprised, nodded. "That's correct. Washington was first inaugurated on April 30, 1789. Before that, for our first thirteen years as a new country, we operated without a President..."

Jeff sighed. It was a good thing he was a lucky guesser. His knack for coming up with the right answer, seemingly out of nowhere, saved his neck on more than one occasion. He risked a quick glance to his right and saw Tess giving him one of those "I don't know how you pulled that answer out of your butt" smiles. She knew he was guessing. It was not easy to fool her. He smiled back, absently brushing his dark brown floppy hair away from his eyes. It didn't matter how much time he spent combing his hair in the morning, five minutes later it would look like it had been through a blender, which was why he gave up attempting to keep his hair neat. Now he was satisfied if it just stayed out of his way.

Jeff stifled a yawn as Mr. Maxwell continued his lecture. The last thing he wanted was for Mr. Maxwell to get onto him for yawning in his class. Normally that wasn't an issue but last night he did not get a lot of sleep, worrying about his sister and his newfound enemy.

****

At lunch, Jeff took his tray and scanned the cafeteria for his friends Greg, Tess, and Ashanti. The four of them always ate lunch together. He finally spotted them in the back corner, talking quietly as they poked at the mystery meat occupying a portion of their respective plates. He walked over to their table with his hands holding the overloaded school cafeteria tray steady. He did his best trying to select the most edible looking samples of unidentified near-food the school cafeteria offered. But, in the end, he chose quantity over quality, as the latter was noticeably lacking. He shook his head. Why in today's advanced society couldn't they create edible—or even identifiable—school lunches? Edible being a relative term. But as a teen, he would eat anything not moving faster than him.

Eating was a secondary concern to the primary purpose of lunch period, chatting and trashing…chatting with each other while trashing everyone and everything else. Sometimes, though, they covered more serious topics such as what colleges each of them were applying to.

The bull session was already underway when Jeff sat down. At first, none of the others took special note of him, as they were heavily engaged in their discussion of which senior girl was the biggest tramp. Tess, as might be expected, was the first to notice Jeff's uncharacteristic silence. "What's wrong, Jeff? You haven't said a word. You also haven't snarfed your delicious lunch yet."

The sound of Tess's voice shook him from his reverie. They had been friends for several years but never started "dating" until this past summer. Now she was almost all he thought about. Her voice sounded a little sweeter than other girls', her long auburn hair was a little prettier, and her face, well, in his humble opinion, she was the best-looking girl in school. And she was also one of the brightest and most talented to boot. Tess and he were in several AP classes together as well as choir, where they were both soloists.

Jeff, Tess, Greg, and Ashanti initially bonded because they were outcasts from the main cliques of the school. Although Tess was well liked among her peers, few called her "friend." Part of it was because Tess came from a much poorer family than most of her classmates, so she didn't have a car or a fancy cellphone, or designer clothes. Nor did she wear ten tons of makeup. And she wasn't ashamed to make good grades. In fact, she enjoyed learning and wanted to excel at whatever she did. All that was fine to Jeff. Indeed, it made her more "special".

Greg, like Jeff, was considered by many to be a "geek", although he had much more charisma, and was thus more popular. However, Greg always preferred Jeff's company over his other friends. They had grown up together—having attended the same schools since kindergarten. Greg was a couple inches shorter than him and had light-brown hair, which was so curly it looked like he wore a Brillo Pad on his head. His frame was a bit wider than Jeff's as well, as he was much more athletic. Greg was also on the high school soccer team.

Ashanti was Greg's girlfriend. They had dated now for almost a year. However, she had been friends with all three of them for years. In fact, she also attended Greg's and Jeff's grade school, having transferred in at fourth grade. Ashanti was short, barely topping five feet, with her curly jet-black hair reaching her shoulders. Her smile radiated from her face like a beacon, brightening every room she entered. Although she was cute, her personality won most people over and was a perfect match for Greg's. Indeed, they were so nice, people called them "the sugar cubes"—sweet and square.

"Huh," came Jeff's bewildered reply.

"Earth to Jeff, come in please," Tess said, trying again to penetrate the haze engulfing him.

"I'm sorry. I was lost in thought."

"That's a first," snorted Greg.

"The first time he's been lost?" asked Ashanti, playing the straight man.

"No, the first time he's had a thought," answered Greg.

"Lay off, guys," Jeff said at last, pushing his glasses a bit farther up the bridge of his nose. "I'm worried about Becca."

The others got quiet, waiting for him to continue. "Last night I caught her trying to buy drugs from Steve Michaels."

Greg whistled.

"Oh my God!" exclaimed Tess. "What happened?"

"I stopped her this time. I'm just worried I won't be there the next time. What's worse, in the process of stopping her, I think I made a terrible enemy in Michaels." Jeff quickly told them the story. They all chuckled at the imagery of the "trashing" of Michaels. However, when he finished, they also recognized the seriousness of the situation.

Greg was first to comment. "Wow. You're right about having two big problems. Becca's at a vulnerable time, and Michaels sure won't take too kindly to what you did."

Jeff nodded slowly.

"Has she tried drugs before?" Ashanti asked.

Jeff shook his head. "No, I don't think so. She says she hasn't, and I believe her. I guess Michaels got a couple of her 'friends' hooked, and now they are pressuring her to try some."

"Michaels, huh. He's bad news," Greg remarked. Steve Michaels was in their class last year, when at school, that is. He dropped out completely last spring. But they all remembered when he terrorized their school. He already had a couple minor brushes with the law—vandalism, shoplifting, the like. But he had never been caught selling drugs, although it was common knowledge he was a dealer. Apparently, now he was much more aggressive in his pushing.

"Have you told your parents?" Ashanti asked.

"No, they have enough to worry about. They would absolutely freak if they ever found out."

"What will you do?" Tess asked.

"I was hoping you guys might have some ideas. I mean, I trust Becca and all. But her friends can put a lot of pressure on her. However, I refuse to let her share David's fate. Plus there's Michaels—he scares the crap out of me. I don't want him anywhere near Becca…or me, for that matter."

"You've got to trust her," Tess urged.

"I *do* trust her. It's Michaels and the others I don't trust."

"Look, how about we keep an eye out for Becca? If we see her getting anywhere near Michaels, we'll text you," Greg suggested.

"Thanks, I really appreciate it. But how can I get her away from those so-called friends of hers?"

"That's a lot tougher. Why don't you invite her to join us some afternoon? Let her know she has other options," Tess suggested.

"You guys don't mind? You used to object whenever I brought her before."

"We were younger then. Kid sisters weren't 'cool.' Things are different now. She'll be welcome," Tess said, putting her hand on Jeff's. Her touch caused stirrings inside him. He forced himself to remain calm.

"Thanks, that would be great." With that, the conversation drifted back into the world of trashy classmates.

****

Thoughts of Michaels, Becca, and drugs eventually receded in Jeff's mind as he went through classes. Finally, the bell rang, signaling the end of the academic day. It also meant time for choir practice—something Jeff really looked forward to—and not only because he got to stand next to Tess the entire time. They were in select choir, which was a special performing ensemble. It was through choir his freshman year he first met her.

But he also liked it because he truly enjoyed singing, despite making him vulnerable to more teasing from his not-so-kind classmates. Singing was his great escape. Nothing bothered him while he sang because he immersed himself into the music. Unfortunately, this time choir practice would not be the escape he desired.

The practice was serious as Mr. Morris, the choir director, rehearsed them hard in anticipation of their upcoming performance in the fall festival. They went through the first four numbers and then it was time for Jeff and Tess's duet. That's when it happened.

Just as they were reaching the song's climax, there was a sharp prick at the back of his head. Finishing the note abruptly, he turned to look at the choir to see who had thrown whatever hit him. But no one looked suspicious. An instant later, Jeff became light-headed and dizzy. Without further warning, he collapsed in a heap on the riser.

"Jeff!" screamed Tess. The whole choir stopped singing.

Mr. Morris, the director, rushed to his side. "What happened?" he asked, the concern evident as he bent down to help the now limp Jeff.

As quickly as it hit, it left. Jeff rapidly regained control of his muscles and struggled back to a sitting position, not quite ready to regain his feet. "I'm fine. I'm fine," he said to all concerned, putting up his hand to ward off all the people gathering around him. "I don't know what happened," he said to Mr. Morris, now holding his shoulders, steadying him against further incidents. "I felt a sharp pain in the back of my head, like something hit me. Then suddenly, I was very dizzy and weak. It completely overwhelmed me. I lost control over my body, but I don't think I ever lost consciousness. I'm all right now, though."

"Did anyone see anything hit Jeff?" Mr. Morris spoke to the choir. "Anyone?" His voice was stern. He would not tolerate horseplay in his choir. No one spoke.

Tess kneeled to examine Jeff as if to assure herself he was okay. Jeff immediately pulled himself together. He didn't want to appear weak and frail to her. Tess pushed back his hand and felt the back of his head, but there were no bumps to be found, although Jeff found her touch very soothing.

"Maybe you should see the nurse," Mr. Morris said to him.

"No, I'm fine. Really." Jeff jumped back to his feet as if to show him how fit he was. "I'm sorry for the disruption. But I'll be okay. Can we continue, please?"

Mr. Morris stared at him for a moment, as if deciding what to do. Jeff nodded to reassure him. Besides, the nurse had probably long since left the school. "All right. But if you start feeling dizzy again, just sit down, okay?"

"Yes, sir."

When the practice resumed, Jeff sang a little stronger than before, wanting to show everyone he was, indeed, fine.

When practice ended, Tess and Jeff gathered up their backpacks and headed for the door.

"That was scary. Are you sure you're okay now?" she asked as they left the choir room.

"I'm fine," he said reassuringly. "Man, it was really weird, though. I've never felt anything like that. For a minute it was as if something came and zapped all the strength from my body. I could hardly move. But

45

then it was gone, just like that," he said, snapping his fingers. "I'm absolutely fine now." Jeff shifted the load from his right shoulder to his left.

"Do you think someone hit you with something?"

"That's what I thought at first, but now I'm not so sure. I looked around on the floor when no one was watching, to see what hit me. But there was nothing that could have hurt me like that. And it was weird. It was a sharp pain initially, but I can't say exactly where it hurt. It was as if the whole back of my head was hit at once. Then the pain went away as suddenly as it appeared, and that's when I got dizzy."

"Weird. Maybe you should see a doctor or something."

Jeff shook his head. "I don't think so. I really don't believe there's anything wrong. I feel fine now." Tess clearly wasn't convinced. "Look, I promise I'll see a doctor if it happens again, okay?" he said, shifting the pack back to the right shoulder.

"Deal."

"Fine." They walked on in silence, each wondering what really happened, but their thoughts were interrupted as soon as they stepped outside. For there, apparently waiting for him, stood Steve Michaels and his rather bulky friend from the previous day. Michaels' companion was an imposing kid whom Jeff did not know, but who appeared to be at least eighteen, with an unkempt mustache and noticeable stubble on his face. He was almost a half a foot taller and considerably wider than Jeff and looked like he could bench press an SUV. Michaels, by himself, had Jeff by a couple inches and maybe twenty pounds—and he was small compared to the WWF clone next to him.

"How's your car, dork?" Michaels asked.

"In the shop," Jeff managed to reply. He resisted saying, 'I heard yours was trashed, though.' No sense further provoking the beast.

Michaels let a thin smile spread out from his tight lips. "You think you're a hot shot now?" He laughed. Then he took a step toward Jeff. "You owe me, big time," Michaels snarled.

"I owe you nothing," Jeff snapped back.

"You're pretty uppity for such a small dork," Michaels said, advancing on Jeff and Tess. "Perhaps someone should teach you some respect."

"Leave us alone!" Tess demanded, putting herself between Michaels and Jeff. Jeff's heart raced at ninety miles a minute as he grabbed Tess and tried turning around, only to find his way blocked by Michaels' buddy.

"Going somewhere, dork?" Michaels called.

"Leave Jeff alone!" Tess screamed.

"Get out of here, Tess!" Jeff yelled. "*Now!*" He used his sternest voice possible in imploring her to leave, giving her a gentle push in the direction of the school.

"What? You don't want your girlfriend to see you get pounded?" Michaels sneered. "Does she faint at the sight of blood?" Then he turned to Tess, who hadn't moved, and eyed her up and down. "Hmm, not bad, dork. What's a babe like this doing hanging around a dork like you?" Michaels took a step toward her.

Jeff quickly grabbed Tess and shoved her much harder away from Michaels. "Tess, run! Get away from here. I'll be all right."

Tess appeared to be torn as to what to do. But after

a brief pause, she turned and ran back into the building.

"No, dork, you ain't gonna be all right," Michaels jeered. "Grab him, Ox."

Before Jeff could move, a pair of strong arms embraced him from behind. He had momentarily forgotten about the appropriately named Ox, and now it was too late. He struggled in vain to get free from the vise-like grip ensnaring him. His backpack fell to the concrete sidewalk with a thud.

"See," Michaels said, moving to within a foot of the struggling Jeff, "you cost me a customer. I don't like losing customers. They mean money, and I like money. You also caused me to spill merchandise…and that's more money. On top of that, you put a dent in my car—more money. No one does that and gets away with it."

Michaels put his face up next to Jeff's. "So, what you gonna do about it, choir boy?"

Jeff was stymied. In a one-on-one confrontation with Michaels he could handle himself. After all, he studied martial arts for over four years, earning a first-degree black belt before quitting to pursue other interests and save money. But he never had used his training in a real fight. Heck, he had never been in a real fight. One of the things they always stressed in his Dojo was walk away from trouble.

Unfortunately, thanks to Ox, it was not one-on-one—more like one-on-five—nor could he walk away as he was firmly in Ox's grasp. Various strategies came to mind. He could probably break free from Ox. He might win the fight. But, in doing so, another fight became a near certainty. Plus, he had to consider any possible repercussions against Becca and Tess, not to mention the possible damage to his own face—given the size of Ox. No need to react rashly now. No, the best course was to try to defuse the situation.

"Look," Jeff said, trying to keep his voice calm. Reasoning with his adversary was his best hope. But that was like trying to tame a tornado. "I wasn't trying to hurt your business." Jeff tried to keep the sarcasm out of his voice as he said "business". "I was sent to get my sister. That's all I was trying to do." There was only one possible escape. "I'm, uh, sorry about the rest. That was an accident, really. I'll pay you for what was spilled."

Michaels glared at him for a while, and then softened his expression and cracked a smile. "I see. Well, maybe I'll let you off easy this time." With that, he started to turn away as Ox loosened his grip. A small crowd of kids had gathered around, but no one dared interfere.

Relieved, Jeff tried to start his heart again as he started to turn around. That's when it hit him. Michaels' fist that is, a sweeping left hook connecting with Jeff's right cheek with a sickening pop, knocking him completely off his feet, glasses flying off his head. So much for Michaels not hitting someone wearing glasses, Jeff thought fleetingly as his butt met pavement. Now a different kind of sharp pain stabbed at his head, only this time, the source was never in doubt. Worse, he was caught off-guard—not only by the suddenness of the attack, but by the fact Michaels was left-handed. He had forgotten that little item. His sensei would have jumped all over him for the mental lapse.

"Then again, maybe I won't," sneered Michaels, as he laughed at Jeff's plight. "Hey, Ox," Michaels said to his giant friend, "feel like pounding a pussy today?"

"Yeah, I haven't squished one all week," came the deep-throated reply.

Jeff, his cheek smarting like crazy, quickly tried to regain his feet. Just as he did, two strong hands grabbed him by the shoulders, pulling him up and pinning his arms behind him as he was lifted several inches off the ground. Michaels walked up to him with a wicked grin on his face. "You see, I might have let you off, but you made me look bad in front of my customers. No one does that and gets away with it."

Still trying to keep things in control, Jeff started to speak, only Michaels quick-punched him in the stomach. Jeff doubled over in pain, with Ox quickly straightening him up again.

Jeff flinched in anticipation of another blow. But none came. Instead, Michaels' face was frozen, jaw hanging down. He appeared to be distracted by something in the sky behind Jeff. Just then, a dark shadow swept across the schoolyard.

"What the heck is that?" yelled one of the kids who were still standing around watching.

"It's a UFO!" screamed another. Michaels and Ox, who also had turned to stare, were fixated on the silent object hovering overhead.

Jeff, seizing the opportunity, quickly broke free from Ox's now-relaxed grip. Grabbing his backpack and glasses, he turned and headed toward the building at a dead run. It was only after smacking into Mr. Olsteen, the Assistant Principal coming out the door with Tess, did he pause long enough to look back to see his airborne benefactor.

It was still there. Floating about three hundred feet

above the playground was the most beautiful sight Jeff had ever seen. Shaped like two inverted pie plates placed on top of one another, it was the classic flying saucer. It didn't seem to shine as much as glow, with the brightest part of the glow coming from the bottom of the saucer. The edge around the craft pulsed with a deep red glare while the rest of the UFO had a silvery sheen. The surface was mostly smooth, although there were a couple half-moon indentations on the part of the craft facing him. There were also unidentifiable protrusions in the center of both the top and bottom.

As if on cue, the object darted off as soon as Jeff spotted it. And before he had a chance to pull his phone from his pocket, it disappeared over the trees, heading west.

Jeff stood there with his mouth hanging open, still smarting from the sucker punch he received minutes earlier. Everyone else, including Mr. Olsteen, stared silently in awe. No wonder Michaels and Ox had been distracted. He, too, was mesmerized by the shimmering ship in the sky.

A car's horn shook them from their collective trance. It was Jeff's mother arriving to pick him up.

Michaels and Ox, noting the presence of Mr. Olsteen, took advantage of the momentary distraction to exit the scene.

"Are you all right?" Tess called to him somewhat dazedly, not taking her eyes off the point in the sky where the object disappeared.

"Yeah, thanks. Thanks a lot. I'll call you later," Jeff managed to say as his brain mentally tracked the foreign flying machine. With that, Jeff hurried off to his mother's car. He didn't want to be around when Mr.

Olsteen recovered enough from his daze to start asking questions.

Jeff gingerly got into the car, making sure to keep the sore side of his face away from his mother's vision. By her expression, Jeff gathered she missed the recent aerial show. Jeff, though, was still thinking about the flying saucer when he got in the car.

"Are you okay?" his mother asked. "You look a little distracted."

"Didn't you see that?" he asked excitedly, responding to her query.

"See what?"

"The UFO! It was right here! Over the schoolyard. You mean to say you never saw it?" he said, a little agitated, knowing his mother would never believe him unless she had seen it herself.

"I didn't see anything," she said, as she pulled out of the school's driveway. "I think your imagination must be working overtime, probably due to all those high-grade movies you've been watching." Her voice dripped with sarcasm.

He was getting nowhere with his mother. Sighing, he sat back and continued to stare out the window at where the saucer had been. The stinging in his cheek, the soreness in his belly, and the memory of his recent encounter with Michaels faded into the background, as all Jeff thought about was the UFO. It *had* been there. He *had* seen it. And, somehow, he was confident he would see it again.

Jeff was lost in thought the rest of the way home.

Chapter 5

"They could all die!" Axel shouted at his father, his calm and cool completely deserting him. "And you *know* that. We're not talking a few hundred or thousand lives this time…We're talking about potentially an entire *sentient species*. How can you stand by and do nothing?"

Axel planned for this "discussion" for over a week now…ever since his first abortive attempt to persuade his father ended in pure embarrassment for them both. This time would be different.

To prepare for round two, Axel researched extensively. There was no chance of persuading his father unless he had the facts right. While his father may be sympathetic to the cause, an emotional appeal carried no weight. No, the only way to win was to use logic, quote facts, and utilize the mental discipline he had been learning these past few months.

Maybe if his father saw he could reason like an adult, then he would listen. He thought about not having Chermal go with him but decided against it. What if he needed Chermal's calming influence? He had been right, although it was turning out not to be enough.

Next was timing. He had to act fast, because Earth did not have much time left. Yet he had to wait for his father to be alone, which was difficult as patience was not Axel's strong suit. While one could have private telepathic conversations in a public place, Axel didn't want his gestures to betray him in front of others, or embarrass his father, like he did before. He might also have a better chance persuading him in private. He was wrong.

His father shook his head sadly, the ridges on his head folding together a bit more than usual. "It's out of my hands," he said with genuine remorse. "You know that." He put his hand sympathetically on young Axelarone's shoulder. "The law is clear. The Alliance strictly forbids us from interfering."

"But billions could die. They *all* could die. Surely, they did not envision this scenario when creating that directive," Axel pleaded as he pulled away from his father. As he did so, he noted absently he was now a bit taller than his father—impressive, as the Thermax was tall for a Delion, reaching nearly five feet. But a height advantage would not get his father to listen to him.

"Our projections say even if some survive, humanity's development could be set back one hundred or more years," Axel argued, attempting to return to the logic and reason that seemingly deserted him. "How can we do nothing?"

Axel made his way to the front of his father's cabin, where there was a real-time three-dimensional holographic image of the shimmering serene blue globe 10,000 miles below. The globe spun slowly. Chermal was working overtime trying to keep him calm.

Axel reflected on the moment he first saw the planet preoccupying his father these past several years. Axel came here kicking and screaming. He wanted no part of studying an alien culture. He was much more interested in firsthand exploration of his own culture…especially the females.

Yet when he got here, Axel was immediately enamored by the planet's inherent beauty, as well as its dominant race's complexities. This was his first extended trip away from home and his first opportunity to really study a primitive alien culture. Now it was real, not just some lesson carrying no meaning to him. It was also the first time he could observe his father in action—as leader of a fleet of Zanchee vessels and head of an important scientific and potentially diplomatic mission. Here his father was not only his father. He was and had to be Thermax, the commander. Even with his son.

Gone, too, was the boredom that led him to his father's office that fateful day…when he "accidentally" learned humanity's fate. His father was furious with Axel for prying about in his office, which certainly didn't help Axel win the argument to prevent the disaster from happening. Yet now Axel's boredom was replaced with a sense of purpose. Somehow, someway, he must convince his father to do what he likely wanted to do anyway.

"I don't expect you to understand now," Axel's father said, patronizingly. "Perhaps someday, when you're a nescrot and have gained more valuable experience, you may." Axel grimaced at the reference to adulthood. "However, there are excellent and important reasons behind the Alliance's laws." His father sighed and softened his voice. The profound sadness behind his words was evident. "I don't like it any more than you do. After all, I've devoted much of my life to studying this planet and have a lot invested in these humans, and I certainly do not want anything to happen to them any more than you do. But sometimes we must live with things we don't like, especially when it's for the greater good."

Axel's double heart throbbed against his ribs, betraying his frustration seething inside. It took all his control not to lash out at his father.

Axel felt something rubbing against his legs. He glanced down to see a ball of fur wrapping around his leg...trying to get his attention. Chermal was looking up at him, radiating calmness and reassurance. It didn't help enough.

Ever since Axel "accidentally" learned about the impending disaster below, it was all he thought about. He and Chermal started stealthily exploring the ship's artificial intelligence system, also known as AI, to learn as much as possible about the event. The resulting devastation was catastrophic and terrifying. He was more shocked when he learned the Zanchee were doing nothing to prevent it.

The rebuff caused him to carefully study Zanchee laws...and their unyielding principals. He had to as part of his studies for Nemseck. But this was something different. There had to be a way to avoid destroying such a wonderful planet and its amazing people. There *had* to be.

Clearly his father cared about the sentient beings below. If anyone could find a way to satisfy Zanchee protocol and save the race below, it was him.

Yet his father immediately dismissed him when he first brought up the subject. He made the mistake of going to his father as soon as he learned what was happening. He compounded his error by confronting him on the bridge, where his father was surrounded by his staff. Axel's emotions must have leaked to everyone within fifty feet of that room. His father had no choice but to immediately reprimand and dismiss him.

His father was steadfast. His father was stubborn—but so was he.

At first, Axel took the dismissal hard. Indeed, if Chermal had not been there to practically force him to calm down, he might have had a major tantrum reminiscent of his childhood. That would have absolutely ruined any chance he might have had. So, he took his anger and frustration and applied it to learning more about the humans and Zanchee law, hoping to find a way to convince his father to act. But now his emotions were betraying him again.

"How can you say that?" Axel said, throwing his hands into the air. "Who are *we* to say what is the 'greater good'?" Axel turned from his father and gestured at the holographic representation of the blue, white, green, and brown planet spinning below. "I doubt *they* would agree. It's certainly not for *their* greater good."

Axel heard it before, a thousand times—"Can't interfere." Why not? Who else was there to save them? Wasn't the destruction of a sentient species too high a price to pay for some stupid principal?

He pointed again to the holographic planet. "Dad, look at this. It's a beautiful planet. And, by your own admission, it is populated with a people having great potential and who one day, perhaps soon, will be ready to join the Zanchee Alliance. Think of all they may contribute. And yet you are ready to let them die, and the planet spoiled. How can you? Aren't their future contributions to the Zanchee part of the 'greater good?' "

Chermal physically batted him on the leg. His control was slipping again. He was even blocking Chermal out. He took a deep breath and tried one last argument.

"Father," he began. Rarely, if ever, did Axel call his dad "father." But desperate times… "If we have knowledge of a catastrophic act, and we have the ability to stop it, are we not as guilty as those who perpetrate the disaster? By *not* acting, are we not, in fact, *actively participating* in the destruction of the planet?"

"Who are we to interfere?" his father replied.

"Who are we *not* to interfere?" Axel countered. "The reason we *must* interfere is because we *can*. We have the ability to stop this thing." The control had disappeared, and his emotions took over. "Dad, we can't just sit here and do nothing. It's not *sen*!"

His father sighed deeply. "I'm afraid we have to, son. We have no choice. Besides, we can't know for certain our projections are accurate. By interfering, we could ultimately make things worse." He again put his hands on Axelarone's shoulders. "You have much to learn about what is *sen*."

Axel broke away from his grasp. "Make things worse? How can they be worse than potentially destroying a planet? Is it *sen* to do nothing, knowing it leads to disaster when doing something at least gives them a chance?" he pleaded.

"There is too much at stake, Axel. It's not only this world. If we interfere here, other races will wonder if they're next. Member races will know our principals are only applied when convenient." Axelasome paused and gazed softly at his son. "Sometimes we have to accept fate."

"I don't accept it!"

"I'm afraid you have to."

Axel turned away in disgust, muttering, "We'll see about that."

Chapter 6

*September 7th, D Minus 210.43 Hours*
*Dallas*

As soon as he got out of the car, Jeff started calling for his sister. "Becca! Becca! Where are you?" he shouted as he barged through the door into the kitchen. "Becca!" he called again, throwing his backpack down in the general direction of the kitchen table and heading toward the family room.

"Becca? Becca? Where are you?"

"Upstairs," came the muffled reply.

"You'll never guess what happened!" he shouted as he tore up the stairs, two and three at a time.

"I'm in the computer room," called Becca. It was no surprise she was in their home's fourth bedroom which had been converted into an office/computer room. Becca and Jeff both spent a lot of time on the family's computer—mostly playing Astroloids and other computer games, but also surfing the net, and occasionally doing homework. The parents had so far resisted their pleas to get them their own laptops.

Astroloids was one of the biggest fads sweeping schools across the country, if not the world, even though it had been around for a couple years. It combined an animated cartoon show with a computer game, mobile platform, and trading cards. Astroloids were aliens of different shapes, sizes, and abilities. There were three categories of Astroloids—good, bad, and neutral. The bad Astroloids were trying to take over the earth, while the good ones were helping humankind defend the earth. Dozens of alien species were in each of these three categories. There were also different cards for each type of weapon. Some weapons worked only against certain species, but not others. All weapons required power. So, there were cards for each species, for ranks within each species, for each weapon type, and for power. Combined they totaled 400 cards, and it was everyone's goal to collect them all. Naturally some were rarer, or more powerful than others making them more valuable. Jeff had been into Astroloids since they came out, but it wasn't "cool" for seniors to be seen playing it—although many did—including Jeff and his friends.

"Becca!" Jeff exclaimed breathlessly as he came into the room. "You won't believe what I just saw!"

"What? The second coming, again?" she replied with no little sarcasm.

"A UFO!"

"What?" she replied, without looking up.

"I'm not kidding. It was right over the schoolyard. I saw it right after practice. Becca, it was *so cool*. It hovered silently over the school parking lot, about three hundred feet in the air. Then it just took off! It was gone in an instant. It was awesome!"

"Get out. I'm not falling for that," she said, never taking her eyes from the computer.

"It's true. Twenty people must have seen it…including Tess and Mr. Olsteen. You should have seen it. It was huge. About thirty feet across, I'd guess. It was shaped like two saucers joined at the edges. And it glowed. Unbelievable!"

"Yes, unbelievable is the word," said Becca still not looking up. "You're not getting me off the computer that easily." Jeff's past of pulling his sister's leg was catching up to him...he had pulled it so many times, it was a wonder she did not have a limp.

"Listen, I'm serious. It hovered for a few minutes then flew off." Jeff paused, then continued. "And I think I know where it was headed." His voice trailed off as he realized for the first time, he really did have a good idea where it was heading. He quieted the little voice inside him asking how he could possibly know.

"Speaking of aliens, I got a Betawick. Beat that!" Becca exclaimed as she continued working the keyboard, ignoring her brother's remarks.

Jeff threw his hands in the air in frustration. "All right, if you don't believe me, maybe you'll believe Tess?" Tess and Becca had always gotten along, despite their three-year difference in age. Becca appreciated Tess treating her as an equal, rather than as a little kid who had to be tolerated.

Jeff took out his phone and quickly dialed Tess's number. He would show her.

The phone was answered on the third ring. "Hello." Tess sounded a little winded. "I was just in the other room." Jeff put the phone on speaker mode.

"Hi Tess, it's me, Jeff."

"I know who it is, silly. How's your chin? You had me worried the way you tore out of there. Are you okay?"

"Yeah, fine. Listen. I need you to tell my dumb

sister about the UFO."

"What UFO?" Tess replied.

Jeff hoped Tess would not hear the giggles now coming from his sister.

"What do you mean, 'what UFO'? The UFO in the schoolyard! You know, UFO—unidentified flying object—the flying saucer you saw with Mr. Olsteen...the one that buzzed us when I was having my *discussion* with Michaels."

"I don't know what you're talking about. Are you all right?" she said, sounding very concerned. "The only thing I saw flying in the schoolyard was Michaels' fist...and I could identify that."

"No, no. Listen. You had to see it," Jeff pleaded. "It was right over the school. Michaels saw it...Mr. Olsteen, too."

"Maybe he hit you harder than I thought. I was so scared! Thank goodness Mr. Olsteen was in the hallway. There's no telling what could have happened if he was still in his office."

"Tess, stop kidding around. Do you really mean you never saw the UFO?"

"Oh, I get it, you're playing a trick on Becca, right? Okay, I'll go along. What do you want me to say?"

Jeff was completely befuddled, and Becca was now outright laughing. "Nothing, nothing at all. Look, I'll call you back later." Jeff hung up without waiting for an answer. What was happening? He had seen Tess staring at the UFO. She was still watching where it disappeared when he got in Mom's car. Was everyone going crazy?

Becca, finally tearing herself from the computer screen, turned around with a smirk on her face. "She won't go along with your joke, will she?" Becca said smugly. The smirk quickly disappeared when she finally took notice of Jeff's face.

"My God, Jeff, what happened to your face?"

"Nothing." Then changing his mind, he continued. "I had a little run-in with your friend Michaels, that's all."

"What happened?" Becca said, sounding genuinely alarmed.

"Seems he objected to my taking away a customer of his and wanted to express his displeasure."

"Oh Jeff, I'm so sorry!"

"That's the kind of people they are, Becca. They don't care about *you*. They only care about drugs and the money to buy more drugs."

Becca was silent.

Jeff looked down at the phone still in his hand. He quickly checked Snap Chat. There were no pics of the UFO posted from anyone at school. He then checked Instagram and Twitter. Nothing. Didn't anyone have time to take a picture?

Jeff thought for a moment, and then decided. "Look, I gotta go somewhere now. Please tell Mom I'm going to Greg's. And promise me not to tell her about this," he said, pointing to his cheek, which was rapidly turning an ugly dark blue.

"I think she will figure that one out on her own."

"Promise me," Jeff demanded.

"All right, all right, I promise."

She would likely keep her word. A couple years ago, there would have been no way to shut her up, short of duct tape. But she was getting more trustworthy and less concerned about getting him into trouble as she got older. Thank goodness.

"Uh, Jeff?" Becca said, returning her attention to the Astroloids.

"Yes?"

"How will you get there? You don't have a car, remember? And mom said you can't drive theirs, either."

Jeff had forgotten that little fact. Well there was still one other option. "I'll take my bike."

That earned another chuckle from his sister. He didn't bother to retort, however, as he was in too big a hurry. He considered momentarily calling Greg to come and pick him up but decided against it. Greg would think he was bonkers chasing after a UFO. Besides, Jeff enjoyed riding his bike, although it had been a *long* time since he last rode.

He dashed down the stairs and into the garage, making sure to avoid his mother in the process. In a flash he was out of the garage and on his bike, a fifteen-speed dark blue mountain bike. He was in such a hurry, he failed to collect a snack on the way out.

Jeff pondered the situation as he pedaled furiously down the road. It didn't make sense. Tess saw the saucer. She was gaping at it with her mouth open wide enough to snare a bird, as was everyone else's in the schoolyard. Why was she lying? Or did she really not remember? Was the world going crazy? Or was it just him? Maybe Michaels did hit him too hard. No, there had been a UFO. How else could he have escaped? He must find out what's happening.

Jeff was sure where the saucer was headed. He didn't know how or why he knew—he just did. And it was more than a feeling—he was certain. He looked down at his watch. It was a little after 4:30. Dinner will be in two or so hours. That should leave enough time to investigate.

Pedaling as hard as he could, Jeff headed down the street. Sweat formed and quickly began flowing down his face. His soaked shirt was rapidly becoming second skin as Dallas' normally stifling summer heat had returned with a vengeance.

He headed up Alexander Drive, which wasn't the most direct route, but had the advantage of having a light at Metcalf. This time of day, Metcalf will be near impossible to cross without a light, and difficult on a bike with one.

While he lived on the outskirts of town, development had rapidly enveloped his neighborhood. When they moved into their current home seven years ago, they were on the very edge of the Dallas area. Now there were houses, apartments, and businesses everywhere. Where did all the people come from to fill up the endless number of houses being built? But come they did. And more houses were going up. When he and Becca were little kids, Mom and Dad took them on walks past the construction. His sister and he loved watching the entire process of clearing the ground, leveling the area, putting in the foundation, framing the house, and finally, finishing it. As they got older, they played around the new construction and pretended to build houses themselves.

But now one had to go several miles to find new construction, as everywhere close was developed. With all the new houses came more traffic. More traffic meant increased danger for bike riders, even on his neighborhood streets as people cut through to avoid the traffic on Metcalf.

Jeff sighed. Now was not the time to think about houses. Focusing had always been an issue for him. There were way too many interesting things out there to distract him. And if there wasn't anything external, his vivid imagination was quite capable of creating his own distractions—much to the dismay of his teachers and parents.

Could his overactive imagination be behind this? Did he dream up the UFO? Certainly others would likely think so. Combine his rich imagination and his love of science fiction, plus having pulled a few hoaxes in his time—especially on his sister. It was no wonder she didn't believe him. No one would. That's why he had to get proof.

He came to the light at Alexander and Metcalf and waited impatiently for the light to change. Several cars were alongside him. Hopefully, they would let him cross without running him over. His watch now showed 4:40. He still had a couple miles to go to get to the quarry. Better step on it.

He was convinced the UFO would be at the quarry, which was due west of the school. This was real, not a figment of his overactive imagination. His head buzzed with all the adrenaline pumping through his system right now. He gripped the handlebars tightly as he tried willing the light to turn green. "Hurry up! Damn it," he mumbled aloud.

After a short eternity, the light changed. Jeff didn't give the cars a chance to zip ahead of him. He whooshed across the intersection and down Alexander in front of everyone. Jeff put the bike in high gear. He had never pedaled so hard in his life, even keeping up with some of the cars that passed him.

He turned onto Reeds, a country road, almost at full speed. Thankfully, there were no cars coming because he could not stop in time. There was a little over a mile to go.

It was 4:53 when he finally pulled up to the dirt road leading to the quarry. A chain stretched across the road, extending between two red posts on either side. A large padlock attached one end of the chain to the post on the right. A large sign saying, "Private Property Keep Out!" hung loosely from the center of the chain.

Jeff dismounted and looked around to make sure no one was watching. Then he walked his bike around the pole. There wasn't a lot of room, but enough, although a few of the thorns in the bushes managed to momentarily and painfully ensnare him. Surprisingly, the quarry wasn't fenced off, relying on the chain and natural heavily thicketed terrain to keep unwanted visitors out. Jeff made it around the pole with only a few scratches to show for his effort. Once on the other side, he mounted his bike again and headed down the dirt road into the quarry itself.

As he got to the rim of the deep pit, he paused to take a good look around. The now-abandoned quarry was large and deep. Jeff estimated it to be about one-half mile in diameter and maybe three hundred feet deep. The quarry had not been mined for several years, even though there were still a few old pieces of machinery scattered about. The rocky dirt road he was on wound its way down to where it disappeared into the dark bluish-brown lake at the bottom. The lake was deep. Sometimes he and several friends snuck out here in the summer and swam in its crystal-clear water. The lake was always cool and refreshing in the hot summer sun. Given the heat today, and his sweaty condition, a dip sounded pretty good.

Jeff scanned the area carefully. Nothing was amiss. There was no apparent place to hide. However, something did not seem quite right, although he couldn't quite put his finger on what.

After spending a few more minutes looking around and snapping a few pics, he headed down. The feeling he was supposed to be here intensified. He was getting closer. But to what?

As he coasted down the incline, one hand on the brake, he studied the surroundings. Nothing noticeable was amiss, yet something still seemed wrong. But what? He couldn't see any outcroppings or caves that might hold the saucer. Unfortunately, he was so intent on scanning the steep walls of the quarry he didn't see the large rock in the path immediately in front of his bike. The inevitable collision momentarily stopped the bike and launched him into the air. Fortunately, he wasn't moving very fast, so he wasn't hurt badly, although there were stinging scratches and his clothes were torn. Just a few more aches to add to his already sore body. His head had thumped against the ground, however, giving him a slight headache. The sound of his mother admonishing him to always wear a helmet echoed loudly in his brain. The bike, meanwhile, skittered down the road, sliding to a stop near the water. *At least no one was here to witness my flying feat*, Jeff thought.

As he dusted himself off and went to retrieve the bike, Jeff gazed again at the lake in front of him. Finally, it dawned on him what was wrong. The water was muddy. The quarry lake was always the clearest water he had seen, but now one could not see beyond the surface. Why? It hadn't rained in several days and no one had worked in this quarry for over three years. He took another photo.

Staring into the lake, he detected out of the corner of his eye a flash of fur running along the cliff. Turning around, he found himself about ten feet from the strangest and ugliest-looking cat he had ever seen. It sat on its haunches staring back at him.

The creature was big, twice the size of Jeff's cat, Sparky. The strange feline had short matted brownish fur, streaked with blue. *What kind of cat has blue fur? Did someone dye its hair?* But that wasn't the only thing strange about the animal. Its paws were disproportionately big. Its head was also shaped a little different from a normal cat.

As he stared at the animal, he began to realize this could not be a cat. For one thing, it didn't have whiskers and its eyes were more rounded than Sparky's, and closer together. They also appeared to have a twinkle Jeff had never seen in a cat's eye. Whatever it was, it stared right back at him with a gaze that seemed to penetrate Jeff's soul, portending an obvious intelligence. Moreover, it appeared to be laughing at him. *My imagination really is overactive!* Jeff thought to himself, although he probably did make a funny sight with gravel and dirt covering him from head to toe after his grand entrance.

"You'll have to forgive Chermal," came a voice out of nowhere, penetrating the stony silence. Jeff nearly jumped completely out of his clothes with the sudden unexpected interruption. He never heard anyone approach. Taking a deep breath, Jeff managed to compose himself enough to turn and face the newcomer.

"Chermal has not been around humans much, and you were rather funny!" the newcomer continued, grinning.

The stranger was a few inches shorter than Jeff and dressed in blue jean cutoffs and a plain white-collared T-shirt, which looked oddly familiar. It should—he was wearing the same identical outfit, only his was torn and soaked in sweat. Weird. Even the dirty socks and worn tennis shoes were nearly the same as Jeff's, only a lot cleaner. The main difference in attire was the newcomer wore what looked like a green bracelet on his right wrist. Jeff was devoid of jewelry.

"Who are you? And where did you come from?" Jeff asked as soon as he gathered enough of his wits to speak.

"You can call me Axel," said the stranger.

"Uh, hi," Jeff stammered, not wanting to be too rude. He was still too spooked to think clearly. "You startled me. I wasn't expecting anyone to be here."

"Are you sure?" Axel said, staring him directly in the eye with a sly grin on his face.

Jeff ignored the remark, as he tried to regain composure. Without taking his eyes off the strange boy and his "cat", he bent down to pick up his bike. Neither he nor Axel said anything for what seemed like several minutes but ticked off less than one. Jeff looked back at the weird cat-like critter, Chermal, whose penetrating gaze never ventured from him. It all was too much to handle.

"I've got to go," Jeff said suddenly, breaking the terse silence. This was way too weird. He needed to collect his thoughts, and here wasn't the place. Whatever he had been expecting, this certainly wasn't it. Besides, it was getting close to dinnertime, and if there was anything he didn't want to miss, it was dinner.

Jeff walked the bike past Axel, who continued to smile disarmingly at him. Jeff didn't know what to say. There was no fear. In fact, he kinda liked the kid, even though they just met. But anxiety overtook curiosity. He was still too shaken up by the day's events. And his stomach was beginning to demand attention.

"Don't worry," Axel said as Jeff passed him. "I'll be here tomorrow. Come back after school and we can talk then."

"Uh, sure," Jeff managed to say. Once again, Axel had startled him…not only by talking suddenly, but it was as though he knew what Jeff was thinking.

"Chermal likes you, by the way. He's looking forward to getting to know you better, too."

That was enough for Jeff. He jumped on his bike without pausing to look back at the strange pair and began pedaling up the long, steep hill. As he did, Axel called after him, "Pleasant dreams." Whatever.

When he finally got up enough nerve halfway up the incline to look back, neither Axel nor his cat were anywhere to be seen. Why hadn't he thought to take their photo? Shaking his head, Jeff pedaled on, thinking he would wake up any time now.

Chapter 7

*September 7$^{th}$, D Minus 210.80 Hours*
*Dallas*

The shock from the bike hitting the curb at his house woke Jeff from his trance. Until then, he was completely on autopilot, so lost in thought he was not consciously aware of where he was or what he was doing. The bump when he went over the curb and headed toward the garage finally brought him back to the here and now. Jeff tried to think back but could not remember any of the ride home. Fortunately, his subconscious must be a good cyclist, since he made it home safely.

What now? Normally, he would run in and tell Becca all about it. But he hesitated. She didn't believe him about the UFO, and now his story about the funny boy with the strange cat would surely convince her he was out of his mind. Especially since he had no photos of them. Worse, she might think he was using the very drugs he was so adamant about her not trying.

He certainly could not tell his parents. Not only would they not believe him, but he would be in trouble for going over to the quarry.

That left Greg or Tess. But what would he say? Would they believe him? Probably not. To be honest, if the situation was reversed, he would assume they were pulling a prank. No, the best course of action was to not to tell anyone, yet. At least until he knew more or had some proof, which meant returning to the quarry tomorrow.

Now that he was removed from the actual event, he wasn't nervous anymore. Instead, he was overcome by curiosity. He wanted to turn around and head back tonight, but that was impossible. It would be dark soon, number one. He would get in serious trouble, number two. And most important, he was very hungry.

Jeff put his bike away and headed inside, still in a fog as he mulled over his possible courses of action, when he bumped into his sister who apparently saw him coming up the driveway.

"Where did you go?" Becca demanded of her brother as she rebounded from the contact just inside the doorway. Her voice denoted both concern and curiosity.

"It's a long story. I'll tell you later," Jeff replied half-heartedly, trying to avoid a conversation he was not yet prepared to have.

"What happened to your face?"

"Huh?" The question surprised him.

"When you left here, it looked like you had a purple tennis ball growing out of your cheek. Now it looks normal."

"What?" Becca now had Jeff's full attention. Up to this point, his mind was at the quarry. Now, for the first time, Jeff realized his cheek didn't hurt anymore. He put his hand up to his face to make sure. Applying pressure to where he had been hit, gingerly at first, then more and more, he failed to find any pain. And he was sure one of his teeth had been jarred loose, but they all appeared fine now, as well. Nor was there any trace of the multiple cuts, scrapes, and bruises on his hands, arms, and legs he had suffered when he took his brief flight over the handlebars.

"Mom will have a cow over those clothes," Becca continued. The clothes were still dirty, and his pants were ripped in the knee from his wreck with the bike, and both pants and shirt were torn from the battle with the bush. But no trace of any scratches on his skin.

"What happened?" Becca's expression turned to puzzlement as she stared at her brother, who was completely bewildered. "What's the matter? Jeff, you're scaring me and it's nearly two months until Halloween!"

"I don't know, Becca," Jeff replied honestly. Another mystery to add to this weird, weird day. But he had to tell her something. "You wouldn't believe me if I told you anyway. Let's say I fell off my bike but wasn't hurt."

"What about your cheek?"

Thinking quickly, Jeff chuckled. "Oh, I really got you that time, didn't I? You actually thought I had gotten punched in the face, didn't you?"

"Did not!"

"Yes, you did, admit it," Jeff said.

"Did not. I could tell it was makeup! I want to know where you got it."

"I'll never tell...Have you gotten as far as me in Astroloids yet?" Jeff asked, quickly changing the subject, thanking his lucky stars Becca apparently bought his story.

"I defeated a Centauzoid!" Becca said

enthusiastically, seemingly successfully off the track. "And I got a quark blaster."

"Wow. You can go through a level five shield with that. I wanna see," he said, heading toward the stairs.

"Not so fast, mister," came his mother's voice from the kitchen. "It's dinner time. Call your father, wash up, and come to the table."

"Awww, Mom. I just want to see it for a minute."

"It can wait until after dinner. Now, get your father. He's in his office."

"Yes, Mom." Jeff gave only the pretense of putting up a fight. There really was nothing he wanted to do more than eat right now…except maybe returning to the quarry. For now, he was thankful he had his sister distracted and didn't have to explain his rearranged face to his parents. But he certainly had a lot of mysteries to solve.

That night he did his homework right after dinner…without prompting from his parents. Just another example of how weird the day really was for him. Finishing in record time, he ran upstairs, closed the door, and settled in at the computer. Since returning to the quarry was not an option, at least for now, research was needed, and he didn't want to be disturbed.

He laid his hands on the keyboard and typed "UFO" then clicked "search." The number of "hits" was staggering. He couldn't believe how many websites there were on UFOs—nearly 250 million hits. Where to begin? Maybe the images tab. Surprisingly, there were videos from the US Government posted among the seemingly thousands of pictures and videos. But none matched what he saw.

Not knowing where to go, he picked another site sounding somewhat official. It had about forty thumbnails of amateur photos of UFOs. Some were obviously faked pictures—even to Jeff's untrained eyes. None looked like the one he saw today floating above the school.

He repeated the process, checking out nearly one hundred sites. There was an amazing amount of information Jeff vowed to come back and read. He created bookmarks for the most promising.

After about an hour Jeff got lucky. For there on the screen was an image of a UFO looking very similar to the one he had seen. Since the picture was taken from a distance it was impossible to tell for sure, but it had the same general shape and markings. Jeff bookmarked the site after noting the picture was taken in Argentina nearly ten years ago. Then, he downloaded the photo into a photo editor where he cleaned it up a bit by sharpening the contrast and getting rid of many of the scratches. Finally, he printed an enlarged version of the photo. It was still blurry, but it clearly was the same craft, or one like it, that was over the schoolyard.

He scanned a dozen more sites with no luck. He took the print and placed it in his notebook inside his backpack, which he'd brought in the computer room as he rushed upstairs.

****

Uncharacteristically, Jeff went to bed early that night. First, he had to reassure his parents this strange behavior was due to being very tired and not because he was coming down with something. At least, he hoped he wasn't.

He didn't even spend the usual hour texting Tess

and checking all the social media sites, once he discovered there still was no mention of the UFO at school. Fortunately, the topic did not come up again in his abbreviated conversation with Tess. She understood he needed alone time to reflect on all that happened. After putting the phone down on the bed table, he closed his eyes and drifted off to sleep.

But it was not to be a restful sleep. The nightmare began.

He and Becca were sitting on the front step of their home, talking. She had been crying again. Jeff wanted to cry as well. An overwhelming feeling of sadness enshrouded him. But he needed to be strong for her sake.

It was nearly lunchtime, although it was dark outside. It was summer, but they both wore jackets as it was cold. Looking up, the sun was barely poking through the dark, murky, ever-present haze. Becca coughed as the dirty air irritated her lungs.

His father came down the street, walking and carrying a bag of groceries. The cars were parked in the garage, useless as they needed gas to run, but there was none to be found. Jeff's car was missing entirely. What little gas they had was saved for dire emergencies.

Jeff was hungry. He was always hungry, but this was different. This was the type of hunger from not eating much for days. Everyone was much thinner now, but not healthier.

As his dad trudged up the driveway, Becca and Jeff ran over to greet him. His dad's face was ashen as he shook his head despondently from side to side. Jeff's mom came outside to join them. His dad's eyes greeted her with unbearable sadness. "There were three fights in the grocery store over a measly can of condensed milk. There's almost nothing left on the shelves. I got what I could, but it took three hours to even get that."

The scene shifted with the family gathered around a small battery-operated TV in the living room. There was no power in the house. Their cellphones were scattered about, useless.

Batteries were rationed, as they were extremely hard to get anymore. It was difficult getting anything now. They only watched TV for half an hour a day. But that was all right, as there was only one TV station still broadcasting, and only for a few hours an evening. It was all news.

Jeff hoped they would get power again soon. It came on for a while, then went off. Dad said something about the power grid being down. Jeff yearned for the days of the past when all he had to worry about was some stupid homework assignment.

The reporter's eyes were heavy and moist. The media had given up any pretense of trying to be uplifting. It was now about survival. The reporter noted martial law had now been declared and troops were arriving to quell the riots breaking out in the nation's cities. The President was shown making an impassioned plea for help at the United Nations, but none was forthcoming. The rest of the world was also suffering. Crops lay dead in the fields. More emergency shelters were set up every day, but there wasn't enough food to go around. Jeff worried they would have to go to a shelter soon. He wasn't looking forward to it.

The President pleaded with the nation not to generalize its collective hate against the terrorist group responsible to include all Arabs. But to no avail. The news went on to show groups of Muslims being rounded up and beaten, shot, and hung, and mosques burned by vigilantes seeking a target on which to vent their pent-up rage.

Senator Horn from what was left of California gave a speech urging the country to drop the bomb on those countries that may have played host to the United Arab Freedom Front. Death for death, he preached.

The news cut to Dr. Valencia, from MIT, who stated thirty newly active volcanoes were known to be erupting along the Pacific Rim, with a dozen more likely to erupt soon. The resulting amount of ash sent into the atmosphere was creating a nuclear winter. Already the earth's temperature had cooled an estimated ten degrees in only a couple months. Massive amounts of ice were forming in shipping lanes. Famine and despair were global.

Scientists talked about the start of the fifth mass extinction in earth's history. But no one said what everyone feared—would *Homo sapiens* be a part of the extinction?

Then they showed the clip...the video bringing terror, fear, anger, and unbearable grief to those who saw it...taken by someone hoping to film family fun in their backyard, but instead capturing humanity's darkest moment. It had been automatically uploaded to YouTube when there still was a YouTube, otherwise it would not exist.

The children's play was interrupted by a brilliant flash of light off in the distance, followed soon by the classic mushroom cloud. The camera shook with the ground, as a wall of debris approached—then nothing. The blast meant to kill millions in Los Angeles, which it did very efficiently with its explosive power and radiation...but it may kill billions due to its fallout, earthquakes, volcanic eruptions, global winter, tidal waves, flooding, and other unanticipated side-effects. Even the terrorists who planted the bomb hoping to disrupt the San Andreas fault could have had no idea of the amount of devastation that ensued as the fault finally let loose the "big one"—or rather big ones. The result was a series of 9+ earthquakes on the Richter scale, whose net effect destroyed most of the west coast and created a massive tectonic shift. In turn, a chain reaction of volcanic eruptions were triggered all along the Pacific Rim. These eruptions spurred more earthquakes, but as devastating as the earthquakes and volcanoes were, it was the resulting tidal waves that had caused most of the initial destruction and loss of life around the world. And now the ash threatened everything and everyone.

The climate changes resulting from the volcanic ash in the atmosphere threatened to completely wipe out the world's harvest. Adding to the misery were seemingly endless traumatic weather events—massive hurricanes, torrential rains, tornadoes, rain in desert areas, draught in rain forests. Billions could starve. Because of the combination of the climate changes and the flooding, entire species would be wiped out, along with, potentially, billions of humans. The casualties mounted faster than anyone could count. And there was no way to stop it.

Another reporter talked about how the world's stock markets had ceased trading. The World Bank called an emergency meeting to try to prevent a worldwide economic collapse, but it was to no avail.

The Earth's governments were collapsing. The US Government, the prognosticators warned, might be next. Cities were deserted, and gangs roamed the streets in search of food. People were fleeing into the country to find sanctuary. The military was barely holding itself together. Even the world's mightiest army needed food to function.

Jeff's dad shook his head and turned off the TV. He looked at his wife hopelessly.

At that moment, there was a crash at the front door. Three armed men burst into the house. "Where's the food?" one of the intruders demanded. Jeff's dad stood and faced them.

"Get out of my house!" he demanded. One of the thugs raised his pistol. There was a small explosion, and Jeff's dad grabbed his chest.

"NOOOOO!" Jeff screamed.

\*\*\*\*

"Jeff, Jeff, what's wrong?" Jeff's mother called as she rushed into the room, alarmed by her son's sudden scream.

"They shot Dad," Jeff said through sobs.

"You just had a bad dream. It's all right now. You're safe."

He was crying uncontrollably. He couldn't help it. Never had he experienced such a horrible dream. His heart still pounded, threatening to burst through his ribs with its intensity. His sheets were soaked.

"You're covered with sweat," his mother said, putting her hand to his forehead. "Well, you don't seem to have a fever. Maybe all that food you ate tonight caused you to have bad dreams." She sat on the bed, stroking his head soothingly.

"It was horrible, Mom. Horrible," he said through sniffs. "The world was coming to an end. No one could stop it. And then Dad got shot in the family room, right in front of us!" It was mortally embarrassing to have his mother see him cry, but he could not stop. The dream was too vivid.

"I assure you, your dad's fine," his mom said softly. "If you listen carefully, you can hear him snoring all the way in here. And, last I checked, the world was doing fine as well. It was just a bad dream." She got up to go.

"Mom, please don't go. I-I don't think I can go to sleep again. I'm too scared." He clutched his mother's arm. The dream seemed real…too real. A part of him chided himself for being such a baby…but he couldn't help it. The imagery burned indelibly into his mind.

"Well, why don't you read for a while? Maybe that will calm you down and give you pleasant thoughts to replace the bad ones."

Jeff nodded slowly. The images haunted him. But he had to try. He gave his mother a weak smile. "I'll be all right, Mom. Thanks…I'm sorry to have bothered you," he said sincerely.

"That's okay," his mother replied. "I'll be right down the hall. Come and get me if you still can't sleep after a while. It's probably because of those cheesy scary movies you watch."

"All right, Mom. Thanks." As she left the room, Jeff picked up his phone and watched funny videos. He needed something to get his mind off his nightmare, as well as the day's activities. Luckily, it worked. After a half-hour, his eyes grew heavy and he put the phone down. He hoped it would be a dreamless sleep.

Fortunately, it was.

Chapter 8

Jeff didn't want to talk about the dream the next day despite Becca's insistent questioning. His screams woke her up, too. But he was afraid it would scare her, even though it was just a dream. Yet, it was so vivid. Never had a dream felt so real...not even his "true" dreams. Several times before, Jeff had dreams about people or events that came true. But he always dismissed it as coincidence or his subconscious working overtime. But none of those dreams were as realistic as this one. Sweat began to form, and his heart raced as he recalled its details.

He was unusually quiet throughout breakfast—not even giving his mother his normal resistance about getting ready for school. He did, however, give his father an unusually long hug goodbye when he left for work.

On the bus, Jeff accessed *The Dallas Morning News* on his phone and searched for UFO sightings in the area.

"What are you looking for?" Becca wanted to know. "I've never seen you take such an interest in the paper—except the comics."

"I'm searching for something," he replied succinctly.

"Well, duh. I figured that one out. Looking for UFO reports?"

Jeff was stunned. How did she know? Then he remembered talking to her about the sighting over the school.

"Uh, no," he lied. Jeff figured if she didn't believe him last night, she wouldn't believe him now. "I forgot I had an assignment for US History. We're supposed to find articles about Congress," he said, trying to deflect Becca's curiosity.

"Then why do I see pictures of UFOs?" Becca replied nonchalantly.

That was one of the problems with having a bright, but annoying sister. Fortunately, Jeff was saved from further embarrassment by their timely arrival at school.

He avoided his friends as much as possible because he didn't know what to say. He wanted to share everything that happened, but it was so unbelievable, he was afraid of losing face. Besides, he needed to get it straight in his own mind first. He still wasn't quite sure what *did* happen versus what he *might* have imagined. The fact that there wasn't a hint of a mention in the morning's paper only made him more cautious—and curious.

Recalling the events of the last two days in his mind between classes made Jeff more spacey than normal. Somehow there was a connection between all the things that happened—Michaels, drugs, the UFO, the strange boy with the weird cat, and his horrible nightmare. He didn't know how or why they were connected, but he was certain they were. And how had his face healed like that?

As he pondered the possible connections in his mind, backpack hanging over his right shoulder, he headed toward Calculus class. That's when he ran smack into Mr. Olsteen, and not a casual bump but a full-scale, knock-'em-over, books flying type of collision.

"Mr. Olsteen! I'm so sorry!" Jeff managed to stammer as he picked up his books, which had scattered from his half-open backpack at impact.

"Mr. Miller. I see you seem to have a nose for trouble."

"Sorry, sir." Jeff frantically picked up his papers. He didn't want to talk to Mr. Olsteen right now. He still wasn't sure what was happening, or what to say.

Too late.

"I wanted to talk with you anyway," Mr. Olsteen said as he helped Jeff gather his things. "Please follow me to my office."

"Uh, I have Calculus right now," Jeff stammered, trying to think of a good reason why he couldn't talk with him right now.

"I'm sure Ms. Levitt will understand. I'll be glad to write you a note. This won't take long," Mr. Olsteen said, insisting.

It was pointless to argue...no sense in making a difficult situation worse. He meekly followed the Vice Principal to his office and took the offered seat in front of Mr. Olsteen's desk. Jeff sat down quietly and waited for Mr. Olsteen to speak.

"I wanted to talk with you about yesterday. What was going on with you and Michaels?" Mr. Olsteen demanded.

"Uh, nothing. Just a friendly discussion," Jeff lied. He didn't know what to say.

"Friendly? If Tess hadn't gotten me and I hadn't arrived when I did, you might have had a 'friendly' visit to the hospital." Jeff sat silent.

"Look, Jeff." Jeff did look. It was very unusual when Mr. Olsteen called someone by his first name. "You are an excellent student here. You have never given us any problems in your three years here. I know you are a very good kid."

"Thank you," Jeff managed to say. What would be the "but"?

"Tess told me something about what happened. We have had problems in the past with Michaels. Jeff, you know we're committed to keeping this school drug-free. Unfortunately, that punk will find himself behind bars if he isn't careful, or worse."

Jeff sat silently.

"I understand it is difficult to 'rat' on someone. And it is more difficult to prove. But if you know anything, we appreciate your cooperation."

Jeff nodded. He wanted to tell Mr. Olsteen everything, but was afraid. He certainly didn't want to bring up his sister's name and have her associated with drugs, even though she hadn't done anything—yet.

"Is there anything more you can tell me, Jeff?" Mr. Olsteen asked, his voice gentler.

"Well," Jeff began. He wanted to ask Mr. Olsteen about the UFO. But his experience with Tess made him more cautious. He decided to be a little more indirect. "Can I ask you something a little off the topic?"

Mr. Olsteen looked at him intently, then, after a dramatic pause finally nodded.

"Have you heard a rumor about a UFO being seen over the school yesterday?"

Mr. Olsteen rolled his eyes. "I would say that is a little off the subject. Unless we're talking about someone's hallucinations. No, I haven't heard any rumors about UFOs."

Jeff sighed deeply. Mr. Olsteen had seen it. He stared right at it. Yet, he wouldn't admit it. Why? What was happening? The UFO was real. He hadn't "hallucinated" it.

"Uh, can I go now?" Jeff asked timidly.

Mr. Olsteen looked at him long and hard before finally nodding. "Just remember, Jeff. We are on your side. You can come to us if you have a problem."

"Uh, thanks, sir. I appreciate it." Jeff quickly got up and headed for the door.

"Just a minute," Mr. Olsteen said sternly. Jeff froze.

"You forgot your note to Ms. Levitt," Mr. Olsteen said, as he picked up a notepad and started scribbling.

"Oh, thanks." Jeff exhaled the breath he had been holding. He had forgotten about the note, so anxious was he to make his escape. He took it from Mr. Olsteen, mumbling his gratitude again, and headed off to class, with yet another mystery to solve.

****

At lunch, Jeff took his usual spot with his friends. He had been racking his brain, trying to think of a way to bring up the topic of the UFO, without seeming crazy—or crazier—to his friends.

They pestered him with questions about his encounter with Michaels yesterday. Jeff told them all he could…up until the UFO appearance. Instead, he used

Mr. Olsteen's arrival as the distraction allowing him to break free, giving Tess credit for saving his hide. They agreed he did the right thing. Trying to fight Michaels in that situation would only have made things worse—win or lose.

After a brief lull in the conversation, Jeff tried his little gambit.

"Guys, you know how my sister is so into Astroloids?"

"And you're not…" Greg replied.

"I can still beat you, anytime," Jeff retorted.

Greg smiled. All four of them were known to play, although, as seniors, it wasn't something you openly discussed unless it was with known players and out of earshot of others.

"Well I was looking at some photos of UFO's the other day, and I ran across this picture." He pulled out the UFO picture he got off the net the night before. "Doesn't this look like the Archimedes fighter?" Jeff asked.

"What are you talking about?" Greg asked.

"I found this picture on the web, when searching for UFO sites. I thought it looked a little like an Archimedes fighter. What do you think?" He handed it around the table. "Wouldn't it be something if actual UFO's served as models for Astroloids?"

"I don't think it looks that much like an Archimedes fighter," Greg said. "In fact, I'm not sure it's a real UFO—it looks kinda fake."

"What do you think, Tess?" Jeff said, handing the picture to her. He studied her reaction carefully, hoping to find any glimmer of recognition.

"I can see where you might think it looks a little

like the fighter—but it's too rounded. The Archimedes fighter is more oval-shaped, isn't it?"

Nothing. No glimmer at all. Jeff had been sure the picture would jog her memory of yesterday's UFO. Either she was very, very good at acting, or she really didn't remember it.

"What's the matter, Jeff?" Ashanti asked. "You look really disappointed."

"Uh, I guess I am. I thought I was on to something."

"Yeah, aliens are behind the Astroloid invasion," Greg said. They all laughed, including Jeff. He put away the picture and returned to his lunch. The conversation drifted back to who was dating whom.

\*\*\*\*

Fortunately, at least in Jeff's current state of mind, there was no choir practice today, so he left school at the normal time. Happily, there was no Michaels waiting for him. Although he almost missed the bus.

When he got home, he grabbed a snack and told his mother he was heading over to Greg's on his bike. Instead, he headed back to the quarry.

As he pedaled, he reviewed the events of the past couple days over and over. Michaels. Drugs. UFO. Becca. The dizzy spell. His face healing miraculously. The dream. Somehow, in a way he couldn't fathom, they were all connected. Something was happening, and it was happening to him.

He arrived at the quarry without incident. This time he was a little more careful getting around the chain. When he came to the edge of the quarry, he peered down into the deep bowl. Again, the lake was muddy. Nor was there any sign of activity around the perimeter.

91

He headed down.

When he reached the bottom, he dismounted at about the same spot as the day before although without the benefit of flying off the bike first. No one was around. He put the kickstand down and walked over to the edge of the water where he attempted to peer through the muck to see what secrets might be hidden within.

"I'm glad you came back." The now-familiar voice shattered the tranquility and startled Jeff. He spun around to face Axel, who cradled the funny-looking creature in his arms. "Although I was confident you would."

While he fantasized about this moment for almost twenty-four hours now, Jeff still didn't have a clue as to what to say. Finally, he just blurted out, "Who *are* you?"

"I told you, my name is Axel," replied the boy calmly, with a slight grin on his face.

"That's not what I meant. I mean, where did you come from? What are you doing here? What's it got to do with me? Why is this all so weird?" Jeff rapidly rattled off the questions he'd been preoccupied with. Jeff looked around. "And how did you get here?" Then, glancing at Chermal, he paused, then asked, "And what is that thing?"

Axel laughed. "So many questions! But I will answer them all...in time. First, let me ask you a question."

"What?" Jeff replied, a little suspicious.

"Did you have any, say, *unusual* dreams last night?"

Jeff's face froze. "How...how did you know?"

"What did you think of it?" Axel asked, avoiding Jeff's query.

"It was horrible, just horrible." The imagery flooded his mind, bringing back the terror. "It scared me to death," he said somberly. "That's what. And it was so real, so vivid." Tears formed in his eyes as the memories echoed in his mind. "It was awful!"

"I know. It scared me too," Axel said reassuringly.

"You had the same dream?" Jeff said, startled by Axel's admission.

"Not the same one, no, but similar—with the same theme," Axel replied. "Come here and sit down," Axel offered, gesturing at a clump of rocks near the cliff wall. "Let's talk."

Jeff followed Axel over to the rocks and took his seat. Axel sat across from Jeff and placed Chermal on the ground in front of him. Chermal sat on his back haunches and stared up at Jeff. Jeff returned his gaze. The warmth coming from the animal was apparent as was the intelligence behind those bright almond eyes. Axel was still wearing the same clothes he had on yesterday, including the green bracelet, reflecting the sunlight brightly.

"That vision bothered me tremendously," Axel continued. "That's why I had to do something about it."

"How do you know what I dreamed? We could have both just had a nightmare."

Axel shook his head. "Tell me if I'm wrong. You dreamed someone set off a nuclear bomb in the desert outside of LA, meaning to destroy the city, but instead ending up destroying most of the planet. Is that about it?"

Jeff nodded slowly, thinking how surreal this

whole episode was. Who was this kid anyway?

"It was very real to you, wasn't it?" Axel said. Again, Jeff nodded slowly. "That's because it was real. Or rather, it's a glimpse into the future of what *will* happen if we don't do something to prevent it."

Jeff stared at Axel, mouth hanging open. He found himself looking from him to Chermal. Who were these guys?

Jeff fought the urge to immediately run away as the fear held within that dream once again rose to the surface and met with his apprehension regarding the strange pair seated next to him. Yet he had to stay.

Axel was telling the truth. He felt the truth in the dream. But strangely he wasn't as afraid anymore. Again, there was a calming warmth seemingly emanating from Chermal, as though reassuring him everything was okay.

"But it was only a dream," Jeff protested. "How do you know it's real? What do you mean 'will' happen? And 'if *we* don't prevent it?' What's going *on*?" Jeff cried out, almost overcome with an explosion of emotions and confusion.

"Just for a minute, go along with me," Axel said. "Let's say you had every reason to feel the dream was accurate and the events portrayed *will* happen. Wouldn't you do everything you could to prevent them from occurring?"

"Of course," Jeff said. "It was absolutely horrible."

"Well, so would I. And I am. Only there are a lot of 'others' who know about this vision, but who will do nothing to prevent it." He spat out the last few words in anger. "That's why I have to help. But I can't do it alone. That's why I need you. And I know you will want to help too."

"But how do you know this 'vision,' as you call it, is real? And what on earth can I do, or 'we' do? Heck, I don't even have a working car right now."

Axel looked at him silently then at Chermal, who returned his gaze. Finally, he looked back up to Jeff. "In all honesty, Jeff, I don't know what we can do. All I know is I have to try, and you are the best one to help." Axel was silent for a moment, before continuing softly. "I also know *we* are the only ones that *can* stop this thing."

"How, how did you know my name?" Jeff asked, recalling he had never given Axel his name. "And why me? Who *are* you?"

"The reason I chose you," Axel said, then looked down at Chermal, "uh, *we* chose you, is because we know we can trust you to do what is right. And because you have the ability to help." Axel stared steadily into his eyes. "As for the rest, I think you know. You tell me." Both he and Chermal stared intently at Jeff.

Jeff stared back at the two for a minute, then threw up his hands and laughed. "This is crazy, absolutely crazy!"

"Go on," said Axel. "Tell me."

"Okay, you will think I'm nuts—which I'm beginning to believe anyway." Jeff laughed. He got up and walked over to the lake, then turned and faced Axel. "Okay, here it goes. I think you two are from outer space. You have a flying saucer parked under the water over there," Jeff said, waving his arms out toward the lake. "And you buzzed me in the schoolyard the other day, and somehow you guys are responsible for my dream last night."

Axel said nothing for a while, then spoke softly. "And if all that were true, what would you do?"

"If I thought it were true, I would jump on my bike, pedal home as fast as I could. Then call the police and tell them to get the heck over here."

Now it was Axel's turn to laugh. "No, I don't think you would do any of that. And that's why you are here. And here alone."

Jeff was quiet.

"Before this goes further," Axel began, "I want you to think carefully about everything. If you are as committed to stopping that vision from becoming real as I think you are, you will want to help me. Before you make that commitment, though, you should know what I'm really asking of you."

Jeff stared at the two sitting across from him. His head spun, but as he listened, he casually put his right hand in his pocket, fingering his phone.

"It could be dangerous, very dangerous. There will be a lot of people and forces working against us. It will mean you may have to make sacrifices. You could get seriously hurt or killed."

As Axel talked, Jeff slowly withdrew his hand from his pocket, phone in hand. He stopped with his hand and phone a few inches outside the pocket. Using feel alone, he aimed the camera at his two companions as his finger hit the shutter button several times, moving the phone around slightly to increase the odds of capturing Axel and especially Chermal in the picture.

Axel, without giving any indication he knew what Jeff was doing, continued. "And what may be hardest of all is that you can't tell anyone about what is occurring. Even if we are successful, you can't tell. Not that I forbid it, but you will find no one will ever believe you—and that will hurt. You may save the earth, but no one will ever know it."

"You're asking a lot from a seventeen-year-old," Jeff said.

Axel smiled knowingly. "I think you can handle it. But you must decide for yourself. Go home now and think about it. Meet us back here tomorrow, after choir, and tell us your decision. We don't have a lot of time."

Jeff looked at Axel, then at Chermal. He wanted to tell them he was ready now. But caution got the better of him. They were right. This was too big a decision to make impulsively. "Will I have another dream tonight?" Jeff asked.

"No…At least, none from us." Axel smiled.

Jeff nodded, greatly relieved. He didn't ever want to see that "vision" again.

Without saying goodbye, Jeff rose and went over to his bike. Pausing only long enough to look back at the two "strangers," he proceeded up the road.

As soon as he made it around the gate, he pulled the phone from his pocket. He opened the gallery and reviewed his latest photos, only to discover they were completely black. Yet he did not have his hand over the lens. Strange.

He got back on his bike and pedaled off into the evening to ponder his destiny.

Chapter 9

Axel left the meeting with his father in a huff. How could his father and the Zanchee refuse to intervene? A whole planet might be destroyed, and they were letting some stupid rule prevent them from helping. Well, it wouldn't stop him.

Not knowing exactly where to turn, Axel went to his Nescian, who was helping him prepare for Nemseck. The Nescian was responsible for training him on mental discipline and taught him *sen*. Axel really enjoyed his times with him, despite the Nescian's habit of speaking in riddles. He helped Axel gain more self-confidence. If anyone could help him with an issue of *sen*, as this was in Axel's mind, it will be his Nescian.

Hopes were quickly dashed as the Nescian provided no help at all in this situation. Wanting enlightenment, Axelarone received frustration. It was as though the Nescian was "brushing him off," which was uncharacteristic. Previously, the Nescian was always willing to listen and render sage advice, although it was sometimes obscure. Not this time. After Axel spilled out his heart, all the Nescian did was nod and give him gobble-gook.

"Search within?" Axel muttered, as he left the Nescian. "Search within? What kind of mumbo-jumbo crap is that?" He turned back, facing the Nescian's room. "You're no help!" he said to a barren wall. "Search within what?" he asked of no one. "Search within the room? The ship? Myself? My room? What is he talking about? I already searched in my father's office—which is what got me into this mess in the first place."

Disgusted and confused, Axel turned back down the hallway, muttering as he went. "I don't have time to play these mind games. And neither do the humans."

Axel retreated to his room, three levels below the command floor. Needing to regain composure, he walked the whole way. Chermal, as always, anticipated his mood and was there, waiting patiently. Axel looked down at the mentiot, his only remaining friend it seemed, hoping somehow Chermal could solve all his problems, as he helped so many times in the past.

It was bad enough having to study for Nemseck, not knowing when it was or what it would cover. Now this. After he successfully completed Nemseck and participated in the ceremonial Seckchi, he could petition the council to review their policies regarding Earth, but by then it would be too late. And until the Seckchi, Axel was essentially a non-entity. Only adults had voice in these matters.

Why did this have to happen now? Why did his stupid dad make him come here three months before Nemseck, if he wouldn't let him *do* anything? How could some stupid principle be more important than a whole planet? It wasn't fair. It wasn't *right*. And, despite what his father said, it wasn't *sen*.

His father made things worse. Not only did he ignore Axel's pleading about the humans, but he also kept harping on Axel's need to prepare for Nemseck while refusing to tell him what he would have to do for it. Nor would anyone else, including the Nescian. Not even the barest of hints. The anticipation itself was part of the test, they claimed, and everyone's Nemseck was different—customized for each individual. But how could he prepare if he didn't know what he would be doing?

So, they had him doing everything in preparation. He spent countless hours working with the QUAIC, learning its every nuance. Countless more hours were spent with the Nescian, learning about his "inner" self and how to improve his metaphysical abilities, and more hours than he could count with tutors of various disciplines. And he spent hundreds of hours studying the enigmatic race around whose planet they were currently orbiting. His father even took him on board the fleet's Time-Warp Ship, which allowed them to journey back in time, so Axel could study first-hand some of the major events in human history. Given, understandably, few Zanchee had access to the TWS, Axel greatly appreciated the opportunity. In fact, he begged his father to allow him to go on more such trips. But now, unless the Zanchee did something quickly, all humanity would be history.

Not for the first time, Axel wished he had someone to talk to. Someone, that is, his own age and not covered in fur. It was tough being the only Nescreet on the *Druize*. And it was only because his father was Thermax he was here. Curse his luck. It was bad enough dealing with his fears about Nemseck without having to essentially go it alone. And now, this!

As these thoughts raged through Axel's mind, a cool, soothing presence touched him. Chermal, as always, was trying to calm him down, pushing for him to step outside his emotional constraints and gain a larger perspective. It was easy for Chermal to have a broad perspective. He could see the future as easily as Axel remembered the past. To Chermal, the past, present, and future were simply convenient designations along a temporal path just as forward, backward, and still were directions along the physical path Axel walked. Time and again, Axel pleaded with his mentiot to give him some hint as to the future, which hopefully would allow him to relax. Chermal refused, making it clear revealing the future changed the future.

Axel assumed a meditative position on the bed. He had to think. If he really was to do something, he would have to be very careful. He could not risk raising his father's suspicions, for he would certainly be stopped. Nor could he count on help from other Zanchee. He was the only nescreet on board, and all the nescrot were loyal to his father. No, it was up to him to save the humans. But what could he do alone? Okay, okay, not alone, but what could he and Chermal do by themselves?

Axel considered sending an anonymous warning to human authorities. But how to go about it? To whom would he send it? And would they believe him?

The only thing to do was run simulations. Axel went over to his desk and accessed the QUAIC terminal. One advantage of being the son of the Thermax was access to the ship's AI and its sophisticated capability to run projections on various scenarios. Caution was needed, however, because he didn't want to tip his hand to his father. Fortunately, scenario projections on the humans was part of his training. He set up the complicated scenario then plugged in "what if" situations such as "What if the authorities are tipped off by one of the terrorists or drug gang members?" The possible scenarios did not include him personally tipping the authorities.

The results were always the same. No matter where the tip came from, its content or source, the authorities would be too slow to respond. Not unless the tip provided specific information such as who, when, and exactly where, and even then, the probability for success was less than 0.1%. Worse, Axel had none of this information, nor any clue as to how to obtain it. The Zanchee projections only said it will happen—but could not provide him names, precise locations, or times.

Nor could Chermal, as great a talent as he was, give him specific-enough details. He could foretell the event, but even he could not identify the individual players. There were too many variables. Now, if Chermal could get close enough to one of the conspirators, he could identify them. But trying to pick the terrorists from 10,000 miles in space on a planet with billions of humans was too great a task, even for him.

So providing a tip would not work. At least, not without getting more information first, and even then, it was a long shot. And how would he get the information? Sure, if he had access to the Zanchee field operatives, he might be able to do something. But that was impossible. He may be the son of Axelasome, Thermax of the fleet, but he was still a nescreet—a nothing—wearer of a green knosett. No one would believe him, follow him, or dare go against the Zanchee Alliance law, or his father, if they would even listen to him. No, if anything was going to get done, he and Chermal would have to be more direct and do it alone.

Or would they? Axel looked down at Chermal, who returned his thoughtful gaze. The Zanchee wouldn't help. But maybe he could somehow get humans to help. Since a tip wouldn't work, he would need a human to work with him. Yet contacting any human would be in violation of almost everything Axel had been taught. He wasn't sure he was quite ready to do that. It was not *sen*, and somehow, even with what was at stake, Axel could not do what was not *sen*. There had to be another way. If he were caught, the repercussions would be severe, not just to him, but also to his father and family. And why would a human believe him? After all, he was, what did they call it…a teen to them, and a short one at that.

Axel rested his head in his right hand, staring at the green knosett adorning his wrist. If only it glowed the red of a nescrot.

Chermal jumped onto the table and rubbed against his knosett. Axel reached out instinctively to scratch him.

"If you ask me," Axel said to Chermal, "it's the nescrot causing all the problems. They were the ones making the stupid laws, which they would turn around and break, anyway. And it is the human equivalent of nescrot who will be blowing up that world.'

The thought hung on Axel. "Human nescrot." If

Zanchee didn't consider their own nescreet important, perhaps they wouldn't consider human nescreet important either. Axel quickly accessed the QUAIC and called up the laws governing Zanchee interaction with sentient species.

Axel read them over quickly. Then he read them again, more thoroughly. Chermal purred softly. For the first time, there was hope. To him it was clear—the Zanchee laws dealt only with interactions with the human equivalent of nescrot.

Axel exclaimed to his furry companion, "Bless the Zanchee blindness! Since Zanchee only consider nescrots as competent to make decisions, they apply the same standards to humans. So, technically, we are forbidden only against contact with human nescrot— that is, human adults. It says nothing about non-adults. It might be implied…but it isn't stated. So, what is the human equivalent of Nemseck?"

Axel accessed the QUAIC again. But the results were a lot more complex than he anticipated. Humans did not have a single defining criterion of what made an adult. Some religions and cultures marked the "coming of age" during a period close to when the human body transitions to its adult form or "puberty" as the humans referred to it.

However, most of the world's modern governments did not recognize puberty as giving one the right to act or be treated like an adult. And though Nemseck may resemble a religious rite, its meaning dealt more with earning rights of adulthood—including the right to vote in the affairs of the Zanchee. So, Axel decided the best definition is one the human governments recognized. Specifically, as he would likely need a human from the country referred to as "The United States," he chose to use that government's criteria.

Thinking he reached a breakthrough, Axel was again stymied when he discovered even the United States Government didn't seem to have a universal definition of becoming an adult. In some matters, like driving a vehicle, they used sixteen. Some of the states allowed thirteen-year-olds the right to make a lifelong commitment—i.e. getting married. Yet, these same states mandated that you had to be twenty-one before you could purchase a social drug called alcohol.

After much thought and one-way discussion with Chermal, Axel determined the best criterion was to use the age when the citizens of the United States can vote, helping determine their own government. That age was eighteen. So, he needed to find a human younger than eighteen.

"All right, Chermal, it appears it's up to the children to save the earth from the errors of their adults. Now, where to begin?"

Axel went over to the console and placed his hands on the input nodules. The quantum computer sprang instantly to work at Axel's command. Axel played out thousands of scenarios as Chermal watched silently. Slowly, a plan emerged.

Chapter 10

Jeff smiled as he thought his parents must be really beginning to wonder what happened to their son when, for the second straight night, he did his homework promptly after dinner without a single reminder. As soon as he finished, he headed right back to the computer.

Jeff did some preliminary searches on his phone. In fact, earlier, while in school, he spent most of Chemistry doing searches on the web, rather than performing his experiments in the lab, leading to a rather embarrassing incident he would just as soon forget. After that, his phone was taken from him for the rest of the day. But now he knew more about what he wanted to look for when he got home.

First, he searched for recent UFO sightings, narrowing his search to the past few days. He looked at both UFO sites and discussion groups. There was only one new item, and it was nowhere near him.

Next, he searched alien contact. Again, there were a lot of hits. But most were like stories out of B grade science fiction novels. Many were about abductions and weird medical experiments being done on the victim.

Not helpful. He tagged a couple sites that appeared a bit more realistic but did not have the energy to read them. Fatigue had overtaken him, likely from the lack of sleep the previous night coupled with the stress of everything that was happening. Time to get some rest.

****

Axel was right about the dreams. There weren't any that night. Mostly because he lay awake thinking about everything that had occurred and what it might mean. Tired as he was, he could not fall asleep. Deep down, he believed last night's dream, no, "vision," was a foreshadowing of events to come. It was real. And he could not let it happen if he could do anything about it. But what? Although he wanted to think of himself as an adult, he really wasn't much more than a kid. For that matter, so was Axel—at least, he seemed to be only a kid. But if he really was an alien, he could be five hundred years old, for all he knew.

He had always been a science fiction buff, with dozens of books occupying his bookshelves and many more stored on his tablet. Science fiction movies and their sequels were his favorites. He often envisioned himself as a hero commanding a star ship, saving the world. Yet, that was fantasy. This was real—at least, it felt real. And that made it different. Very different. What did he know about saving the world? Or nuclear bombs? Or any of that stuff? He was scared. Scared of the possible future if he did nothing. Scared of what would happen to him if he did something. Scared of failing.

Perhaps it was his fondness for science fiction preventing him from freaking out at the thought of actually meeting an E.T. He always believed they existed and were likely behind many of the UFO sightings he heard about. Having now met one, he found himself more excited than scared. But his enthusiasm over the contact was heavily tempered by his fear of the reality behind that dream.

He wanted desperately to talk to Greg and Tess, and especially Becca, about what happened. But tell them what? Axel was right. They wouldn't believe him. Adults certainly wouldn't. He was, after all, only a teenager with an overactive imagination.

And what about the danger? On one hand, the thought of a dangerous adventure à la his favorite science fiction heroes thrilled him. But again, the nasty reality of what it might really mean if something should happen to him scared him silly. He wasn't ready to die—heck, he hadn't been alive very long. Death wasn't the only thing to be feared—what if he wasn't killed, but instead severely hurt…like being paralyzed, or getting a serious head injury? Most kids his age thought themselves invincible—he knew better.

Jeff remembered Dwight from grade school, who was paralyzed from the waist down. Dwight was a great kid, but no one wanted to be around him. It was as though they feared him. Scared because he was different…afraid because he reminded them of their own fragility. How would Jeff manage in the same position?

Then again…how could he live without his father? Or the millions or billions who could die if he did nothing? It wasn't a hard decision. It was a hard reality.

Then there was the other little matter. Why him? Why did Axel choose Jeff Miller to be the savior of the world? He was honest with himself. He was bright, but there were smarter kids. He knew martial arts but was far from being an expert. He had some talents, but there were kids more talented. Besides, what was he going to do, sing the bomb away? So, what made him so special for Axel to pick him and not someone else? And he was selected—Axel said as much. And he was telling the truth. Of that, he was sure.

As he tossed and turned, Jeff had another inspiration. Given it was a nuclear bomb he was supposed to help stop from exploding, perhaps he should read more on nuclear weapons, including how they worked. He picked up his phone off the charger next to his bed and started searching. Again, the amount of information was overwhelming. He picked a few sites providing basic information he could understand and started reading. Finally, his eyelids grew heavy and he fell asleep.

****

Jeff found it extremely difficult to get up the next morning for school. Not only had he not slept much and was exhausted, but school no longer felt important. Not with everything else going on—like saving the world. He already had a pretty serious case of senioritis, and now this. He desperately wanted to skip school and head straight for the quarry. But Axel told him to meet him at the same time today—so evidently Axel wanted him to go to class. Better to play it safe than jeopardize his standing at school, much less get into considerable trouble with his parents, until absolutely necessary.

For the second day in a row, Jeff avoided his mother as much as possible that morning. He didn't want to face a thousand questions as to why he looked so tired and why he hadn't slept well. No sense getting her alarmed. So, Jeff dressed without the normal five reminders, fixed his own breakfast, and even avoided the usual morning bickering with Becca. Instead, he mumbled something to both his mother and sister about an upcoming test and buried his nose in a textbook.

Truthfully, he had no idea what textbook his nose touched as his eyes were so glazed over from the lack of sleep. When the bus came, Jeff boarded quickly and silently. He hoped to take an entire bench to himself so he could stretch out, but Becca foiled his plans.

"All right, Big Brother, your act may fool Mom, but it doesn't fool me," Becca commented as she sat down next to him. "What's going on?"

"Nothing," came his automatic response.

"Well, either you're wearing mascara now and it's running, or you didn't get much sleep last night. Either way, it's newsworthy, knowing how well you sleep."

Jeff was beaten. "You're right. I didn't get much sleep. I was worried about this test today."

"Would that be the one you were studying for this morning?" Becca asked.

"Uh huh," Jeff replied, as he unsuccessfully tried to stifle a yawn.

"Interesting way of studying you have, staring at an upside-down textbook. Is that something you pioneered? By the way, what is your test in?"

Jeff sighed. "Okay, okay, I don't have a test today. I didn't get much sleep last night because I'm worried about you," Jeff told her half-truthfully.

"Me?" Becca replied, innocently.

"Yes, you." Jeff was thankful for a good excuse to use. "I'm scared to death you will ignore my advice and start doing drugs like your so-called friends." Jeff warmed up to the lecture. It wasn't hard. He really was frightened for Becca. "I'm scared of what they will do to you—both the actual effect of the drugs, and of defying all that you have been taught to honor, love, and respect."

"I'm a big girl now. I can handle myself."

"You're only fourteen. You're not old enough to decide whether to throw your whole life away yet." Jeff had a hard time keeping a straight face as he said that remark, though, remembering at fourteen he also felt he knew everything.

"I'm not throwing my life away…just the fourteen-year-old part," Becca said flippantly, trying to lighten the mood.

"Yeah, right. Look, Becca, I'm serious. I'm very worried about you."

Becca turned away.

"Becca, it's not worth it. I don't care what anyone says."

"You sound like a commercial. Will you break out a frying pan and an egg next?" Becca said sarcastically.

"If I have to. But I will use the frying pan on your head."

"That sounds more like the brother I know and love," Becca said, chuckling.

Jeff joined her. It felt good getting it off his chest. He was also pleased at successfully deflecting Becca's curiosity away from what else was bothering him. Two days ago, his main concern was a new zit trying to form on his nose—now there was keeping his sister off drugs, avoiding getting beaten up by someone who looked like the missing link, and also this little matter of saving the world.

\*\*\*\*

Jeff managed to stay awake—barely—through his morning classes. And given calculus was one of them, that task was extremely difficult. Finally, it was time for lunch.

As soon as he sat down at the lunch table, he faced an inquisition. His appearance apparently was somewhat disturbing. His friends, like his sister, were concerned about Jeff's ragged look and lack of sleep. Having been successful once with the tactic, might as well tell them the same thing he told her. The difference was they believed he was also concerned about another physical confrontation with Michaels…which was true.

Sure, he knew karate—but he hadn't practiced in two years. And while he was confident he could handle himself against Michaels, the gorilla significantly changed the odds. It wouldn't hurt to start brushing up on his martial arts skills.

The other reason everyone was concerned was today was choir practice. And it was after choir on Tuesday that Michaels and Ox had been waiting for him. Tess suggested the best thing would be to make sure he left as part of a group. Along with Tess, there were several others in choir who could be counted on. Ashanti again volunteered to help keep an eye on Becca. Unfortunately, Greg had soccer practice and couldn't help.

Jeff still avoided bringing up Axel. He badly wanted to tell them. After all, his friends and sister were such big parts of his life that he wanted to share everything with them. But it was too unbelievable. And he didn't want them to think he was crazy. So, he kept his silence—for now. Hopefully, he could get some proof or something to help back up his story when he finally told them.

Lunch reinvigorated Jeff, as food often did. He was still very tired but more alert. As the day wore on, the adrenaline surged through his system as thoughts of Michaels and Axel continuously danced through his head.

**\*\*\*\***

Finally, it was time for choir. Despite his anxiety about what might follow, Jeff looked forward to choir. It wasn't just the singing. It gave him more time with Tess.

And there she was, flashing a big grin in his direction that ignited a fire within him. What started innocently as a good friendship had blossomed into a true romance—until all this came up. He quickly smiled back and took his seat next to her in the front row. Mr. Morris claimed he had them in front because they were soloists, but Jeff suspected it was to prevent them from talking to each other. Jeff mouthed "later" in response to her questioning expression.

Her hand brushed against his in response as they took their places. It both calmed and excited him, though in very different ways.

The fall show was coming in two weeks, so Mr. Morris was rehearsing them hard—calling them to order as soon as he entered the room. The first number was a rousing piece that really got the choir perked up. Luckily, it had that desired effect on Jeff, who was still dragging.

The next song featured a duet with him and Tess. They harmonized well together, and the song always gave him goosebumps. Not just because it was a beautiful song, but because he was singing it with her. Being a romantic ballad only added to its special meaning. And they sang it well together. Jeff stole a glance at Tess and discovered her smiling back at him.

The song was going great. The choir sounded excellent, and Tess and Jeff never sounded better as the song reached its climax featuring Tess and Jeff hitting and sustaining a high C.

That's when it happened.

It came out of nowhere…suddenly and without notice. Everything was sounding so great. And then…

"Sssqquueeeeaaakkkkk."

The choir froze. Tess stopped in mid-note and stared at him, mouth hanging open. Jeff turned twelve shades of red—all at once. Everyone stared at him. Then someone laughed, and the rest joined in.

"What was that?" someone in the back row said in a stage whisper.

"I, I have a frog in my throat," Jeff stammered.

"Sounded more like a mouse," said another in the back. More laughter.

Jeff cleared his throat, somewhat loudly. Of all the times to get a frog in his throat. His being overtired must have had a bad effect on his vocal cords.

Mr. Morris quickly got the choir back under control by rapping hard on the music stand.

"Shall we try that again?" Mr. Morris asked, continuing to tap the podium. Jeff wanted to disappear. Last practice, he fainted, now this. Would he ever just be able to sing?

Fortunately, for Jeff's shredded ego, they made it through the next time without any hitches, faints, or squeaks. The one good thing about the episode, it distracted him from his other issues, at least for a while.

The moment proved shorter than Jeff would have preferred. Fortunately, though, Tess hadn't forgotten her promise. So, when Jeff got ready to leave choir, he found himself surrounded by six other choir members, and they all walked out together.

The caution proved fortuitous, for as soon as they left the building an altogether-too-familiar voice boomed out, "Hey, Miller. See you bribed some of your sissy friends to protect you."

Jeff turned to see Michaels leaning against the school building. Ox was next to him. So were a couple kids Jeff recognized from school. Apparently, he had the unfortunate timing of having choir during Michaels' "business hours" and near his "office."

"One of these days, Miller, you won't be so lucky. There won't be all those choir sissies or vice principals around to protect you. Just you and me. Then we'll see how tough you really are," Michaels taunted.

Jeff ignored him as best he could. He continued to walk to the traffic circle, talking to Tess about the choir practice. But his ears burned. He wasn't the only one.

Tess's mother was there first, so Jeff opened the car door for her. Tess was about the only person in the senior class who didn't have a car. In fact, she didn't know how to drive. Her parents were very strict and told her they wouldn't allow it until she turned eighteen—much to her complete chagrin. "Call me later, Jeff," she said as she got into the car, but not before giving him a quick peck on the cheek. "We can talk about everything then."

"Yeah, sure," Jeff managed to say. He gave her a parting wave as he shut the door and headed to the curb where his mother's car had pulled up.

"I see you and Tess are getting along nicely," his mother said as a way of greeting. She gave him a conspiratorial grin and wink.

Jeff tried ignoring her, too. Being a teenager wasn't easy.

Chapter 11

Doug gathered the various files strewn across his desk and tucked them under his arm, along with a legal pad. The Dallas regional FBI office was his "home" office, although he didn't spend much time there. Given he was rarely in the office, let alone at home, it was just as well he was now a bachelor.

Doug mentally reviewed the events of the past couple days as he headed toward the conference room. He had certainly poked the hornet's nest. While DC did not take the threat as seriously as Doug felt warranted, they had not ignored him either. So now he found himself leading a jury-rigged subtask force. One good thing about 9/11, it forced the various agencies in charge of the country's security to work more closely together. Doug was already part of a multi-disciplinary anti-terrorism task force. His new subtask force was now a part of that as well.

Waiting for him in the conference room were Seth Rosenburg of the CIA, Hakeem Nassir of the NSA, Julie Longley of Homeland Security, Tyrone Hill of the DEA, and Hector Rodriguez of the Department of Immigration and Customs Enforcement. All had top secret clearances, allowing them to share information freely with each other.

"I want to thank you for getting here on such short notice," Doug said as he entered the room. "I know you've been briefed. And brief is the right word, because we simply do not know much. What we know for sure is three very bad, very powerful people, who head exceptionally dangerous organizations, have been seen meeting secretly for some unknown purpose.

"I need not remind you the anniversary of 9/11 is coming up. And I'm sure Raheim would like nothing more than to celebrate the date by topping the carnage.

"The key to discovering what he's planning is determining what these three organizations could possibly have to gain by working together." After a dramatic pause, he continued, facing Seth. "Perhaps one of the keys may be knowing whether the Russian government is working with Krenchenko. Seth?"

"We know that the Russian president and Krenchenko go way back. We also know they both are heavily invested in several specific companies. But there is no direct evidence Krenchenko is working with the Russian government."

"Can we put a priority on finding out?" Doug asked.

"I will push it up the chain of command," Seth replied.

****

The team spent the next two hours brainstorming and developing a variety of theories. But they all had holes. There was no logical reason why these three organizations would work together. The Russian mob, if anything, saw Bivardo as a competitor. It was almost unthinkable they were working together. What could Raheim possibly offer them to get their cooperation, assuming Raheim was the ringleader, although Doug was certain that was the case.

The lack of specific chatter related to the meeting picked up by the NSA indicated the organizations were keeping a very tight lid on whatever was happening. It was highly likely only the very top leaders knew what was occurring.

All three organizations were flush with money, despite Bivardo's recent seizures of his fortune by the US. The loss represented only a portion of his assets. He still had plenty of money. So, it was unlikely the deal was strictly financial, although the possibility still remained.

Doug handed out assignments. Seth and the CIA would concentrate on Krenchenko. Ty and Julie would work on Bivardo. And Doug would continue concentrating on Raheim. Meanwhile, Hector and Hakeem would encourage their agencies to be on high alert for anything suspicious that could be tied to any of the three targets.

Doug had agents trying to track the three pilots of the planes that took off from Monterrey. But so far, none of the planes made a reappearance. No doubt, the registration numbers were fake, and the planes repainted since then.

Others were trying to back-trace where Bivardo and Krenchenko were before meeting with Raheim, but without any success so far. In short, they had nothing.

## Chapter 12

*September 9<sup>th</sup>, D Minus 164.4 Hours*
*Dallas*

As he had the day before, Jeff changed quickly and clambered on his bike as soon as he could. He thought about calling Greg to go with him but decided against it. For some reason, he felt he needed to go alone. He hated lying to his mother about where he was going but there was no other alternative. So off he pedaled to confront his destiny—wherever it took him. When he and Tess finally talked, he would have a lot more to tell her than she could possibly imagine.

\*\*\*\*

He made it to the quarry without incident. It was as he left it. There was no overt sign of Axel and his fuzzy friend, or, for that matter, anyone else. The lake was still muddy.

After carefully negotiating the thorns by the chained entrance, Jeff turned his bike down the dirt road leading to the lake. A sense of calm came over him with the wind caressing his cheeks as he headed downhill. Surprising himself, he wasn't scared or anxious. Instead, he was at peace and self-assured. He was doing the right thing. He had a purpose. It was as though he matured ten years in two days dealing with all these things—and he hadn't fallen apart...yet.

Once again, Axel appeared out of nowhere as Jeff parked his bike at the lip of the lake.

"You made the right decision," Axel began. Chermal rubbed against his legs. "I know it wasn't easy. But I'm very glad you came. Chermal knew you would."

"How...? Never mind. All right, I'm here. Now what? What can I possibly do? How can I help you? What can you do? What can we do?" Jeff fired his questions as he walked toward the strange pair. "Can you tell me what's going on?"

Jeff came to a stop a few feet away. Axel stared at him for a moment. A deep-throated sound, halfway between a growl and a purr, came from Chermal.

"Before I tell you any more, we must do one final test."

"Test? What test?" Jeff said, somewhat agitated.

"We must make sure you can handle what we need you to handle."

"And what is that?"

"I can't tell you yet. You will have to trust me."

"You ask a lot without giving me much to go on."

"I understand. And there's more. This test could possibly harm you. We don't think it will, but there is that risk."

"What kind of test? I won't have to run through a ring of fire or wrestle snakes or something, will I?"

Axel laughed. "No, nothing like that. It is a mental test. We need to examine your mind."

"You're not going to cut me open!" Jeff exclaimed, backing up a few steps, images flashing through his mind of some of the darker science fiction series episodes he had seen.

Again, Axel chuckled. "No. In fact, we won't touch you...physically. We need to test your psychic potential."

"Psychic potential? As in ESP?" Now it was Jeff's turn to laugh. "Boy, do you have the wrong guy! I can't read anyone's mind. If I could, I would never have let Becca get into trouble or allow Michaels to sucker punch me like that."

"Don't be too sure. Many people have psychic insights without realizing what they are. I'm sure you have had occasions where you knew the answer to a question before it was asked?"

"Well, yeah," Jeff said thoughtfully.

"Or know the phone will ring a second before it does and who was calling before you picked up the phone."

"Yeah, I guess so."

"Have you ever had déjà vu? Where you felt you have been somewhere before, even though you never have."

"A couple times."

"And don't you often seem to know what your sister is thinking, or where she is, without having any way of really knowing it?"

"Yeah, but I'm not a psychic! I just know her really well...too well, at times."

"I understand you're not like those psychics you see on TV or read about. But we believe you have tremendous potential. Now we need to make sure."

"So, what do you want me to do, read some cards or something?"

"No, just sit down and relax. You may feel a sharp

pain, followed by a dizzy spell."

"Like the one I had during choir?" Jeff asked with sudden insight.

"Precisely. Only this time, it will be a little more intense. Can you handle it?"

Jeff took a deep breath, then nodded. There was no backing out now. "Okay. What do I do?"

"Sit down there and relax as best you can."

Jeff looked at Axel, and then at Chermal. He certainly didn't like the thought of someone, or something, probing his mind. Then again, he didn't like the idea of someone blowing California into the ocean, either. "Okay," he said, making up his mind.

As Jeff sat down, Chermal took a position directly in front of him. "I want you to close your eyes," Axel said, "and think about someplace you really like."

Jeff thought for a moment, then decided the best place to imagine was the beach where he and his family went every summer. He and Becca loved laying out on the beach and swimming out in the ocean. He pictured the hot sand, the beating sun, the salty air, the pounding surf…

No sooner had he formed a mental picture of the beach, then came the same prick he felt at choir. Only this time it was followed by a throbbing pain, then darkness.

****

When he came to, it took a few moments for Jeff to gather his wits. He was still by the lake, only now lying down.

"What happened?" Jeff asked as he sat back up and straightened his glasses.

"You passed the test," Axel replied.

"By passing out? Great," Jeff said somewhat sarcastically. "I'd hate to see what would have happened if I failed." Then he looked up at Axel. "Does that mean you'll tell me what's happening now?" he asked.

"Are you sure you want to know?" Axel asked.

"Can you trust me with it?" Jeff asked in turn.

Axel paused, then nodded. "Yes. I'm sure we can."

Axel gazed down at Chermal, and then nodded again. Jeff held his breath, expectantly. He did not anticipate what happened next, however.

Right before Jeff's eyes, Axel began to change. Slowly and subtly at first, then more rapidly, his entire body morphed.

It started with the hair on top of Axel's head, which appeared to grow back into his skull. No, that wasn't it. It was more like Axel's head grew out, taking in the hair as it grew. It was both fascinating and terrifying. He mentally patted himself on the back that the sight of someone transforming right in front of his eyes did not send him fleeing in absolute terror.

As Axel's head grew larger, so did his eyes. They became bigger and wider, swallowing the eyebrows as they grew. Their shape also changed, becoming more almond, while beginning to bulge from his face. The whites of the eyes faded into a dark pool, reminding Jeff more of an insect's eyes than a human's. "Bug-eyed," as it were.

As his eyes grew, Axel's nose retreated into his swelling head. His lips became thinner, almost non-existent. The size of his mouth did not change, but it appeared smaller given the almost complete absence of lips and the now super-sized cranium.

The changes were not limited to Axel's head. As Axel's head grew larger, his entire body shrunk. He had been around three inches shorter than Jeff, but after transforming he was now about Becca's height, or nearly a foot shorter than Jeff.

Axel's hands also changed. His fingers grew longer and thinner and developed an extra knuckle. To Jeff's mute amazement, a sixth finger appeared on the other side of the once little finger, almost directly opposite the thumb. Miraculously, even Axel's clothing metamorphosized. No longer did he wear the same outfit he had for the last three days, he now wore a seamless off-white toga running from his toes to his neck complete with soleless shoes of the same color.

When the transformation was complete, Axel gazed sharply into Jeff's eyes. "Now you know for sure."

"How?" Jeff managed to ask, completely bewildered by what he witnessed.

"Don't worry—I'm not a shape-shifter like you see on the cartoons or those old science fiction flicks you like so much. I have always looked this way. But I convinced your mind I appeared 'human'."

"ESP?" Jeff asked tentatively. "My dad says that's a bunch of malarkey."

"Judge for yourself," was Axel's reply.

"So, your spaceship…"

"Is under the lake, as you surmised."

"You're one of the 'gray' aliens I've read about," Jeff said. Axel merely nodded.

"I am a Delion, from the planet Delios, which is about 51.4 light years from here, in about that direction," he said, pointing into the northwest sky.

"We are part of the Zanchee Alliance. Our fleet is parked in geosynchronous orbit, about 10,000 miles above us in space. We have been here for some time, studying Earth in general, and humans in particular. But that's all we are here to do, study. We hope Earth eventually will be ready to join the Alliance, but that time has not yet arrived."

It was difficult to process all that Axel said. The entire situation was overwhelming. A million questions flew through his mind.

Best to focus on the task at hand. "Can you tell me what's going on now? Why me? Why doesn't anyone else remember seeing your saucer? What happened to my injuries? My pictures? And how will we prevent the dream from coming true? And how do you know it will come true if we don't act?" Jeff rattled off his questions, more to relieve the tension than to satisfy his curiosity.

"It's a long story," Axel began.

There was something strange about how Axel spoke, but Jeff could not put his finger on it.

"And I can't tell you everything, at least not yet. In fact, I can't tell you a whole lot. For one thing, there is still a lot I don't know and for another, you're not ready yet to learn. But I will try as best I can."

Jeff suddenly realized what bothered him about the way Axel spoke. He wasn't! At least, not with his mouth—it never moved.

"Telepathy!" Jeff blurted aloud as it finally clicked into place.

"That's right," Axel replied. "I have always spoken to you telepathically. We call it 'teleping.' However, to not give myself away, I planted a 'suggestion' in your brain that I spoke with my mouth and not through your mind."

Instead of hearing the words, Jeff found them simply forming in his mind. They were crystal clear, like his own thoughts, but somehow different. Jeff took an involuntary step back as he stared again at Axel and Chermal.

"This is so weird..." was all Jeff could manage to say.

"I understand. All of this is hitting you at once. But I don't know any other way to do it. We don't have very much time," Axel commented.

"All right. But tell me one thing. How do you know what will happen? I mean, how do you know the dream is real?"

"I guess the best way to describe it to you is we have developed very sophisticated simulations based on our observations," Axel explained. "And our observations include those in both the physical world and the metaphysical."

"You mean psychic—like ESP? Like the way you are talking to me now?"

"Yes, sort of. You'll learn more during your training."

"Training? What training?"

"You need to be trained so you can best help us...so you can make better use of your potential."

"Training in what? I have already studied karate."

Axel laughed, which was weird because he didn't physically laugh, but rather Jeff had the mental image of Axel laughing. "I'm not talking about physical training—although that may come in handy as well. Rather, I'm referring to 'psychic' training."

"Psychic? Me?"

"That was one of the reasons we chose you. You have tremendous latent psychic potential. That's why you got dizzy when we did the psychic scan a few days ago, and why you passed out a minute ago. However, you have never exercised that potential. In fact, you have been blocking it. Chermal and I will teach you how to use your talent."

"Chermal?" Jeff's head spun with all the things being thrown at him at once. How could an oversized cat train him to be a psychic?

"Chermal is a mentiot," Axel said as he stroked the faux feline. "They exist as much in the metaphysical world as in the physical. My race, the Delions, have been using mentiots for thousands of years to help us develop our psychic abilities. Not only are they able to communicate to us telepathically, but they have the ability of enhancing the latent psychic abilities in other creatures—including us, with whom they become 'attached.' When we are born, each of us is given a mentiot as a companion. I can't exactly explain how they do it. But they do. They are bright, but never express themselves in words—rather, they convey complete thoughts and emotions. You won't hear Chermal in your mind, like you do me. Instead, you will have an urge to do something—or suddenly know something you didn't before. However, their abilities are not limited to telepathy. They can read the future, what you call precognition; see things far away, what you call clairvoyance or remote viewing; and move objects mentally, or psychokinesis. They can also teleport—think themselves someplace else and materialize there."

At that moment, a new thought entered Jeff's mind that was neither his nor Axel's. As Axel had described, he didn't 'hear' words, but rather suddenly felt a strong sense of attachment from Chermal, along with a feeling of pure warmth. The sheer power of the thought almost overwhelmed him. What kept him from staggering was the feeling of affection connected with it. It was obvious the feelings came from Chermal, now rubbing up against his leg, just like Sparky. When Chermal returned his gaze, the intelligence behind the eyes was apparent.

"I think we've given you enough to think about for one day. Why don't we meet here tomorrow? Can you be here earlier?"

Jeff shook his head. "No, I have school tomorrow, followed by choir. And then our family always goes out to eat on Friday. But the day after is Saturday so I will have the whole day free." If Jeff had his car back, he could arrive earlier in the day. But it wouldn't be ready until Monday.

"I could skip school…"

"No. Not necessary at this point. Right now, it is important you continue your daily routine as much as possible. However, I can't say that will always be the case. But for now, let's work around your school schedule."

"In that case, it will have to be Saturday."

"Fine. Why don't both of you come here Saturday morning."

"Both of us?" Jeff asked, confused.

Chapter 13

*September 9th, D Minus 164.35 Hours*
*Dallas*

Becca waited until Jeff disappeared down the driveway before getting her own bike. She was determined to discover what was going on with her brother. She and Jeff had been very close until this year when they drifted apart. Some of it was admittedly her fault. She began to hang around people Jeff didn't like. But he was also excluding her more and more when he was with his friends, so they were even.

But this was different. Something was really bothering him. Whatever it was, it was serious. Jeff might fool their parents, but not her.

At first, she thought it might have been her fault...that he might be trying to do something to stop Michaels—which scared her to death. But that didn't make much sense. After all, what could he do? Still, the possibility she might have had something to do with it made it more important she find out what was happening.

Jeff was certainly acting very secretive, closing the door when he was on the computer, and shutting his notebook whenever she came near. Plus, he was acting strange—the thing about the UFO, the bruise that was there, then wasn't, and doing his homework right after dinner, without complaining. Talk about weird. But, oddest of all were the after-school trips he took. He said he was going to Greg's, but that was a lie. For one thing, Greg lived in the opposite direction from where he rode every afternoon. Initially, she thought he might be heading to Tess's, but when she saw her earlier that day, Tess asked her what was going on with him. So, she was as mystified as Becca. Unless Tess was putting up a smokescreen, which was not likely. Whatever was happening, she was determined to find out. And if it was Tess—well so much the better. She needed more ammunition to tease him with anyway.

So, as soon as he was half a block down the road, she got her bike and headed after him. There was a little tinge of guilt about spying on him, but only a tinge. After all, hadn't he been spying on her? Turnabout was fair play. Never mind his saying he hadn't intended to spy on her.

Trailing him would be easy, assuming he didn't go too fast. By pedaling hard she could keep up with his normal pace, but she would lose in a race. Hopefully, it wouldn't come down to that. Jeff was unlikely to notice her, either. He was such a space she could practically ride side by side with him and he still wouldn't notice.

She was mildly surprised when Jeff turned down Alexander and headed toward Metcalf. Now Becca's curiosity was really aroused. Tess couldn't live over here—it was a different school district. So where was he going?

She stayed one hundred feet or so behind Jeff when he got to the light. Then she carefully observed the cross-traffic. As soon as they started slowing down, she took off, figuring the light must be about to change. Sure enough, it did. Jeff darted across as soon as it turned green. Becca made it across as well, just as the light turned yellow. As expected, Jeff never noticed his sister tailing him.

They turned down old Highway 10 and headed out of town. She hoped they didn't have much farther to go. He was going a lot faster than normal, meaning she had to pedal twice as hard to stay with him. As it was, the gap between them steadily increased. At least the exercise would help her conditioning for soccer.

After a few miles, Jeff pulled off onto the dirt road leading to the abandoned quarry. What on earth was he doing?

By the time she got there, he had disappeared. The road was a dead end, so the options were limited. She quickly turned down the lane and pedaled until she got to the chain across the road. There was nowhere for him to turn off this road once on it, so he had to go here. She dismounted and carefully hid her bike in the bushes. Then she scurried over the chain and headed down the road on foot. She kept to the side of the road so she could duck quickly into the surrounding bushes if she heard anyone coming. With no one in sight, she jogged down the trail toward the pit. Fresh bike tire tracks confirmed this was where he had gone.

Jeff was nowhere to be seen, meaning he probably went down into the quarry pit. Cautiously, she walked to the edge and peered down. There he was, getting off his bike at the end of the road, near the lake. No one else around. What was he doing? Her curiosity was killing her.

Keeping to the side of the path nearest the cliff, she

jogged down the trail toward her brother, who had now moved along the quarry floor to a point nearly underneath her. When she came to a spot that should be directly above him, she stopped and crept to the side of the road. When she got close to the rim, she got on her hands and knees to avoid detection and moved toward the edge. As soon as Jeff became visible some twenty-five feet directly below her, Becca got all the way down on her stomach and inched forward for a better view.

Becca's heart pounded while adrenaline surged through her system. If nothing else, this adventure was exciting.

She was shocked to see Jeff was no longer alone. How was that possible? She hadn't seen the other boy approach, or, for that matter, seen him at all when she scanned the area shortly before. The other boy was about three inches shorter than her brother. He was wearing jeans and a plain T-shirt. Something was vaguely familiar about the outfit—but then again, everyone her age wore similar clothes.

There was also a very large cat sitting on its haunches near the smaller boy's feet. It seemed to be listening to the conversation between Jeff and the boy. That was weird. Sparky might sit still, especially on top of her homework, but she never paid attention to what anyone said—at least without a can opener in their hands.

Jeff was speaking, but not loud enough for her to know what he was saying. She tried edging a little closer, but it didn't help. So, she contented herself with watching.

At first, they were simply talking. But then Jeff sat down very deliberately. Suddenly, Becca felt a sharp pain in her skull and at the same time Jeff grabbed his head. Before she could figure out what was happening, she got terribly dizzy and closed her eyes, praying for the lightheadedness to stop.

As quickly as it came, the dizziness disappeared. When the world stopped spinning, she cautiously opened her eyes. After getting her bearings back, she saw Jeff was lying down. Becca immediately scrambled to her feet, never taking her eyes off her brother. Standing, she paused as Jeff was getting up himself. Huge sigh of relief. He was okay. Whatever happened to him must have gone away as quickly as her dizziness had.

Jeff stared at the other boy and his large cat. While she could not hear the other boy, who was facing away from her, it was apparent Jeff was listening to him— nodding his head from time to time.

Finally, Jeff spoke. It sounded like "How?" but she wasn't sure. A little while later, she heard what sounded like "apathy" or something like it. Whatever it was, he was disturbed. He waved his arms about and stared at the cat, which seemed to return his gaze. Then, suddenly, the cat stared straight up at her! She could swear it winked. Fortunately, neither the boy nor Jeff noticed.

This was getting a little too weird. The scene reminded her of *Alice in Wonderland* and the Cheshire cat. Maybe it was time to go.

But instead, she felt a strong urge to stay. With a burst of confidence and no trace of fear or concern, Becca headed down to join her brother and the strange pair below.

Chapter 14

Greg stared across at Ashanti and Tess, who sat opposite him at the kitchen table in his house. The table was their impromptu operations center. Tess called the others after choir to voice her concern and frustration. The three of them hastily agreed to meet at Greg's house. Ashanti gave Tess a lift. They told their parents they were working on a project together. Which was true. The project was called Jeff.

"What do you think is going on with him?" Greg asked in a hushed voice. Even though no one else was within earshot, the nature of their conspiracy seemingly demanded a whisper. Besides, he didn't want to risk any of their conversation being overheard—especially by a certain younger brother who delighted in giving him grief.

The three of them hoped Jeff would not learn about their clandestine meeting since it would only increase his anxiety about his situation. They all were very worried about him. Despite the front he put on, it was obvious something was bothering him a great deal.

"I have no idea," Tess replied. "He has been avoiding me the last couple days. I called him yesterday

135

about a homework assignment and all he talked about was the homework! It was like he couldn't wait to hang up. That definitely was not like Jeff."

Ashanti giggled. Greg ignored her and replied, "I know what you mean. Today, for the third straight day, he asked me to cover for him with his parents. He's been telling them he was coming over to my house after school. Where is he going that's such a secret? I mean, it's not like him. He tells me about everything." That last comment earned him a curious look from Tess.

"That's a good question," Tess replied after a brief pause. "I have no idea at all."

"Has anyone talked to Becca?" Ashanti asked.

"I saw her briefly this morning before school," Tess replied. "She is as mystified as the rest of us. Whatever is happening, he's keeping it to himself."

"Well, I know he's upset about Michaels. Could that be it?" Ashanti asked.

"Possibly," Tess replied. "That certainly could account for him acting strange. But it doesn't explain where he's going after school."

After a few moments, Greg spoke up. "Maybe he's back in training," he suggested.

"What do you mean?" asked Ashanti.

"He used to study karate. In fact, he made black belt. I was there when he tested."

"That's right," Tess replied. "But he hasn't taken any lessons in, what, two years."

"True. So maybe this 'incident' inspired him."

"You don't think he will try to do something stupid, do you?" Ashanti asked.

"Like what?" Tess replied.

"I don't know…like maybe going after Michaels."

Tess shuddered. "I hope he's not that dumb. For one thing, Michaels is never alone—he always has that brute with him. And, God knows whether Michaels is carrying some sort of weapon," Tess said. Tears welled up in her eyes as she thought about the possible consequences of a physical confrontation with Michaels.

"Michaels is bad news," Greg said, somewhat oblivious to Tess's distress. "He lives with his older brother, Tom, who is about twenty-two. I gather his parents split several years ago, and neither parent wanted anything to do with their kids. Tom dropped out of high school to take care of him and Steve and has had brushes with the law. Rumor has it, Tom is now a big-time dealer. In fact, he drives around in a new Mercedes. I guess he's getting Steve involved in the new family business."

"You know, Steve and I went to the same grade school before we moved," Ashanti said. "I remember he was a pretty good kid back then. Very quiet. I guess being abandoned by his parents pushed him over the edge."

"Well, he certainly isn't quiet now," Greg noted. "But that brings us back to the question of what to do about the situation—and Jeff."

"We can't let him confront Michaels," Tess exclaimed, fear and concern overwhelming her.

"What do you recommend?" Ashanti asked.

"I have no idea, other than I think we should talk to Jeff about it. Maybe we can get him to open up if we work together," Greg replied.

"We could try tomorrow at lunch," Ashanti suggested.

"I don't think so. Whatever it is, I doubt he will be willing to talk about it in the school cafeteria where nosy ears are everywhere," Tess said. "I think we need to talk to him, alone."

"I agree," Greg said. "But when?"

"What about tomorrow night? We could do a double date," Ashanti suggested. They frequently went out together, so what she was proposing was reasonable.

"I can't tomorrow night," Tess replied. "I have to work both Friday and Saturday night." Tess worked part-time at the burger joint down the street from the school.

"How about Saturday during the day?" Tess suggested.

"That's a good idea. Listen, my cousin works at Hurricane Harbor. He told me before he could hook us up with some free tickets," Greg said.

"Great!" Ashanti replied enthusiastically. She loved going to water parks.

"Well, I don't have to go in until seven, so that works for me," Tess added.

"Do you think he will come?" Ashanti asked.

"A free trip to Hurricane Harbor? Of course he will," Tess said. "I can tell him I have a new swimsuit as an added incentive."

Both Ashanti and Greg laughed.

"We should also invite Becca," Tess added.

"Good idea," Greg said. "I'm sure my cousin will give us another ticket. He owes me."

The three spent the rest of their meeting planning.

Chapter 15

The sight of his sister stumbling down the road caused Jeff's jaw to drop almost into his chest. "What are you doing here?" he immediately yelled to her. Then realizing she couldn't hear him, he repeated the question to his two companions. "What is she doing here? Did you bring her here?"

Axel shook his head in a very human fashion. "No, Chermal and I had nothing to do with it. In fact, I'm as surprised as you are that she's here."

Not satisfied, Jeff continued. "What does she know?" His voice was a mix of surprise, anger, and concern.

"Nothing. But now that she's here it will be easier for her to help you than you constantly worrying about her while trying to keep her in the dark." Axel glanced over at Chermal, whom he suspected knew a lot more than he let on about the sudden appearance of Jeff's sister.

"No. NO. She's only fourteen years old," Jeff protested. "This could be dangerous, as you pointed out not so long ago. I don't want her mixed up in anything that could hurt her."

139

"Dangerous for you, yes. But there are many things she can do that will not put her at significant risk," Axel replied. "And this way, you will not have to worry about her possible involvement in those other activities…Besides, she also passed the test," he added, somewhat sheepishly.

"You tested her as well?"

Axel nodded as he looked over at Chermal. "Actually, Chermal was the one who did the testing. I honestly didn't know she was here until a few moments ago, like I told you," Axel admitted. "Her test was not as rigorous as yours, but it was sufficient to let us know she can help. Besides, Chermal says it was meant to be."

"What do you mean by significant?" Jeff asked, as the word finally sank in.

But before Axel could respond, Becca arrived on the scene. "Uh, hi, guys," she said, as she made her way over to where Axel and Jeff stood.

\*\*\*\*

Becca took in the scene before her. Jeff stared at her, appearing shocked and angered by her appearance. But the other boy looked more amused than anything. And then there was that strange cat. Was that blue fur?

"Becca! What are you doing here?" Jeff demanded.

"I followed you," she replied with an impish grin.

"Why?"

Becca flashed her cute innocent smile, the one that allowed her to get away with so much at home. But she remained silent.

"Man, that makes me very angry!" Jeff said in a raised voice. "You had no right to do that."

"I'm sorry, I really am," Becca replied, flashing her

baby-blue eyes in that almost puppy-dog way. Seeing him relax a little, she continued, "It's just that I was really worried about you. You've been acting so strangely lately. And I needed to find out why. I had to know if I was responsible." The last was only half-true. She was confident there was a lot more going on than just Jeff's concern about her. And now she was certain.

****

Chermal's calming presence washed over Jeff, which helped reassure him. He took a few deep breaths, which, along with Chermal's mental tranquilizer, allowed him to relax. He tried to clear his head. Too much was happening at once. What was he supposed to do?

*"Tell her,"* Axel telepced to him. *"It's all right. She can help us."*

Jeff nodded. He sucked in another deep breath and then looked back at his sister. "Well, since you're here, let me introduce you. Becca, this is my friend, Axel," he said, gesturing toward Axel, "and his—" Jeff paused, trying to think of the right word. "—companion, Chermal." Turning toward his new friend, he continued. "Axel, this is my nosy little sister, Becca."

"Glad to meet you," Axel said.

"Same here," Becca responded with a grin. Then she turned to Jeff. "So, what's going on?"

"Axel needs our help," Jeff began.

"Help? To do what?"

"Nothing much…just save the world," Jeff blurted out, a little melodramatically. He was sorry almost immediately.

Becca laughed. Neither Axel nor Jeff joined her as

141

they both maintained a serious demeanor.

Speaking softly, yet firmly, Jeff spoke to his sister. "Becca, this really is serious. I can't tell you everything right now, mostly because you won't believe it anyway," Jeff said, gravely. "Heck, I don't know most of it. But you must believe me when I tell you this *is* very important. Axel thinks you can help us, although I don't know how. If you decide to work with us, it will require your complete cooperation. Most importantly, you can't tell anyone. Even if you decide not to help, you must promise to keep quiet."

****

Becca looked at Jeff, then Axel, and then back at Jeff. His expression was stone cold...deadly serious. Then she gazed at the strange cat at Axel's feet. Did it wink at her? She looked back at her brother, whose expression remained grave. Becca didn't know what was happening, but she believed it was important...or at least Jeff was convinced, which was good enough for her. "Not even Mom and Dad?" Becca asked, mostly to get a reaction.

"Especially not Mom and Dad," Jeff replied.

"Wow. You guys really are serious. All right. I promise...so what's this all about?"

****

"Before making any commitments, Becca, I want you to know this could be dangerous," Axel said. "I don't want either of you to take the danger lightly. I can't be sure what dangers you will face."

"Now you're scaring me," Becca said.

"Good. I intended to." Then privately, he teleped to Jeff. "*I trust your judgment as to how much to tell her, and how best to go about it.*"

"I agree," Jeff said aloud.

"You agree to what?" Becca asked.

"Uh, I agree it will be dangerous," Jeff said, recovering from his error.

"Well, I'll need to know more before I can say 'yes' to anything," Becca said cautiously.

"At least promise not to say anything to Mom and Dad until you know more."

"*Maybe if she had the dream too?*" Axel asked silently.

"No, that will be way too scary for her," Jeff replied, again a little too loudly.

"What are you talking about? What's way too scary for me? What's happening?" Becca asked.

"What's too scary is the thought we might miss dinner!" Jeff said, trying to break the tension. "We better be getting home."

"Awww, we're just getting started!" Becca said. "Come on. Tell me what's going on."

"I'll tell you more after dinner. I promise. Right now, we should be getting home."

"Oh, all right. Let's go."

Jeff turned to Axel and asked, "What time do you want us here Saturday?"

"Will ten a.m. be okay?"

"Works for me."

"Me too," Becca added.

Jeff gave her a long stare. "Okay, we'll meet you back here at ten Saturday morning." Then turning to Becca, he said, "All right, let's go."

"Okay." Her tone and facial expression suggested disappointment.

"Go on ahead. I'll meet you at the top. I need to

talk to Axel for a minute."

Becca gave Jeff the stare straight from the freezer. But she relented. "Ohhalllrrriiigghtt." She turned and headed up the dirt path.

As soon as she was out of hearing range, he turned to Axel. "I don't know about this. How can Becca help? She's only a kid!"

"And you're such a wizened old man," Axel replied with no little sarcasm.

"Well, compared to her, I am. And you said it might be dangerous—I don't want anything to happen to her."

Axel was silent for a moment, his face wrinkled with worry. He then looked down at his furry friend. "What will happen to her if we do nothing? Or if we fail? Think about that," Axel replied, as though trying to convince himself as well as Jeff. Then he added, a little more softly, "We certainly will do what we can to minimize any risk to her and to all of us. Besides, Chermal feels she should be with us, and he is never wrong."

"I don't know about any of this," Jeff repeated, emotionally torn. "I mean, what can we do? Heck, I can't even vote or legally drink a beer, and you want me to help you save the world? How can I possibly help?"

"To be honest, I am not sure *how* you can help," Axel admitted. "I only know you *will* help, and your role is essential. The exact plan is admittedly still in flux."

Jeff stared at Axel in total disbelief. Once again, he was struck with the idea Axel wasn't that much older— if any—than he was. "How can you *know* I can help and not know how?" Jeff said angrily. "First, you tell me the world will end unless we prevent it…now you're telling me you don't know what we can do to stop it? Are you crazy?"

"I know it sounds crazy to you. What I can tell you is this. We have thoroughly studied the situation and *know* three things. One, this is a nexus point. Various patterns are converging on this physical space and time."

"You mean Dallas."

"Yes. We also know we cannot do it without help."

"And the third thing?"

"You have the ability to help us. The test confirmed it. That's all I can tell you right now."

"You're asking us to take an awful lot on faith. Hell, I don't know if any of this is true."

Axel said nothing.

Then Jeff felt it, the feeling of total confidence and surety of knowing not only could they succeed, but they *would* succeed. The feeling wasn't his, nor was it coming from Axel. He looked down at Chermal, who returned his gaze. Jeff could swear he was smiling.

"We will succeed," Axel said. "Chermal *knows*."

Jeff sighed. There was something in the way Axel said "knows." It was as though he really did know. At least, Axel felt he did. "Okay, we will be back Saturday. Now I have to figure out what and how to tell Becca."

\*\*\*\*

It was after six by the time Jeff and Becca arrived home. Their mother was none too happy with their rather tardy arrival. They explained to her they decided to take a long bike ride together since it was such a beautiful day. That excuse earned them a raised eyebrow. "Since when did you two ever go bike riding together? At least without me forcing you?" their mother asked.

"Well, Greg was busy, and we wanted to do something outside," Jeff hastily explained. The reasoning may have been weak, but it served its purpose.

"Dinner will be ready in about thirty-five minutes. Why don't you get a head start on your homework until then?" their mom suggested.

"Sure thing, Mom," Jeff replied, as both he and Becca made their way upstairs. They missed the eyebrow reaching new heights. Needless to say, it was a bit unusual for them to be so agreeable to doing homework, especially before dinner.

****

When they got upstairs, Becca hustled Jeff into her room and closed the door. "Okay, spill the beans. What's going on with you and that weird guy with the even-weirder cat?" Becca demanded.

"And what were you doing following me?" Jeff demanded in return.

"I knew you were up to something," Becca replied. "And I was afraid it had to do with me," she added softly. "I didn't want to be responsible for your getting hurt or anything." She paused, then added, "I'm sorry, Jeff. But I really was worried." Her "puppy dog" eyes worked to full advantage.

Jeff sighed. She was right. He had been acting strange. Should he be angry at her for being so sneaky—or pleased she cared enough to risk following him? Ultimately, it didn't matter why she was there—

the important thing was she *had* followed him and now, for better or worse, she was "in". Axel and Chermal both believed she could help. Moreover, if his dream was real, what choice did he have?

"Okay, I'll forgive you. But please don't do that again. It could have been dangerous. And if you hadn't been hanging around Michaels…" The puppy dog eyes worked harder. "Okay. Let's drop it. I will try to trust you more, as long as you do the same."

"Deal," Becca said heartily. "Now tell me what's going on."

"You won't believe me."

"Try me."

Jeff took a deep breath, trying to figure out exactly what to tell her.

"Do you remember the movie about ET wanting to go home?" Jeff began finally.

"Yeah, so?" Becca replied.

"Well, Axel *is* an extraterrestrial or 'E.T.'. That is, he is *a friendly* E.T."

"What are you talking about?"

"E.T.—extraterrestrial—an alien from outer space."

Becca stared at him for a long time, and then finally broke into a grin. "What? Come on, Jeff! You will have to do better than that."

"I'm serious, Becca. Axel *is* an alien from a different planet. His spaceship is under the quarry lake. You saw how muddy the lake was, well that's why. Remember when I told you I thought I saw a UFO?"

Becca nodded with her mouth hanging open, yet her eyes suggested she was leery of being taken in.

"Well, that was Axel."

"Ha, ha. Next you will tell me he really was looking for you to help him save the world."

"Exactly," Jeff replied.

Becca stared at him for a moment, then laughed. "Boy, you almost had me going there for a minute!" Despite her laughing, Jeff could tell she wanted to believe.

Jeff shrugged. "Okay, don't believe me. I don't care. I told Axel I didn't think you should be a part of this anyway."

Becca stopped laughing. Then they stared at each other awhile. Jeff racked his brain. This was going to be difficult. How do you get someone to believe in the unbelievable?

She looked as if she couldn't quite convince herself to believe him. He couldn't blame her. After all, he had told her many a whopper in the past.

"Becca, I know this all sounds preposterous to you. Heck, it is preposterous. But it is also true."

"Why should I believe you?" Becca asked.

"Because it's the *truth*…and you know it is true, if you just listen to that little squeaky voice inside you.

"But I know it's hard to accept," Jeff continued. "I'm not sure I do totally, either. It's like I'm living in a fantasy or something. It's all too unreal." Just having someone to talk to about his own doubts, even if she couldn't help him—at least not yet—was a big relief.

"Exactly!" said Becca. "It is too unreal. So why believe you?"

"All right, don't believe everything. I understand. But, at least for the time being, can you *pretend* it's true? And go along with us? See where it takes you. And while Axel looked human, you must agree

148

Chermal—that's the 'cat' you saw next to him—was very strange. That's because it is alien too…

"Look, I give you my most solemn vow I will not tease you for believing me. And, as a good faith gesture, to prove to you how serious I am about this, you can have my entire Astroloids collection—to hold, mind you, not to keep. If I'm playing a joke on you or something, then my Astroloids are yours to keep, or do whatever you want."

"I think you've been watching too many science fiction flicks," Becca said, as she studied Jeff's face carefully.

"Okay, so let's pretend Axel is an alien," Becca said slowly. "Why in the world would they be contacting you? What do they want? And how will *we* help them?"

"I'm not really sure why I, or we, were chosen," Jeff answered honestly. "It doesn't make sense to me either. All I know is that Axel said I *was* selected. He said it had something to do with my psychic potential."

"Huh?"

"My psychic potential. You know, ESP, telepathy, and all that."

"I know what psychic means. I just don't see you having any potential."

They shared a nervous laugh together. Despite whatever risk there was, it would be easier having Becca there to help. If for nothing else, it would be good having someone he could confide in. This secret was like runaway yeast in the oven of his mind—it kept growing and growing until it threatened to explode his head.

When they stopped laughing, Jeff got serious

again. "Axel says they will train us to develop our psychic abilities."

"Wow," was all she could think to say. "On the level?"

Jeff nodded.

"Wow."

Chapter 16

When Jeff arrived at the lunch table the next day with his tray customarily overflowing, there were expectant smiles on each of his three friends' faces. "All right, what's going on?" Jeff asked, suspicious of their conspiratorial grins.

"Greg got us all tickets for Hurricane Harbor," Tess blurted out.

"Really!" Jeff said excitedly. He really liked waterparks, and the thought of Tess in her swimsuit... "When?"

"Tomorrow," Greg replied, still grinning.

Jeff's face fell. "Tomorrow? I can't make it tomorrow." His dismay in not being with his friends was moderated considerably by the excitement of what he would be doing on Saturday morning.

"But you have to come," Tess pleaded. "Becca is invited, too."

"That's wonderful, but I'm afraid neither of us can make it. We both have somewhere to go tomorrow."

"What could be more important than seeing me in my new swimsuit?" Tess asked.

That hurt. He had to come up with something fast

151

to allay their suspicions. "Uh, Becca and I have to go visit our Aunt Ruth. She's in the hospital," Jeff said, half-truthfully. She was in the hospital, but the hospital was over a thousand miles away.

"I see. What about Sunday?" Greg asked.

"Ummm, maybe. I don't know. Can I call you tomorrow and let you know?"

Greg, Ashanti, and Tess stared at each other. Jeff realized the problem. He normally would have jumped all over getting free tickets to Hurricane Harbor. Their concerned glances said it all. He needed a distraction.

"Uh, sure," Greg managed to say.

Knowing his friend was concerned, he decided to relieve some of the tension. "Have you gotten any new cards lately?" Jeff asked. "I recently got a Thombolt 90! I know I can smoke you now."

Greg smiled. "Only in your dreams. You know you can't beat me."

The tension left the table as the discussion became more animated over who had the best deck of Astroloid cards. Jeff kept up his side of the argument, but all the while he thought of what to do about his friends. He hated not including them. He hated more having to lie to them. But what could he do? Axel said it might be dangerous. Did he have the right to involve them in something dangerous? On the other hand, how would he feel if it were one of them? Would he want to be left out? This was not an easy decision. Nothing was easy anymore. Besides, he didn't know enough yet. Better to wait until he knew more. Right now, he had more questions than answers.

\*\*\*\*

As the day wore on, Jeff felt more and more

removed from school. Axel was always on his mind, as was his dream. School was so trivial. How could you compare learning calculus with saving the world? What difference did it make when Vermont joined the union if humankind might end in a week? More pointless were the concerns of his classmates. Who cares who likes whom? Or, who snubbed whom? Or even, who had the best Astroloid deck. All their worries were so…so juvenile. At least, compared to what was happening to him. But then again, what *was* happening to him? It's unreal. Which made it more puzzling why Axel insisted he go to school today. One would think saving the world was a bit more urgent than today's calculus assignment.

These thoughts carried over into choir. At least in choir he was exercising his talents and enjoying Tess's company. It didn't seem quite as pointless. He was also one of the featured singers, which further stroked his ego.

So, it was with a rather enlarged head Jeff once again started in on his duet with Tess. But nothing quite deflates an inflated ego faster than…

"Sqqquuueeeeeaaakkkk." It happened again. Same song. Same note. Same giggles. Same laughter. His face turning the same shade of red as before.

"The mouse is back!" snickered someone in the back.

"Someone call an exterminator," joked another wisecracker.

Jeff did his best to regroup while Tess buried her face in her hands. She appeared almost as embarrassed as he was. Mr. Morris banged again on the music stand to try to restore order. His expression was almost as funny as the squeak, being a mixture of concern, amusement, and anger over the choir's reaction.

"Perhaps we should start again," Mr. Morris said in a stern voice. Jeff nodded.

The rest of the rehearsal went smoothly, fortunately for Jeff. However, as they were being dismissed, Mr. Morris asked Jeff to stay behind. Jeff feared what he had to say.

"Jeff, I want to talk to you," Mr. Morris said as the choir filtered out. "Please sit down."

Jeff sat down on the riser's second row. "I'm really sorry about that, Mr. Morris. I don't know what happened. I know I can hit that note. I've done it hundreds of times. I…I had something stuck in my throat."

"I know," Mr. Morris said sympathetically as he sat down next to him. "Jeff, you know sometimes stress can cause our voice to do strange things. I've heard you sing. I know you can hit that note consistently. So, I think something else is happening. Have you been under a lot of pressure lately?"

"Huh?"

"Are you nervous about the duet? About singing with Tess? Or is there something else that's going on in your life?" Mr. Morris asked sincerely.

Jeff refrained from saying what he was thinking. *Well let's see. What could possibly be causing stress in my life? My sister almost buying drugs from thugs? A goon and a Neanderthal are looking to do permanent damage to my face? Meeting secretly with an alien? Terrorists setting off a nuclear bomb? The world possibly ending soon? Being asked to help save humanity, but not having a clue as to how?*

"It's not uncommon for performers to feel stress before a big performance," Mr. Morris continued. "And I know the Fall Festival will be the biggest audience, by far, you've ever sung before. So, I'm sure you're nervous about it."

"Ummm," Jeff managed to stammer. "I guess that must be it."

"Jeff, I'm sure you will do fine. I assure you if I didn't think you could handle it, I wouldn't have given you the duet. But you need to relax. Neither you nor I want a repeat performance of the squeak during the Fall Festival performance."

Jeff nodded.

"But I don't want this to cause you too much stress. If you feel you can't handle it, let me know and I will get someone else to do the duet."

Jeff wanted to stand up and shout 'You idiot…if Axel and I don't come up with a way to stop the terrorists, there won't be a Fall Festival—perhaps ever again.' Instead, Jeff managed to swallow hard and say, "I, uh, I don't think that will be necessary."

"Well, think about it over the weekend. At this point, I'm willing to let you make the decision—as long as we don't have any more episodes. But I'm afraid if it gets any worse, we will have to, uh, make a change."

"I understand." Jeff surprised himself at how calmly he took the news. Even a few days ago, he would have been absolutely devastated with the barest hint he might not be able to sing with Tess in the Fall Festival. But, now, it didn't seem quite as important to him.

Mr. Morris smiled. "Okay. Jeff, I know you can do this."

Jeff nodded somberly. "Thanks. I'll let you know Monday."

Mr. Morris smiled and then dismissed Jeff with a wave of the hand. As he arose, a wave of emotions hit him. He ignored them. As if there was nothing else happening in his life.

Tess waited for him outside the room. "Well?" she asked. "What did he say?"

"Mr. Morris feels stress may be causing my voice to crack," Jeff said softly, feeling somewhat embarrassed.

"Really?"

"Yeah, really."

"I can understand you find it stressful to be singing with such a tremendous talent."

"Yeah, right," Jeff said. "Mr. Morris is concerned about the Festival."

"Oh." Her voice suddenly sounded full of sympathy and concern. "Does that mean he won't let you sing?" She put her arm in his as a way of saying she was sorry for laughing. Jeff patted her hand in response.

"He said he will let me make that decision—at least for now. If I get any worse, he will have to make the decision for me. He gave me until Monday to think about it."

"That's good," Tess said. "So, what do you think you will do?"

"I don't know. I just don't know. I mean I really, really want to sing. But…geez, what if it happened again—right in the middle of the performance? I would just die."

"Speaking of dying, dork," came a loud,

unexpected, and most unwelcome voice from behind. "I think I could arrange that."

Jeff was so caught up in his choir dilemma he totally forgot about Michaels, who apparently was waiting for him.

Jeff turned around, Tess's arm still in his, to face his tormentor. Michaels was not alone. Ox was right beside him.

"Leave us alone!" Tess yelled at the bully. She tightened her grip on Jeff's arm. "We didn't do anything to you!"

"Oh, but your boyfriend did. And he owes me plenty, don't you, dork?"

"What, you need some more trash?" Jeff replied, without thinking very clearly of the consequences.

Michaels, to his credit, didn't charge Jeff as he might have been expected to. Instead, he grinned a half-smile. "Hiding behind your girlfriend, dork?" Michaels sneered, then looked around the schoolyard. "Where are all your other sissy choir friends?" He took a step closer to the two. While Michaels talked, Ox started moving around to the left side. Michaels stared straight into Jeff's eyes. "Hmm, there are no choir sissies or vice principals around to save you this time, Miller. So maybe we can finish our 'discussion' from the other day." He took another step closer. "You got my money, dork?"

Automatically, Tess stepped back, dragging Jeff with her. Jeff's eyes never left Michaels. However, they lost track of Ox, who slipped behind them. "Grab her, Ox!" Michaels shouted. "Let's make sure she doesn't go for help, this time."

Ox quickly closed the gap between him and Tess

and grabbed her before she could react. One giant arm wrapped around her waist, as his other big paw clamped over her mouth, preventing her from screaming.

"Let her go!" shouted Jeff.

"Sure, dork, just as soon as I get what I came for."

"And that is?"

"This," Michaels said, as he threw a left hook in the direction of Jeff's face. But this time, Jeff was ready for it. Despite the rust, his years of martial arts training paid off as his right arm automatically flashed up to block Michaels' hook, while his own left fist darted toward Michaels' nose. It connected with a sickening crunch. Without pausing, Jeff pivoted on his right foot and hit Michaels with a reverse kick in the groin, sending Michaels backward, doubled over in pain and falling on his butt with a thump.

Jeff immediately turned his attention to Ox, who still held Tess tightly, although with his mouth hanging wide open and a completely blank expression on his face. Seizing the advantage, Jeff took a quick step and kicked out with his right foot and then swept his leg back across the back of Ox's knees, taking his support completely out from under him. Ox immediately tumbled backward. As he fell and in order to catch himself, Ox instinctively loosened his grip on Tess, who fell on top of him. Tess reacted quickly, giving Ox a sharp blow to the stomach with her elbow, as she twisted free from his grasp. As soon as they hit the ground, with Tess still on top, she rolled off the stunned human gorilla and clambered back to her feet.

"Let's get out of here before they recover!" Tess shouted, as she grabbed her book bag, which had miraculously not opened.

"Good idea!" Jeff said, joining her in a fast trot away from the groaning pair. Ox scrambled to his feet but appeared indecisive as to whether to pursue them or take care of the still-moaning Michaels. His hesitation allowed them to get away cleanly.

"You were wonderful!" Tess gushed as soon as they were out of sight. "Thank you so much!"

"You were pretty impressive yourself!" Jeff replied, still catching his breath. "Where did you learn to throw an elbow like that?" Jeff's admiration for his girlfriend, already sky-high, climbed further.

"It comes with growing up with two older, and much bigger, brothers," Tess said, smiling. She didn't add she also practiced on her younger and more annoying brother.

Their mothers were waiting for them in the traffic circle when they arrived somewhat out of breath. Before getting into her car, Tess made Jeff promise to call her that night to talk.

****

Jeff waited until Becca was occupied watching TV before making the call to Tess. He was apprehensive about talking with her, though. The waterpark, and his lame excuse for not being able to come, would be a topic of conversation. He still wasn't sure what he would say but avoiding her would only create more problems.

The first thing Tess brought up, however, caught Jeff completely by surprise. It wasn't about Michaels, or the waterpark, but rather about his voice. As if he had any control over the matter.

"So, have you decided what you will do about choir?" Tess asked innocently.

"Not yet, but I'm leaning toward risking mortal embarrassment and singing at the Festival. I mean, I haven't had any other, uh, incidents. And I can't be sure Mr. Morris is right about what caused my, uh, problem. It may simply be I really did have a frog in my throat!"

"Yeah, right. Face it, Jeff, you have been under a bit of stress lately."

"In more ways than one," Jeff said, more to himself.

"What?"

"I mean, all of a sudden we are facing very adult issues," Jeff said, trying to recover from his slip.

"Like drugs…and thugs like Michaels."

"Yeah," Jeff said, mentally scoring one for himself for the nice deflection.

"What are you going to do about him?"

"I think I'll start by going out a different door after choir."

"Good idea!" They both chuckled.

"Seriously, I'm open to suggestions. But it's not just me anymore. I'm afraid you have now gotten yourself marked as well. So, what will *you* do?"

"Good question. I am not sure, either. I mean, if we go to the authorities, whomever that may be, we may get ourselves in deeper. And if we do nothing, we are just inviting more trouble. So, what *can* we do?"

"I guess the first thing will be to make sure we take a different route out from choir," he said, smiling to himself. "Maybe if we avoid him long enough, he will forget about us and go on to torment somebody else…or be stuck in jail."

"Maybe. I don't think it will be easy to avoid him, though. And now he has added incentive."

"I know. I'm very concerned about him going after you, especially now. Please make sure you never go anywhere alone."

"The same goes for you."

"I can take care of myself," Jeff said reassuringly.

"I saw that. But next time, he may have more than Ox with him."

"I promise I'll be careful."

"Okay, so what's the real reason you and Becca can't come tomorrow?"

Jeff was again totally taken off guard by Tess's sudden change of topic. She was quick with more than just her elbows.

"I told you already," Jeff replied, trying hard to remain calm.

"What, you have to visit your grandmother?" Tess asked.

"Yeah, she's not feeling very well."

"That is *not* what you told us!" Tess said in her best "Ah ha" voice.

"Huh?" Jeff replied, completely flustered. What had he told them at lunch? He racked his brain.

"That wasn't the excuse you gave us at lunch," Tess repeated.

"It wasn't?" Jeff asked innocently.

"No, it wasn't. At lunch, it was your aunt. So, what's going on? Or do I need to ask Becca? You know she will tell me."

"Okay, Sherlock, you got me," Jeff said. Tess would make a great lawyer someday.

"Well, what is going on?" Tess continued to press. "I know it must be serious for you to skip a free trip to the waterpark."

Jeff paused to collect his thoughts before proceeding. "Tess, I honestly can't tell you now. But I promise I will as soon as I can...I mean, I would like to now, but the fact is, you won't believe me if I do!"

"Try me!"

"Not yet. Please, give me a few more days, and then I will. I promise."

"And this involves Becca?"

"Yes, but it has nothing to do with Michaels. And that's all the questions for today, detective. Look, I will tell you everything. Just give me time. Please? And please don't ask Becca—she doesn't know the entire story."

"You give me little choice. But tell me one more thing. You're not in any kind of trouble, are you?"

"I thought I said no more questions. No, I'm not in any trouble. Now, no more questions!"

Jeff managed to escape any additional inquiries for the rest of the conversation. But he couldn't put Tess off for long. By not telling her anything, he increased her determination to discover what was going on. Yet, he also could not tell her anything—at least not until he knew more about what was happening. However, it was an issue he was certain to bring up with Axel the next time he saw him.

Chapter 17

Axel banged his hand down in frustration on the console. "No matter how many scenarios I run, the results are always the same. Mass destruction. Billions dead. But I can't think of anything else to do."

Chermal gazed at him serenely.

"I know I'm upset—of course I'm upset! I know, I know. I can't think straight when I'm upset. But what else can I do? Everything I think of fails. And our projections show the device will explode in less than one earth day. There just isn't enough time."

Axel paced, trying to mentally calm down. "There has to be a way. What am I overlooking?" He glanced at Chermal again, meeting his calm, reassuring gaze. "There *is* a way, isn't there?" Chermal said nothing.

He continued his pacing. "I've run every scenario I can think of…but without father's help…or breaking our laws right and left, I don't know how. And even then, I don't know what I could do." Axel returned to the console. "Anything we could do takes a long time to implement, but we simply don't have it. We don't have the time. But there's got to be a way. There's got to be."

Axel wailed as he banged his fist down again on the offending console. "There's not enough time." He was about to bang again when inspiration hit. "Not enough...time...*time*..." He turned and faced Chermal. "*Time!*" he said excitedly. Chermal's expression did not change.

"If we had more time..." Axel said to his furry companion as a sly grin formed across his face. "And we both know how we can get more!" Axel turned again to face the console. He attacked it with renewed vigor.

After several hours of hard work, Axel finally shouted with glee, "I think I've got it. It just might work. But we'll need to hurry." Chermal uttered a low growl...which was about as vocal as he ever got.

"I know I will be risking a lot. It could be very dangerous. Even if we succeed, it most certainly will get me into serious trouble...my career over before it started." Axel paused as he reflected more. "It may also get Dad into trouble. I guess it's possible they would blame him...and he could lose his command. But what is that compared to saving billions of human lives?

"Chermal, I must try to stop this carnage...even if it means giving up everything, including my life, in the process. This is *sen.*" Axel stared straight into Chermal's eyes, who returned his penetrating gaze. "I see you agree. So you *will* help me? Okay. Now we need to plan how we can 'borrow' that extra time. We need to do this right the first time. There won't be a second chance." With that, Axel returned his attention to the console.

Chapter 18

Tess was already at Ashanti's by the time Greg arrived since Ashanti gave her a lift after choir practice. They agreed Ashanti's was the best place to meet, since her house was located between Greg's and Tess'. Besides, they met at Greg's last time and his younger brother was still giving him "grief" about having two girls over. Ashanti's mother bought in on the excuse they were working on a class project. Never mind the three of them did not have a single class together. It also had to be strange they were meeting on a Friday afternoon, normally the last time any parent expected their teenaged children to work on a school project. Fortunately, Ashanti's mother wasn't nosey.

Tess quickly filled Greg in on what happened to her and Jeff earlier. The story stood on its own merits without her normal "embellishments." Yet the image of Michaels getting kicked in the groin earned a few chuckles. Greg whistled softly when she was done.

"Whoa, this is getting way too serious," he commented. "What are you guys planning to do?"

"I don't know!" Tess said, nearly sobbing. "Jeff's right in saying just about anything we can do likely makes matters worse. He's hoping if we can avoid Michaels long enough, he will eventually forget about us."

"From what I know of him, that's not likely. Did anyone witness what happened?"

"Not that I know of. Of course, Jeff and I didn't stick around to find out."

"I don't blame you. You're right about Michaels. He won't forget, and he won't give up."

"I think you should tell the police. Or at least school officials," Ashanti said.

"And what will they do?" Tess asked angrily. "We have no evidence. They can't arrest him—it's our word against his. And what's the school going to do? He doesn't go to school here. And, if he should find out who ratted on him…" Tess let the rest of the sentence go unfinished. There was no need to further emphasize the negative consequences that would bring.

They sat quietly awhile, until Greg finally broke the silence. "Maybe we could get some evidence." His mind started to whirl.

"What are you talking about?" Ashanti asked. "Whatever it is, I don't think I like it."

"I mean, if we can get some evidence on Michaels, we can either use it to put him away…or force him to stop harassing you two."

"This sounds awfully stupid…and dangerous," Tess said.

"What else can we do? And is it any more dangerous than doing nothing?" Greg asked.

"I guess that depends on what you have in mind," Tess replied.

"I'm not exactly sure. I mean, I just thought of the

idea. I only know if we can get something concrete on Michaels, it will force him to leave us alone...or put him away. Either way, problem solved."

"I think you watch too many detective shows," Ashanti commented.

They were quiet for a minute. "What kind of evidence?" Tess asked, breaking the silence. Greg did not have an immediate answer.

"What about videotaping?" Ashanti suggested after a long pause. "My dad has a video camera with 300 times zoom lens. With that, we can be a long way away and still record the action."

"That sounds great!" Tess said eagerly.

"I don't know..." Greg said hesitantly. "It would have to be pretty clear as to what he was doing. He could always claim he was just giving someone some sugar."

"Yeah, right."

"No," Ashanti said. "Greg's right. We really need something more. If only we could tape the conversation."

"We can," Tess said. Greg and Ashanti just stared at her.

"Listen, all we have to do is get someone to pose as a buyer and have them record the deal."

"Who in their right mind would do that?" Ashanti said, shaking her head. "After all, the evidence will be against them, as well. And if it didn't work, they would be in serious jeopardy."

"How about if I did it?" Tess said.

"No good." Greg said, shaking his head. "He already has it against you. You'd best avoid him. And I think that goes for all of us. He knows we are all friends. And, besides, Ashanti is right…it's too dangerous."

"So, what do we do?" Tess asked.

"Hmmm. I was just thinking," Greg said. "You ever watch football games on TV?"

"Not if I can help it," Ashanti replied. Greg glared at her.

"I do sometimes. So?" Tess replied.

"Ever notice those satellite disk-looking things they point at the players?"

"Sound cones?" Tess asked. "That's a great idea. Only, how will we get one? They aren't cheap."

"I think I know where we can rent one. There's an electronics rental outfit in the Meadowmont Mall. I bet they have one. They have all sorts of electronic equipment people can rent."

"All right, let's check it out. But let's all agree we do this together, or not at all. I don't want anyone trying to be a hero and getting themselves seriously hurt over this," Tess said.

"Agreed," Greg said. Ashanti nodded her consent.

They spent the rest of the afternoon planning before Ashanti dropped Tess off at her work.

Chapter 19

Tom Michaels stared at the man sitting across the conference table from him. What he had heard was simply unbelievable.

"You want us to go to California to be *muscle?*" he asked incredulously. "Man, I'm no muscle. Get yourself some other sucker." Tom looked around the room to see all six of the other "District Managers" nod their heads in agreement.

Victor Martinez, Regional Vice President of Transdigital, part of the expansive Bivardo Empire, rose from his chair. As he did, his fist slammed down on the table.

"You will do what you are told, or you will not be working for me!" Victor's voice roared. The three men standing behind Martinez slid their hands into their vests, making it clear no one had better start anything. Placing his hands on the table, he continued in a slightly softer voice. "You're not 'just' muscle. You were selected because of the skills you have to offer and the services you can perform. You and your people will undergo special training to hone those skills. There is also special cargo you will take with you." Then

Martinez stared directly at Tom. "Do what you're told, and you will be amply rewarded. You don't and you won't be 'employed' anymore. And if you don't work for me, you don't work for no one. Got it?"

"Okay, but can you at least tell us why we can't just fly to LA, if it's so important. And what's this training all about?" one of the men around the table asked. "I mean, we stand to lose a lot of revenue, ya know?"

"First of all, you're not paid to ask questions." Martinez glared around the room. No one dared move.

It looked like Martinez didn't understand it either. He must be scared, too. Out of the blue, he was told to deliver, by truck, "special" cargo to some out-of-the-way place in the desert, along with thirty men who could be completely trusted and shoot straight.

Martinez continued, "While we are going to Nevada first to train, I understand we are preparing for a major operation in California. That's all I know. But that's enough for me, and it will be enough for you, too."

"It's okay, Victor." Tom turned to stare at the person who had stepped forward. He had been standing in the back of the room, behind Martinez' bodyguards. The man was obviously from the Middle East, but his fluent English and accent indicated he was likely schooled in America.

"Permit me to introduce myself. I am Mohammed Farcie. I understand your concern, and I would feel the same way." Farcie paused as he looked in each man's eyes around the table. He had their complete attention.

"This is an extremely complex and sensitive operation. It represents an unprecedented collaboration between our two, uh, organizations. If successful, and I'm confident it will be, it will propel your company to the forefront in your industry. Upon successful completion, we anticipate a dramatic increase in the demand for your 'product,' as well as a reduction in the competition, allowing you to substantially increase your profits.

"You can be assured each of you will be amply rewarded for your time. You will each receive a $50,000 bonus upon completion of the operation, which should take no more than a week. Each of your men will get a $5,000 bonus.

"As to why we need people from Dallas rather than using purely local talent. Simple. Due to the nature of this operation, we need more manpower than the local offices can provide, plus we need complete security and are quite frankly concerned some of the people in the LA office may not be trustworthy. You won't be alone. We are bringing in people from all over the country.

"I appreciate you are talented people who have accomplished a lot to rise this far within your organization. And I understand this operation is not what you are used to. But what we need most is your leadership skills."

He paused. "We also must ensure successful delivery of this cargo to LA. *Nothing* can happen to it."

Farcie held up his hand as if to stop the inevitable questions before they could be asked. "I cannot tell you more about the mission or the nature of the cargo. But you will learn upon your reaching our training grounds. I am sorry we cannot tell you more, but the reason for all these security precautions will become obvious once you reach your destination. Succeed in this mission, and you will be amply rewarded. Failure is not an option."

Tom was about to speak up again in protest when Jack Reynolds, another District Manager, spoke up.

"I hate this!" Jack looked at Farcie then back at Martinez. "And why are we working with these *Arabs*? You can't trust them!" He spat out the last sentence, pure hatred pouring out from his eyes.

In response, Farcie smiled. Then in one fluid motion he pulled out a pistol that had been tucked away in his jacket. It had a silencer attached. A soft "pop" was quickly followed by the sound of Jack falling over backward in his chair, a bright red circle appearing on his forehead, his lifeless eyes staring upward.

"Any more comments or questions?" Farcie asked the now stunned group. "Good."

Tom started to get up when he noticed none of the bodyguards reacted at all to Jack's murder. The other District Managers remained seated. Any reaction might easily be fatal.

Martinez, looking a little shaken, spoke up on cue. Composing himself as best he could, he assumed his normal commanding voice. "I want each of you to pick four of your best men. We prefer you pick those able to handle a variety of firearms—and can shoot straight. But the most important trait we are seeking is loyalty and obedience. They must be willing to do what you tell them, without pause or question." Martinez paused to scan the room. Everyone nodded agreement. He avoided looking at the now vacant spot at the table.

"We will travel in groups. I will be in the lead car. There will be two trucks, one with weapons for us, the other with our cargo. That truck is not to be touched. Farcie will be in that truck, with several of his men and four of ours following immediately. Two cars will follow about two minutes back. Jim, you and your men will follow with the second truck. The rest of you will follow about five to ten minutes later. We are driving, as the destination is not exactly convenient to an airport.

"Because of security concerns, we do not want you traveling in large groups, except for two cars immediately behind the truck. And do not get stopped for speeding on the way. A ticket could prove fatal.

"It is paramount these trucks get through, especially the larger truck with the special cargo. If it is stopped for any reason, you are to do what is necessary to prevent it from being searched. Follow cars will be alerted and proceed expeditiously to provide further support. You will do *whatever* necessary to make sure that truck gets through. Is that clear?" There were reluctant nods from around the table.

Farcie picked up from there. "You will be given detailed instructions on where your destination is on Saturday, as soon as the trucks arrive with the cargo. You will leave immediately thereafter. Arrival at the training facility will be at varying times on Sunday and early Monday, so make sure you follow your schedule. Once there, you will learn more about the operation and the nature of your training."

"I will meet again with each of you tomorrow morning," Martinez said. "I will call you with the time. I also want to meet with each of your picked men, as well as approve the person you are leaving behind to maintain operations in your absence. We will meet in the field 'office.' That's all."

Martinez and Farcie left the room, followed by

Martinez' personal bodyguards. Farcie apparently traveled alone. Jack remained on the floor, unattended. No doubt, they wanted him to remain as a reminder. A "clean-up" crew would come along after they left and remove any evidence Jack had been there.

Tom sat stunned in his chair, staring after the departed leaders. His fellow District Managers talked in hushed tones around him as they gathered themselves to leave. He just sat and stared, trying to make sense of it all. Whatever this operation was, it had to be big. Martinez liked Jack. For him to sit and watch him be so unceremoniously eliminated without blinking an eye meant this Farcie had lots of juice and scared the crap out of Martinez. Which meant it should scare him too.

What possible operation required so many men from so many different cities? What were they being trained for? Where in the desert were they heading? What was the cargo? And why did they need an army to guard it? Why couldn't they trust the LA organization to provide security? Why were Arabs involved? Who was working for whom? How would this operation increase demand for their "product" or reduce competition? It didn't add up. Even the pay, $50,000 for seven days, did not make sense. Not that he was complaining. Extra money always came in handy. But why that much just to make a delivery, receive training, and help with security? Unless it was going to be a lot more dangerous than they let on. Unless they didn't expect to have to pay everyone...After all, the company didn't pay you if you were dead.

Chapter 20

The next morning, Becca and Jeff took off for the quarry at 9:30. They wanted to go earlier but it would be too suspicious if Becca gave up watching Astroloids on TV and Jeff got up too early. It was their Saturday morning ritual, after all—Becca watched Astroloids, and Jeff slept in—often till noon. But as soon as Astroloids was over, Becca rushed in and woke her brother. Much to her surprise, he got up without protest. Normally, getting her brother out of bed on a weekend took something just short of an Act of Congress.

Jeff showered and dressed in a hurry and joined his sister downstairs. He quickly snarfed three bowls of cereal while Becca packed food for their trip. When they were done, they found their mother upstairs and told her they were going bike riding. After giving them a "what's gotten into you" look, she admonished them to be careful. They left with their mom still shaking her head.

**** 

Axel was nowhere to be seen when they arrived at the quarry. As they made their way down the access road to the bottom, Jeff tried to keep one eye on the

175

area where they had been meeting in hopes of seeing where Axel might be hiding. But neither Axel nor Chermal were to be found. Yet, as soon as they got to the bottom and off their bikes, a familiar voice greeted them from behind.

Becca nearly set a new high jump record when Axel's voice interrupted the serene silence.

"Thanks again for coming," Axel said in greeting.

"All right, I give up," Jeff said to him, throwing his hands into the air. Unlike Becca, he was not shocked by Axel's sudden appearance. But he was completely befuddled by it. Axel gave him a quizzical look in return.

"Where were you hiding?" Jeff asked. "How do you always manage to sneak up on me?"

Axel smiled, then tilted his head slightly. "It may be better to show you. But I caution you, it may be a little disorienting." Without waiting for a response, Axel looked over at Chermal and nodded.

With no other warning, Jeff's world went suddenly dark. There was an intense, but very brief wave of nausea and dizziness, causing him to close his eyes. But as quickly as it came, the discomfort dissipated. Cautiously, he opened his eyes and experienced his second shock in two seconds. No longer was he in the pit…at least not outside. He was in a brightly lit room, with no visible source for the illumination. The room was semicircular, with an apparent radius of twenty feet and an illuminated domed ceiling. The walls were featureless and off-white in color.

Jeff immediately glanced to his right to make sure Becca was with him. She was, standing stunned with a look of amazement and awe on her face and her mouth hanging open. To her credit, she was not screaming in fear.

What was stranger than the visual appearance of the room was the near complete lack of sound, other than what the four of them were making. There was no background noise from machinery, not even the hum of lights.

Also missing was any trace of odor. For perhaps the first time in his life, Jeff breathed air completely devoid of smell. It was a little disturbing.

Axel stood in front of him, grinning like a Cheshire cat. Speaking of which, Chermal sat at Axel's feet.

"What happened? Where are we?" both Becca and Jeff asked, almost simultaneously.

"You're on our ship...under the lake," Axel replied calmly.

"Jeff, what's happening?" Becca cried out, her voice denoting more shock than fear. Jeff quickly put his arm around her. Although he was a bit shaken by what just happened, he couldn't show it in front of Becca.

"I told you, Axel and Chermal are aliens," Jeff said in a remarkably calm voice. "We are on board their UFO, which is parked under the lake," he continued almost matter-of-factly. He surprised himself, as well as Becca, with his stoicism.

Becca's eyes widened more...which was only barely possible. "You really were telling the truth? I don't believe it. This can't be happening!" Now she sounded more enthusiastic.

"It is happening. It is real. Although I have a hard time believing it myself," Jeff replied. He was incredibly relieved at how well his sister was accepting the situation. She was excited, although obviously a little frightened. Yet, most any other girl her age, or boy for that matter, would be hysterical by now. In fact, Becca should have been more upset than she appeared. Then he glanced down at Chermal, whose face bore a wry grin, confirming Jeff's suspicion he was at least partly responsible for their lack of fear.

"How did we get here?" Jeff managed to say. "Did you 'beam' us over?"

Axel laughed softly. "Sorry to disappoint you, but no. There's no 'Scotty' here. You asked how I managed to suddenly appear out of nowhere. Now, you know."

"No, I don't. I don't have the foggiest idea," Jeff replied.

"You were teleported."

"You mean you did this with a telephone?" Becca said, completely lost.

Jeff and Axel both laughed. "Don't be so silly," Jeff chided. "Teleporting means to move from one place to another by means of telepathy—or at least by using ESP or something." Then, turning to Axel, he said, "Right?"

"Basically. With teleporting, you use your mental powers to control forces enabling you to move from one place to another instantly—in this case, moving all of us."

"You can do that?" Becca asked in total amazement.

Axel nodded. "Especially with Chermal's help. You may eventually learn how to teleport yourself, once you've had the proper training."

"*No way!*" shouted Becca gleefully.

Axel smiled. "Yes, there will be a way. But there is

a lot of hard work to do first."

While Axel talked to Becca, Jeff took a moment to take in more of his surroundings. In the middle of the room were four chairs—or a close approximation of chairs—arranged in a semicircle matching the curvature of the wall. They were made from very thin material, about one quarter inch thick, that was almost translucent. The seat of each chair was mounted on a narrow pedestal made of the same material as the seat. Jeff assumed the pedestal allowed the seat to swirl 360 degrees. The seat was a little closer to the floor than a normal chair. The back of the chair, also made of the same thin material, was about thirty inches in height and curved slightly. The back seamlessly became curved sides going all the way to the front of the chair, with the forward parts lower, forming arm rests. In front of each chair was a small panel, about one-quarter inch thick and about fifteen inches by twelve inches in size. The panel was about two and a half feet above the floor and angled toward the chair. The panel, however, floated in the air with no visible support. It was likely some sort of control board, although there were no obvious buttons or knobs on its surface. It was completely blank, and dark green in color.

Other than the chairs, the room was devoid of furniture or consoles and the ceiling, walls and floor were completely barren and smooth. The floor appeared to glow, although much less than the walls and ceiling. Upon closer inspection, miniscule black dots in a seemingly random pattern were scattered across the floor.

"What is this place? Why are we here?" Jeff asked.

"As you have surmised, this is the control center of

the ship. The reason I brought you here is simple. You asked."

"I only asked how you appeared out of nowhere. I didn't ask to be taken to your ship."

"Ah, but that is what you wanted, wasn't it?"

Jeff nodded reluctantly. Axel was right; it had been what Jeff wanted but was too timid to ask. Judging by Becca's reaction, she was glad to be here too, although still unsettled.

"Besides," Axel continued, "we need a controlled environment to begin your training."

"Can I ask how this ship flies? I mean, how do you pilot it? I don't see any controls, unless those panels have some sort of controls disguised on their tops. And how do you see where you are going? There's no windows or view screens."

"Lesson one. You need to perceive things as they are…rather than trying to force them into something that fits your scheme of things."

"Huh?"

"You assume there must be a window or 'viewscreen' to see because that is what you expect, based, I suspect, on what you've seen on TV or in the movies."

"Right…I mean, don't you need a window or viewscreen to see where you're going?" Jeff said, completely puzzled.

"Only if you are using your eyes."

"How else can you see?"

"By using your mind."

"I don't get it. How can my mind see?" Jeff was completely lost.

"In your case," Becca chimed in, "you will

probably need strong glasses."

"Very funny," Jeff said, as Axel grinned at her quick wit.

"That's not far from the truth," Axel said. "You both will need special 'glasses' to help you see—or rather perceive—until you develop the skills yourself."

"Okay, now you've really lost me," Jeff said, imagining the kind of glasses he would need to wear to improve his mind's vision.

"In the case of vision," Axel explained, "people need glasses when light entering the eye moves away from the retina and causes the image to be distorted. Glasses refocus the light, making the image clearer." Jeff and Becca both nodded.

"You and Becca receive psychic input all the time. Everyone does. Only it is not 'focused,' so it is hard to interpret and understand. It becomes distorted and fuzzy so its meaning may not be clear. Therefore, your brain discards it. Occasionally, an image will come in more 'focused,' and you have a 'psychic experience,' like knowing who is calling before you answer the phone.

"Chermal was my glasses when I was a child. He still helps me as I continue to learn. But we don't have more mentiots for you two to use. Instead, we will give you a special crystal that will become your 'lenses.' They will help 'focus' the psychic input so you can better understand it and control it. As your brains get more used to receiving clear psychic input, they will stop automatically filtering it all out. You will eventually learn how you can control it, change its focus, if you will, without needing the lenses."

"Wow!" Becca said enthusiastically. "You really mean it? This is *soooo lit*."

Jeff's mouth hung slightly open as he absorbed what Axel told him. A thought still bothered him, though. "That still doesn't explain this ship," Jeff said.

"In simple terms, you don't *see* where you are going in this ship, you '*perceive*' through your psychic senses. This ship is controlled through use of psi, or psychic energy if you prefer, not by means of levers, wheels, buttons, and switches you are so used to."

"This I gotta see," Jeff said.

"This you have to *perceive,*" Axel corrected.

Chapter 21

*September 15<sup>th</sup>, D Minus 19.21 Hours*
*Druize*

Getting on board the TWS would not present tremendous problems. There was little need of security on the *Druize*, given the ship contained mostly beings with considerable psychic capabilities who could detect most anything that could go wrong before it happened. Plus, everyone on board was extensively screened before being allowed to embark. The main security for the ship was externally oriented—preventing unwanted entities from getting on board or detecting the ship's presence. So, getting around inside the *Druize* was not a problem, especially for the son of the Thermax. Unlike humans, the Zanchee had little reason to be paranoid, especially on the *Druize*.

Axel was also confident he and Chermal would have no problems piloting the TWS, even though he had never done it. Axel had flown other craft. In fact, he was developing quite a positive reputation. Both he and Chermal were familiar with the TWS patterns, had studied *how* to do it, and practiced on simulators. They both flew recently in the TWS and, as always, Axel had carefully studied the Amaritz, or pilot, and every move he made as he guided the craft. Axel was confident he could fly it—at least for as much as they needed. He just hadn't done it before.

No, the main problems were two-fold. The first was to get the TWS to recognize him as being "authorized" to pilot it, and the second was to get the TWS off the mother ship without triggering two million alarms. While he did not know how his father could stop him once they were underway, Axel had little doubt he would find a way. So, they needed to escape undetected.

The second problem could be solved by simply returning the TWS where and *when* he "borrowed" it after accomplishing what he set out to do. It would be extremely tricky, but Chermal agreed it could be accomplished with minimal risk of discovery. Besides, even if they were caught, as long as he accomplished his mission, it would be worth it.

The first problem, however, was considerably more challenging. It required Axel and Chermal performing the Zanchee equivalent of "hacking" into the ship's controller. Unfortunately, it was more difficult to "hack" into a Zanchee AI controller than a human computer system. It also required a "hack" considerably more complex than any Axel had previously attempted.

The Zanchee AI Controller utilized what in human terms would be called a quantum-based computer, or QUAIC. Instead of using electronic "switches" to store information in binary form—"on" and "off"—as human computers do the Zanchee AI used quantum particles and their characteristics, referred to as "spin," to store information. This allowed processing and storage capabilities literally billions of times better than current human technology. The AI operated as its own entity—

capable of independent thought. Its purpose was not only to guide the user through its vast library of stored knowledge but also to make decisions based on that knowledge and apply it to whatever task was at hand. Being quantum based allowed the AI to reach these decisions virtually instantaneously.

Perhaps more importantly, the third key difference was the Zanchee system utilized psychic energy, or psi, to access and control the QUAIC. Since everyone has a unique "psychic" signature, this provided the ultimate in security. As psi is a fourth dimensional energy, it allows the user to be light years from the AI, yet still have instantaneous access. Thus, the AI located on the *Druize* was in constant communication with the Master QUAICs on the Zanchee home planets—all in "real" time. That is, in what is perceived to be the "current" time in the linear time frame of the 3-D universe.

Axel did have clearance to utilize the ship-based AI—but only on the lower levels of access. He did not have the authority to get to those parts of the QUAIC that would enable him to get into the ship's security systems or control the TWS. Neither did Chermal. Yet, for them to succeed, they needed to do both. And because it was impossible to duplicate a person's psychic signature, there was no way to access the QUAIC without going through an authorized person. At least none Axel or Chermal could think of.

Axel mulled over this dilemma for a considerable amount of time. The easiest way to solve the problem would be to find a crewman authorized for the appropriate levels of the QUAIC and have them do what they needed. However, this was extremely risky. First, it would be nearly impossible, if not impossible, to find someone so authorized willing to help Axel to, in effect, undermine his father. The crew was extremely loyal to his dad. Even those who might be sympathetic to Axel's cause—i.e., saving the planet spinning beneath them—Axel wasn't sure they could be trusted not to tell his father about his plans. Moreover, could he find a nescrot who would *listen* to a nescreet, even the son of the Thermax, much less work with one? And if he did find the right person, it meant placing him or her in extreme jeopardy—especially if Axel's plan failed. Finally, he could not be sure the AI itself would not alert his father to the unusual requests required for the plan to work.

Axel glanced at a chronometer he set for earth time. It counted down to the predicted time of the explosion. He had less than twenty earth hours to prevent the catastrophe.

Fearing he had come to a dead end, Axel fretted over the options. That's when inspiration, in the form of Chermal, hit or rather pawed him. While Axel frantically ran various scenarios through the console, Chermal suddenly, playfully swatted his leg. Axel ignored him. But when he did it again, a bit harder, Axel looked down and saw playfulness in him he hadn't seen in months. As soon as Axel glanced his way, Chermal took off for the door. Once there, he stopped and looked back at Axel. "I'm in no mood for games right now," Axel told his furry companion. "You know how important this is." Chermal's responded by returning to Axel's leg and giving it another swat, this time a little more meaningfully.

Chermal again darted for the door. "All right, you win," Axel said, chasing after him, thinking he needed a break. It had been a long, long time since Chermal engaged him in a game of chase. But that was apparently what he wanted, so Axel took off after him.

Chermal led him down the corridor and disappeared into the rec room. Axel bounded after him. But when he got there, Chermal was nowhere to be found, although Axel still "felt" him, so Chermal was still in the room. Chermal "cloaked" himself in such a way Axel couldn't perceive his location. Puzzling. "I see, you want to play hide'n'seek like humans. Okay, but only for a little while. Then back to work."

Axel searched all the obvious hiding places around the room, and there were plenty. But Chermal was nowhere to be found. Stumped, Axel again scanned the room, trying to figure out what he missed.

That's when Chermal dropped in. For just as Axel was ready to give up, Chermal fell from the ceiling, landing directly on top of Axel's head, before continuing to the floor.

Recovering from the surprise "attack," Axel found Chermal sitting on his haunches, looking up and smiling at him. He made no move to escape when Axel swept him up in his arms. The game and lesson were over.

Axel glared into Chermal's eyes as understanding dawned, and with it, a new burst of energy and enthusiasm. *I don't know what I would do without you!* Axel teleped his mentor as he gave him a hug. *I didn't find you because I was thinking two dimensionally. That's why I never looked up. But you were playing three dimensionally.*

*In a similar fashion, I've been contemplating accessing the QUAIC with the same limitations, accessing it in the same fashion I always have…that is, in 'real' or current time. I keep thinking of time in three-dimensional terms, which has time moving only in one direction. Which is stupid because that was why we were using the TWS in the first place!*

*Instead, I need to think four dimensionally and view time as more of an ocean instead of a river flowing only downhill.*

Axel paused as the plan unfolded in his mind. *Theoretically, I could access now the Master QUAIC on Delios as it will exist at some point in the future. If, at that time the future me is an authorized user, I could enter the appropriate QUAIC level. Then have it send a command back in time to this QUAIC, providing me current authorization!*

*It depends entirely on my being an authorized user in the future.*" Axel looked at Chermal, whose eyes shined their approval.

*Okay, we just have to assume I do. It's our only chance. Which means, it may be Earth's only chance.* Axel returned to the TWS, picked up Chermal, and placed him on the console in front of him. Chermal's short tail swished back and forth in approval. *I will really need your help on this. It goes way beyond anything I've attempted before. Communicating with the Master AI is one thing, but to access its future self and have it send back instructions to this time…wow.* Axel paused. *But I believe it can be done.* Then looking again at Chermal, who radiated confidence, he said, *Okay, I know it can be done!*

He and Chermal spent the next several hours planning and prepping. Every detail, every thought, needed to be rehearsed. Given the time constraints,

Axel's concentration had to be complete. There would be no second chance, for him or earth, and its doomsday clock was about to strike midnight.

****

It was time. First task was doing the mental exercises required to get him in the proper state of mind to maximize his psychic self. As he prepared, Chermal's strength enveloped him. With the strength came Chermal's calm and confidence, which were nearly as important as the mentiot's considerable psychic ability.

Axel, with Chermal's assistance, formed a mental picture of what he anticipated looking like in thirty years. This was the youngest age Chermal and he were most confident he would have the authority to fully access the Master QUAIC, or MQ, and the Time Operations within. He was pleased the mental picture of the Delion he would become would be quite attractive to female Delions.

In addition to the physical characteristics, Axel needed to imagine what his mental makeup would be like after thirty years of additional training and hard-won experience. Given he had no idea what experiences those might be, he used his father as a guide. Since he closely resembled his father physically, with similar personalities, it stood to reason he would share his behavior and mental characteristics.

Axel needed to do more than simply imagine what he would look and act like in thirty years. He must essentially *become* that person. That is, he needed to *think* like the wizened nescrot Axel would think. There could be no doubt to the future MQ that the person communicating with it is—would be—Axel's future adult self. Unfortunately, he would not have one thing the future nescrot would have—thirty more years' worth of memories. He had no choice but to risk those future memories would not be critical to his current success. Given his psychic signature would be the same as his future self, there should be no need for the AI to probe his memories…at least he hoped.

As the older Axel's image, both physical and mental, took shape in the younger Axel's mind, he felt the changes happening within. Confidence in his abilities increased, while he grew more cautious about the universe around him. Because the success of this mission required Axel's future self to become a leader of some note, it gave the nescreet Axel more assurance, with a touch of arrogance demanded of being a leader. His bond with Chermal deepened to a degree Axel didn't realize was possible. A part of Axel was surprised at how calmly he took in the changes. The nescreet Axel would normally be bouncing up and down with his success.

At last they were ready. Chermal gave Axel the subtle signal to begin. Together they reached out in both space and time to the Delion of thirty years in the future. Chermal always knew where and when to look for what they sought. It did not take long before they confronted the AI of the future MQ.

As anticipated, the AI was essentially the same as he remembered. From what Axel gathered, it hadn't changed much in 2,000 years. So, he wasn't expecting it would be different in the future than when he left Delios three months ago—or was it thirty years ago?

After contacting the MQ, Axel identified himself and opened his mind to its psychic probing. As expected, the probe simply identified Axel to the MQ, thankfully without examining Axel's memories—which were thirty years short.

Axel held his psychic breath for the few eternal nanoseconds it took for the MQ to confirm his identity. There were no beeps or lights flashing to let Axel know he was approved. Instead, the universe simply opened for Axel to examine—or so it appeared. The incredible sheer volume of knowledge flowing through the collective mind with which he was joined, completely staggered Axel. If Chermal hadn't been there with him, the shock of the moment might easily have damaged Axel's young brain. No manner of training could have possibly prepared him for that moment, certainly not his limited exposure to the infinitely less powerful QUAIC on board the *Druize*.

But Chermal *was* there and Axel felt him act quickly to narrow access to the MQ so he wouldn't be so overwhelmed. although Chermal appeared to struggle to keep the contact open while he worked. Adding to the difficulty was their desire to limit their contact with the AI to reduce the risk. Tighter and tighter, Chermal helped him focus, until the information stream became manageable. As planned, when Chermal was confident Axel could handle it, he gave Axel a mental nudge, telling him it was time to proceed.

It was hard tearing himself away from the universe now open to him. The nescreet in him wanted to explore. But a new maturity filled him now. He took comfort knowing this wonder would someday be his to explore. But today, he had a higher purpose. Today, he must act to save a world.

As he gathered his wits, he realized the enormity of

the task still awaiting him. It was one thing to access the MQ in the future. It was still another to have the MQ access the ship's QUAIC in *this* time frame and then give the ship's QUAIC the necessary commands.

The first task was to find that part of the MQ responsible for Time Operations. With Chermal's help, they found the access point quickly. Now came the difficult part.

For him to access this part of the MQ, which was one of the most sensitive and secure areas for obvious reasons, two things were necessary. First, his future self must be authorized to have access. Axel could only hope he would become such a person—for only those at the highest levels of command had such access. Second, he had to go in alone. The security in this part of the MQ required only single entities to enter. No one could bring a "guest"—even that person's mentiot.

After consulting for a few moments with Chermal, who gave him his reassurance, Axel took a couple deep breaths and relaxed deeper into his chair. While meditating before his attempt, he kept his mental image of his future-self firmly in mind. Finally, he was ready. Tentatively, he reached out to the psychic "Sentinel," the AI guarding entry into Time Operations.

Axel recoiled slightly at the touch before quickly recovering. The Sentinel possessed enormous power, which was directed at whoever tried to access the portal. Axel steeled himself as much as possible against the anticipated power surge, but nothing could have prepared him for what he experienced. In a fraction of a heartbeat, a presence did not just "touch" his mind, but enveloped it, swallowing it whole into an unfathomable being where Axel became less than a grain of sand among all the beaches of Earth. In that breathless moment, the Sentinel was in every part of his mind. But there was no attempt to control or alter it. Indeed, the benign presence was intimidating only in its sheer power.

But before Axel could formulate a thought, it was over. He was in.

Again, Axel squelched the child in him that was thrilled at his having gotten in and what it meant about his future. As the nescrot Axel, he pushed ahead.

Now that he was in Time Operations, he had to get it to do what he wanted. Not only had Axel never worked with such a powerful system, but the very nature of Time Operations made it more complicated. Axel needed to formulate exactly what he wanted in as precise a detail as he could and then pass it along to the Time Operations AI.

What he needed was for the future Time Operations AI to pass along to the present-day Controller AI on the *Druize* that the present-day Axel was authorized to access the TWS and its QUAIC. Simple.

Chapter 22

*September 11th, D Minus 121.71 Hours*
*38,000 feet up*

Doug gazed out the window at the land far below rushing past at 513 miles per hour. No matter how many times he flew, and he had flown many, many times, he still enjoyed the view from 38,000 feet. It helped keep everything in perspective—seeing how tiny human constructions were in relation to the world. The sky was clear, with only a few puffy clouds floating below with their shadows dancing across the landscape. A smile formed. No matter how big one thought he was, each of us was still an insignificant speck against the background of the world, which was an even-more insignificant speck in the cosmos.

Doug shifted his six-foot-one-inch frame around, trying to get a little more comfortable. He cursed under his breath that the agency made him fly "economy" on this flight. He certainly had enough frequent flyer miles for an upgrade. But, no, the bureau was being austere and allowing their agents fly first class was seen as politically insensitive. So, he had to fly economy. At least, at an athletic 205 pounds, Doug fit into the seat, which was more than some people, including many of those he had the displeasure of sitting next to on some flights. At times, he suspected there was a conspiracy afoot whereby the airlines deliberately sat the 360-pound blabbermouths who only bathed once a month next to Doug while the gorgeous single women were always seated somewhere else.

Fortune was with him on this flight, however. The seat next to him was unoccupied, giving him a lot more room. Well, if he couldn't have an attractive woman next to him, an empty seat was the next best thing. Having the extra space was a rare treat indeed.

Doug's mind wandered as he absently gazed out the plexiglass. He wasn't likely to see any terrorists outside his window, although Lord knew he saw them seemingly everywhere else. Since being reassigned to the special joint agency anti-terrorist task force, Doug hadn't taken a single day off. Fortunately, he loved his work. He even liked the danger because he believed in what he was doing. Although, a day off every now and again might be nice, but not likely to happen in the foreseeable future.

Suddenly, something caught his attention in his peripheral vision…a brief but blinding flash, like bright sunlight reflecting off a shiny surface…but where? He scanned the skies. At this altitude, there weren't many aircraft flying higher than they were, but the reflection came from above. He stared out into the cloudless blue-white sky.

Doug bent down to retrieve the case tucked underneath the seat in front of him. Opening the front pouch, he pulled out a set of small, powerful binoculars. Without shame, he lifted them up to the window and stared out. He might look silly doing this, but there was still a child inside him that he was determined to never let die.

It took a few moments, but he found the source of the reflection. There was something there, and it was flying very high—at least 25,000 or more feet higher than the plane he was in, but it appeared to be traveling in the same direction and maintaining the same relative speed.

He carefully studied the craft looking for what caused the bright reflection. There was something peculiar about it. For one thing, while it appeared metallic, he couldn't see any wings. Sometimes, depending on the angle of the airplane, it could be difficult to see wings. But at this angle, they should be visible unless the craft was banking. But if it were banking, it should be turning, and this craft wasn't.

Also, the shape wasn't right. It was too fat. It was shaped more oval than any airplane Doug knew.

But something else bothered him, something he couldn't quite put his finger on. As he puzzled over it, he brought the binoculars down to examine the object again with his naked eye. Then it hit him. The sun was behind the craft. There was no way for it to cast a reflection from that craft onto Doug's plane. Yet there was no mistaking it had—or, it flashed a very bright light in his window.

Doug focused the binoculars back on the craft. Just as it came into view, it teetered from side to side, like a plane waving its wings, although there clearly weren't any. Then the craft suddenly changed direction. Impossibly, it veered off at a 45-degree angle, instantly. There was no turning or banking, one moment it was heading straight ahead, the next, it angled off.

Then it changed direction again. This time it was

coming directly at Doug's plane. It grew larger and larger and its oblong shape became clearer. Then it changed direction again—straight up—at an impossible speed. Even with the binoculars, it was almost instantly out of his sight.

Doug sucked in his breath. Whatever he saw, it was not an airplane. Nor was it likely a craft of human origin.

He looked around the cabin of the plane to see if anyone else had seen it. But no one had been looking out the window. He momentarily considered going up front to ask if the pilots saw anything—or if an unusual object showed up on radar. But as soon as he thought of it, he dismissed the idea. To do so would mean drawing unnecessary attention to himself, and to even get to the pilots would have required him to flash his badge, blowing his cover. Besides, something told him they didn't see anything and, even if they did, they never would admit it.

So once again, he had seen a UFO, but he had absolutely no proof or witnesses to show for it. Doug put away the binoculars and sank back into his chair. What he did was important, essential perhaps. Yet it still paled in comparison to solving some of the biggest mysteries out there. Like who was flying that UFO and what were they doing here? And what caused that flash of light he took for a reflection?

Doug sighed. Maybe someday, he would seek out the truth. But for now, he had bad guys to catch. And, somehow, he didn't think UFOs were on the terrorists' minds.

Doug glanced at his watch. It was 10 a.m., Pacific Time. He was landing at LAX in less than an hour. Jim

Nobles, the Special Agent in charge for the Los Angeles Bureau of the FBI and an old friend, would greet him at the airport. Doug would brief him privately as they drove back to the Bureau offices in LA. There, Doug would brief the three agents assigned to assist him.

However, in addition to Bureau resources, Doug now had local police, Homeland Security, NSA, the DEA, the CIA, as well as Immigration working various aspects of the case. Doug smiled to himself. Immigration. Of all the things they suspected Abdul Raheim of, the only thing they could arrest him on now was entering the country illegally. And that was only if they caught him in the US. And then, the best they could do was detain him shortly before deporting him. Unless they gave him a one-way ticket to Gitmo. But even if they just detained him, at least it would give them an excuse for seizing him and everything he had with him. Doug hoped that would be enough.

Of course, Abdul might not be in Los Angeles anymore. His "blip" only appeared briefly before mysteriously disappearing again. So, Abdul was apparently sticking close to whatever was shielding his signal. Yet, the signal reappearing meant the bug was still working and had not yet been discovered by Abdul. It also meant it could reappear again at any time…and anywhere.

It was not lost on Doug at all that today marked the anniversary of the worst terrorist attack in history. And now he was in pursuit of another terrorist who might be plotting something equally bad or worse.

They had worked on the assumption whatever was going to happen, would happen today. But Doug's gut said no. He knew Raheim. He wanted to maximize the terror, meaning announcing his plans, then daring the US to stop him. Yet nothing had been forthcoming.

Nor had his task force found anything substantial, other than confirming all three organizations, Raheim's, Krenchenko's, and Bavaro's, were in a heightened state. Hakeem reported there was an unusual amount of "chatter" coming out of all three. But neither the NSA nor CIA came up with anything concrete.

Doug looked back out the window, again wondering what was out there.

Chapter 23

*September 11th, D Minus 121.82 Hours*
*Dallas*

Greg paced back and forth on the playground waiting impatiently for Tess and Ashanti to appear. His car was parked in the lot on the east side of the building, out of sight from the playground and Michaels' preferred spot for doing business. The backpack weighed heavily on his shoulders—both physically and psychologically. He wiped the sweat from his palms as his heart pulsed with both excitement and fear and from the adrenaline coursing through his arteries, boosting his already high energy state. What they were doing was dangerous but must be done to save his friend.

He hardly slept the night before, thinking about today's adventure. And now that it was go time, he was more nervous. Worse, their initial plan wouldn't work.

Before arriving at the school, Greg got the sound cone from the mall, while Ashanti picked up Tess. The cone cost him $50 for just one day but was worth it. He could easily earn it back mowing lawns tomorrow.

Greg ate a big snack at the food court before heading over to Peterson Elementary. As with his best friend Jeff, food was an important part of Greg's life.

He made sure to fill his backpack with plenty of additional snacks and water. He didn't want to chance going hungry. After all, he might be gone several hours.

The schoolyard was empty when he arrived. But he was a few minutes early. He told Tess and Ashanti to meet him at 11:00, and it was only now 10:50. Shifting the weight of the backpack so it was more comfortable, he scanned the schoolyard. The only people visible were a couple younger kids with their mother heading for the playground. Neither his friends nor, notably, Michaels, were anywhere in sight.

Peterson Elementary was one of Michaels' known hangouts—one where he liked doing his "business." Unfortunately, Greg didn't know what his "hours" were, so he had no idea how long they might have to wait. There was always the possibility he wouldn't show. But if he came, chances were he would be in the same spot as always, which was by the back fence on the other side of the schoolyard from where Greg was now.

The original plan called for them to either observe Michaels from one of the cars—if they could park close enough—or find a good hiding place as close to Michaels' "spot" as possible from where they could videotape his transactions. But now he was here, it was clear there wasn't anywhere suitable. The guy at the electronics store said they needed to be within fifty yards to pick up the conversation clearly. Unfortunately, Michaels chose his spot to do business well. It provided an unobstructed view in every direction for several hundred yards—probably so he can make a quick escape if necessary. Even with a sound cone and a 300x camcorder, they needed to be closer than across the schoolyard.

As he pondered their options, Tess and Ashanti walked up. Both wore backpacks strapped to their shoulders. Ashanti had the camcorder. Tess brought snacks, as well as a soccer ball they would play with as a cover while waiting. Greg hadn't trusted Tess would bring enough food, which is why he brought some as well.

"Guys, there's a problem," Greg said, as the other two got closer. "I don't see anywhere we can set up."

Both Tess and Ashanti looked around. The only possible hiding place close enough was in the bushes behind someone's house. They agreed that was not a good choice. Especially when they noted a particularly big dog chained in the backyard. They also agreed parking close enough to record wouldn't work, either, as Michaels would notice people in the car. He would be much more suspicious of cars than of kids playing in the playground—especially since Greg was pretty sure Michaels would recognize Greg's car and possibly Ashanti's. It was a shame neither of them had a car with heavily tinted windows, like some of the kids. Then they could park close and not have to worry about Michaels being able to see inside the car.

"What do we do now?" Tess asked.

"I'm not sure. Does anyone have any idea where Michaels is now or when he may come here?" Greg asked.

"I was told he usually comes by here in the late morning on Saturday. I have no idea where he is coming from, or where he goes from here," Ashanti said. Tess nodded her head in agreement.

"I guess we could wait here for him to show up,

then follow him and see where he goes. Maybe the next place will be better. If not, we can always set up Monday at school."

"That's true. But it certainly will be more difficult. Not only will we need to rent the sound cone an extra two days, but it means carrying all this expensive equipment around school—or leaving it in the car all day. Neither alterative sounds particularly attractive," Ashanti said. "Besides, this whole thing gives me the creeps. The sooner we're done, the better."

"I agree," Tess responded. "Let's wait and see what develops."

Reaching a consensus, they walked over to the soccer field and carefully put their backpacks down. Tess dug the soccer ball out of hers and kicked it toward Ashanti. Greg took up his position as goalie.

The wait was not long. About a half hour later Michaels pulled up in his cherry-red Miata, with its top down, and parked about three hundred yards away from Greg and the two girls. To their surprise, Michaels was not only alone, he did not get out of his car. Fortunately, though he scanned the area thoroughly, he apparently didn't recognize the three of them. Both Tess and Ashanti had their hair up, and Greg wore a headband and an old pair of glasses instead of his contacts to help make them more difficult to recognize.

A short time later, as if by magic, several kids appeared and gathered around the car. The shop was now open for business.

The ball whizzed by Greg's ear as he was distracted by the gaggle of kids gathered around Michaels.

"Don't stare!" Tess scolded as Greg sheepishly

retrieved the ball. "Just continue playing."

Greg nodded. It was important they not draw undue attention to themselves. They kept playing, but simply stole a glance every now and then.

Every time Greg glanced at Michaels, there was a different kid with him. He shook his head sadly about the implications of such a steady business. The flow of customers remained constant for about thirty minutes. Then a glance revealed Michaels talking on a cellphone. Judging by his exaggerated motions, he was not enjoying the conversation. Michaels suddenly brought the phone down, almost slamming it against his car before stopping and putting it in his pocket. He must have said something to the kids gathered around him as they quickly scattered. The Miata's engine roared to life and he drove off.

As soon as he heard the engine start, Greg told the girls, "Okay, guys, let's roll!", both of whom had been surreptitiously watching the events unfold and were already moving. Tess quickly grabbed the ball and stuffed it back into her backpack. Greg took off at a dead run for his car, leaving his backpack behind. The girls grabbed it and their own and made for the gap in the fence where Greg picked them up. Tess kept an eye on the Miata as it made its way down Park Lane. A fortuitous light held him up.

"He turned onto Maple," Tess shouted to Greg as she and Ashanti dived into Greg's blue Ford Focus.

"Whoever was on the other end of the phone conversation sure got him fired up about something. He did not look happy as he took off!" Greg commented as he likewise hit the gas.

"I hope we can keep up," Ashanti said.

"Fortunately, although he obviously was agitated and in somewhat of a hurry," Tess commented, "he wasn't really speeding. I don't think he wants to risk getting caught with all his 'merchandise' by doing something stupid—like getting a ticket."

"Unfortunately, I may have to bend a few of those laws to catch up to him," Greg commented, as the speedometer reached 55 in the 35 zone before he slowed for the turn onto Maple.

"There he is!" Ashanti shouted, needlessly. She was in the passenger seat next to Greg. "He just turned onto Davis. He might be heading toward the turnpike."

"Good. We only have to keep close enough to watch where he turns," Greg panted, still a little out of breath from his dash to the car. As he spoke, he pressed down hard again on the accelerator.

"Careful," Tess commented. "You don't want to close on him too fast, or he'll notice."

"Right," Greg said, as he eased off slightly on the gas.

"He turned onto the North Dallas Tollway, heading north," Ashanti noted. Michaels' choice in cars made him easier to spot and follow.

"Got it." They weren't too far behind now.

Greg held back as far as he could, while maintaining visual contact with Michaels. It wasn't easy, though, as cars continuously zipped in and out of the traffic lane ahead of him, momentarily blocking his view. Fortunately, the freeway was three lanes wide at this point, so they could weave around the trucks looming ahead.

Greg had seen hundreds of movies where one car tailed another. It always looked easy on the screen. But now, traffic proved reality was much more difficult. At one point, they found themselves directly behind Michaels. If he had looked in his rearview mirror then, game over. Fortunately, Greg quickly got into a different lane and again put a few cars between them and him.

It was great the girls were with him. They kept track of Michaels' Miata, while he concentrated on driving and traffic. Thanks to modern electronics, the tollway no longer had toll booths. You either had a toll pass or they billed you based on your license plate. That made it easier to follow him.

After about four miles, Ashanti noted Michaels moved over to the right lane. "I think he will exit at Wichita Avenue," she said.

Greg nodded and pulled into the right lane, about four cars back from Michaels. Sure enough, he made the exit. Greg slowed and followed.

Luck was with them as a charcoal PT Cruiser also pulled off the turnpike between Michaels' and Greg's cars. Moreover, it stayed behind the red Miata at the light at the bottom of the exit ramp in the left-hand turn lane. Greg breathed a heavy sigh of relief because the light was a long one. The PT Cruiser likely prevented Michaels from noticing them, and the long light gave them a chance to relax a bit. The pain from gripping the steering wheel so hard provided evidence of the tension they all felt.

When the light changed, the Miata peeled out. The PT Cruiser was right behind him. Greg lagged back a bit to create more space between himself and Michaels.

Michaels continued down Wichita Avenue, heading out of town. "Where could he be going?" Tess asked. "It seems unlikely he would deal so far away."

"That's true," Ashanti replied.

"Should we stop?" Greg asked.

After a short pause, Tess responded, "Well, we've come this far. Let's see where this takes us. If we don't like where he stops, we drive on."

"Agreed," Greg said, with Ashanti nodding.

After a few miles the road narrowed from four lanes to two, and traffic thinned. This proposed quite a dilemma. Greg needed to stay close enough to see where Michaels was going, but far enough back not to attract his attention.

One by one, the cars between Michaels and Greg disappeared, causing him to fall farther and farther behind. Then fortune turned from bad to worse as a traffic signal, one of the few on the road this far out, turned yellow just before Michaels got there. He accelerated right through. There was no way to make the light before it turned red. So, Greg could either run the red light, risking a possible ticket or worse, a collision, or stop and hope Michaels would not get too far ahead.

Greg glanced at Ashanti. Without asking, the expression on her face told him what she wanted him to do. He stepped on the brake.

The light was frozen red. Every second was like five minutes to Greg. The Miata was fading into the distance, and they would not catch him if the light didn't change soon.

Tess was the instigator. She pointed out there were no other cars visible—on either road. Now she didn't exactly tell Greg to run the light, but her observation was rather prudent. He looked at Ashanti, who gave him a barely perceptible nod. Greg stepped on the gas.

Nor did he spare it. Greg figured he already broke the law by running a red light. He might as well bend it a bit more by exceeding the speed limit—by about 30 mph. He silently prayed no one—particularly anyone wearing a blue uniform—was watching.

Michaels' Miata grew larger and Greg slowed down. Just as he did, the Miata's brake lights came on. Greg slowed more as Michaels made a right-hand turn. Greg waited until Michaels disappeared around the corner, behind a building, before proceeding.

When Greg got to the intersection, he saw Michaels had turned into an old industrial park filled with seemingly abandoned warehouses. By the time the trio arrived, Michaels was nowhere to be seen. The parking lots were empty. Greg turned in and pulled into the first parking lot. There were several rows of warehouse-type buildings visible. But from his brief glance, it appeared most, if not all, were no longer in use.

****

"What do we do now?" Ashanti asked.

"He has to be here someplace," Greg replied. "He must have gone into one of the buildings. Let's go down each row and see if we can see his car, or maybe hear or see something indicating where he is."

"I don't like this," Tess commented. "I have a bad feeling about this place. Maybe we should turn back."

"I know," Ashanti agreed. "I get the same feeling."

"Look," Greg reasoned, "we've come this far. I'd hate to turn around now."

"I don't know, Greg," Ashanti replied. "This is spooky. Besides, we stand out like a sore thumb here.

There are no other cars."

Greg was silent for a minute. Ashanti was right. They couldn't just drive in and look for him. However, the industrial park was not so big that he couldn't cover it on foot. He also noted there was a convenience store across the street.

"Do you have your cellphone?" Greg asked Ashanti. She nodded. "Good. So do I. Tell you what. I will explore the area on foot. Ashanti, you take my car, and you two wait over there out of sight," he said, pointing to the convenience store, "in case he comes back. I'll walk around to see if I can find him or figure out what's going on. If either of us spots Michaels, we'll text the other." Ashanti again nodded. "Okay then. I'll see you in a little bit." Without waiting for a reply, Greg grabbed his backpack and headed off.

He was pleased Ashanti did as instructed. He had been afraid the girls might follow him. The place also gave him the creeps. Something didn't seem right. But he made a commitment and intended to follow through. Besides, he needed to return the sound equipment tomorrow.

Greg hiked down the broken pavement noting the overgrown weeds on either side of the road were tall enough to hide just about anything. The second warehouse, like the first, featured a few intact windows and a bunch of broken ones. A weathered "For Sale" sign adorned the side of the building. The phone number was no longer readable. "Great marketing," mumbled Greg as he passed by. He vaguely remembered seeing on the news one of the last businesses left this "park" last year, complaining the developer never kept the place up. Obviously, they had a point he thought as he walked around one of the many potholes in the road.

Behind the second building were five rows of smaller metal buildings more tightly bunched. All abandoned. The buildings shared the same basic design—tall weeds and broken windows along the front red brick façade, with taller weeds along the metal sides.

Greg stopped by the side of the third and last building in the first row and surveyed the situation. To get to the second row of buildings, he must either cross the parking lot in plain view of anyone watching or venture into the field and risk snakes and who-knows-what. However, if he went through the field, he would still be visible to someone looking in that direction. Might as well avoid the snakes.

Greg trotted quickly across the parking lot. His plan was to go down one row then the next, looking carefully at the gaps between buildings to see if he could spot any activity.

When he reached the third row, fate intervened. He was near the end of the row when he heard a car making its way down the road connecting the rows of buildings. Immediately, he ran to a gap between two buildings and practically dived into the weeds, just as the car came into view.

He was about thirty yards from the road as the car passed, close enough to get a good look at the black Mercedes as it drove by. The car appeared as if it had just been driven off the lot—brand-new with not a speck of dirt on it. However, it didn't have dealer plates, so it had not come directly from the dealer's—at least, not legally. The windows on the car were heavily tinted, preventing Greg from seeing inside.

The car slowly ambled past. The potholes slowed the black beast to a crawl as it carefully avoided them, lest it soil its spotless sheen.

Keeping close to the building, Greg followed the car as it made its way down the road. It turned into the alley separating the fourth and fifth rows of buildings. He quickly ducked down into the weeds as the car crawled past his location between the first and second buildings on the row. As it passed, he was able to see through the windshield into the car. There was a driver and a passenger in the front. It appeared there were others in the back seat, but Greg could not be sure.

The car turned into the loading dock area of the third building on the fifth and last row. That building was much larger than the others. As it pulled in, the garage door opened, allowing the car to drive straight into the building. A highly faded "Transdigital" could be made out on the sign above the door. It was the only building without broken windows.

Hustling as fast as he could, while sticking to the shadows of the buildings, Greg made his way over to the building across from the one the car went into. He made it, right as the door was closing. Before it closed completely, he got a quick glimpse into the building. Though brief, his glance was enough to reveal several cars—all expensive looking—parked inside. There were also at least a dozen people. All of them scary in appearance. He also noted one other thing inside— Michaels' Miata.

Greg's heart pounded against his ribs as he stared across the alleyway at the mysterious building. What should he do? It was one thing to talk big, but now he was confronted with reality…and it was completely different. Whatever was happening in the building, it was bigger than just Michaels. It was way more than Greg and his friends bargained for.

Greg felt for the phone in his pocket. He was about to pull it out to call the girls when his world went black. Greg never heard the thug sneaking up behind him. He only felt his head explode, then his consciousness quickly slipped away.

Chapter 24

Axel had Jeff and Becca sit in two of the chairs, while he remained standing in front of them, Chermal at his side. The chairs were the most comfortable Jeff ever sat in, despite their thinness. They molded themselves to fit the contour of his body.

"Before we begin training, there is something you want to ask me," Axel stated rather than asked.

"In fact, there are a few million things I want to ask," Jeff replied. "But I guess the thing that's got my attention is this teleporting thing. I know you said it involves using your mental 'powers' and all, but how does it *work?* I mean, I know enough about physics to know it should be impossible to think yourself somewhere else. There must be a zillion laws of physics you just broke."

Axel smiled in response. "That's because you are thinking in terms of your three-dimensional physical world. But the universe exists in more than just three dimensions. Psychic energy, or psi, in fact, is one of the primary binding forces existing in the *fourth* dimension. Just like gravity helps bind things in the third dimension, psi binds things together in the fourth."

213

"I still don't see how that gets you from one place to another instantly."

"Allow me a quick demonstration," Axel said. Instantly, a piece of ordinary copier paper appeared in Axel's left hand and a seemingly normal ballpoint pen appeared in the other. "For this demonstration, I am borrowing a piece of paper and pen from your room, if that's okay." As he said that, Jeff took a closer look at the pen. The characteristic teeth marks on its end confirmed its identity.

Axel proceeded to mark two "X"s on one side of the paper. He then handed the paper and the pen to Becca. "Becca, I want you to show me the shortest distance between these two 'X's".

"That's easy." Becca said confidently. "Everyone knows the shortest distance between two points is a straight line." She took the pen and held the paper on her knee as she drew a line connecting the X's. She then handed the paper back to Axel.

Axel examined the line she drew and then handed the paper and pen to Jeff. "Do you agree that's the shortest distance?"

Jeff stared at the page. There had to be something he was missing, but he couldn't see it. After examining it for a moment, he commented, "I guess the line could be a little straighter."

Becca sighed. Axel smiled. He took the paper back from Jeff. "Well, you'd be right if you were just two dimensional." Axel looked at Becca. "Do you understand what I mean by *dimensions*?"

Becca nodded, then recited from memory. "The first dimension is simply length, like a straight line. The second dimension adds width. A square is two-dimensional. The third dimension is length, width, and height, so a cube is three-dimensional."

"And the fourth is time!" Jeff added enthusiastically.

Again, Axel smiled. "Very good, both of you. If we looked at only the *surface* of this paper—" He held up the page with the "X"s facing them. "—how many dimensions are there?"

"The surface has only two dimensions, doesn't it?" Jeff answered. "While the paper is three dimensional, its surface has only two dimensions. Because it only has length and width."

Axel nodded. "Now let's imagine for a moment you are a two-dimensional creature, say 2-D man, living on the surface of this page. In fact, let's imagine you live here," Axel said as he pointed to the left-most "X" on the page. "For you, the quickest route to the other 'X,' is indeed roughly the line Becca drew."

"However, it is not the shortest route for us, since we are *three* dimensional." Axel took the paper and held one end in each hand. Slowly and dramatically, he folded the paper so the two "X"s were touching. "You see, for us three dimensional creatures, the shortest distance is to fold the paper so the 'X's are touching."

"Ahhhhh," said Becca and Jeff simultaneously as the light bulbs suddenly illuminated in their minds.

"Now, let me ask you another question. Have I made the trip shorter for 2-D man?"

Becca answered before Jeff. "No. He still has to travel along the line, and the line isn't any shorter."

Axel nodded approvingly. Jeff smiled with pride at his sister's cleverness. "So," Axel continued, "even though these two 'X's are physically touching each other in the *third* dimension, poor 2-D man still has to go along the surface, right?"

Jeff and Becca both nodded, but Jeff's expression portended puzzlement. "By folding the paper, aren't you changing it into being three dimensional?"

"Only for those for whom the third dimension exists. But poor old 2-D man is blissfully unaware his world has changed. For by simply folding the paper, we have done nothing to change its surface, have we?"

"No."

"And 2-D man lives only on the surface. He doesn't know about the fold because it is folded along a dimension he is completely unaware of—except maybe theoretically.

"Okay, now watch." Axel then proceeded to wad the paper up into a tight ball, which he then tossed to Jeff, who caught it adroitly. "All right, Jeff, if you are still 2-D man, what has changed?"

Jeff looked at the crumpled-up piece of paper. He carefully tossed it up in the air and caught it as he pondered. With sudden insight, he blurted out, "Nothing."

"That's right," Axel praised. "Nothing has changed for 2-D man. For him, his world is still flat as a pancake and he still has to make his way down Becca's street to get to the other 'X'. For although to us his world is crumpled into a tight ball in three-dimensional space, we did nothing to change the two-dimensional aspect of the surface of the page. All the changes we made were done through the third dimension. So, for 2-D man, his world remains flat and unbroken. He is completely unaware he could move just a short distance *through* the *third* dimension to get to any other spot in his two-dimensional world. Indeed, we could almost touch every point on his 2-D world with every other point through the *third* dimension and 2-D man would never know."

"I get it!" Becca said excitedly. "So, what you mean is our three-dimensional world could be crumpled up in a tiny 4-D ball and we, being 3-D, would never know it." Axel nodded enthusiastically.

"And, depending upon how crumpled up our 3-D world is," Jeff continued for Becca, "we may be touching several other 3-D spots, or connected to several—or theoretically, all other spots, through the fourth dimension. So, if we could access the fourth dimension…"

"You could instantly go from one location in your 3-dimensional universe to another," Axel said, completing Jeff and Becca's thought. "Although that is a tremendous over-simplification, it is essentially what happens. Psi, being a fourth-dimensional energy, is not restricted to three-dimensional space limitations—or time."

"Okay, but I'm still not sure how you move from one place to the other. We're still three-dimensional, as is that paper and pen."

"Exactly," Axel said. Another plain piece of paper appeared in his hand. On it he printed an "X," a "Y," and a "Z" in a staggered manner. "If you are 1-D man, that is, living in a single dimension, could you go from 'X' to 'Y' to 'Z'?"

Jeff and Becca both shook their heads. "A single-dimensional creature could only go along one dimension—either straight forward or straight back."

Axel nodded. Then he drew two straight lines. One

connected "X" to "Y" and the other connected "Y" to "Z." He then drew a third line extending down from "Z" in the same direction as the line from "X" to "Y". "Will you agree if 1-D man starts at 'X', he can go to 'Y' along this line?" He said pointing to the line connecting the two.

Jeff and Becca nodded. Axel continued, "and you will also agree a 1D man could go from 'Y' to 'Z,' as that is also a straight line." Again, they nodded. "So, all that has to happen for a 1D man to go from 'X' to 'Z' is for him, or her—" He looked at Becca. "—to be rotated along the second dimension. That is, reoriented. The 1-D creature may not be aware of this 'displacement' as he is still heading along a single dimension—only it is now in a new direction. At point 'Z', it could then be returned to its original direction by rotating it again through the second dimension Because 1D man may not be aware of the displacement as he is still heading in only one direction."

"I think I understand," Jeff said. "So to get 2-D man to go from one 'X' to the other 'X,' " Jeff said, holding up the wadded paper he still had in his hand, "all he needs to do is be turned along the third dimension and then returned to his original orientation. He won't need to change into a 3-D creature, just utilize the 'extra' dimension as a convenience."

Axel's grin widened. "I knew I had two good students. That's exactly right. The other point to understand is that when 2-D man is traveling along this new dimension, he is not visible to his 2-D mates left on the surface of the paper. To them, he simply disappears at one 'X' and magically reappears at the other 'X'."

"That's what happened to us." Becca said excitedly.

Axel nodded. "Yes, that disorientation you felt was you being rotated through the fourth dimension then rotated back, using psi. And you two will learn more about how to control it."

"Great! Let's get started," Becca enthused.

"We have been," Axel said as he smiled. "The first step is to learn more about how ESP and psi work."

"What's the next step?" Jeff said anxiously.

"Learning more." Axel held up his hand, which now held a watch. "Mind if I borrow this?"

Startled, Jeff looked down at his wrist. His watch was missing. Or, rather, it was no longer on his wrist but now in Axel's hand. "Uh, yeah, I guess," Jeff managed to say.

"You'd make a great magician." Becca commented.

"Thanks, I think." Axel then examined the watch, whose wristband was still latched. "You will both agree this watch is three-dimensional, correct?" Both Jeff and Becca nodded. "Now let's try to imagine how a 3-D object appears to a 2-D person."

Axel held up his left hand, which, magically, held another sheet of paper. "Okay, let's suppose you're 2-D man living on the surface of this paper. Now, you encounter our 3-D watch. What will 2-D man see?"

"It will depend on what part of the watch intersects the plane of his 2-D world," Jeff answered, somewhat smugly.

Axel gave him a half-grin. "Okay, so if the watch intersected our 2-D world like this…" Axel took the paper and brought it against the watch. To Jeff's and

Becca's amazement, the paper simply slid around the watch, so the watch stuck out through the page on both sides. The paper surrounded the watch face only. "If the watch intersected the 2-D world here…what will the watch appear to be to 2-D man?"

Becca and Jeff both answered quickly. "A circle!"

Axel nodded. "Very good." He then took the watch away from the paper, as though the paper didn't exist. Then he reinserted the watch so it was perpendicular to the page, with the paper going through the watch face and the watchband opposite of the face.

"Now how will it appear to 2-D man?"

"I know," said Jeff. Picking up the pen and the folded sheet of paper he still had on his lap, he drew a long oval and then a little way over, drew a smaller rectangle with rounded edges. Holding it up to Axel, he said, "I guess it will look something like this."

"Excellent." Axel commented. "Now what can you tell me about what you just drew?"

Jeff stared at it for a moment, then realized what Axel was probably getting at. "The circle and the rectangle are not connected."

"So, to 2-D man," Axel said smiling, "this watch, which is solid in our 3-D world, appears to be two completely separate and distinct objects."

"That's right." Becca said with a gleam in her eye. "There is no way for 2-D man to know they are connected. And, given the oval represents the metal watch, and the rectangle the plastic band, there is no reason to think they are related."

"Great!" Axel said. "So far, so good. Now, let's throw you a little curve." With that, he took the paper away and proceeded to wad it up into a tiny ball. He then reinserted the watch, so it intersected the paper at dozens of points. "Now what will it look like to our 2-D friend?"

Jeff laughed. "It will look like a jumble of objects of varying sizes and shapes."

"And, again, they will not appear to be from the same object," Becca added, her voice full of excitement.

"That's right," Axel said with a bit of pride. "Okay, next question. If 2-D man lives on this 2-D world"—he held up a piece of paper—"and, say 2-D woman living on this 2-D world"—he held up another piece of paper—"what happens if the two worlds came together? What would 2-D woman look like to 2-D man?" Magically, the second piece of paper was inserted at a right angle into the first paper.

Jeff thought about it for a moment then spoke out, "A straight line!"

"That's not very flattering," commented Becca.

Axel smiled. "In reality, the line may or may not be straight, depending upon whether 2-D's 2-D world is flat or curved. But the line, itself, is one-dimensional—having no width. It may appear curved to 2-D man, because 2-D woman's world was curved, but it has no width."

"Let me get this straight—pardon the pun," Jeff said. "Your intersection of two 2D worlds creates to us a 3D object, but to the people on the 2D worlds, the intersection is one dimensional."

"Exactly."

"Clear as mud," commented Becca. Her grin giving away she was not being serious.

"So now imagine there is not just one three-dimensional universe, but a limitless number of them existing within four-dimensional space. Some of these universes may intersect each other, as these two 2-D worlds did. What does one three-dimensional universe look to the other?"

"It appears two dimensional," Jeff answered, stroking an imaginary beard, "because they can only intersect in two dimensions. If they intersected at all three dimensions—they are the same space."

"Exactly. And how would a 4-D object appear to a 3-D person?"

"It will also appear three-dimensional. But like the watch was to two-dimensions, we will only see one three-dimensional surface. We could not see it in its entirety. In fact, it could also look like two, or several, different objects," Jeff said reflectively, as he pondered the possibilities.

"Good." Axel separated the two pieces of paper, then took the single piece of paper with the x-y line drawn on it and made it so the paper looped around and cut through its own surface. "Now let's say the 2-D universe was folded onto itself through the 3-D world. What would the x-y line appear to be to 2-D man at the point of intersection?"

"A single dot."

"So 2-D man might not know his universe was folded?"

"I guess not."

"And if our 3-D universe was similarly folded, how would we know?"

Jeff and Becca looked at each other. Neither had an answer.

"Ahh. You are beginning to understand. Now, let's

go one more step. So far, all we have talked about is physical matter. But what about energy? Let's go back to our poor crumpled 2-D man for a minute." Axel bent down and picked up the wadded piece of paper containing the original two "X"s. As he straightened up, he revealed he held a flashlight in his other hand. Jeff recognized the flashlight as also coming from his room.

Axel turned the flashlight on and shined its light on the wadded paper. "Okay, what does 2-D man see? Assuming for the moment the photons from the light excite the 2-D atoms in 2-D man's world so they, too, become illuminated."

"Well, for one thing," began Becca, sitting up straighter, "2-D man has no way of knowing where the energy came from to light up his world as the flashlight exists outside his 2-D universe."

"And," said Jeff, picking up from his sister, "since his 2-D world is crumpled in the third dimension, only patches of it will be lit up by the flashlight. So, it appears as random bits of light. He has no way of knowing it came from a single source."

Axel smiled. "Exactly. But the more interesting item may be what 2-D man 'sees.' How does a 3-D energy affect a 2-D surface? I'll let you think about that one for a moment. For now, let's just say as you can only see a small portion of a fourth-dimensional object, the same is true for a fourth-dimensional energy. Only a small portion of it is discernable in a 3-D world. And just like a four-dimensional object may have many, many different three-dimensional surfaces—and will appear to us to be a different object, so it is true of fourth dimensional energy. It may have many different three-dimensional aspects to it. And it may not be obvious to us 3-D creatures these are different aspects of the same energy, as opposed to being different energies. Such is the case with psi.

"Another point to consider. To rotate a three-dimensional object through the fourth dimension requires an enormous amount of energy—if that energy is from the three-dimensional universe. Just like it would for 2D man to be rotated through the third dimension. But such an exercise, as you saw, required very little effort from us, because we used energy from our three-dimensional universe.

"The same is true when we teleport. This is done using psi.

"Psi is a fundamental fourth-dimensional energy. And as such, it is only partially observable in our three-dimensional universe. All of those things you think of as ESP—telepathy, clairvoyance, telekinesis, precognition, and so on—are all aspects of a single energy source—psi."

"So how can we three-dimensional creatures use it? Or hope to control it?" Becca asked.

"Well, as three-dimensional creatures, we will never fully comprehend psi, or any true fourth dimensional object or energy. However, we can use it. Even though 2-D man may not be able to figure out why or how his 2-D world has become suddenly illuminated"—Axel again held up the paper wad and flashlight—"he can still use the lighted patches to his benefit. And, once he has discovered what parts of his world are now brighter, he can use them better."

"So how do we find these patches of light?" Jeff asked, leaning forward.

"Good question," Axel answered. "The answer is

that the light is all around you. You only need to become more sensitive to its presence. Some people—both of your species and mine—seem more naturally equipped to handle psi. That is, they are more receptive to it. The reason for this could be they have better receptors, or perhaps they are simply *less* effective in filtering it out."

"We filter *out* psychic information? That doesn't make sense," Becca said. "I don't remember filtering out anything."

"You are not aware of it. But don't you recall ever having any 'hunches,' or knowing who is calling you before you answer the phone, or what someone will say before they say it?"

"I guess, but I don't know that I filter it out."

"Let me ask you a question, then. Do you 'listen' to everything you hear?"

"Becca never *listens* to what anyone says," Jeff quipped.

"As if you do," Becca retorted.

Ignoring their bantering, Axel continued. "You are probably not aware of how effective your brain is at filtering out information it doesn't consider important. Have you ever been at a crowded party where there are lots of conversations going on at once—or at a stadium, or any public place where there are a lot of people?"

"Sure."

"What does it sound like?"

"Just a bunch of noise," Jeff said. "You can tell people are talking, but it becomes an unintelligible mumble."

"Right, but then have you ever heard someone call your name, without raising their voice, from across the room in that situation. And suddenly, you can pick out their voice?"

"Yeah!" Jeff saw where this was heading.

"So, although all the other voices seem unintelligible, somehow your brain can pick up someone saying your name—even though they may not be talking any louder than anyone else."

"That's right!" Becca said. "How does it do that?"

"Because your brain becomes sensitized to certain patterns it recognizes are important, such as the sound of your name, or the sound of a familiar voice. So while your brain is 'hearing' all that noise, it only processes those sounds—or signals, if you prefer—it recognizes. Those are then processed to your consciousness. In the same way, your 'psychic receptor,' if you will, processes psychic input, but only allows those signals it recognizes as being important to go through to your consciousness. You can imagine if you could sense psychic energy as well as, say, light energy, how overwhelmed you would quickly become."

"So how can we train it to process more information?" Jeff asked, squirming in his seat.

"The problem is your brain has been well-trained in what sounds may be more important, but it has had no training in what psychic noises may be important. To train it, we need to follow a two-step process. First, we will 'boost' the signal strength. That is, increase the psychic energy flow to your brain so it is not as easy to ignore. Second, we will train you to become more sensitive to it. You are not used to processing psychic energy, so your psychic sense is mostly dormant. We need to exercise it, so you can use it better. Train your psychic sense to focus."

"You're going to teach us to meditate, aren't you?" Becca asked.

"Well, the meditative state is an excellent way to become more sensitive to psi. As you shut down your other physical senses, your brain becomes more aware of input from a different source—psi." Axel paused for effect. "But that's not all we will do. Unfortunately, we don't have the luxury of spending the next fifteen years training you to be adept, as is the case with my people. So, we must take some necessary shortcuts."

Becca raised her hand, then spoke up. "Before we do anything else, I have a question."

"This isn't school," Axel responded. "You don't have to raise your hand…Although on further reflection, I guess it is kind of like school at that." Smiling, he continued. "What is your question?"

"When Jeff first came here, he was sporting a very large bruise on his face, and when he returned it was gone. Further, his clothes were torn, but there were no scratches. Were you somehow responsible for that?"

Axel smiled. "It was more Chermal than me. The truth is Jeff healed himself of both the bad bruise and the scratches. All we did was speed up the healing."

Both Jeff and Becca looked at him with puzzled faces.

Turning to Jeff, Axel continued. "What we did was speed up your body's normal healing process. Chermal can make parts of your body speed up dramatically, without it adversely affecting your other systems. Kind of like a localized time bubble. In fact, once you reach Level Three of your training, you will have the ability to do this yourself. Keep in mind, time is an aspect of the fourth dimension."

Jeff and Becca's mouths reached an all-time record for jaw opening.

"Now, about those glasses we discussed." Axel turned and walked over to Chermal, who had remained sitting in the same spot. They stared into each other's eyes for a few moments while Axel's back was to Jeff and Becca. When he turned around, he held two necklaces. On each was a single oval stone. The stones were a milky white and appeared to glow dully. A subtle swirl of ever-changing color flowed within them.

Axel walked over to Becca and Jeff and held out the necklaces.

"Wow" was all Jeff and Becca could say.

"Before you put these on, let me tell you what they are. These are gramirls. They are native stones on Chermal's planet and are fourth-dimensional gems with a strong aspect in our three-dimensional plane. As such, they act as a conduit for fourth dimensional energy—namely psi—into our world. Think of them as your psychic glasses. These crystals are your lenses into the psychic realm. They can boost the psychic energy for you up to some fifty-fold. However, going from a near stop to full intensity is extremely dangerous. Because you are not used to using your psychic senses, we need to take it gradually. Otherwise, it could literally drive you insane, possibly kill you." Jeff wasn't sure if he was kidding or not.

With that, Axel waved his hand over the crystals. As he did so, they became noticeably duller. The swirling pattern disappeared. "I have adjusted the crystals so you may use them, but with caution." He handed the necklaces to Jeff and Becca.

The gramirl was warm to Jeff's touch. Even though

it was considerably duller than when Axel first showed it to him, it still was beautiful. The stone was mesmerizing. "How do I use it?" Jeff managed to ask.

"*PUT THE NECKACE ON!*" Axel said.

"*You don't have to shout!*" Becca and Jeff said simultaneously.

"*ACTUALLY, for the first time in a while, I'm not 'shouting,'* " Axel replied. "*I am 'talking' much more normally. You are just hearing me better. Remember, I was never 'talking' at all. You were always 'hearing' me telepathically.*"

"*Wow.*"

"*Initially, Chermal and I will filter the psychic energy flowing through to you, so it won't be so overwhelming. Go ahead and put the necklaces on. You need to get used to them.*"

Jeff and Becca both complied, although somewhat reluctantly. They were each mesmerized by the stone and wanted to keep holding it.

As Jeff put on the necklace, a whole new world opened to him. The feeling was so intense it was almost physically painful. At the same time, no single sensation stood out. It must be like what happens when a blind man suddenly sees, so incredibly extreme was the new-found stimulation. No, it was more like if a person who could not see, hear, or smell suddenly gained all their senses, at the same time.

"*Do not be alarmed at the fact these new sensations seem so jumbled,*" came Axel's steadying thoughts. "*Your brain needs some time to learn how to make sense of the new information it is now receiving. You must learn to translate everything you perceive into its three-dimensional equivalents.*"

*"So, let's make things a little easier by dampening your other sensory input so you can concentrate on the psi."* With that, the room instantly became black. Becca let out an involuntary "yelp", for the darkness was unlike anything she ever experienced. Jeff's feelings echoed Becca's outburst. It wasn't just dark, it was completely devoid of light.

*"Don't be frightened,"* Axel reassured. *"We are all still here. And now you will, for the first time, also experience a complete absence of sound."*

Jeff screamed, only he didn't. He tried to—in fact, he thought he was—but no sound came out. There was no sound, period. Not even the sound of blood rushing through his ears he normally heard when everything else was quiet.

*"Okay, now I've got your full attention."* Axel's thoughts came through like a bolt of lightning in a pitch-black sky. Without any other major sensory distraction, Axel's psychic voice boomed into the silence, instantly becoming the focus for both Becca and Jeff.

*"Jeff, how many fingers am I holding up?"* asked Axel.

*"How would I know? It's pitch-black in here."*

*"Relax and reach out. Focus on my 'voice.' Find me mentally. Let the picture form in your mind."*

Jeff took a deep breath and then let it out slowly, forcing his body to relax. As he did so, he pictured Axel in his mind. He imagined Axel still standing in front of him and Becca, as he had been when the lights went out. Yet, somehow, that didn't quite seem right.

*"You moved!"* Jeff exclaimed.

*"Excellent. Where am I now?"*

Jeff concentrated hard.

"*No. You're trying to force it,*" Axel said. "*Your psychic 'receptors' are in the cerebellum, part of your 'old' brain, the part of the brain common to most animals. Your consciousness, or your inner voice, is located mostly in your cortex, or 'new' brain. So, by concentrating, you actually mask psi from your brain. You need to 'let go' of that voice. Relax and perceive.*"

Jeff took another deep breath. This wasn't easy. How do you force yourself not to think? He took another deep breath, relaxing his muscles as he did so. Images kept flashing through his mind. He ignored them. Another breath. This time he let the air out slowly. Axel's last words reverberated in his mind. Jeff allowed them to echo, growing louder with each replay. Jeff imagined he could physically hear the words being spoken to him.

"*You're over there,*" Jeff said, pointing his arm to his left.

"*Very good! Now how many fingers am I holding up? Just let the picture form in your mind.*"

Axel's voice came through clear as a bell. Jeff visualized seeing him smiling at him as he spoke. He was holding up his right arm. Three fingers extended from his palm.

"*Three.*"

"*Do you agree with him, Becca?*"

There was a long pause, then Jeff heard Becca say, "*yes.*"

"*Okay, now think a minute. Jeff, did you hear Becca say 'yes'?*"

"*Yeah.*"

"*And Becca, you can hear Jeff?*"

"*Yes.*"

"*How?*"

Jeff was stunned for a minute. If there was no sound, how did he hear Becca? There was only one answer.

"*Telepathy!*" Jeff and Becca both 'shouted' at once.

"*We can 'hear' each other telepathically!*" Becca nearly shouted in her excitement.

As the realization sank in, an almost euphoric feeling came over him. It was one thing to speak telepathically to an alien, it was entirely different to be sharing thoughts with someone whom he loved and was so close to.

His joy increased as he pictured Becca seated beside him.

"*I can see you! You're waving at me.*"

"*Yes!*" came Becca's energetic reply. "*And you've got a grin going from ear to ear. And you're slouching. Though it doesn't take a psychic to know you'd be doing that.*"

Jeff laughed. He could tell Becca was laughing as well.

"*Excellent,*" Axel exclaimed. "*The more you telep to each other, the easier it will be.*"

" '*Telep?*' "

"*Speak telepathically to one another.*"

"*Oh.*"

"*Okay, now we will try clairvoyance—or remote viewing. I want you to reach out to someone who is very familiar and important to you. Simply try to picture what they are doing. But pick someone who you don't know where they are. Don't try to imagine where he or she is, though, just focus on the person you are trying to reach.*"

Both his parents were home, so he decided to try to perceive Greg. Again, he took a deep breath and relaxed. Greg's image came to mind and he then let the thought drift without trying to focus on it. At first, he had a vague feeling of Greg's presence. Then suddenly, an image came to mind.

"OH MY GOD!" Jeff shouted into the silence. "Greg's in trouble!"

Chapter 25

*September 11th, D Minus 119.82 Hours*
*Dallas*

Greg's first sensation of renewed wakefulness was pain...pain from his head...pain from his wrists...pain from something constricting his chest.

Slowly, he gained a realization of what must have happened. He remembered hiding behind the bushes...and then the world went blank. Judging from his current situation, the bad guys must have seen him.

He started to open his eyes, but then heard voices. Deciding it might be advantageous to appear still out-of-it, he kept as still as he could. Meanwhile, he took inventory of his situation.

From the pain and pressure, he figured he was tied to a chair, with his wrists tightly bound and his arms pinned behind the chair. There was a rope digging into his chest and another rope binding his feet together. The musty smell confirmed he was in a seldom-used building. The heat plus a slight breeze told him there was no air conditioning, but there was a fan somewhere. The lack of a gag meant they were so sufficiently isolated his captors were not worried about his screaming for help. And judging by what he had seen of the industrial park, that was probably the case.

It took all his concentration to remain still and quiet his breathing. Hopefully no one noticed him stirring. Maybe by playing "comatose," he might learn something useful. Although using the information would first require escaping...or being set free. One thing at a time.

Having gotten over the initial shock of his situation, Greg focused on the voices. One was quite agitated.

"You know this kid?" said the voice, rather loudly.

"Yeah, his name is Greg Daniels. I think he's a senior at Dirkson."

Greg recognized Steve Michaels' voice.

"You want to tell me why a seventeen-year-old kid is following you around? With a parabolic microphone and recorder, no less?"

"I have no idea."

There was an apparent slap, followed by an involuntary yelp of pain. At least Michaels was suffering some along with him.

"That's not good enough! You better come up with something more, or so help me..."

"Okay, okay," Steve Michaels replied. "He's a friend of this kid that I've kinda been hassling."

"The one who broke your nose?"

There was no audible reply. Greg worked hard to suppress a smile.

Any inclination to grin disappeared instantly as the sound of a cellphone ringing reverberated around the room. Its ring was instantly recognizable. No doubt the girls were checking in with him. Hopefully they would do what they were supposed to and call the police when he didn't answer the phone. The ringing continued.

"Judging from the number, it's another cellphone," Steve mentioned.

"Bill, go check around. Make sure there aren't any other *friends* of my brother hanging around. The kid had to get here somehow—so either find his car or find the people who drove him."

Greg wanted to scream "NO!" But it would serve no purpose, other than to clue them in to the fact he hadn't been alone. He prayed the girls had already left…and had the smarts to have called the police. At least now he knew the mystery voice belonged to Steve's brother, Tom.

A door opened and closed. It sounded as though someone came into the room, as well as someone leaving.

"What the hell is *this*?" came the angry sound of a new voice. "I go to make a phone call and come back and find you have some kid tied up?" The voice was likely from the person who had just come into the room.

"One of my men found him snooping around outside," replied Tom.

"So, he clobbered him? A kid? What are you thinking? Afraid he will beat you guys up? Then you had the stupidity to bring him in here?"

"We didn't know what else to do. Bill found him outside, with a parabolic microphone."

"What?" The man's tone changed instantly. "How much did he hear?"

"We don't know."

"How did he get here?" The voice, which Greg guessed belonged to the boss, was, if possible, becoming more agitated.

"Apparently, he followed my brother."

"And what the hell is your brother doing here?"

"Well, you wanted us to leave immediately. I haven't had time to brief him on what I needed him to do while I was gone."

"So, you had him come here?" The unidentified man was yelling quite loudly. "How *stupid* can you get?"

"It gets worse," Tom admitted, somewhat subdued. "His phone just rang."

"And you think it might have been someone checking in on him, right?"

"The call came from another cellphone. I sent Bill out to check."

"I know he didn't call anyone in the past hour," Steve said, somewhat meekly. "I checked his call register." Greg mentally admonished himself for not having a lock screen on his phone. It was too much hassle having to unlock it each time he used it, especially since he used it all the time.

"But that doesn't tell us if anyone else knows he's here," said the mystery voice. "So how much does he know?"

"We're not sure," replied Tom.

"Well, why don't you ask him?"

"He's still out," Tom replied.

"You really are an idiot." The footsteps came toward him. They stopped right behind his chair. Greg tried as hard as he could not to react.

But then came the unmistakable sound of a gun being pulled from its holster. It was followed by the angry man's voice.

"Okay kid, you have five seconds to talk to me, or

you'll never see your mommy again."

Greg didn't know what to do.

"Five…"

Sweat formed on his brow. He was scared out of his mind.

"Four…"

A cold steel cylinder pressed against the back of his head. He couldn't continue his masquerade. Greg didn't know whether to scream, or cry. What the hell was happening to him?

"Three…"

His breathing involuntarily quickened. His little "game" was over. And he had lost.

"Two…"

Greg did not know much about guns. In fact, he had never seen a handgun up close—and didn't particularly want to. Nonetheless, he was pretty sure he knew what the loud, sickening, metallic *click* coming from behind his head meant. The gun, whose muzzle was pressed against the back of his skull, was now cocked and ready to be fired.

"One…"

"Okay, okay," Greg said, breaking the tension building around him. He opened his eyes and tried scooting up a bit more. He glanced around the room to get his bearings. He was in what had likely been an office. Only the room was barren of furnishings, save for the chair he was tied to. Steve Michaels sulked in one corner of the room, staring down at the floor. His brother, Tom, stood about three feet in front of him, appearing very disturbed. To his left were a bunch of monitors showing scenes outside the building, with a man watching them carefully. Greg cursed himself for not looking hard enough for security cameras. Greg could not see the man behind him, and he got the distinct impression he wasn't supposed to.

"Better start talking, and fast, kid. I don't have a whole lot of patience," came the voice behind him. "What were you doing outside with this parabolic mic? And don't give me no b.s."

Scared stiff, Greg mustered all the courage he could to answer him, all the while wondering what the heck he stumbled on to. This wasn't a simple drug transaction. Greg quickly decided the truth would be the best approach.

"As you guessed, I was following Steve. I wanted to collect evidence to use against him. He was hassling some friends of mine, and it was the only way I could think of to get him to stop." Greg quickly added, "I wouldn't turn him in or anything, simply let him know I could…if he didn't leave us alone."

The gun's cold steel pressed deeper against his temple. "Who else was with you?" came the voice.

Before Greg could answer, the door opened. Greg turned his head in time to see Tess and Ashanti being herded in at gunpoint.

Chapter 26

As anticipated, Axel had no problem entering the dock area, since everyone on the ship knew him. More importantly, they knew who his father was, so the crew always extended him the greatest courtesy. Except for just a few areas, Axel had run of the ship.

Axel approached the TWS with Chermal in tow. They passed several crewmen on the way, but their mental screens were effective. No one stopped them. Instead, they exchanged pleasant greetings. Fortunately, Axel controlled his own emotions, stifling the anxiety welling up inside him over what they were about to do.

The TWS was housed in its own bay, separate from the hundreds of other craft on board. To get there required walking across a large, empty space. But no one paid attention to them.

The trickiest part was getting onboard the TWS. Teleporting would be readily detected and arouse suspicion. This left the old-fashioned method of sneaking on. As internal security had never really been an issue on the *Druize*, there was no guard, per se, watching the portal to TWS. However, Axel did not want to be observed boarding her.

Axel and Chermal timed their visit to coincide with a shift change. Axel figured as the crew were shuffling about, they would be less likely to notice Axel and Chermal boarding the TWS. Moreover, since the incoming shift would not know Axel was there, they would not miss them when he and Chermal disappeared into the TWS.

Their success depended on there being no one on board the TWS. To make sure, Axel decided to risk having Chermal scan the ship first. As they hoped, the TWS was empty.

Axel waited impatiently for the shift change claxon to sound. Without ceremony, the crew in the dock area began filtering out as new ones made their way in. Now was the time. Axel and Chermal unobtrusively made their way to the TWS. Taking one more look around to make sure no one was watching, Axel opened the portal and quietly snuck onboard the circular craft. Chermal was right behind him.

The TWS was slightly larger than most exploration vehicles as its missions could include emergency evacuations of personnel and equipment. Thus, it had a rather large cargo area that could be converted to extra personnel space. The normal ship's complement included a crew of eight. Yet, in a pinch, it could hold up to one hundred.

Like most exploration craft, it only took one person to pilot the craft. "Flying," though, was not really an accurate description of the movement of the TWS. Nor was "pilot" an accurate translation of the Zanchee term "Amaritz." The Amaritz was more of a guide, showing the TWS where and when to go, rather than physically steering it there. The rest of the crew included a commander; an Amaritzn, or co-pilot; two Hetchs, or space-time navigators; an engineer; and two scientist/technicians. Usually, one of these was a time scientist, versed in both the past and potential futures. There were normally only four at any one time in the command room.

Since Axel and Chermal were not planning any long jumps in the TWS, Axel felt they could get by without a Hetch—at least, he hoped so. Chermal could navigate as much as needed. The on-board QUAIC should be able to handle the necessary calculations. Axel was confident in his and Chermal's ability to direct the craft where and when they wanted it to go. The thing was, Axel wasn't entirely sure where that was. He and Chermal had come up with several critical junctures where/when it might be possible to stop the disaster.

Axel's plan was simple. Go to those critical time/space junctures and search them for the right people who might be able to help. This was where he would need Chermal's sensitivity. Chermal would know the right mind when he found it. Axel just wished he had Chermal's confidence they would, indeed, find the right person. He had to believe Chermal was right. They would succeed. There was no other choice.

Axel and Chermal headed immediately for the command center of the TWS. As he sat down in the Amritz's chair, the command console obediently slid into place. The key moment was at hand. Would the QUAIC respond to Axel's commands? There was only one way to find out.

Axel placed the palms of his hands on the console, which lit up upon his touch. Although the QUAIC responded to psychic input, physical contact was required to activate the system. This served as an extra security measure, requiring the Amritz to be physically present in order to guide the craft. So far, so good.

Axel took a deep breath. He was committed now. Axel glanced at Chermal, who wagged what there was of his tail. The meaning was clear. Do it.

Axel gave the command to start the psionic generator, which was used to propel the TWS through space and time. With a huge sigh of relief, Axel noted that it started without a hitch. They had to act very quickly now, as the start of the psionic generator would be noted by those attending the TWS's bay.

The quickest way to escape without being stopped, especially since they lacked a Hetch, would be to make a simple time jump, maintaining the same physical reference point, or PRP. If the PRP was not kept constant, a jump in time would also result in a huge jump in space. Even traveling back just eleven days, which is all Axel wanted to do, would result in being several million miles from earth, as the earth continuously moves around the sun, the sun moves around the galaxy, and the galaxy moves around the universe. To counteract this movement, it was necessary to do the time shifts while maintaining a fixed relationship with a PRP, which was continuously moving around in physical space. The problem was since the *Druize* maintained the same geosynchronous orbit around earth for the past several years, just going back a few weeks would result in their reappearing on the *Druize*—which would be disastrous, especially since the TWS would likely have been here then.

Axel decided to solve the problem by doing three

shifts. The first shift would move them back in time to 1904, well before the *Druize* arrived and a time when no Zanchee were known to be visiting earth, while keeping the same spot relative to earth. Then they would relocate to the physical point they wanted to go. Finally, they would shift forward to the desired time.

Chermal purred. It was his way of saying, "let's go." He was right. It was now or never. Axel gave the mental command to the QUAIC to shift.

Axel was not prepared for what he found. He had never experienced such complete mental silence. One moment, there were thousands of Zanchee whose minds touched Axel's, albeit loosely. Then there were none. Silence. If it weren't for Chermal's constant reassuring touch, he might have lost it. As it was, the emptiness was frightening. But with Chermal's help, Axel regained control of his emotions and focused on the task at hand.

Axel perceived outside the TWS. Space. Nothing but space. Below them, some 10,000 miles, hung the beautiful blue globe, the planet Earth. It had worked! The TWS's QUAIC had taken his commands. They were free of the *Druize*. They were, at least temporarily, free of the Zanchee. They were free from his father.

Axel and Chermal had plenty of time to plan their next move...over one hundred years. A part of Axel wanted to take advantage of some of that time and explore the new old world below him. But that would cause Axel to lose focus. There would be other times for exploration.

He could try to track down the great-great-great grandparents of the suspected Arab terrorists responsible for disaster and simply prevent them from meeting. But that was not the Zanchee way. It was not *sen*. And it would not be his way. Besides, such a move was dangerous with a high probability of failure, especially since they could not be sure of how many people were responsible for the disaster. Or who they were. Much less trying to follow their ancestors around to make sure they didn't meet some other time. Eliminating one might not be enough to stop the event from occurring. Plus, any change made here would have a rippling effect through time. The risk was too great of doing unforeseen harm to the world Axel was desperately trying to save.

Axel moved the TWS over what would become modern-day Dallas. There wasn't much down there now. Especially at night, there was little evidence of civilization, although the cities, considerably smaller than during his time, still glowed with some lights, they were far, far dimmer than what he was used to.

Dallas was first of the six potential target cities. In the various sims they ran, they succeeded more times using Dallas than any other base.

Axel looked one last time at the extensive frontier below. Beneath him was a vastly different time. A time of horse-and-buggies and early automobiles, when travel by air was a mostly foreign concept, let alone the idea man would develop a weapon so powerful it could destroy the world, then have the sheer stupidity to use it. Axel longed to go down there…to be lost in their simplicity, to warn the people of the dangers of the twentieth century that lay before them…a century that would bring tremendous change…so many advancements, including, unfortunately, better ways of killing their fellow man. To Axel, humankind would take several gigantic strides forward over the next one hundred years, but there would also be several deadly steps back.

Chermal purred again. Chermal could probably feel his longing. But they had a job to do, the most difficult parts of which lay ahead.

Axel engaged the QUAIC to do yet another sim. They could not afford any mistakes at this juncture. Now he had much more time to plan, and he intended to take advantage of it. Once they returned to their own time, their problems would become four-fold. First, they would again become vulnerable to detection by the Zanchee. If they were detected, Axel assumed they would somehow be stopped. He could not allow that to happen. To minimize detection, Axel spent considerable time analyzing the Zanchee monitoring system, as well as studying the Zanchee activity over the past several days. Because of the heavy psionic shield possessed by the TWS, about the only way it could be detected was when it was moving, and then only by either direct observation—in effect, someone seeing the ship—or by detecting the psi flux created by a moving psionic shield. Axel could reduce the first risk by timing his trips when no Zanchee would be in the area. Since he had the records of where all the Zanchee were over the last several days, it would be possible to time it precisely. The psi flux would likely only be detected if someone were specifically looking for it. So, if he timed his travel to occur while the TWS was apparently safely still onboard the Druize, there would be no reason for the Zanchee to be looking for psi fluxes. Unfortunately, when Axel analyzed the data, there were only a few very narrow windows of opportunity for them to operate. They would have to act quickly once they returned to near-present.

Next, they had to find the right person to help them. That would not be an easy task, especially given the short time available to find them. Not only must the person have a high psi quotient in order to be able to do what would likely be required, but they also had to be the right age. They had to be the human equivalent of a nescreet, which meant being less than eighteen years of age. They had to be of the right character, willing and able to help. And, lastly, they had to be trustworthy. Trusted not only with this terrible burden, but also to use their newfound powers wisely after this crisis passed. This could potentially be a big problem—but risking a *potential* problem was a good gamble in order to solve a very real, and deadly, existing one. Many in the Zanchee fleet would doubt there could be such a person among the humans.

Once the right person was found, they needed to be convinced to help, without scaring them to death. That could prove to be challenging. Further, the best approach would depend upon the person they found, making it difficult to prepare.

The next task would be to train that person, so they had the ability to help. Adequate training required time…lots of time. And Axel had never trained someone else. Heck, he was still learning himself. Yet, Axel was confident he, with Chermal's help, could do it.

Once they were ready, the final problem was the little matter of discovering where the bomb was located and figuring out a way to stop it from exploding.

Chapter 27

Doug arrived at the regional FBI headquarters in Westwood, near the campus of UCLA. Jim had called and apologized for not being able to meet him at the airport. But that was okay as he needed to rent a car anyway, wanting an unobtrusive vehicle instead of the standard FBI issue.

"Welcome to LA, Mulder," Jim said, extending his hand in greeting when Doug was shown to his office.

Doug smiled. "You'll never let me live that down, will you?"

"Are you kidding? Of course not," replied Nobles, who looked remarkably like Samuel L. Jackson, at least to Doug. It was appropriate Nobles was the SAC—special agent in charge—of the LA Divisional office where he could be with the other movie stars.

"I still say it was a UFO we saw."

"You've been watching too many reruns of the *X-Files*, my friend. Although I still see you're chasing aliens...only this time they are the human kind."

Doug nodded. "Yes. And I have a bad feeling about this one, Jim. Very bad."

"Another one of your famous hunches, Mulder?"

Ignoring the remark, Doug continued. "Something big is going down. It's not like Raheim to be buddy-buddy with the Cartel. Their culture does not tolerate illicit drugs…it's a sin they take *very* seriously there. For them to be working together cannot be good for the US."

Jim nodded. "You ready for more bad news?"

"Not really…"

"Seth just called. He said you were right. There may be something happening in Russia."

"What did he tell you?"

"About thirty days ago, a 15-megaton thermonuclear device seemingly turned up missing in the Russian arsenal. Their military claims the device isn't missing, insisting it was a grievous 'clerical' error. However, there is suspicion it might be true. The leading suspects are the Chechen. And none of our sources have indicated Russian Mafia involvement. If they were involved, they have kept remarkably quiet with very few people involved. So far, Washington has been willing to accept the official Russian version, as we have no evidence to the contrary."

Doug stopped dead in his tracks. "Jim, the Russian Mafia is full of ex-KGB men. They have the wherewithal to not only pull something like this off, but to keep it a secret as well. The question is why? What would they want…? *My God*!"

"What?"

"Jim, we need to call Washington, *now*. The President needs to be brought in on this immediately!"

"What are you talking about?"

"Jim, remember when I worked the Kosloski case? It was about domestic espionage involving thefts of military secrets?"

"Yeah, so?"

"That's when I first ran across our friend, Krenchenko. One of the things supposedly stolen was the ultimate stealth device."

"Huh?"

"I don't know how it works or anything. It's obviously very top secret. But I did learn it was a device that scrambled virtually all spectra of wavelengths. Thus, it not only scrambled radar, but infrared and virtually everything else except visible light. And I'm not too sure about that."

"Fascinating. So?"

"Well, won't it also keep things from broadcasting out…such as our bug's signal…"

"Okay, so that might explain why we lost the signal."

"There's more. What you may not know is when he was with the KGB, when the Soviet Union started to break up, he helped round up some of the Soviet nuclear experts not in Russia. These men have not been heard from since."

"My God!"

\*\*\*\*

"I can't take this to the President, for God's sake," said Deputy-Director of the FBI, Ross Klingman. "You have absolutely no proof, only wild speculation."

Doug stared at the speakerphone, unable to believe what he was hearing. Veins in his neck pulsed as he struggled to contain his anger. "Listen." He restrained from adding 'you idiot.' "We lost the signal from Raheim's implant for nearly two days. Then, it suddenly appears in LA, only to disappear again in one hour. I saw him with Victor Krenchenko, ex-KGB who is known to be affiliated with the Russian Mafia. Russia is missing an atomic bomb. Krenchenko is thought to have kidnapped former Soviet nuclear experts when he was with the KGB. And Bivardo certainly has the ability to sneak such a weapon into the country—"

"And you have your wild theories. I know. Listen, Stanton, you have no *proof.* Washington said there is no missing nuclear warhead, that it was simply a clerical error. There are hundreds of possible explanations for Raheim's bug to wink on and off, including a malfunction. Hell, we don't even have proof Raheim met with Krenchenko. The shot you took of him only showed his back and a part of his face…Nice work, by the way," he added sarcastically.

"It was Krenchenko. I know Krenchenko well enough to recognize him when I see him."

"Look, Stanton, you really expect me to go to POTUS with some crazy-ass story about the UAFF getting together with the Colombian drug cartel and the Russian Mafia to bring a nuclear bomb into the United States? You're crazier than the TV Mulder. Why would they want to bring a bomb into the US? If the UAFF got its hands on a nuclear weapon, don't you think their first target would be Israel?"

"Because the fallout of a bomb that size exploding in Israel will kill hundreds of thousands, if not millions, of Arabs…" The pressure from Nobles' tight grip on Doug's arm was barely enough to keep Doug from adding 'you stupid idiot' to the end of his sentence.

"All three of these men have big axes to grind with the US, including Bivardo," Doug continued, trying to get Klingman to understand. "We have hundreds of millions of dollars of his assets frozen, and his uncle and cousin in jail. How can you *not* take this to the President?"

"Stanton, you've come up with some crazy ideas in your career, but this one tops the cake. No wonder they—"

"Where did you say Director Stinson is?" Doug interrupted, in a harsh tone.

"He's unavailable," came the stern reply.

"Don't you think he should be made aware of at least the *possibility* that LA will be blown all to hell?"

"I'll let him know. Call me back when you get me some hard evidence."

"At least let me have some more manpower."

"I'll keep it under advisement. I believe Nobles already has three agents assigned over to your case, plus your little task force."

"Raheim could be anywhere."

"I'm sorry, but until you get me some more evidence, that's all I can do." His voice didn't sound all that sorry. "Maybe your buddies with NSA or CIA could help." The last line was delivered with sarcasm. Klingman was old school, meaning he had no love for the other agencies and a deep mistrust especially of the CIA. These joint task forces were like a slap in the face to him. How he ever got assigned to the Anti-Terrorist Joint Task Force was a complete mystery to Doug.

Stanton reached over and pressed the speaker button on the phone, disconnecting them from the Deputy Director.

"I told you not to speak with Klingman," Jim said.

"I had no choice. He won't let me speak with Stinson." Shaking his head, he continued, "His arrogant stupidity could condemn millions."

"Doug, you've got to see it from his side. He's been told there is no missing bomb. And you know we can't run to the President with every terrorist plot we uncover. Especially when we have no proof they exist."

"This is not some run-of-the-mill terrorist plot, Jim. We're talking about a 15-megaton nuclear bomb detonating in the second largest city in this country. Millions of lives could be at stake."

Realizing he was alienating his only ally, Doug softened his tone. "Look, Jim, even if there is only a five percent chance, or a one percent chance I'm right, can we afford to take the risk?"

Jim shook his head. "I'm on your side, Doug. I'll continue to try to get through to Stinson. Talk to your buddy with Homeland Security…maybe they will take this more seriously. I'll try to assign a few more agents to the case on the sly. If anyone asks, they will be looking for Krenchenko. But we must be very careful about this. We can't afford to have any leaks. I don't need to tell you the panic knowledge of a nuclear bomb in LA would cause."

"I understand, but that panic is nothing compared to the chaos that will erupt if Los Angeles should suddenly disappear from the face of the earth. Jim, you know my instincts have always been accurate."

"*Almost* always."

"I'm not wrong about this, Jim."

"Okay, okay, let's for a moment suppose there is a missing thermonuclear device. I still don't see how UAFF, the Cartel, and the Russian mob are connected. It doesn't pass the smell test. It especially doesn't make sense the Cartel having any part of a nuclear threat.

After all, Los Angeles is a very profitable center for them. The same goes for the Russian mob."

"I don't think the Cartel believes the UAFF will explode a nuclear bomb. In fact, they probably received numerous 'assurances' from Raheim they won't use it. The way I figure it, the UAFF needs the Cartel's ability to smuggle things into the US to get the bomb and any technicians they need into the country. They also may need their manpower to provide protection. The UAFF undoubtedly told the Cartel the bomb will be used to extort money from the US, gain the release of political prisoners, and make the US apply pressure on Israel to release more land. It also sends a clear message to Israel the UAFF has nuclear capability and are not to be messed with. It is also possible the target may not be LA, but rather a military base, which may be more palatable for Bivardo.

"It's my guess Raheim brokered a deal between the Cartel and the Russian Mafia, who have previously been inimical to one another as they perceive each other as threats. The Russian Mafia wants access to the Cartel's drugs and distribution network. The Cartel wants in on the action in Europe. Neither have any love for the US Government."

"I don't know, Doug, seems like quite a stretch."

Doug's reply was interrupted by a telltale beep emanating from his pocket. It meant his receiver once again picked up the signal. Raheim was on the move.

Chapter 28

As soon as he screamed, the image disappeared from his mind's eye. But it was still etched in Jeff's memory. "My God," was all he could say as beads of sweat formed over his brow. For a moment, Jeff forgot where he was and who he was with. The image of Greg tied to a chair with a gun pointing at his head obscured any other thoughts. Increasing his despair at his friend's predicament was the feeling it was all Jeff's fault. Somehow, even though he didn't directly perceive him, Steve Michaels was likely in the room with Greg and probably behind what happened. Greg had likely taken it upon himself to try to help Jeff and plunged headfirst into trouble as a result.

"*Jeff! Jeff! What's wrong?*" Becca's loud mental shout startled Jeff back to the moment.

"What's wrong?" Becca repeated out loud.

Before he could answer, Chermal's calming presence exerted itself on him. Instinctively, he wanted to jump up and scream. How could he calm down? Here he was on a UFO with an alien and his best friend was tied up with a gun to his head. Yeah, that's pretty calming.

Yet, he had to relax. Panic wouldn't take that gun away. No, it was time for clear thinking. Focus on Chermal's calming thoughts. Relax. Screaming wouldn't help. He took a deep breath, then another.

"*Jeff, relax,*" Axel directed, not realizing telling someone to relax in these situations often had the opposite effect. "*When you're too agitated it becomes difficult to focus...You need to gain control of your feelings.*"

"*But Greg's in serious trouble!*" he replied with considerable agitation as he struggled to retain control. "*He's tied to a chair, and there's a man holding a gun to his head!*"

"*I know this is difficult, Jeff. But you can't help him unless you calm down,*" Axel said soothingly. "*Focus on your breathing in order to relax and then we can help you.*"

He nodded. Then realizing it was still dark, managed to reply "*Okay...I'll do my best. What do you want me to do?*"

"*When you're ready, open yourself up to Chermal and me. Once you feel our presence more strongly, I want you to refocus on Greg. This time, we'll come along with you.*"

Axel's confidence buoyed Jeff's hope. Axel and Chermal were Greg's best hope. But how could he relax at a time like this? His heart thumped hard against his chest. His best friend was being held at gunpoint while he was on a UFO with an alien from outer space. Sure, that's relaxing. Again, the calming influence came from Chermal, helping him to focus. Focusing on the wave of calmness, he relaxed his death grip on the armrest.

Axel's tone was confident and reassuring.

*"Concentrate on your breathing. Feel each breath. Slow your breathing down. Follow the air coming down your trachea and into your lungs. Feel the air escaping from your nostrils. Try to quiet that inner voice. Know only your breathing. In through your mouth...Hold...Out through your nose...In...Hold...Out..."*

With each breath, his muscles relaxed. But he tried not to let it distract him. He forced all thoughts save those pertaining to his breathing from his mind. Again, he breathed deeply, slowly. His chest expanded, ribs pushing outward with each breath intake. The diaphragm constricted, forcing the air back out of his lungs. Again. Again.

As he became focused on his breathing, he lost track of time. He even lost track of where he was or what he was doing there.

Then, suddenly, he was no longer alone. Axel and Chermal were there with him, perceiving each breath with him. Without being told, he knew he was ready.

*"We will be with you when you visit Greg. But we will only be observers. It's up to you to maintain the contact. Do not try to do anything yet. We must first gather information. For this reason, it will be very important for you to stay focused and not let your emotions control you."*

What did Axel mean about not doing anything yet...What could he do? He was miles away. But as soon as the thought popped up, he got rid of it. Relax. Again, he focused on his breathing and Chermal's calming influence until Axel teleped again.

*"Very good. Now it is important you maintain contact with Greg. No matter what you see, you must*

*focus on him, or you will not be able to help him. You must also keep control of yourself and your emotions. Can you do this?"*

Jeff nodded. Axel continued. *"We will be with you all the time. I will tell you what to do. Are you ready?"*

*"Yes,"* he teleped back.

*"Let's go, then."*

Jeff again focused his mind on Greg. Immediately, the image of Greg bound tightly to the chair formed in his mind. A gun still pressed against his head.

*"Expand your viewpoint,"* directed Axel.

He wasn't exactly sure how he was to "expand his viewpoint." Axel didn't bother to tell him that. So, Jeff decided to imagine he was viewing Greg through a camera with a zoom lens. Then he pictured "zooming" out.

It worked. Gradually, more of the room came into view. There was the man holding the gun. He was in his late thirties, five-foot ten, with dark hair and a Latin complexion and wearing what appeared to be a very expensive black suit. Next, Jeff tried panning his viewpoint, moving around the room. First, he "moved" his point of view to be next to Greg, so he saw what Greg could see. Starting to his left, there was a man watching a bunch of security feeds, and then Michaels' oldest brother, Tom, standing about three feet away, appearing very displeased. Next to him, almost cowering, was his nemesis, Steve, who looked to his left, wide-eyed. Jeff shifted his viewpoint to see what captured his attention.

His heart almost stopped completely. For there, sprawled on the floor hugging each other desperately and sobbing, were Tess and Ashanti. They were being guarded by another big goon.

Without Chermal and Axel's radiating confidence and calm, he would have lost it right there. But he didn't. Somehow, he maintained control. He kept contact.

*"Listen to what they are saying…"* came Axel's mental instruction.

Jeff almost cursed his own stupidity. He had been so thrown by being able to "see" what was happening, he didn't think about the fact maybe he could hear as well…

With Axel and Chermal's encouragement, Jeff "listened" intently. Again, he imagined he was observing the scene through a camera, but this time there was a microphone attached. He mentally adjusted the "gain."

\*\*\*\*

"We told you, we didn't tell anyone!" came Tess's desperate pleading.

"Let them go!" Greg shouted. "You've got me. You don't need them!"

"They've seen me, and they know you're here," came the reply from the man behind him.

"They won't tell anyone. We don't know what's happening! *Please,* you've got to believe me!"

"I don't like this," Tom remarked. "I don't like this at all…"

"It was your stupidity and the stupidity of your brother that created this mess!" responded the man. "And it will be up to you to fix it."

"But they're just kids!" replied Tom.

"NOOOOO!!" cried Tess and Ashanti together, as they realized what was being discussed. *"Pleaasee."*

"Let them go!" pleaded Greg.

"*Shut up,*" the man with the gun shouted. Then, turning to Tom he said, "Since it was your brother who led them here, I think he should do it."

Steve jumped back, shaking his head. "No, no, please…"

"You wanna be a tough guy, punk?" said the man. "Well, now we'll see how tough you really are. Or do you want to join them?"

Jeff directed a thought to Axel. "*We've got to do something. Quickly! I think they are about to kill my friends!*"

Again, the calming influence from Chermal. Then came Axel's directive. "*Focus your mind on the man with the gun. He's the boss. You must convince him it is not in his best interest to have them killed.*"

"*How?*"

"*Focus your thoughts…Make them his…*"

Jeff's mind was blank for a minute. He heard what Axel was saying. But it didn't make sense. There was a man with a gun threatening to kill his best friends—all because of him.

Jeff focused back on his breathing. Panicking now would not help his friends. What did Axel tell him? Make his thoughts theirs? How…? What thoughts?

Then another voice spoke to him…a very familiar voice. "*Jeff,*" came his sister's telep. "*I know what he means. You need to think of a reason not to kill them, and then broadcast that thought to those killers.*"

He had forgotten Becca was there. Bless her! She had already more than justified her presence. Jeff would later reflect on this moment, and marvel again at how calm his sister was, and how she had been able to think clearly when he was about to panic.

Becca's penetrating idea was enough to lift the fog from his brain. She was right. Simply thinking killing was wrong would not get the job done. There must be a reason which the mystery man would accept as his own.

Thinking fast, Jeff realized Greg, Ashanti, and Tess were more valuable as live hostages than as dead kids, weren't they? Perhaps they could use their disappearance as a ruse? There was also the potential problem someone saw them coming this way by chance. And he can't be sure the kids didn't tell someone where they were or what they were doing.

He refocused himself. The thought he needed to prepare must be void of any emotion. It must also refer to his friends as "the kids" rather than identifying them by name. The mystery man, even if he knew their names, would not likely use them in his thoughts.

Drawing a couple deep breaths to relax himself again, Jeff composed the thought he wanted to send. Then he focused his mind on the mystery man behind Greg and concentrated on his thought.

"*Don't try to force it,*" directed Axel. "*Just let your thought float lightly. Put yourself in the man's position. How would he think? Try thinking his thoughts…then adding your own.*"

Jeff tried doing what he was instructed. It was very difficult trying to think like someone who was ready to kill your best friends.

He started by trying to understand why someone would want to kill three kids. The man was concerned about being identified. But why? Most of the time, simple fear was enough to keep kids quiet. Unless he was afraid that perhaps they had stumbled onto his plans. Whatever these plans were, they were important enough to kill for.

*If it was so important the operation not be stopped, could he take the risk the kids weren't spotted here? And the disappearance of three kids might cause all kinds of hell to break lose.*

*He needed to hedge his bet. If the authorities traced the kids back here, they could possibly act fast enough to stop them. In that case, he needed some way to slow them down. Offering dead bodies would be of no help.*

Jeff was so absorbed in the "thoughts" he was broadcasting he was completely unaware they totally missed his intended mark.

Chapter 29

Greg squirmed helplessly as the mystery man, no longer afraid of being seen by him, stepped over to the now-terrified Steve Michaels. Ashanti and Tess, both trembling, held each other tightly. Greg was proud that while they were frightened for their lives, they were not panicking. It was as though they knew somehow things would work out. Suddenly, Greg realized he felt the same way…strange.

In fact, Michaels looked worse than the girls, taking an involuntary step back as the mystery man held out his gun for him to take. He started to shake his head. Greg could *almost* feel sorry for him.

"Take it!" commanded the mystery man.

"I—I—can't!" Steve cried.

"Perhaps you should join your friends then." The man withdrew the gun and turned toward Tom. "This is your problem."

"Wait!" Tom shouted. "We need them alive."

The mystery man began to raise his gun, this time pointing at Tom.

"Listen to me. Even if they didn't tell anyone where they are, those girls were by the convenience

263

store for quite a while. What if someone saw them? You know the disappearance of three kids will stir up lots of trouble."

The man started to waver a bit. "Go on," he commanded.

"If there is any possibility of their being able to trace those kids back to us—through my brother or whatever, then we may need something more than dead bodies to keep them at bay."

The man stared at Tom for what seemed like hours, although it was only seconds. "I don't think so," the man said, as he cocked his weapon and pressed it against Greg's head. "But you're right, we can't shoot them. We must make it look like an accident." He turned to the girls cowering on the floor. "I bet you guys don't get high, do you?" Without waiting for an answer, he went over and picked up Tess's arm. "Just what I expected…no tracks." He turned toward one of the other men standing in the back. "Bill, go get some needles and make up a batch of pure liquid sky. I think these poor rookies were never told they had to cut the good stuff, and so in experimenting, they make a simple, but alas fatal miscalculation."

"NOOOO!" Tess screamed.

"What's going on here!" came the sound of a new voice. Greg had been so busy praying and preparing for death he had not noticed a new man entering the room. Whoever it was, he owed him his life. The man spoke fluently, but with a clipped accent. As Greg turned his head slightly to take him into view, he noted his savior looked Middle Eastern. He was about five-foot nine and dressed in what appeared to be an expensive tailored suit.

"Mr. Farcie," the surprised mystery man exclaimed. "We were, uh, getting rid of a minor problem."

"By killing children? This is not the way we do things. Your man is right. They are potentially much more valuable to us alive rather than dead. You will bring them with you."

"That will not be easy, driving them half-way across the country. And three kids missing together is bound to make the news—possibly nationally."

"Then you do not take them into any public places," Mr. Farcie replied. "Your, uh, company must have many offices along the way, no?"

The mystery man was silent for a minute. "Yes," he finally replied.

"Then it is settled. I suggest you take the kids in a van and leave immediately. The rest of the convoy will leave as scheduled." With that, the man turned and left the room.

"Okay, you heard the man," the mystery man said. "The kids will ride in one of the vans. Make sure they are guarded at all times, Hector."

The mystery man turned toward another thug brandishing a gun, although this one wore glasses and was a little less intimidating than the others. "Hector, drive the van with the kids. Take Katherine with you. You will be a happy family, traveling to Las Vegas on vacation. Tom, have one of your boys not making this trip take their car to Laredo and dump it. With luck, it will appear they simply ran away to Mexico. At the very least, it will buy us time."

"Right."

"And Tom, your brother is coming with us as well.

265

Put him with his friends in the van. Bill, you will ride in back with them—and keep them quiet, using whatever means necessary. I will be in the van close behind. Call me on my cell if there are any problems. Tom, you will take one of the cars." Then the man stared directly at Greg. "If any of the kids give you trouble, kill them. We just need one left for hostage purposes. Feel free to dope 'em if you need to." The air turned cold.

The man continued, directing his words at Hector. "You will leave in five minutes. I will call you in a bit with contact points. We will follow in another fifteen minutes. The two trucks will follow us, along with two convoy vans. Those of you assigned to the convoy remember the first truck *must* go through. Take whatever action necessary to assure this happens. The rest of you have your schedules. You know where the rendezvous point is?"

Hector nodded.

"Before you go, I suggest you get these kids to the bathroom. I imagine they may need to 'freshen up.' " He chuckled, then continued. "Okay, let's get moving."

Chapter 30

Jeff turned to Axel as soon as he knew Greg and the girls were safely loaded into the van.

"Okay, now what? How do we rescue them?"

"Can't we take this ship and intercept them?" Becca asked. "I mean, don't you have any ray guns or anything?"

Axel shook his head. "I'm sorry, but that's just not our way."

"But we've got to do *something*!" Jeff cried out.

"As I told you, *I* can't do anything. None of my people can interfere directly with your culture. It is strictly forbidden."

"But you already have! You're here…I mean, we're here with you!"

Axel smiled. "I said 'directly.' One of the, hmm, I guess you would say 'loopholes' in our law is that it is written for nescrot, that is, for adults. I am but a nescreet, or a 'juvenile.' "

"So, it doesn't apply to you?"

"Not exactly. As I haven't gone through Nemseck yet, I am not expected to fully 'understand' our laws, although I am to be 'guided' by them. I am still held accountable for my actions. However, the way the laws are written, they say we are not to directly influence the actions or interact with the 'Nescrot' in the cultures we are studying." Axel smiled mischievously. "But you two are not yet adults according to your own laws, so you are not considered nescrot. And because I am also nescreet, I cannot be expected to understand the law should extend to include interacting with Nescreet as well."

Jeff chuckled, despite the slight perceived insult at being called 'not an adult.' "You would have made a good lawyer."

"Please do not insult me so."

Jeff and Becca both laughed out loud. They needed the release of tension Axel's humor supplied.

After a moment, Jeff turned serious again. "That still doesn't tell me how we will save Greg and the girls."

"Not 'we,' 'you.' You will have to save them. We can assist, but because this involves human adults, you must be the one to act. That is why we recruited you." Axel didn't want to tell them at this point, one of the reasons he needed human help was because he couldn't be more than one hundred feet away from the TWS. He had to stay within the psionic shield, not only to avoid detection but because he was at this time also still onboard the *Druize*.

"But how?"

Before Axel formed an answer, a purring sound interrupted him. They all turned to face Chermal.

"He's right," Axel said. "You don't want to rush into this. We need to plan carefully, and you need to get more training so you can help them."

"But we don't have time! They're in danger!"

"We have time. I believe it is almost 1,300 miles, using your units of measure, from here to Las Vegas. As they will not want to attract attention from the police, it will take them nearly twenty-five hours, even driving straight through, to get there. That gives us plenty of time to plan, and to train. They won't risk doing anything to Greg or the girls until they get to their base outside Las Vegas."

"But—"

"Can't we just call the police?" Becca interjected. "Tell them about the convoy and the hostages?"

"I am afraid not, for several reasons. First, they are committed to getting that cargo through. It is unlikely the police will take us seriously enough to take aggressive action. Thus, it could lead to a lot of bloodshed and police casualties. Second, they will not hesitate to kill the hostages. And third—"

"They're the ones!"

"What? Who are what ones?" Becca asked, perplexed by Jeff's outburst.

"Those men who have Greg. They are the ones responsible for what will happen in LA, aren't they?" Jeff asked Axel.

Chermal purred. "We're not sure," Axel said in response to Jeff's question. "But Chermal and I are picking up the same vibrations you are. In particular, the man they called 'Mr. Farcie' seems to know about the bomb, but we can't get anything specific. That's why we must be extra careful. Right now, they are our only lead. We've got to learn more before we do anything."

"Why can't you read the guy's mind and find out

the information we need?" Jeff asked.

"Unfortunately, it's not that simple. We can only 'read' what a person broadcasts, that is, what they are consciously thinking about. Although it is possible to perhaps read a person's brain without their consent, it is not *sen*, it is not our way, nor is it safe for either party." Axel paused. "There is also another risk we must consider."

"What's that?" asked Becca.

"If we move the ship, we greatly risk detection by the Zanchee. You see, I, uh, 'borrowed' this ship," Axel confessed. "It's heavily shielded, so it can't be detected while it's stationary. But when it moves, it will be much more readily detectable.

"When you saw me the first time, over the school, I planned the trip to coincide with a period when the risk of detection was minimal. There may not be another such window much before D-zero."

"D-zero?" asked Becca.

"Detonation," Axel said.

Jeff gave Axel a hard stare.

"Detonation?" Becca asked. "Jeff, what is really going on?"

Jeff drew in a deep breath, before continuing. "Remember when I told you Axel needed our help to stop terrorists? Well, what I didn't tell you is they are planning on using a nuclear bomb to blow up LA."

"What!"

"It gets worse. The bomb sets off a chain reaction along the San Andreas Fault. Millions, if not billions will die."

Becca's face turned white. "How, how could you possibly know all this?"

"Axel and Chermal can see into the future," Jeff replied.

"The Zanchee know this will happen," Axel said. "But they won't do anything to stop it." Axel balled up his fists in a very human gesture. "They say our laws forbid it. So, it is up to us nescreet to prevent this tragedy!" Something resembling a growl could be heard. "Us three nescreet *and* Chermal, that is."

"I know we must look at the bigger picture," Jeff said. "But I can't ignore my friends. They're in serious danger and scared to death. And I don't like the thought of them being given drugs."

"I understand," Axel said sympathetically. He was quiet for a minute as he looked at Chermal, apparently silently conferring with him. "Chermal says they will be safe. They are not likely to get doped unless they give their kidnappers any problems. One sedated person is easy to handle, but three can create its own difficulties given the need to make regular stops.

"Yet, I understand your anxiety and realize they are probably terrified right now. Perhaps if we contact them and let them know they will be safe and we will rescue them when we can, they will feel better."

"How are we gonna contact them?" Jeff said in frustration. "Call them? I don't think those terrorists will let them answer the phone."

"Again, you are too limited in your thinking. Tell me, how are we communicating right now?" Axel made a point to project the image of his lips not moving to hammer home the point.

"Telepathy. Of course. But how? It's one thing to telep to you—you're ready to receive me. They aren't. And how will they know it's me? They have never experienced telepathy before."

"As for the first question, we'll show you. As for the second, it will be up to you to convince whomever you are teleping with that it's you they are hearing and not their imagination. I suggest picking the person you feel will be easiest to convince."

He had been friends with Greg since first grade, so he knew him the best. However, he also was very close to Tess. And Tess was more accepting of "strange" ideas. Tess would be easier to convince it was him "speaking" to her telepathically and not just her imagination. Maybe the idea boys and girls think differently would assist her recognizing his thoughts as not originating from within her own mind.

"Tess," Jeff said. "I think it should be Tess we contact."

"All right. But we need to wait a bit. Right now, they will be too confused and frightened to be receptive. Let's give it an hour or so."

\*\*\*\*

"*Okay.*" Axel said. "*Relax like you did before and picture Tess in your mind just as you did with Greg.*"

Jeff closed his eyes and thought of Tess. The gramirl warmed against his chest as the image of her formed in his mind. Gradually, he visualized her sitting on the back seat of a van. Ashanti was next to her with Greg on the other end of the seat. Steve Michaels was in a bucket seat in the row ahead of her. None of them were talking, nor, thankfully, were they restrained by anything other than the presence of the goon, apparently named Bill, seated next to Steve. In the front row were two more people Jeff did not recognize. One of them was a woman, appearing to be in her late 30s or early 40s. The driver was about the same age as the woman. Unlike the thug seated behind him, who looked like he was a reject from the WWF, the driver looked more like a businessman.

Broadening his "view," Jeff saw the van was on Interstate 30, heading west.

"*Focus on Tess*," came the mental suggestion from Axel.

Jeff narrowed his focus back to Tess. He noted the still-terrified expression on her face, which was about ten shades whiter than normal. She clutched Ashanti's hand rather tightly. Ashanti's other hand had a firm grip on Greg's hand. Michaels, seated in front of them and next to the goon, did not look much better. All of them were quiet.

Jeff fought the anger welling up inside of him at the sight of his three friends in peril. He slowed his breathing, knowing he had to be relaxed and calm if he was to help them.

"*How do I contact her?*"

"*Start by directing your emotions toward her. Project your affection for her, your warmth, but also your confidence in her safety.*"

Jeff tried directing his thoughts toward Tess. "*You will be fine, you will be fine,*" he said repeatedly in his mind. However, there was no reaction from Tess.

"*Don't try talking with your mind. Not yet,*" Axel instructed. "*Just direct your feelings toward her, without words. Emotions are much more powerful. Once you establish contact in this manner, it will be easier to strengthen the bond so that communication will be possible.*"

Jeff took a deep breath, and then exhaled slowly.

He reached inward. Chermal's reassurances radiated within him. He took those emotions and projected them toward Tess, along with his own strong feelings of friendship and affection he had for her. He remembered their first date…and their first kiss. He remembered holding her tightly in his arms. He thought about how much he cared for her…

"*That's it*," Axel commented. "*Keep projecting those feelings*."

Jeff concentrated on his feelings. How much Tess really did mean to him. How she made him happy by simply smiling at him.

"*It's working*." blurted Becca. "*She's relaxing her grip*."

Becca's words barely registered on Jeff. He was too tuned into Tess. The more he thought about his feelings for her, the closer he felt to her. She felt the same way about him. The more he thought about her, the happier he felt. He knew she was smiling, too.

"*Now, tell her you are with her*," Axel directed. "*But continue to project your feelings, along with the words. Pretend you are talking with her over the phone. But don't try to 'shout.' If anything, whisper*."

Jeff did as he was instructed. "*Tess, I am here with you*," Jeff teleped. "*Don't be afraid. It really is me. I am communicating with you telepathically. Everything will be okay*." Jeff kept repeating the same thoughts over and over again.

Tess just smiled as she stared out the darkened window of the van.

"*Tell her you will prove it is really you*," Axel said. "*Tell her a red pickup will pass the van in about ten seconds. There will be three people in the truck. It will be followed by a blue Ford Taurus, with a family of four.*"

Jeff relayed the information, along with his continued reassurances everything would be all right, and he really was there with her.

A red pickup passed the van, followed by a blue Taurus. As they did, Tess's eyes grew wide.

"*She's not convinced,*" Becca commented. "*She probably passes it off as coincidence, or the fact she could see them with her peripheral vision.*"

Jeff nodded.

"*Tell her the next car passing the van will be a green Toyota Camry. It will have Oklahoma plates, with "GOLPHER" on it.*

When the aforementioned car passed the van, Tess let out an audible gasp.

"*Reassure her again!*" Axel said. "*Tell her to relax, to open herself up to you so you can talk.*"

"Jeff?" Tess asked tentatively. She spoke out loud.

"What did you say?" Ashanti asked.

"*YES!*" Jeff teleped her, excited at the breakthrough. "*It's me. I can hear you.*"

"How?" Tess said. "This can't be happening."

"I know," Ashanti replied. "It's just not real.'

"*Tess! I do hear you,*" Jeff teleped again. "*But you don't have to talk out-loud. Ashanti will think you're crazy. Of course, she would be right.*"

Tess laughed. "Now I know I'm crazy. I'm talking to myself." Ashanti just stared at her.

"*No, you're not, Tess. It's really me,*" Jeff teleped. "*I can't tell you everything right now. But I can tell you it will be okay. I promise. Remember how weird I've been acting lately?*"

*"Boy, do I,"* Tess thought to herself. Tess figured she might as well play along. At least her imagination was a lot more interesting than staring at the back of some thug's head.

*"I'm glad I'm more interesting than a thug's hairdo,"* Jeff replied.

*"Jeff??"* Tess didn't know whether to be happy or frightened.

*"I know this is hard to believe. But you will just have to trust me. That's one of the reasons I've been so weird lately, I have been learning telepathy."*

*"This is unreal. You can't be real."*

*"I am and there are others with me, Tess, including Becca. Our 'teachers' are very powerful, uh, psychics. They have given me a special stone with the power to augment my own meager psychic ability. That's how I can contact you."*

*"Where are you?"*

*"I can't really tell you now. But I'm safe. I'm still in the Dallas area."* He paused, then continued. *"Tess, I know what has happened to you."*

*"I don't know what is happening to me! How can you know?"* Tess started to get very emotional again.

*"Calm down, Tess. It will be all right. I promise. The men who kidnapped you are drug dealers, as you may have suspected. However, they are involved in something much bigger."* Now was not the time to tell her everything. It would only add to her anxiety. *"Tess, you will be okay, I promise. My friends are powerful. We won't let anything happen to you three. But we can't act right now. You have to trust me."*

*"How can you get us out? How can I believe you?"*

Jeff was stumped for a minute. How can he

convince her? Then he remembered his own recent experiences. With a glance to Chermal, he teleped, *"Tess, trust your feelings! Reach down past your fears. You know I'm telling you the truth. You know I will get you out of this."*

Jeff perceived her starting to relax.

*"How, how long?"* Tess asked, tentatively.

*"Tess, I honestly don't know. We still must figure that out. All I can tell you right now is this is more involved than just you three, and we must be extremely careful. But I also know it will work out, and I will get you out safely.*

*"I will tell you more later, as you get more comfortable with the, uh, situation,"* Jeff promised. *"I will contact you on a regular basis. Don't be frightened. It will be okay, I promise,"* Jeff repeated. *"If anything changes, shout out to me with your mind, I'll hear you."* Axel nodded his affirmation.

*"I'm very sorry I can't free you right now, Tess."* Could she sense the tears tracking down his face? He continued, trying to be as upbeat as possible. *"But we have to plan this carefully. We need more information first, which is why it may take some time. You will be fine as long as you three cooperate with them. And I want you to cooperate, don't do anything foolish—and don't let Greg try to be a hero, either. Right now, I need you to keep Ashanti and Greg calm."*

*"I'll do my best,"* Tess said. *"I just can't believe this is happening to me."*

*"I know, neither can I,"* Jeff said honestly.

Chapter 31

Jeff and Becca chowed down on some grub while Axel bent over the control station. The suppressed hunger rose to the surface as soon as Axel suggested they take a break. Becca was amazed, as she had never known Jeff to forget about food.

The food was good, which shouldn't be surprising, as Axel "borrowed" it from their refrigerator. That Axel could simply "think" food to the table gave Jeff a whole new appreciation of his psychic ability. *Maybe, being psychic won't be so bad after all.*

It took Axel a while to convince Jeff they could not simply take off after his friends. He desperately wanted to do something, anything, to help them *now*. But with Chermal's assistance, Axel finally got through he needed to be patient. Resigned to waiting, he turned his attention to the next most pressing thing to him…food. While Jeff and Becca ate, Axel ran simulations on the TWS's AI.

As soon as Jeff ate his fill, which was considerable, he looked over at Axel, who appeared to be in a trance. "What is our plan?" Jeff asked, hopeful there was one. "How soon can we leave to rescue them?"

Axel opened his eyes and returned Jeff's stare. "Unfortunately, it won't be soon. The first thing we need to do is continue your training. I'm afraid it will take quite a bit of time before you are ready. In every simulation I've run, it is quite clear we will only have one chance to rescue your friends if we are to stop the terrorists, and our timing will have to be perfect, or we will fail. It will do your friends no good to be saved from their captors only to perish in a nuclear blast or its aftermath. However, my projections—" Axel paused, then looked at Chermal. "—as well as Chermal's perceptions, tell me they will be safe until we can rescue them, assuming they don't try anything stupid."

Axel continued. "As I told you earlier, there are only a few 'windows' we can work, or the Zanchee will detect us and stop us. We cannot afford for that to happen." Axel paused. "What's more, if their kidnappers are the terrorists, then any rescue attempt could cause them to act differently than what we are expecting—which may make it impossible to stop them. Taken together, I'm afraid the earliest possible window for us to successfully launch a rescue will be Thursday, at D-Minus 4.10."

"That's cutting it pretty close," Jeff exclaimed.

"What about the police and the FBI?" Becca asked. "Can they help? Won't they be searching for them?"

"In my projections, they can't find them in time. Chermal agrees. At first, the authorities will assume they ran away…after all, they are seventeen and have a car. They will also be thrown off the track by finding Greg's car in Laredo. The authorities will spend most of their time and resources looking in Mexico and locally. Although the disappearance of five teens will undoubtedly make national news, we do not think they will be successful. Besides, if the police or FBI should act to try to free your friends, it could easily cause the terrorists to explode the device early…before we could act to prevent it. That's why we cannot interfere until we are ready."

It took a second to register, then Becca spoke up. "Five? But there are only three of them."

"He's including us," Jeff said. "Isn't that right?"

Axel nodded. "I'm afraid so, for a couple reasons. First, in order to pull off this rescue *and* stop the terrorists, our projections say you will need to reach level three psi control. That takes a lot of training—and hard work on your part. Second, because of your friends' disappearance, there is a significant probability you two will not be able to 'sneak' over here like you have."

Jeff and Becca both nodded slowly. Axel was right. Their mom, not to mention the school, would go crazy at their friends' disappearance. There was no way their mom would let them out of her sight—and since his car was still in the shop, it would be more difficult. Besides, the extra publicity generated from five kids missing, instead of three, may help increase the efforts being made to find them. This should help his friends.

"What happens to my folks?" Becca asked. "They will be so worried! Mom will freak. They will be absolutely devastated."

"Chermal will help keep them calm and maintain their faith, but some pain is unavoidable, as will be true also with the others' parents. But, keep in mind their pain will be temporary. If we fail, there will be billions whose pain is permanent." Axel looked at Jeff. "I told you when you first came this won't be easy."

"True, but it's so hard when you hurt someone else, intentionally or not. Especially when it's someone you love so deeply." Jeff fought to keep the tears from forming.

"Yes. But you will see your parents again as well as your friends," Axel reassured. "We will be successful." He paused, and then added, "We have to be."

Jeff was silent for a moment. Becca sat, stunned. She fought hard to choke back the tears. Despite Chermal's silent reassurances, she was not successful.

A thought struck him. "There's something more you haven't told us," he stated, looking at Axel.

Axel was silent.

Jeff continued. "You can't leave the ship…or the area immediately around this ship, can you?"

Axel nodded slowly.

"And," Jeff went on, "it isn't because you are afraid of being detected by the Zanchee. There is something special about this ship. Isn't there? What is the other piece of this puzzle?" Jeff asked.

Axel said nothing.

Jeff stared intently at Axel, then at Chermal. Realization dawned on him. "Time! You told us Chermal can perceive into the future…That our concept of time is based on our three-dimensional universe, but in the fourth dimension, time flows both ways. That's how precognition works…"

"There are an infinite number of futures. He sees only the most probable. But that future can be changed."

Jeff nodded. He didn't really understand it

completely, but he was learning. "But there's more, isn't there?"

Now Axel looked over at Chermal. His face registered surprise.

Jeff smiled as he sensed the truth in what he was thinking. "This ship is a time machine, isn't it? That's why you know so much about our future."

Becca's mouth went wide as she stared first at her brother, then at his two strange friends. Today was one big shock after another.

Axel smiled. "We did indeed choose well." His smile widened to a grin. "But it's not quite the way you are thinking. Yes, this ship can travel through time. But I did not come from the future, at least not the far future. I left my ship right before the explosion took place. But you are correct. That is why I cannot leave the ship as its heavy shielding protects me...from me. It would be disastrous for me to exist in two different locations in the same time. The same is true for you. That's why I can't simply send you back in time to warn your friends.

Becca was first to react. "I don't understand. If you can go back in time...can you also go ahead in time?"

Axel shook his head. "You're thinking if we can go ahead in time, why not go to a point after the explosion is supposed to occur and learn if we were successful in preventing it? Right?"

Becca nodded and added, "You could discover how we did it, then we could come back to this time and do it!"

"Unfortunately, it doesn't work like that. It is true we can go ahead in time...to one of the *potential* futures. But the timeline we would follow would be the one where we had not had an influence—because at the time we left, we hadn't. So, all we would see are the consequences of us *not* acting—which we already know. Not until an action has already been done can we go ahead in time to see its consequences."

Jeff and Becca both nodded, although neither were exactly confident they understood it fully.

"However, this brings us back to the subject of training. To get you to Level Three takes a lot more time than we currently have. The solution is to create more time."

"How?" Becca asked, hanging on every word.

"We go back to a period before the Zanchee were here. That will give us a lot more time to train. However, we still will not have unlimited time."

"Why is that?" asked Jeff.

"Whenever you travel back in time, there is a risk of accidentally altering the future…the time paradox. A simple innocent action, such as killing a butterfly, could trigger a chain reaction through time that could lead to your own non-existence…or create other problems we simply cannot afford to deal with. This is appropriately called the "butterfly effect" in your literature. As we will need to remain on Earth for training for reasons of expedience and supplies, the longer we remain, the greater the risks. Because of this concern, the TWS has a safety feature built in requiring it to return to the present time in approximately eight of your weeks. I do not have the ability to override this mechanism.

"As a result, we need to get you to Level Three in less than two of your months."

"Do you think I can be ready by then?"

"It has never been done before to my knowledge.

But never has the need been so great. We will do it," Axel affirmed. Axel didn't want to add that he had never trained anyone before—let alone take a compete novice to an advanced Level Three. But he wouldn't be alone—Chermal would be there too.

"What about Becca?" Jeff asked. "I don't like the idea of her having to go…of her being away from home for so long."

"Unfortunately, I don't think we have a choice. It will be more difficult on your sister to return home, knowing she cannot tell her parents what is happening, or where you are. Besides, Chermal feels she will be needed…especially now we have to rescue your friends in addition to stopping the terrorists."

Jeff looked at Becca. She was pretty tough, but being away from Mom and Dad would be very rough on her. "How about it, Becca? Do you think you can handle it?"

Becca nodded. "I don't know I could do it by myself," she admitted honestly. "But I know with you here, and with what's at stake…I'll handle it."

His sister was fighting hard to keep the tears back. What would their parents think? How would they feel? He could imagine their agony. Yet Becca could handle it. His heart swelled at her bravery.

"What about my friends?" Jeff asked.

"Although we will not be physically here in this time, Chermal will always be in constant touch with them. You can telep them on a regular basis. Remember we will be gone for eight weeks, but less than one week will pass for them, so if you telep them only once a day, to them, it will be every three hours."

"How can we telep them if we are in a different

time?"

"Remember, psi is a fourth dimensional energy. Time flows differently. With Chermal's help, we will reach them in this time.

"Both Chermal and I feel they will be fine, especially with you keeping in regular contact. But if their situation changes, we can always sync it so that we come back, as you say, 'in the nick of time.' "

All three of them laughed. "How long do you think it will take to get me to a Level Three?" Jeff asked.

"Hopefully, less than eight weeks," Axel said with a straight face. "You have a lot of potential, and we will take every shortcut we can. But it will still require you to work almost non-stop. Becca, too, will go through the training. But it will not be necessary for her to get to a Level Three, so her training will not have to be as rigorous."

"So where will we go to train?" Becca asked.

"Not where, when" Axel replied. "We will remain essentially in the same spot, although not 300 feet down as we are now. But at a different time. We are going to Dallas of 1904. There's another pond, not too far from where we are now that will make a great hiding spot."

"Why then?" asked Jeff.

"For two reasons. One, we don't want to go too far back in time. The further we go, the higher the risk that we set off a chain of events that could affect this present. Second, Chermal and I have already been there and did some preliminary scouting."

"When do we leave?"

"We already have."

Chapter 32

Doug checked the tablet twice to make sure. But there was no mistake, the beep was coming from LAX airport. He cursed under his breath. Days had gone by with nothing and then suddenly, out of nowhere, the signal had reappeared—only to be at the freaking airport he just left.

Jim Nobles confirmed what Doug feared. There were no agents at the airport. Who would have believed that Raheim would be so bold as to use one of the busiest and most watched airports in the world?

Quickly, they faxed a photo of Raheim to the airport police. They could only hope there was enough time. But he couldn't wait for them to act. He rushed down to his car and headed off to the airport.

Unfortunately, he was in a rental car and not an official car. There was no siren or lights to get him through the traffic. And, as his bad luck would have it, the 405 turned into a parking lot not long after Doug entered.

Keeping one eye on the tablet plotting Raheim's progress and the other eye on what was ahead of him, Doug steered the car onto the shoulder attempting to make his way around the stalled cars.

Unfortunately, a truck driver in the right-hand lane did not appreciate Doug's efforts to avoid the crowd and pulled his rig halfway onto the shoulder, effectively blocking Doug's way. Doug laid on the horn, but it did no good. There was no way around him, and he wasn't budging.

Swearing in all four languages he spoke fluently, and in three others in which he had a more limited, albeit colorful, vocabulary, Doug put the tablet down long enough to grab his cellphone out of his pocket. Fortunately, he had the foresight to have Nobles' cellphone on speed dial. Grabbing the steering wheel with his knees in case the traffic unexpectedly started moving again, he put the cellphone on speaker while attempting to zoom in closer on the tablet.

"Jim. It's me. Raheim is moving to the International Terminal. He does not seem to be in any kind of hurry."

"I have the airport authorities watching for him. Can you give me more of a fix?"

"Yeah, give me a sec." He zoomed in closer, with Raheim's position superimposed on an airport map. "He's at Gate C8."

"Got it. I'll let the airport authorities know."

"Uh, Jim, I need a favor." The car was completely stationary now as the freeway had become a ten-lane parking lot. "I'm stuck on the 405. There's a massive traffic jam. And some jerk of a truck driver won't let me go around on the shoulder."

"Where are you?"

"I just crept past a sign that read 'I-10, 1 mile.' "

"Okay, I'll see what I can do. I'll call in a favor."

Doug was more impressed with Jim when a police helicopter buzzed overhead a few minutes later. The copter circled for a minute, then landed in a parking lot adjacent to the freeway.

Doug pulled the car as far off the shoulder as he could and ran toward the waiting helicopter. He paused only long enough to flash a quick, but not so friendly, universal sign toward the truck driver.

Rushing a bit too quickly, Doug tore his pants as he scaled the fence separating the freeway from the parking lot. Swearing for the umpteenth time in the last fifteen minutes, he could almost hear the truck driver laughing at his plight.

The helicopter pilot's smile quickly faded as he saw the scowl on Doug's face. He scampered into the seat next to the pilot, who handed him a headset. Doug mumbled quick thanks as the copter jerked once, then ascended quickly into the sky.

"I appreciate the lift," Doug managed to say, while trying to keep his stomach in place. "I assure you the urgency is warranted."

"I'm sure," the pilot responded. "Really, we owed one to your associate. Jim Nobles has helped us out a time or two."

"I appreciate it just the same," Doug said, meaning it sincerely. Cooperation between the police and the FBI was not always a given. Doug redialed Jim's number while staring at the tablet.

"Nobles."

"Jim, I show that Raheim is outside the terminal and stationary. He is either on a plane, or under one."

"I'll pass it on."

"Thanks, I'll be at the airport in—" He turned to

the pilot who held up one hand. "—five minutes. Have someone meet me at the heliport, wherever that is."

"Will do. I'm on my way there myself."

"Don't take the 405."

"Thanks for the tip."

As he hung up the phone, Doug continued to stare at the screen as though he could reach out and touch Raheim. But he couldn't.

Doug looked down at the city moving quickly beneath him. It was a good thing he didn't get airsick. He only wished he had more time to enjoy the view.

As he stared ahead at the rapidly approaching airport, he mentally reviewed the situation. Something was not right. He could feel it.

※ ※ ※ ※

A stocky man about six-foot two and wearing a suit and tie greeted Doug as the copter thumped down on the airport's helipad.

"I'm Rick Ganen, head of airport security," the man said, sticking his hand out as Doug scampered away from the helicopter wash and met him at the door.

"Doug Stanton. Pleased to meet you. I greatly appreciate your cooperation in this matter."

"Anything to help the FBI," the man replied, with little enthusiasm.

Uh oh. This one was not quite as cooperative as the LA Police had been.

Doug looked down at his tablet. The blip was moving. "Raheim is on the move. Do you have your men on location?"

Rick nodded as he picked up a radiophone that was strapped to his belt. "Sydney, this is Rick, come in."

"Sydney here."

"What's the status?"

"Everything is clear here. I went on board flight 227 and checked everyone out, personally. He's not on board. We're checking the ramp area now."

"The FBI man says he's on the move again."

Doug stared at the tablet. "It looks like he's running toward the runway."

"The FBI man says he's heading toward the runway."

"Impossible," came the reply over the radio. "There's nothing on the runway but that jet."

Doug stopped in his tracks. "You didn't let that jet leave the gate, did you?" he demanded.

Rick clicked the radio again, "Sydney, did flight 227 just leave the gate?"

"Yeah. I told you, I checked it thoroughly. There were only two Arabs aboard that flight—and both were women. You didn't tell me to stop the flight, and I had no other reason to delay it."

"You've got to stop that plane!" Doug practically screamed. This wasn't his day.

"That won't be easy." Rick said. "Once it's left the gate and unless we have some kind of evidence—"

Doug shook his tablet in front of Ganen's face. "This is your evidence! He's on board that plane. Now stop it before I have you on Federal obstruction of justice charges," Doug snapped. Nope, this wasn't his day.

Ganen looked at Doug's face. There was no bluff there. He got back on his radiophone. "Walter, this is Ganen."

"Yeah."

"I need you to recall flight 227. We have an

emergency situation."

"Can you tell me the nature of the emergency?"

Doug had had enough. He grabbed the radiophone from Ganen's hand. "Yeah, this is Doug Stanton, with the FBI anti-terrorist force. There is a man on board that flight that represents a severe threat to the US, and if you don't turn that flipping plane around in two minutes, I will personally come up to that tower and throw you off it. Got it?"

"Loud and clear. Where do you want the plane?"

He had to think fast. If they returned to the gate, there was too much of a chance Raheim could find a way to sneak off. He handed the radiophone back to Ganen. Doug's anger dissipated as he finally felt like he was getting some breaks. "Is there a place you can have that plane parked away from people?" Doug covered up the microphone on the radiophone. "He could easily have a bomb on board, and he won't hesitate to blow himself up, if he could take several hundred with him."

Ganen nodded. "Tell the pilot to go to T-32 and hold. Have him tell his passengers a warning light came on and they have to check it out, but there is nothing to worry about."

"Will do," came the reply.

"Okay, where do we go?" Doug asked.

"Follow me."

Ganen led Doug down four flights of stairs and down a long hall. Using his passkey, Ganen opened a security door leading into an underground garage for airport vehicles. "Wait here," Ganen instructed, as he ran into an office facing the garage area.

He was back in less than two minutes, carrying a couple uniforms. He threw one at Stanton as he moved down the rows of vehicles until he came to a maintenance truck. "Put this on," he instructed as he did the same with the second uniform. "We told them it's a mechanical problem, so we'd better look the part, in case your guy is watching. It will also make the other passengers feel a bit better when we come onboard."

Doug nodded appreciatively. Maybe he had misjudged this Ganen fellow. "Lead on," he said, as he zipped up the uniform unitog. "I trust your judgment," he added.

"Good," Ganen said as he similarly zipped up his, then climbed into the driver's side of the truck. "Get in."

They pulled out onto the taxiway running alongside the terminal. Pulling over to the edge, and mindful of any aircraft that might be on or turning onto the taxiway, Ganen drove past the umpteen gates of the terminal. He did not drive recklessly but maintained a quick pace as he moved onto a service road paralleling the main taxiway.

They drove for what seemed like 100 miles as the roar of jets taking off and landing a few hundred yards away threatened to steal Stanton's hearing for the rest of his life. Finally, they reached the plane, which was parked at the end of the taxiway, far away from the terminals and the airplane traffic patterns.

"How do we get onboard?" Doug asked as he gazed up at the nose of the 757.

"We take the elevator," Rick replied, as he got out of the cab and climbed up onto the back of the truck.

As soon as Doug had climbed up to the flat top, Rick positioned himself at a control box located on the side. Within moments, the entire top of the truck lifted upward toward the main body of the plane. As they rose, a door opened on the side of the plane. A brunette flight attendant poked her head out and gazed at them as they slowly ascended.

When they leveled off, there was a two-foot gap between the plane and the platform on which Doug and Rick stood. Doug was about to jump when the platform began to slide toward the door. "Like the post office, we deliver," smiled Rick as Doug looked back at him. "Don't forget your tool kit," he added, pointing to a tool kit sitting close to where Doug stood.

"Uh, thanks," Doug said, as he made his way into the galley of the plane. The brunette stewardess was waiting.

"Please do not do anything to alarm the passengers," the stewardess, whose nametag bore the name "Sonya" on it, whispered to Doug as he stepped on board. "They think there is a minor service problem."

"I'll be careful," Doug said, as he pulled the tablet out of his pocket and laid it on top of the opened tool kit. "If anyone asks, tell them I'm trying to track down an electrical short in the lighting system that apparently triggered an alarm."

Sonya nodded, then stepped aside to let him through. Rick followed Doug onto the plane but remained in the galley area as Doug headed into the passenger compartment.

Doug had to be careful. He did not want to cause any unnecessary commotion, nor give himself away to Raheim, should he be on board. But despite his electronic evidence to the contrary, something told him he wasn't.

Doug hoped any passengers who happened to see the tablet lying on the tools would mistake it for an electrical meter or some other gadget that airplane mechanics used. He carefully examined the floor lights as he made his way slowly down the aisle to look as authentic as possible. But as he did so, he kept a steady eye on his tablet, watching the signal strength gradually increase as he neared his target.

Fortunately, Doug was very experienced in locating "bugs" in crowded rooms without anyone knowing what he was doing. When the tablet indicated he was within two feet of the "bug," Doug didn't look up at the person seated there. He didn't have to. He had memorized most of the faces as soon as he stepped into the passenger compartment. He did note the seat number, however. 18A.

Upon reaching the tail of the plane, Doug stopped. He found a panel secured by screws at the flight attendant's station. Grabbing an electric screwdriver from the toolbox, he quickly opened the panel. Doug breathed a sigh of relief when the opening revealed several electrical connections.

He grabbed a random tool from his kit and stuck it and both his hands inside the panel opening. After waving to the wires for what seemed to be an eternity but to his watch was only 74 seconds, he pulled his hands back out and resecured the panel.

"All set," he said as he made his way past Sonya. When he got back to the galley, he motioned to Rick to leave. They both made their way out of the plane and back onto the platform.

When they got back into the cab, he turned to Rick. "Call the tower. Tell them they can let the plane go.

Please apologize for the inconvenience."

Rick glared at Doug a long time before grabbing his radiophone to relay the message. He spoke to the tower as he maneuvered the truck back onto the service road and headed back toward the main terminal.

In the meantime, Doug pulled out his cellphone and called Jim. "Jim, I need everything we can get on the passenger seated in 18A on board American Flight 227 to Chicago. The passenger is a Caucasian female, currently blonde, about 24 or 25, petite, and I guess about five-foot-four."

"I may need a court order," Jim replied.

"Then get it. I want to know everything about her, including what she had for breakfast, before that plane lands in Chicago. Then I want her tailed when she gets there. Do not let her know she's being followed. It shouldn't be too hard, though, as she has the 'bug' in her purse. However, the agents are to maintain visual contact as much as possible, in case she dumps the purse. They are not to intercept her until I give the word."

"I'll call Mark Brevit in Chicago and set it up. Can you tell me what's happening?"

"Jim, she had Raheim's bug in her purse. That means Raheim somehow found it and had it removed. I believe he planted it to try to put us off track. He probably anticipated the plane would get off the ground before we could intercept."

"So, you think the girl…"

"Is totally innocent, yeah. He or one of his men probably just 'bumped' into her at the airport and slipped the bug into her purse. But I want her checked out thoroughly, just in case. If everything is okay, then we need to interview her and see if she can tell us anything about how she might have gotten the bug. I doubt she will be much use, however. Raheim is too professional for that.

"In the meantime, I want to check with the gate attendants for that flight. Maybe we'll get lucky and they saw something. But I doubt it."

"Okay. I'll meet you at the gate. I'm just now pulling into the terminal."

"Roger, I'll see you there."

"The name is Jim," came the response, and the line went dead.

\*\*\*\*

Doug edged his car into the traffic exiting LAX. It took a little over two hours to talk to all the personnel they could think of at the airport who might have seen someone. They turned up nothing, as predicted.

Rick got the footage from all the security cameras, which were plentiful, for the past six hours. These would be scrutinized at the FBI office. But they would not likely reveal anything useful either. It was highly unlikely Raheim made the transfer in person. Since it required a surgical procedure to remove the bug in the first place, there was no need for Raheim to chance going to a public place just to plant the bug.

\*\*\*\*

"What now, Doug?" Jim asked after they arrived back in his office.

"I guess we go back to old-fashioned shoe leather."

"When do you think he found the bug? Was this a set-up? He could be anywhere."

"I don't think so. He likely just recently discovered the 'bug'. He's still here, somewhere."

"Another one of your famous Mulder hunches?"

"Yep. And I don't like it at all."

Sitting there, Doug suddenly had an inspiration. "Jim, have the lab boys pay particular attention to the vehicles dropping off passengers. That blip did not start until it appeared at the airport, meaning it was shielded until then. Focus on panel trucks. Maybe we'll get lucky. Tell them as well the transfer probably occurred before she went through security, but after she got her ticket. Otherwise, they would not have known she was a passenger."

"Got it."

Chapter 33

Greg awoke with a start as the van hit a small pothole on the freeway.

It was pitch-dark outside, the sky full of stars. It was amazing…so many more visible here…wherever here was. He glanced down at his watch, which read 2:20 a.m. They had been on the road over twelve hours.

Ashanti was sleeping peacefully, her head resting on Greg's shoulder. Tess was beside her, sleeping with her head on a balled-up old sweatshirt the lady captor gave Tess in an uncommon display of niceness.

Greg was somewhat confused by his own emotions. On one hand, he was scared to death. The mystery man, once they finished this job in LA, whatever it is, would not need them as hostages anymore. And they knew too much to be simply released.

Yet, having Ashanti's head on his shoulder made him feel good. He was needed. He liked that she cared for him, and he discovered just how much he cared for her as well, which made him angrier with himself for getting them into this situation in the first place. Why did he have to be so stupid?

Tess stirred a bit, and then resumed the slow, steady breathing of a deep sleep. He was impressed by Tess. Both she and Ashanti had appeared so terrified by what happened. But suddenly, Tess became like a rock. She kept telling Greg and Ashanti she "knew" everything would be okay. Because their captors strongly discouraged their talking at all, Tess could not tell them why she was so confident. But she really believed they would be fine. She wasn't just saying it to make them feel better or convince herself. And that confidence was infectious. Greg and Ashanti both felt better. Now he was convinced things would work out, although unsure why he felt that way.

The three of them agreed to cooperate fully—within reason. None of them wanted to be doped. They also needed to be fully alert and functional if they were ever to escape.

Greg's thoughts turned to home. At this point, his parents were probably getting very worried. It was not like him to stay out so late without having told them he was going out. And they certainly would have called or texted by now, and because he did not respond it would only increase their concern. He wished he could somehow communicate to them they were all right...well, at least unharmed. But it was not likely they would have called the police...yet. Even if they did call, the police could not do much until they had been gone at least twenty-four hours. Without evidence of foul play or ransom demands, the police would assume they ran away. But they were still minors, so authorities would have to take it somewhat seriously. And their parents would know better.

Steve was slumped over in the seat in front of Tess,

his head against the window. The dreadful noise coming from his direction indicated he was sound asleep. Greg looked over at him. He was starting to feel a little sorry for the jerk. He clearly was as frightened as the rest of them. And no doubt he felt betrayed. Greg got the impression Steve wanted to talk with them, but Bill the baboon would not allow it. Still none of them would be here if Michaels hadn't been just a complete jerk—not to mention, a pusher. But then again, Michaels refused to take the gun. Greg would not, could not forget that. Maybe there was some good inside him, after all.

Voices coming from the front of the van allowed him to push the sad thoughts from his mind. He noted the lady was now driving. Her "husband" was in the passenger seat, and he was upset with her driving skill as demonstrated by a recent pothole adventure. The jolt apparently awakened him from a rather pleasant dream.

Greg smiled. That conversation sounded familiar. They had the married part down pat.

He turned his thoughts again to the issue of escaping. Getting away would be almost impossible, especially since there were three guards, all armed. Whenever they stopped for gas, the three of them were continuously watched. They were not allowed out of the van, except when they got to the company "offices," which appeared to be mostly houses in isolated areas. When Ashanti complained about having to pee, the response was to hand her a jar and to tell her either use it or wait until they stopped at one of the scheduled stops. She waited, as did the rest of them. So far, they had made three such "pit" stops. In each case, the house was deserted when they arrived. Whoever was in control was not taking chances.

Perhaps one of the girls could make a break for it the next time they got to a service station or one of the company houses. He and the remaining girl could try to distract the guards. If one of them could get away, they could alert the authorities. But to get out of the van required getting around Bill the baboon. And whenever Bill left, Hector Whomever took his place. Steve was treated no differently than the three of them. He was as much a prisoner as they were and knew it.

Greg considered flagging a motorist while they were on the freeway, perhaps by using their fingers to make a smudge sign on the window. But no opportunity presented itself yet.

At the last house they were in, he found a pen on the floor of the bathroom. He also stuffed some toilet paper in his pocket to write on, meaning they could write a sign on the toilet paper. But Tess, surprisingly, vetoed the idea when they had a moment to talk. She said not only was it not worth the risk, but it was unnecessary, and that "they" knew where we were. Only, she never got a chance to explain who "they" were, as the Neanderthal they called "Bill" woke up from his snooze and promptly shushed them.

A new conversation between the two in the front seat shook Greg from his reverie. He strained to hear what they said, knowing any information he could learn might be helpful to them down the road. Because the goons likely thought all the kids were asleep, they might be a little more revealing in their conversation. He was right.

"So, what do you think this is all about, Kate?" said the "husband."

"Beats the hell outta me, Hector. I'm just doing what I'm told. I don't like we're taking these kids, though. That's just not right."

"I know what you mean. I don't like it none, either. Thankfully, they haven't given us much trouble. I don't wanna have to be the guy to waste them. Especially Steve. He's been a fair operator. It's not right for Martinez to do that to Tom."

"I'm not sure it was Martinez."

The two were silent for a moment.

"You know, I don't understand any of this," Hector said. "I really don't like working with those Arabs. They give me the creeps. And the rumors about Reynolds..."

"I know, me too."

"You're pretty close to Martinez. He give you any clue?"

"Honestly, I don't think he really knows. And I'm not sure he cares. He's getting paid pretty handsomely, as we all are."

"Yeah, but is it worth it?"

"It's not like we had any choice."

"True."

"But why are we heading to the desert, for God's sake? What on earth could be out there worth all this trouble?"

"We're going for training."

"Yeah, training. Training for what? And what is our mysterious cargo? Any ideas? And what do the Arabs have to do with Martinez, or Transdigital? Are they new suppliers? New customers?"

"I get the idea this job has little, if anything, to do with drugs," Katherine replied.

"Then what?"

"I wish I knew." Then she glanced in the mirror to see if anyone was awake. "I can tell you this much though...I saw some of the 'cargo' before it was loaded into one of the trucks."

"And..."

"There were weapons. Lots of weapons...and not only guns, but big things like rocket launchers, and a bunch of electronic stuff. And they were Russian. Or at least the boxes they came in looked like they had Russian on them."

"Weapons? This is getting worse and worse. We're no mercenaries."

"I overheard Martinez talking to Stevens in Detroit. He thinks Bivardo has gone over the deep end...totally crazy."

"Yeah, well, Martinez isn't so far behind."

Katherine nodded.

"Any idea what he's planning though? I mean, what do we need with all those fancy weapons?"

"I have no idea. I know the government froze hundreds of millions of dollars in Bivardo's assets. Maybe he's thinking about getting it back—by robbing a big bank or something."

"Where do the Arabs fit in?"

"I'm guessing they are the ones with the weapons. I do know this. That big truck that pulled in...it was manned by Arabs, and they won't let anyone within fifteen feet of it."

"What do you think is in it?"

"I have no idea, unless it's more weapons like the ones I saw."

"But what do the Arabs get from all this?"

"Money, drugs, a piece of the pie? Who knows?"

"Yeah, well, that don't help me none. It's not like we got profit-sharing or anything," Hector said. "I don't like this, not one bit."

"Neither do I," replied Katherine.

*And neither do I*, thought Greg.

Chapter 34

Doug met with Jim, Seth, Julie, and Ty at the LA FBI office. The other members of the task force joined in via conference call. Sadly, none of them had good news to contribute. Their bosses shared the same skepticism Doug's boss did. And now that the eleventh came and went without any atrocity, they were less inclined to act. It was becoming clear they were pretty much on their own.

An intense review of the security tapes turned up nothing. There were no obvious contacts between the passenger and someone dropping off the bug. However, they did see she went to the restroom before going through security. There were no security cameras in there. So now agents were busy trying to track down all the women who went into that restroom in the few minutes before the passenger went in, but left after she came in. This was a massive task, and they simply did not have the manpower to do it expeditiously.

All three of the targets, Bivardo, Raheim, and Krenchenko, disappeared without a trace—as had those three planes and the pilots who flew them. The only lead they had was the beep from Raheim indicating he was in LA. Or at least he was two days ago.

"This is not good, gentlemen," Doug said in a classic understatement as they reviewed the case.

"You may like this even less," Jim replied. "I have to pull Walters off this case."

"What, are you insane? We need more manpower, not less."

"I'm sorry, orders from the top. You heard about those five kids who disappeared in Dallas?"

"Yeah, I thought they probably ran off to go to some rock concert or something."

"It's high-profile. Drawing lots of media coverage, which translates into major pressure on us to do something."

"Yeah, so? That was Dallas, this is LA."

"The only lead we have is a report from some truck driver who says he remembers passing a van with kids in it matching their description on I-40 near Kingman, Arizona. They were heading west. He remembers it because as the van passed him, he happened to look and see one of the kids staring at him from the back of the van. She appeared terrified and worn out. He says the image of her face burned in his mind. But there was nothing else out of the ordinary with the van. He recognized the face instantly when he saw it on the national news last night. We've been asked to supply additional manpower to check it out."

"That's a pretty thin lead."

"Granted. But it's all we have to go on."

"Jim, I know saving five kids is important. But we may be talking about hundreds of thousands of kids here, if that maniac has a nuke. You've got to get some more manpower."

"Doug, I'll do my best. But"—He waved to the tablet sitting uselessly on the table—"our best hope disappeared. He could be anywhere in the world. And we have nothing else to tie him to this area. Nor do we have any proof he has a nuclear weapon...especially since both Moscow and Washington are denying one is missing. In short, we have nada. And if we alert the LA police of our fears, the story is bound to get out. Besides, there is little, if anything, bringing more manpower to the case will do."

"Yeah, until he vaporizes LA." He stared down at the now useless tablet. He then looked up at the agents seated at the table. "I'm telling you, the key to this puzzle is figuring out what kind of leverage or influence Rahcim has over Bivardo and Krenchenko." Doug turned to Seth. "Does the CIA have anything on Krenchenko that might make him want to jump into bed with Bivardo or Raheim?"

Seth replied, "Not a clue. Further, our sources within the UAFF state flatly they do not believe the UAFF has a bomb, although they acknowledge there is something happening—only they are not high enough in the organization to determine exactly what. And if they had a bomb, the feeling is it will be much more valuable to them as a deterrent than to use it on the US. They know the wrath it will cause. Not only from the US, but likely from every other country in the world. However, at least two of the top men, Raheim and his right-hand man, Mohammed Farcie, have vanished."

Jim also nodded absently, then spoke up. "That is basically the reasoning DC is using. No one there believes they will actually use it either, if they had one, which they are not accepting as fact, or even a strong possibility."

At that moment another agent stuck his head in the door. "Jim, we have something on the vehicle, but I don't think you'll like it."

"Come in, Bill, and tell the group."

"After reviewing all the tape, we think we know which truck delivered the bug to the airport. It was an unmarked white Mercedes light truck. However, they were using some kind of infrared device that blurs the license plates on our camera. So all we have is a general description of the truck."

"That won't do us much good. They could have easily painted that truck by now. Not enough to even put out a BOLO," Jim commented.

"Pull every traffic cam in the area. Let's see if we can track that truck. Right now, it's our best lead," Doug suggested.

The agent nodded and left.

Doug looked over at Ty. "What about the DEA? Anything on Bivardo?"

"Nothing concrete. While there may be some logic behind a Russian Mob-Cartel alliance, we have seen no evidence of one forming. And most believe each organization is too greedy and suspicious to ever trust the other." He paused, then continued. "However, we do see a lot of activity happening within the Bogotá cartel. Something is seriously going on there. Key people went missing at each 'District Office' as they call it. Rumors are circulating they are preparing for something big, but they are keeping a tight lid on it. So far, we have no idea where they are going or what they are up to, other than it is somewhere out west."

"We need to establish who is running the show,"

Doug stated. "I think we can eliminate Bivardo as the ring-leader. He was likely brought in to supply the cover and smuggle the weapon into the country. That leaves Raheim and Krenchenko as the possible mastermind. Thoughts?"

"We know Raheim has motive," Seth replied. "But what bothers me is how could he have known to contact Krenchenko?"

"Right." Doug replied. "It is not likely Raheim knew Krenchenko. It is more likely Krenchenko reached out to him."

"What are we missing here?" Jim asked the group.

"A motive," Doug answered.

Chapter 35

The afternoon sun beat down relentlessly upon the tin roof of the dilapidated Quonset hut, turning it into an oversized oven set on high, seemingly transferring all its heat energy to the already-stifling interior. An undersized fan provided minimal relief from the oppressive temperature. The building had no windows.

Greg mopped his forehead with his wadded-up shirt, already soaked from previous attempts. More beads of sweat soon formed to replace those he just removed. The three of them sat on the floor with their backs against the wall as the room was devoid of furniture. They were in what must have been an office at one time. The room had three doors—one leading to a bathroom, one to the outside, and the other to the interior of the building. The latter two were deadbolted shut. From time to time, they heard noises coming from the other side of the interior door, indicating the space was being used for something. It had to have another entrance though, as no one came through their space to get to it.

Having traded modesty for additional comfort, they were clad only in underwear, which clung tightly to their sweaty bodies. A pail half-filled with warm water was in the middle of the room, which they used to quench their thirst and replenish the fluids continuously leaking from their overheated bodies. The pail was constantly being replenished from the faucet in the bathroom. Empty wrappers and containers, once holding an eclectic ensemble of mostly junk food, lay scattered about the floor.

Normally, the thought of being clad only in underwear with two pretty girls similarly attired would be rather stimulating. But these were not normal circumstances. Sex was about the last thing on his mind, which, for him—or any seventeen-year-old male—was saying something. But he and Ashanti were never alone, for one thing. And these weren't exactly romantic circumstances for another. At least when they slept, she always curled up next to him, which was very nice. Of course, the bedding consisted of a couple blankets laid over the hard, painted concrete floor.

Their captors were not trying to be inhumane. Indeed, they made sure there was plenty to eat, although they were not willing or able to give them their choice of food. Greg was amazed at the things he would eat when hungry enough. Never again would he be so finicky about food. The Spartan conditions they found themselves in were more a result of lack of facilities and the need to keep them in a secured area, than it was an intentional desire to torture them, although the results were nearly the same. Katherine, the woman who drove the van, provided them a deck of cards, which served as their only means of entertainment, other than talking.

Greg was thankful for one thing. None of the

captors ever laid a hand on the girls. Apparently, they were told if they touched either of them, they would die. Simple, but effective. However, that didn't keep some of the men from leering at the two teens, making Greg nervous and thankful for the edict—but worried about what would happen once the "mission" as their captives were calling it, was completed.

At least now they could talk freely. Thank goodness for small favors. Steve Michaels was a frequent guest, although "guest" wasn't quite the right word. It was more like co-captive. His brother could only gain his release for short periods of time. As a result, Steve spent most of the day with Greg and the girls, as well as every night. He did get to eat with his brother most of the time, but claimed the food was no better. He also mentioned his brother's accommodations were similar to theirs.

Greg had been surprised by Steve. Before, he was just a thug preying upon innocent kids. But now he had become human. He apologized to Tess for the way he had hassled her and Jeff, citing the need to maintain a certain tough guy image, or he would lose his position in the organization, which now appeared lost anyway. Tess, to her credit, accepted his apology, although she did not exactly warm up to him. The fact he now seemingly shared their fate did not appear to change Tess's mind he was mostly responsible for their being in this situation.

However, underneath Michaels' perpetual scowl was a decent kid trying to get out. As Steve confided more and more to them about his tormented childhood, Greg understood why Steve followed his brother into a life of crime. For them, it was the only way they saw to escape from the madness coming from poverty coupled with an alcoholic and mostly absent father and an abusive mother.

When Steve was eight, he accidentally shot and killed his best friend, Joe Kinder, when they found one of his father's handguns and began playing with it. Steve never thought it was loaded. But that was why Steve refused to carry a gun—even though his brother strongly encouraged him to do so. Steve figured Ox was almost as good—and far more intimidating. Greg agreed. Steve admitted he was still haunted by nightmares of that shooting. He could never rid his brain of Joe's startled expression when the gun went off, prematurely ending his life.

Steve's father died of liver disease when he was eleven. His mother soon after succumbed to the pressure of raising three difficult kids by herself and literally went crazy. She had enough sense to deposit Kimberly, Steve's then eight-year-old sister, at her grandmother's, before disappearing for good. But Steve's grandmother wanted no part in raising the two boys. Steve was only twelve at the time. Tom had been forced to raise Steve, though he himself was only seventeen.

Not wanting the two of them to be split apart, or kicked out of their house, Tom dropped out of school and turned to pushing drugs to pay the rent and buy groceries. The landlord, who got paid in cash, did not seem to mind there was no adult in the house, as long as the rent was paid on time.

Greg could not approve of what Steve and his brother did, but now understood the pressures that had driven them. Greg admitted he did not know what he would have done if he had been faced with the same situation. Not for the first time, he thanked God for his family.

Outside, another loud "BOOM" echoed, rattling the rafters with its intensity. Greg could only imagine the nature of the explosion.

Steve, for his part, was not allowed to see all the weapons Tom's associates were being trained on. But he did confirm they were Russian in origin. He also noted Dallas was not the only "office" supplying men or equipment. Combined, there were well over one hundred people at the camp, with more coming in. This included three Russians handling most of the training, assisted by several Arabs. His brother was silent as to what they were training for or why they had the weapons in the first place. Steve did tell Greg his brother was being trained on some electronic gear, however, and not on the weapons. Tom had always been good with computers, electronics, and the like. Steve also knew he was being held hostage to assure Tom's cooperation. Tom told him as much. Apparently, Tom and Steve's actions regarding Greg and the girls stirred questions of loyalty in Martinez' mind. It also likely meant whatever task they were being trained for was not to be to Tom's liking. So, Martinez wanted leverage to assure Tom's full cooperation. Tom was well liked and respected among his peers. If Tom cooperated, so would they. It was working.

Steve expressed his amazement at how Greg and the girls kept their composure through all of this. Of course, they couldn't tell him the reason was they were regularly communicating with Jeff and knew they would be rescued.

Greg had not believed Tess when she first told Ashanti and him about her mental conversations with Jeff. They both thought she was crazy but went along with her. But then she started telling them things she had no way of knowing—like what they would be served for their next meal, and what color shirt the guard would have on, that sort of thing. Gradually, Ashanti and Greg had to admit something freaky was going on. Finally, Tess convinced Greg enough, so he could relax and receive Jeff telepathically himself. While he was a little envious Jeff selected Tess to be the one he contacted first, he also knew Jeff made the right choice.

Admittedly, his first teleping experience was a little disturbing, as well as being completely unbelievable. But as he got used to it, he found it totally amazing and wonderful. Ashanti, though, could not get used to the idea. She was quite content to let Tess and him have all the fun. She said she didn't want anyone, not even Jeff, invading her mind. He and Tess tried to explain that was not what it was like, but it was no use.

Even harder to accept than the teleping, at first anyway, was that Jeff and Becca were working with aliens. Initially, the thought of aliens was not only unbelievable, but disturbing. Yet, after thinking about it more, nothing else could explain everything that was happening—especially Jeff's newfound powers. Once they accepted this new reality, all three of them became much more confident rescue was possible. Who knew what powers and technology these aliens possessed?

Jeff teleped them regularly, which helped them cope with all the surreal things happening to them. They also teleped with Becca, although Tess more so than he. She told them she was also being trained, but not as rigorously as her brother. But she was amazed at what she could do.

Jeff told them the Arab he had seen was a terrorist and planned on doing something horrible, but he didn't divulge exactly what. But he did tell him thousands would die if they were not stopped, which was why they had to be so cautious. No one needed to be reminded of 9-11, even though it occurred before any of them were alive. Greg strongly suspected the possible death count was much higher than what Jeff let on, but he did not question the basic fact. Jeff also assured him no one would touch the girls, making all three of them more comfortable.

Jeff explained they would be rescued…but they had to time it perfectly, or it would fail. That was why it was taking so long. Knowing aliens were involved and there was a lot more at stake than their kidnapping also explained why it was taking so long to be freed. Even though Greg still didn't understand why Jeff couldn't simply call in the police, he trusted his friend's judgment, as did the girls. Steve, however, was not told of these "private" conversations. As a result, he did not have their confidence in being rescued. Of course, for him, he was still very confused as to why he was now being treated as a prisoner by the same people who had been employing him to push their poison on others.

Greg reflected on his last telep with Jeff. He could "hear" Jeff so much more clearly now. Before, it was difficult to discern what thoughts were coming from Jeff versus what were created by his own mind. But now, it was very easy to distinguish. Indeed, the teleped conversations had become more like a normal discussion, as though Jeff was seated across the table from him in a quiet room. Before, it was like talking to someone at a huge party with loud music blaring. Greg wasn't sure if it was because he was getting used to the idea of teleping or simply a result of Jeff's becoming more powerful and adept as a result of his training. He suspected it was a little bit of both. Tess reported the same clarity in her conversations with both Jeff and Becca. The fact Jeff was getting stronger gave them further hope.

Greg and the girls admitted to themselves it was a little scary having a friend with these abilities. Yet, when they pushed their fears aside, it was still the same Jeff they had always known...only more mature and confident.

Greg and Tess even tried teleping each other, with some modest success. Now they had experienced telepathy, they thought maybe they could develop their own abilities more. They practiced by taking turns holding up a playing card and having the other one guess what it was. They were getting fairly good at it, although admittedly Tess was doing better.

Another loud explosion, this one greater in intensity, shook the walls. It was enough to startle Ashanti, who had been half-asleep. The smell of spent gunpowder wafted in the air.

"That one sounded too close for comfort," she said.

"I just wish they would stop," added the newly awakened Tess. "I don't understand what all these drug dealers need with such explosives and high-tech weaponry."

"Steve overheard them talking about a big shipment coming into LA. My guess is the shipment is

317

meant for someone else, but these guys are planning on taking it for themselves. Steve also noted there was a bitter rivalry among some of the Cartel. Perhaps this Bivardo guy is trying to take over someone else's turf."

"This is too unreal," Ashanti lamented. "One week ago, our biggest worry was controlling our zits…Now, we are scared for our lives, being held captive by drug thugs who are apparently backed by crazy Arab terrorists who seem to be getting ready to launch a war, while we are awaiting being rescued by our seventeen-year-old friend who has suddenly developed superpowers and is buddy-buddy with ET. This sounds like some B-movie plot. I keep waiting to wake up."

Greg reached over and pinched her on her thigh.

"OW! What was that for?"

"Weren't you going to ask to be pinched to see if you were dreaming?"

"No!" Ashanti replied, hitting him softly on the shoulder.

"Sorry, I guess my psychic powers aren't that good," Greg said, grinning.

The sound of the deadbolt being turned ended any further interplay between the two. As the door creaked open, Steve, half walking, half being pushed, made his way into the room.

When the door closed, and the lock clicked back into place, Steve made his way over to the other three.

"The man is crazy!" Steve said as he sat down. "Absolutely insane." Steve tried to keep his voice down, but his emotions betrayed him.

"What is it?" Greg asked.

"Martinez will shoot me if he knew I told you guys. In fact, he would shoot me if he knew I knew.

But, hell, I don't think any of us will survive long anyway."

"What did you find out?" Tess asked, calmly.

"This guy Bivardo, you know, the head drug czar. He's planning on making a big splash Friday. I overheard some of his lieutenants talking. They are dividing his 'troops', I guess you call them, into three teams. You know he has almost 150 people here?"

They shook their heads. That was a lot more than Greg had figured. "Well, he does. And he's got all these high-tech weapons, in addition to these fancy guns and stuff. He's planning on striking back at two of his enemies at once—the US Government and the Disenzio family. This Friday, he's planning on robbing the Federal Reserve Bank, and at the same time, intercepting this huge shipment of drugs coming in from Asia the Disenzio family has lined up. There are a few other 'hits' as well.

"The lieutenants say it will be a cakewalk, as everyone will be watching the news or some crap. I guess his Arab friends are planning on some kinda big diversion."

"Any idea what?"

"Just that it seems to have something to do with one of the military bases near here."

"Geez," Ashanti said, "that's pretty bold, taking on the military like that."

"Yeah, and very stupid. Like I said, the guy must be crazy."

Chapter 36

Jeff stared intently at the coin lying flat on the control console in front of him. The face on the quarter stared back, unmoved. And that was the problem. It wasn't moving.

"I can't do this," he complained. "It's just not working."

"You are trying too hard," Axel commented. "It is not a question of will. It's a question of doing. You don't *order* the coin to move—you simply *perceive* it being somewhere else. Remember, the psychic energy is controlled by the older part of your brain, not by your consciousness."

"I'm trying—"

"Yes, trying. Not doing. Don't try. Do."

"You sound like a cliché," Jeff commented. "Next, you will call me 'Luke'," he mumbled as he returned his attention to the quarter. How do you perceive it somewhere else? How do you give up consciously trying to will it to relocate? *Okay, don't try to move it,* he told himself—*just picture it in a different place.* Jeff looked over at Becca, who was taking in his predicament while seated at the Amritzn's console.

320

Taking a few breaths, he relaxed his body and his mind. Closing his eyes, he visualized in his mind's eye Becca sitting a few feet away. He focused his awareness on her face. Slowly, he expanded his awareness, taking in more and more of her and the console. The coin would be on the console, tail-side up. So, he casually turned his attention to the console top to perceive the coin there, face down. He became curious as to what was on the coin's back side, so he decided to look more closely. As the image became sharper in his mind, he made out the triangle shape on the back and the "2000" at the bottom. It was from South Carolina.

"Open your eyes now," Axel instructed.

Jeff did. George Washington no longer returned his gaze. The coin disappeared. Amazed, Jeff looked over at Becca, who now stared at a quarter, turned face down, on the console in front of her.

"I did it!" Jeff shouted. "I really did it!"

"Wow," Becca exclaimed. "I can't believe it!"

"What, no faith in your brother?" Jeff mock-scolded her. They both chuckled.

"Don't get too cocky," Axel stated. "We still have a long way to go before we're done," he said with a scowl.

Jeff and Becca immediately got serious again.

Then Axel smiled. "Congratulations, though. You've now passed Level One."

"Level One? But you said I have to become a Level Three. We've been at this now for weeks!" Jeff complained.

"Actually," Becca replied, "I think it has been eleven days."

Axel put up his hand to stop Jeff from snapping

back at Becca. "We are making good progress." Chermal purred his agreement. "You can do this, Jeff. You've made it over a big hurdle. I think you will find things getting a little easier."

"I hope so. I know we are running out of time…even though we have over one hundred years."

"We will make it," Axel assured him.

"Speaking of time," Becca said, "It's killing me to be in here, knowing real living history is all around us outside. I'm just dying to go out there."

"We can't think about those things right now," Jeff reprimanded. "We have more important things to be doing. We can't afford to be selfish. We must focus on the task at hand."

"Hmmm," Axel said. "I think a little exploring may be an excellent idea."

"Huh?"

"You must now learn to become invisible."

"Invisible? Are you kidding? You can do that? How?"

"Oh, I'm not talking about turning transparent." Axel replied with a smile.

Jeff sat up straighter. Axel now had their full attention.

"Have you ever been in a situation where no matter how hard you tried you couldn't get anyone to notice you?"

They both nodded. Both could think of several examples, such as trying to get the teacher to call on them when they knew the answer, but only getting called on when they didn't.

"At those times, doesn't it feel like you're invisible?"

Again, they nodded.

"What we will teach you is how to become virtually invisible to everyone, not by disappearing, but by getting everyone to totally ignore your presence."

"Everyone already ignores Becca," Jeff said, getting a quarter tossed in his direction in response.

"We will take a field trip to the Dallas of this time period. If you can walk around dressed as you are in twenty-first century clothes in the Dallas of 120 years previous, without everyone stopping and gawking, or otherwise causing a scene, then you will have succeeded in making yourself practically invisible."

"Cool, but how do we do it?"

"By projecting nothing."

Becca and Jeff stared at Axel.

****

Axel had more than training in mind when he suggested the field trip. It would not only be useful training, but they could use a break given the non-stop intensity of their work. Besides, he was as eager to get outside the ship as the others now he was no longer concerned about being detected by the Zanchee or worried about a second Axel existing in this time period.

He was pleased with the pace of training, although it was tough on all concerned. The eight-week timeline was really somewhat arbitrary. Yes, they had to return to the present, but as long as they stayed for a day and remained hidden, they could return and repeat the eight weeks. But each trip forward ran the risk of detection by the Zanchee. And there was another concern. While technically as long as they returned to their September, Jeff would still be seventeen. However, his physical body was still aging. A second eight-week stent and Jeff's physical body would reach eighteen years. Would that make him an adult to the Zanchee? No, the best thing was to get the training done in one round.

But that didn't mean they had to work continuously without break. This trip would provide both a needed mental break and a valuable lesson.

****

Jeff was a little disappointed to find himself along with Becca instantly transported to a dark alley, which he assumed was near the middle of downtown Dallas. The disappointment came not from now being in an alley in the early twentieth-century Dallas, but in how they arrived. In the back of his mind he pictured them riding into town perched proudly atop three beautiful mares, like royalty arriving to survey their dominion, or at least like the cowboys of yesteryear back from a long cattle drive. The fact Axel had never been near a horse, let alone ridden one, hadn't really entered Jeff's mind.

When they arrived, he was first struck, not by the old-fashioned buildings now in near new condition, but by the air. He expected it to be crystal clear. But it wasn't. If anything, it was hazier. The smells were entirely different as well. Gone were the smells of modern civilization—the pollution and the exhaust. In their place were the smells of horses—and horse byproducts—plus dirt, smoke, coal, wood, and early twentieth-century industry.

"Wow," Becca commented. "I don't know what I was expecting, but it wasn't this. This is sooo cooool!"

"Notice the smell?" Jeff asked.

"Yeah, it's really different. I can't believe it. And look at these buildings. They look new, even though they're so old."

"They are new—to this time period. They are only old in our minds."

Both were struck with the mix of brick and wood frame buildings. They were astonished to see buildings reaching twenty and more stories above their heads. Neither had known exactly what to expect, and the reality was surprising.

When they stepped out from the alleyway, they found the streets were not made of dirt but were covered with brick. Some were even paved. Jeff had not known paved roads preceded the advent of the automobile.

Staring out onto the street, it was as if they had walked into a movie set. There was a set of railroad tracks running down the center of the street. Above the tracks were what appeared to be powerlines. This was also surprising, as Jeff had not realized electricity was a big part of the early twentieth century. A glance at Becca confirmed she was as surprised as he.

The idea of having a railroad track running down the middle of the street, needless to say, was extremely strange. There was something familiar, only what was it? As he reflected, a sharp elbow in his side broke his concentration.

"Hey, why did you do that?" Jeff asked his sister.

"Look!" was all she said as she pointed down the street. For there was Jeff's answer. Ambling slowly and noisily down the middle of the street was a classic trolley car coming directly at them, sparks flying from the rod rolling along the electric wire.

Immediately, Jeff recalled reading about the old trolleys so commonplace in American cities at the turn of the twentieth century. He had seen pictures of them. But, never having been to San Francisco, this was his first "live" look at one. He couldn't take his eyes off the big red car, jammed with people. A bell in front announced its coming to all concerned.

Becca practically pulled her brother out of the way as the trolley crossed the intersection and headed directly at them. Jeff's mouth still hung open as the car passed—its passengers similarly gaping at the strange trio on the street below. One man, apparently feeling friendly to people who were obviously strangers, tipped his cap as they went by.

That was another strange thing for him. Somehow, in the back of his mind, he pictured Dallas during this time period being like an old frontier town, full of cowboys, saloons, horses, and dirt roads. Heck, they hadn't yet seen anyone dressed like a cowboy. Most of the people were dressed in turn-of-the-century business clothes. Many of the men carried attaché cases of some sort, with a derby hat or bowler perched on top of their heads. There were no guns strapped to their waist. Jeff smiled. There were probably more men of his time period carrying guns in downtown Dallas than here. There were few women to be seen. Of course, the stores were not open and fewer women worked outside the home.

Yes, there were horses, but only those pulling carriages. Jeff and Becca looked wondrously as carriages drawn by one and two horses made their way past, the horses' hooves lifting proudly with each step as they clippity-clappity made their way down the brick street.

What there were a lot of were bicycles, again

surprising him. Apparently instead of using horses, most of the people rode bikes into town. Jeff was amazed to see all the adults riding bicycles, adorned in their finest fashions and business suits. It certainly was different from Jeff's time when few adults ever ventured onto a bike anymore, unless they were adorned with unseemly tight-fitting specialized clothing and looking ridiculous.

Yet another new noise drew Jeff's and Becca's attention. It sounded like an old pump motor Jeff had seen down on the farm. "Chickity chickity" it chugged. As it grew louder, the source of the sound became visible as it rounded the corner.

Jeff saw where they got the name, "horseless carriage." The automobile approaching them looked far more like the carriages they had just seen than a car, with its large, spoked wheels and headlights looking like lanterns, mounted high in front of the open passenger compartment containing high-backed seats. The passengers sat high up off the road as the carriage was several feet off the ground. There was no steering wheel, only a stick the driver used to control the early auto's direction. A large crank protruded from the very front of the car.

Apparently, the sight of an automobile was not commonplace yet. For as the horseless carriage made its way down the street, its two passengers sitting erect and proud and decked out in their finest apparel, people on both sides of the street stopped and gawked. Many waved.

Unfortunately, the car was not the only thing getting undue attention. At first, everyone they passed stared at the unusual trio with their equally strange pet cat. And why not? They stood out like a sore thumb, dressed in early twenty-first century clothes, including modern tennis shoes, while walking down the middle of an early twentieth century Dallas street. Everything about them stood out—not only their clothes, but their hair styles, the way they walked, the way they talked, Axel's unusual look, and Chermal's indescribable appearance.

Jeff and Becca were getting frustrated at the fact they were apparently bad at projecting "nothing." Axel and Chermal were getting a little tired of continuously having to "blank" people's short-term memories so the foursome would not be readily remembered. Their frustration overshadowed their sheer joy in being part of a living museum.

"Maybe this is a mistake," Jeff said as a group of individuals huddled together, possibly discussing Jeff's group's appearance. "Maybe we're not ready for this!" Already they had to duck down one alley to avoid a group of teens who looked like they were ready to challenge the unusual group.

"You give up too easily," Axel commented. "And you are both trying too hard. Your very effort to 'project nothing' is really causing you to be more noticed. You both need to relax and believe nothing is wrong. Convince yourselves and you will convince others. Focus only on appearance for now."

Jeff tried to do as he was instructed and knew Becca was as well. *There's nothing wrong with my clothes*, he told himself. *Everything is fine. Everything is normal.*

"You're still thinking too much," Axel chastised. "Don't think...just feel. Feel you are unimportant. That you are not worthy of any attention. That you are, in fact, nothing at all."

"Kind of deflating to the ego, isn't it?" Becca commented to her brother. Jeff shot her a glare in return. Then he realized not only would he have to feel he was unimportant, he needed to feel everyone in their group was also not noteworthy. That was harder.

"Very good," Axel noted. "Empty your mind of thoughts of yourself and the rest of us. Concentrate on your surroundings, and how you blend in…how you belong. Don't think about their strangeness as it will only reflect on your own. Just absorb the details."

Jeff understood. He began to note the similarities between his surroundings and TV westerns he watched, feeling more comfortable with his immediate environment as he concentrated on the familiar and not the different.

The gramirl warmed against his flesh. It helped broadcast his nothingness to those around him. Absently, he noted Axel smiling with apparent approval. Jeff ignored him and continued down the street, allowing his subconscious to control his movements and keep him in the company of his companions.

They walked on, unnoticed.

Chapter 37

Doug peered through the binoculars at the warehouse loading dock across the street. From his vantage point in an unmarked van parked in the alleyway, he could see past the open garage door and into the warehouse itself. Workers scampered back and forth, unloading a semi-trailer truck parked at the dock. Everything appeared perfectly normal for a computer-supply warehouse.

Doug was grasping at straws. He had the other two agents assigned to him staking out two other warehouses in the area that could be traced, albeit indirectly, to Bivardo. They had been at this now for three days, without turning up so much as an illegal parking citation. Nothing, absolutely nothing. To say it was frustrating to him was like saying LA had a few cars.

Doug picked up the half-eaten hamburger and took another bite. His ex-wife was right, he thought as he absently wiped the remains of his meal from his lips, this job was killing him. Eating too much junk food was bound to knock off anyone.

His pocket's ringing shook him from his reverie.

Without taking his eyes off the warehouse, Doug grabbed the phone from his pocket, pressing his index finger against its fingerprint scanner as he did so.

"Stanton," he said as a way of answering, absently noting the red indicator on his phone lit up, indicating a scrambled call.

"Doug, this is Jim. Get back here now. The fits really hit the shan!"

"What did?"

"The State Department just received a threat from your buddy, Raheim." There was a long pause. "He says he will nuke one of six targets if his demands are not met. He sent along a picture of the nuclear warhead shown with a copy of today's *USA Today* to prove he can do it."

Doug started the van and pulled out into the street while he kept the phone to his ear. He took no satisfaction from the fact he had been right about Raheim.

"What are his demands?"

"He has a long list of prisoners he wants released, both by the US and Israel. He wants an immediate pullout by Israel in all Israeli occupied land and a billion dollars deposited to a Swiss account."

"Anything related to Bivardo?"

"No. There's no mention of Bivardo, his assets, or his family members. I guess they are not wanting the alliance public. Of course, a billion dollars is a lot more than what we froze in Bivardo's assets."

"How much time?"

"He's given us till one p.m., Pacific time, tomorrow."

"That's not a lot of time…"

"It gets worse. He says that if we haven't made a good faith deposit of $250 million by midnight tonight Pacific time, he'll release the information to the press, along with the photo."

"Good God! That alone will cause a massive panic."

"Yeah, and not only in LA. He's named San Diego, San Francisco, Las Vegas, Camp Pendleton, and Edwards AFB as other possible targets."

"Curious. Four major cities and two military targets. Why not all cities or all military?"

"I guess to maximize the terror."

"Yeah, but then why not have six cities? Why include Camp Pendleton and Edwards?"

"To throw us off the track."

"Or maybe to pacify his allies. I doubt Bivardo wants to destroy a large customer base by killing millions of citizens."

"So, you think the target is military?"

"I think that's what he wants us and Bivardo to think."

"You don't think so?"

"No. Call it another hunch, but I believe his target is LA."

"Well you'll have your chance to explain your hunch to the top brass. This time, I assure you, you will have everyone's attention—not to mention the manpower you've been wanting."

"I hope it's not too late. I'll be there in twenty minutes, if I don't get stuck in another LA traffic mess." With that, he closed the phone and put it back into his pocket.

Chapter 38

Greg, Ashanti, Tess, and Steve were sound asleep on the floor of their prison/room when they were rudely awakened by the sound of a loud explosion.

Greg jumped nineteen inches off the floor, impressive considering he started prone. As his consciousness returned, the room's lights hit his eyes like a sledgehammer, causing him to squint. Three Arabs stood in room looking at them. Two held submachine guns pointed in their general direction, and the third had a pistol, which he brandished about over his head. Greg surmised the handgun was the source of the explosion.

"Get up!" shouted the Arab holding the pistol in heavily accented English. "You four are coming with us."

"What's happening?" Steve managed to ask groggily. "Where's my brother?"

He was answered with a hard backhand slap by the man holding the pistol. "Get moving," he said again, waving the pistol toward the door.

They obeyed, getting quickly to their feet and pulling on their shoes. Since the desert nights were cool, they were fully clothed, which was fortunate, as it was much cooler outside.

The morning sun was making its way up into the fiery red desert sky. The mountains in the background, painted red in the early light, made a beautiful backdrop. The air was crisp and clean. Unfortunately, they didn't have much time to enjoy the scenery as they were rather rudely pushed toward a medium-sized truck parked in front of the Quonset hut. A larger semi-trailer truck was parked in front of it. Both appeared freshly painted.

Greg stole a quick glance around as he they were herded into the back of the smaller truck. The base, or whatever it was, appeared deserted. There were only four buildings, all of them Quonset huts like the one that had been their home for the past however many days it had been. But there were no other vehicles in sight. No lights shone from any of the buildings. As they got in, the other truck moved off.

As soon as they scrambled inside the back door of the truck, the door swung shut, leaving them in total darkness. The sound of a padlock being applied to the door broke the silence, sealing them in. There was no access to the front of the truck from the back, so they were effectively boxed in. The truck started moments later. With a grind, indicating a shifting of gears, and a jerk, the truck began to move.

Ashanti started to sob. He reached out, found her, and put his arm around her. "Everything will be okay," he said, in a not-too-convincing fashion.

"What the hell is happening?" Steve said angrily. "Where's my brother?" he shouted, presumably toward the front of the truck. There was no reply.

"The walls of this truck seem very thick," Greg noted, as he tapped the side. He wanted to prevent a panic by getting everyone to talk. "I think this is a refrigerator truck or something."

"Great," Tess replied. "The better to preserve us."

"It means," Ashanti said through her sobs, "that it's probably airtight. We may not have a lot of air."

"It also means no one is likely to hear us, unless they have an ear pressed against the truck," Tess said.

Greg nodded, then remembered no one could see the gesture. "You're probably right," he said. "Even so, I will try to get a message out."

"What are you talking about?" Steve asked, somewhat agitated. "How the heck will you get a message out?"

"I'll think of something," Greg replied, knowing Tess and Ashanti knew exactly what he meant. *"Jeff. We need you!"* he shouted telepathically. He only hoped he would be heard.

*"I'm here."* Jeff teleped in reply almost immediately. Jeff came through more clearly than ever before. *"What's happening?"* Jeff asked.

Ashanti, Tess, and Steve talked softly in the background. Silently, he commended the girls for their composure, as well as for distracting Steve while he concentrated on Jeff.

Quickly, Greg relayed to Jeff what had just transpired.

*"They are making their move. This is good,"* Jeff told him.

*"Good? How do you see that?"* Greg replied.

*"Well, before you were in the middle of an extremely well-armed camp. Getting you out would*

*have been very difficult. But now you only have one guard, and he's driving the truck."*

*"How do you...never mind,"* Greg teleped. *"But there were three of them."*

*"The other two are in the big truck, containing the warhead."*

*"Warhead?"*

*"Don't sweat. It's under control,"* Jeff teleped back. Greg hoped he was telling the truth.

*"Where are you?"* Greg asked.

*"When am I is a better question,"* Jeff replied.

*"Huh? Yeah, when will you rescue us? I don't mind telling you this is getting mighty tense. We're locked in the back of a truck, in complete darkness bound for God knows where. And it's a refrigerated truck, so we might be short on air."*

*"Los Angeles."*

*"What?"* Greg asked, totally confused.

*"That's where you're headed."* There was a pause. *"Axel tells me we will be rescuing you in about fifteen minutes, your time. Tell the others to be ready. I'll telep you right before."*

*"Okay...But how will you rescue us?"*

*"I'm not sure yet. I have another week of training first. But I'm sure it will be good. Gotta go now. You'll be seeing me soon."*

Now Greg was very confused. What did Jeff mean he had another week of training in order to rescue him in fifteen minutes? Once again, he wondered if he and Tess had imagined all these conversations with Jeff. Maybe they really *were* crazy. But then again, what did he have to lose?

"Guys," Greg said, interrupting the conversation

that had been continuing uninterrupted. "I got through. We will be rescued in about fifteen minutes. Be ready to run."

It was a shame it was pitch dark. Greg could only imagine the look he was getting right now from Steve.

Chapter 39

*September 16th, D Minus 8.45 Hours*
*Los Angeles*

Doug refilled his cup with more coffee, stifling a yawn in the process. He glanced at his watch, noting it was shortly after 4:30 in the morning, local time. That meant Doug had been up almost twenty-four hours straight and with only seven hours sleep total over the past three days. He took another sip from the cup. At least the coffee was decent here. Much better than at the Dallas Regional Office. He was also thankful the small conference room was located near the restrooms. That came in handy when you're drinking a pot of coffee an hour.

He made his way back to the small table, where his friend Jim was seated, along with Seth and Ty. Jim, if anything, looked more worn out than Doug felt. But sleep was not an option. Not when the stakes were so high. Muffled conversations, some quite animated, came from the main conference room down the hall. That room had become the war room. Big shots were there from the military, Homeland Security, CIA, FBI, and the DEA, along with the President's National Security Advisor. In addition to the people physically present, they were connected directly to the President's situation room in Washington. A large HD monitor nearly filled one wall, currently displaying the DC group. High-tech speakers made it feel like everyone was in one large room together.

Doug and Jim had been asked to make their reports, and then were shepherded out of the room. The big boys would handle it from here they were told. They were allowed, though, to stay on the same floor, in case they were needed. All other staff had been removed.

Each agent had an open laptop in front of them. A large monitor in the back of the smaller conference room displayed a map of the Los Angeles area. Each laptop had a large file containing all the information they had on Raheim and the United Arab Freedom Front. Another file contained information on Bivardo, and a third on Krenchenko. A desktop computer, with secure links to DC headquarters, anchored the table at the other end, with a secured printer attached by cable.

"I still don't get it," Jim said as Doug sat down.

"Which part of this totally incomprehensible puzzle do you not get?" Doug responded.

"Why haven't we heard from Raheim? The deadline for the money passed nearly four and a half hours ago. But we haven't heard a word." Then waving his hand toward the door where the voices were coming from, he said, "There are several people in there convinced this is either an elaborate hoax or a major bluff to try to extort money from the US."

"It's not a hoax. Or a bluff," he assured them.

"Then why has he not made a move?" Ty asked.

"Maybe it has something to do with us having a complete blanket over virtually every media outlet in the state, if not the country?" Seth interjected. "And any attempt to contact the media may result in our being able to track him down?"

"Or, it was meant to throw us off the track," Doug interjected. "The UAFF's style has always been to issue warnings before they strike. That way, they can blame their victim's lack of response to their demands as the reason for whatever atrocity happens. It also means no one else can claim 'credit' for their actions. By giving us six potential targets, he knows he's spreading our resources out. He's also twisted enough to to think he's giving us an even chance."

"It also gives them the opportunity to watch how we respond," Seth interjected. "Perhaps setting up the real event, which could be weeks or months away. And a false alarm now will mean a smaller response then."

"But why not alert the media, as he threatened to do? Won't the resulting panic also serve his purpose?" Ty asked.

"Unless he's playing some other game we don't know about, yet," Doug said. After a pause, he continued voicing his stream of conscious. "Perhaps he never intended to collect the ransom."

"Meaning?"

"He fully intends to explode the bomb," Doug said solemnly. "We just don't understand the rules of this new game." Then bending back over his laptop, he added, "The answer has got to be in these files, somewhere. I just know it."

"Christ, we've read these files over and over until we have practically got them memorized word for word. Still nothing."

"Hmmm." Doug paused. "Maybe we've been

looking at this all wrong from the beginning. We have been trying to deduce what these *organizations* are getting out of this, and why they are working together."

"Yea, so?"

"But what if it's not the organizations at all. What if it was strictly personal?" He gestured at his laptop. "One thing we know about each of their organizations is they are very authoritarian. Each of them demands one-hundred percent loyalty and obedience. In essence, the organizations will go along with whatever the leaders want."

"Okay, they have strong leaders, so what?" Ty asked.

"Humor me. Let's review it one more time. See what we have. Let's start with this. All three leaders, Bivardo, Krenchenko, and Raheim have a deep hatred for the US. We all agree on that?"

Nods all around.

"So, it might not have required as much arm twisting or negotiating if Raheim convinced them they will be getting their vengeance.

"The key to all of it is Raheim. I'm certain he is behind this entire operation. So, let's concentrate on him. But this time, let's focus on the man, not the organization. Although I think the UAFF is certainly involved, Raheim is pulling all the strings. Something tells me there is a personal motivation here, not just political."

"All right. I don't know what else we can do," Jim said, taking a long drink from his cup. He pulled Raheim's file back up on his computer. "We know he has a strong hatred for the US."

"Okay, let's begin with that. Here is a man who

came to the United States for school. He even graduated cum laude from Penn State, and then went on to get a master's degree in Geology, right?"

"Right. Then he went back home and went to work for his government's oil resources. It was there he met up with the al-Qaida run by Osama Bin Ladin," Seth added.

"Which is where everyone assumed he developed his hatred for the US. But I think Bin Ladin just refined it. What if he already had it within him?"

"Why? He spent six years here. There is nothing to indicate he had any difficulties while studying here."

"What about his family? Didn't he have a sister come here, too?" Jim interjected.

Seth scanned through the file. "Yeah, she also went to Penn State. She's three years younger than him. She met someone while she was here, apparently, and stayed after she graduated."

"He's a religious man. Maybe he didn't like his sister being perverted by western culture," Ty said.

"I guess," Seth replied.

"What happened to her?" Doug asked.

"The file doesn't say."

"Let's find out." Jim went over to the desktop computer and tapped in his access code. He then went to FBI archives and did a search. No record was found.

"Well, she doesn't have a file, so she's kept clean. Let me tap into the IRS database. See if she's been paying any taxes." Given the crisis before them, the team had been given clearance to access about any government database available. It took Jim a few minutes to find what he needed. "Hmmm. According to these files, she's deceased. She died in 1998. Last known address was Hampstead, New York. The last filing indicated she was part of a joint return with a Robert Martin's. Going back, they were married the previous year. No other dependents were listed."

"How did she die?" Doug asked.

"Just a sec. I have to go to another database to find out. Damn. As fast as these computers are today, they never seem fast enough!" Jim waited impatiently for the New York records to come online. It took a few more minutes to figure out how to do his query appropriately. "Here it is. Hmmm. Coronary failure…blah, blah, blah. High levels of cocaine were found in her blood. Doug, she died of a drug overdose. In the words of one of your heroes, 'fascinating.' "

"Yeah, it is. Any bets on the organization that probably supplied the drugs?"

"Nope. But if Raheim has a grudge against Bivardo, why not simply kill him? He's certainly had the opportunity."

"Raheim's motto is not an 'eye for an eye and a tooth for a tooth,' it's more like 'a thousand eyes for a cavity.' He won't want Bivardo simply killed but destroyed…then maybe die an agonizing death."

"We're dealing with a psycho."

"A psycho with a grudge and a nuclear weapon. Not a good combination," Ty added.

"Jim," Doug asked, "does it say *when* she died?"

"Yes…Oh, oh. It was September 16th at 4:00 p.m. Uh that is 1:00 pm Pacific time."

"That doesn't give us much time," Doug exclaimed.

"I still don't understand what he's planning," Seth said.

"My guess is we are looking at a giant double-cross. He's used Bivardo to help him get the warhead here and to provide a base of operations. Probably had him help provide security and other things, too. Then, he gives Bivardo a false target, to lure him to the actual site."

"Okay, so which is the false site, and which is real?"

"My bet is that Edwards is the false target. Being a military base, it will be the easiest one for Bivardo to believe is the real target and the easiest one for Raheim to get Bivardo to accept. He loses fewer customers that way."

"Okay, I'll buy that."

"This may also explain why he hasn't alerted the media. He doesn't want a panic."

"Why not?"

"Because the warhead isn't at the target yet. My bet is it is, or was, near Edwards, the pseudo-target. He will wait until Bivardo and his men clear out, then move it to the real target, probably by truck. If he creates a panic, then he will have extreme difficulty getting into the city, as all the roads will be clogged. And we both know how bad the traffic is around here under normal conditions." Doug smiled slyly. "Furthermore, he won't want some of his intended victims—Bivardo and his cronies—fleeing the trap."

"Okay, if you're right, where's the target?" Jim asked.

"Like I told you before, I think it's here, Los Angeles."

"I still don't see how Bivardo fits in. How will Raheim lure him to LA?" Seth queried.

"Bivardo is extremely ambitious. He's not satisfied being a member of the Cartel. He wants to *be* the Cartel. My bet is Bivardo is planning on doing something big here in LA. He's planning on using the nuclear explosion as a cover…it certainly will get everybody's attention, including all the crooks."

"What is he planning?"

"I'm not sure. But with Bivardo, it has to be big. Remember, too, he has no love lost for the US government. Maybe he will try to get his money back."

"I thought that's what the billion dollars was for," Ty said.

"They know they won't get that. The easiest way is to simply steal it. Who has that kind of money?" Doug asked

"I don't know. Maybe the Federal Reserve Bank," Jim replied.

"Yep. Let's make sure it's covered, but have it done quietly. We don't want to alert them. My guess, though, is he's going after more than just money. I bet he's also planning a hit on some of his competitors." Turning to Ty, Doug asked, "Have you heard of any major drug shipments coming in?"

"No, but I've been focused on Bivardo. I'll check with HQ."

"I'll also contact the New York office and get someone over there to speak with this Robert Martin. See if he can shed any light on the situation," Jim said, then looked at his watch. "It's 7:30 in the morning there. He should be there by now."

Seth nodded, then asked, "Ok, that may explain Bivardo and Raheim, but what does Krenchenko get from all this?"

"That's a bit tougher to figure out," Doug admitted. "Certainly, he has no love lost for the US, but that doesn't explain what's happening. He is taking a huge risk knowing the US will be out for blood if that bomb goes off. If they can trace that bomb back to the Russian Mafia, they will be hunted down by both Russia and the US."

"Could Russia possibly be behind him?" Jim asked.

"Russia would be risking an all-out nuclear war," Doug stated.

"True, unless they have strong 'evidence' the nuke was stolen, including a few dead bodies, which we understand was the case. Russian sources claim there is a lot of evidence Chechens were responsible, although no one from this country has seen it," Seth pointed out.

"And the US's anger will be directed, at least initially, on the Arab terrorists…" Jim said, following the thought. "Because we will want revenge, there will be a major call for all-out war in the Middle East. If we started two wars over 9-11, I can only imagine what we might do after a nuke detonated on US soil."

"And there is already some suspicion the Saudis are secretly funding the UAFF. That suspicion may be enough for us to turn against our biggest Arab ally."

"And with a little 'push' that Russia could certainly help start, American anger will likely be directed against *all* Muslims," Seth noted.

"And Russia will be there to be the friend to all Muslims…"

"And all oil they control…"

Doug managed a half-smile.

"Yea, but I'm not sure Russia is prepared for the

backlash that will occur if the other Arab nations discover it supplied a terrorist group with a nuke," Seth replied. "Besides, I really do not think they are wanting to risk WWIII if Raheim should explode a bomb they supplied. And we have not found any evidence that Krenchenko is working with the government."

"Could it be financial?" Jim suggested.

"I don't think so. Raheim does not have that kind of cash," Seth replied.

"Perhaps they are planning on moving in on the drug trade in a big way if one and maybe two of their primary competitors are taken out," Ty pointed out.

"Good point, but still, I don't know it's worth that much risk…But there still could be a financial component. What do you think will happen to the stock market if a nuke went off in LA?" Doug asked.

"Initially it will close for fear of a run…but, still, the market will likely take a huge hit…especially for those companies either headquartered or with a heavy presence in LA," Jim answered.

"And if you anticipated that crash…"

"You could make a fortune selling short!" Jim exclaimed. "That could be it. Krenchenko will not do it directly, but he has many shell companies that could do it for him. I'll have DC get on it in the morning."

"You mean later this morning?"

"Yeah…"

"You know, the president of Russia could be involved…with or without the rest of the government's—especially the military's—knowledge. He could be playing the same financial game."

"I'll add him to the list," Jim stated. "Okay, now that you've got it all figured out, where's the warhead?"

"You know, I have an idea about that," Doug answered.

"I'm listening."

"Something you said about Raheim started me thinking…"

"About?"

"He has a master's degree in Geology."

"Yeah?"

"Well, Los Angeles is a very big city. A single nuclear warhead, even a fifteen-megaton hydrogen bomb, will not completely destroy it. Oh, with radiation and all, it certainly will kill maybe a million or more. But not everything…"

"And?"

"What is everyone in California afraid of?"

"That's easy. The big one…A giant earthquake."

"I'm no geologist, but what do you think a nuclear bomb detonating on one of these major faults would do?"

"Jesus Christ!"

"We will have to wake up a few more people. Find a geologist who can tell us where on the fault line a nuclear explosion would do the most damage. That's where you're likely find the weapon."

Doug searched through the maps on the table. "Doesn't the San Andreas fault run near here?"

Jim displayed a map of the area on the large screen. He then called up a geographical map showing the fault lines. "The San Andreas fault runs parallel to the coast, right on the other side of the mountains," he said, tracing a line along the map. "The closest point to Los Angeles is here—" He pause and pointed to a spot on the map. "—San Bernardino."

Doug fumbled around on his laptop until he came up with a map of San Bernardino, which he put on the main screen. "I see four airports here."

"Airports?"

"Raheim isn't the suicidal type. That's for his cronies," Doug explained. "He will want to see the results of his revenge. I'm betting he has a small plane waiting for him at one of these airports." As he talked, he got up and headed toward the door.

"Where are you going?" Jim demanded.

"Rialto airport. If he's there, I'll find him. You do what you can to convince the big shots, and make sure those other airports are covered. We're running out of time." With that, Doug left.

Chapter 40

Axel slowly raised the Winchester rifle to his shoulder and sighted his target. One finger of his right hand pressed lightly on the trigger with the other four fingers wrapped around the barrel as his thumb held back the hammer. The rifle, although over one hundred years old to Jeff's time, was practically new, as Axel "borrowed" it from this time. He stared coldly at Jeff as he centered the target in his sight. Chermal sat passively at his feet. The target would not be hard to hit. After all, it was only twenty-five feet away.

Axel's finger rested on the trigger. Slowly, but steadily, he pulled his finger toward his body, squeezing the trigger in the process. His target simply stared back at him. Becca squirmed as her brother calmly awaited the bullet that could end his life.

Jeff remained motionless, perched upon the boulder located a few hundred yards away from where the ship was hidden. He looked down the barrel at Axel's steely gaze and confidently awaited his fate. A bright intense flame flared from the barrel. If he waited to hear the loud report, it would be too late—the bullet would have found its target.

Jeff sat motionless, watching as the bullet exiting the rifle, spinning slowly and serenely as it made its way toward him. The patterns of the suddenly super-heated air being parted by the bullet's path as it escaped from the barrel turned the area around the would-be fatal projectile bright with red and yellow colors. Wisps of smoke began to trickle out of the end of the barrel, trailing after the bullet that continued its deadly journey. A part of Jeff appreciated the beauty of the moment.

It would be so easy to make the bullet "disappear," to teleport it somewhere else, somewhere safe. But that was not what this exercise was about. He waited. The bullet continued its deadly course.

The bullet kept coming, spinning. One foot, two feet, three feet. Without his eyes ever leaving the projectile, he casually rose. He stood next to the boulder that had been his seat and watched as the bullet continued its path toward his former location. He could simply reach and grab the bullet, spinning slowly beside him, or easily flick it away with his finger. Instead, he let the bullet continue past him as he casually made his way over to Axel. As the bullet smashed into the boulder, it folded up, then bounced back much more slowly in a haze of powder. Pieces of rock flew slowly off in all directions from the bullet's impact. Just as the bullet fell to the ground, harmless, Jeff reached and grabbed the rifle from Axel, being careful not to break Axel's fingers in the process.

****

Becca stifled a scream as Axel picked up the rifle, aimed, and shot at her brother from practically point-blank range. Even though she had been told Jeff was ready and it was safe, she wasn't so sure. It was hard to believe. What if something went wrong? What if he really wasn't ready? Her brother sat motionless on the rock. It was as though he was in some sort of trance. As the sound of the rifle cracking reached her ears, her eyes were still locked onto Jeff. But he wasn't there. Startled, she looked back toward Axel, only to see her brother, grinning from ear to ear, holding the rifle.

"Don't you ever scare me like that again!" she shouted, angry because she had been so frightened. But her joy in her brother's success and safety quickly succeeded her anger. She ran over to him and threw both arms around him in an embrace worthy of any wrestling hold seen on TV. "You did it!" she exclaimed.

\*\*\*\*

Jeff nodded, relieved. He passed the test. He slowed time, his time, down to where it almost stopped. To everyone else, Jeff had been moving faster than the eye can see, but to him, he moved at normal speed. It was everything else that slowed down.

His giddiness was quickly interrupted as a streaking ball of fur flashed straight at him. Leaping from about three feet away, and claws outstretched, the feline flew at Jeff's face. Without a second of hesitation, Jeff reached up with his free hand and snatched the creature in mid-leap.

"Nice try, Chermal!" Jeff declared, still smiling. He then pulled the cat-like creature in toward his chest, holding him firmly with one hand. Taking his hand from around Becca, he scratched Chermal gently behind the ears, like he did with his family's cat, Sparky. The alien had the same appreciation Sparky did for the gesture as a purring-like sound emanated from Chermal's body.

****

Axel and Becca both laughed at the strange pair. Jeff merely smiled. Becca's admiration for her brother continued to grow. They had both come so far in the past eight weeks, but her own progress paled in comparison to her brother's. She was still trying to master simple telekinesis.

But Jeff had changed in more ways beyond developing his seemingly superhuman powers. There was a new air about him, a maturity well past his years. He had a job to do, and the stakes were very high. Yet even with the apparent weight of the whole world on his shoulders, he never complained, never stopped trying to get better. They were working against an impossible deadline, and he was determined to beat it.

When Becca talked to him, he explained he was so focused on whatever it was they were training on at the time, he pushed everything else from his mind, including what was happening to his friends, over one hundred years into the future.

Axel came over to Jeff, with his hand extended. "I believe your custom is to shake hands when congratulations are due."

Jeff looked down at the proffered hand with a kind of blank glaze over his eyes.

"Jeff," Becca said affectionately, "I think Axel is trying to tell you…you passed. You made it!"

Axel nodded his affirmation. Slowly, a grin that threatened to swallow the rest of his face began to spread from ear to ear as Jeff grabbed the extended hand.

"I wish we had more time to celebrate," Axel said. "But Chermal informs me it is now time to go."

\*\*\*\*

When they returned to the ship, the three humanoids took their seats. Chermal followed, taking his customary position next to Axel. As he sat, Jeff reflected briefly on his last conversation with Greg and the girls. It took place over a week ago, for Jeff. But when they returned to their own time, only fifteen minutes would have passed for Greg and the girls. The four of them—he included Steve—would be scared, but at least they knew he was coming.

Axel explained they would travel to the targeted physical point, just over the California border with Nevada, while they were still in this time period. Then they would make the jump to the twenty-first century when Greg and the girls would be very anxiously awaiting their arrival. By doing it this way, they would minimize the risk of being detected by the Zanchee when they returned to their own time.

Jeff expanded his awareness to "watch" the flight. After all, it wasn't every day you got to ride in a flying saucer.

There was no sensation as the craft lifted gently from its hiding place at the bottom of a small pond. Jeff and Becca observed in fascination as the water cascaded down the sides of the ship when it made its escape from its watery hold. The few trees rimming the pond slipped quickly beneath the ship as the open sky beckoned. Jeff yearned to ask Axel to take them on into space so he could have the thrill of looking down on the blue, green, brown, and white globe he called home. But there was a time and place, and this was not the time.

Jeff loved flying, although he hadn't had many opportunities. He and Becca averaged about one trip a year, to visit either set of grandparents. When they flew, the two of them always fought to see who got to sit by the window. Whenever possible, they both got window seats. When they didn't, whoever had the window often had the other's head leaning across, stealing glances at the terrain below.

But now it wasn't necessary. Both had an unrestricted view as their psychic senses gave them a full panorama of the majestic scene surrounding them. The trees quickly became dots. The wooden structures, train rails, and dirt roads marking the soon-to-become metropolis of Dallas came into view, then quickly faded as the craft traveled upward and onward.

In this time period, they had the sky to themselves, save for the native creatures calling the sky home. Jeff and Becca both savored the moment, as they watched the ground slipping rapidly beneath them. Since they felt no motion in this inertia-less craft, it was as though the earth sped away underneath them.

Although focused on the task ahead, Jeff allowed himself a moment to enjoy the unraveling scenery below as they crossed the country at unthinkable speed. He noted how unspoiled much of the land was in this time period. Large areas of grasslands and far more trees than the time he was used to. The familiar checkerboard pattern marking cultivated fields was mostly absent, as were the ribbon lines marking highways. There were no large brown clouds hanging over the cities. Indeed, at this altitude, it was hard to spot the small nests of civilization below.

In a matter of minutes, they traversed the plains and headed toward the mountains. The mountains were breathtaking in their majestic splendor, their ragged peaks topped with white. And then, in a few more minutes, the long winding crack in the earth called the Grand Canyon came into view, its beauty unmatched in the eyes of the young travelers flying above it. Both Jeff and Becca had always wanted to go there, and now they were seeing it for the first time, from some 30,000 feet in the air while on board a flying saucer!

The view, though magnificent, was rather short-lived as they arrived at their destination in less than thirty minutes. They found themselves surrounded by desert, with no signs of civilization anywhere.

"I want to warn you again," Axel said, as they hovered over the barren land, "I have no idea how long we will have before the Zanchee find us. If I think they have detected us, I may have to activate a total psionic screen—in which case, neither Chermal nor I will be able to communicate with you. In other words, you will be on your own."

"I understand," Jeff said solemnly. "Let's do it."

With no sense of movement, the world below changed. Save for the fact there was now a highway below them, and the landscape was slightly different, it was hard to tell how much had changed when they returned to their own time. Such was the nature of the desert that they were flying over.

"Axel," Jeff said, "I can feel them. They are in that truck, there." Jeff pointed at a moving dot.

"The warhead is not with them," Axel pointed out. "It is in another truck, several miles ahead. Chermal managed to separate them by having the man in the second truck have a rather urgent call of nature." Becca smiled.

"I don't care. I must get my friends first. We still have nearly five hours to stop the bomb."

"You're taking a huge risk. If I can't—"

"I have to do it this way," Jeff said. "I have to get my friends."

Axel sighed. There was no arguing. Indeed, he couldn't be sure that Jeff's way wasn't the right way. "What do you want us to do?" Axel said.

"Take us down. I think the sight of a flying saucer might be enough to get most cars or trucks to stop, don't you?"

Becca smiled and nodded. "Even in California!"

"Okay, Chermal, when the truck comes to a stop, I need you to teleport me into the truck's cab. I'll take it from there. Becca, you stay here." A meow-like sound confirmed that Chermal would do his part.

"What?" she asked, incredulous he had left her out of his plan.

"Becca, if anything should happen to me, you will be our last hope to stop the bomb. You have to stay here."

Becca stared at her brother, but he was right. Slowly, she nodded.

"Let's go."

The TWS banked sharply, and then descended toward the desert highway, which Jeff knew to be California 127. "I think we can put on a bit of a show," Axel said. "I'll activate all the running lights. That should create quite a display."

They leveled off about one hundred feet above the ground, matching the pace of the truck moving along the highway. Gradually, they overtook the truck and moved to a position about fifty feet above the surface and about one hundred yards in front of the truck, keeping pace with its forward movement. As good luck would have it, the truck was alone on the two-lane highway.

As Jeff mentally prepared for the rescue, Becca suddenly interrupted. "Jeff, when I perceived the truck with bomb, I picked up something. There are two Arabs on that truck. Neither speak English. Yet I distinctly picked up an English phrase from them."

"What was it?"

"It'll sound strange. I kept picking up 'It's not your fault.' I don't think they are referring to someone's conscious. It means something."

"Thanks. Keep with them. I will be back shortly."

As they hoped, the truck came to a screeching stop, pulling onto the shoulder of the road. Axel held the TWS's position, directly in front of the truck. Jeff said, "Okay, Chermal, teleport me into the cab of that truck!" He got a low growl for a response. Jeff managed one last look at his sister's eyes as he winked out, but just before he teleported, the telltale claxon went off. The Zanchee had found them.

Chapter 41

To Becca, the world suddenly went black. "What happened?" she cried out.

"The Zanchee found us," Axel replied calmly. "I had to activate the psionic shield. It is our only hope."

"What about my brother?" she said, fighting to keep down the panic rising within.

"Chermal managed to teleport him on board the truck before we had to seal off. He will have to do without us for a bit," Axel replied, as he bent over the console, fingers and mind flying over the controls.

"What will you do?"

"Working on it," Axel said. Although he and Chermal knew this moment might come, he was still unsure exactly what they could do. The obvious thing would be to do a jump back in time. However, with the shields fully raised, he would be flying blind—which made it extremely difficult and dangerous to jump.

Axel worked the QUAIC. There had to be a solution.

He was running out of time.

The TWS was no match for the *Druize*. It would not take them long to penetrate his shields.

He conferred silently with Chermal. They would be risking everything, but Axel could see no other solution. Chermal radiated assurance.

"Becca," Axel said, looking up from the console. "There is only one hope we have, but it entails considerable risk."

"Tell me."

"We can try jumping back in time."

"Why is that risky? We just did it only a few moments ago."

"Because we have to do it blind. With the psionic shields fully up, we will be unable to perceive where and when exactly we are jumping. We can't locate the PRP—a physical reference point. Without a PRP as a guide, we will have no idea what will be occupying this space at the time we are going to. We could as easily materialize in the middle of the sun or another planet."

"Isn't space mostly, you know, space? That is, isn't it a vacuum? I think the odds are rather small of our hitting something."

"True, space is mostly a vacuum. But unless we jump more than a few hundred years, we will still be inside this solar system. And there are lots of things here that are dangerous, besides planets. Asteroids, planets, comets, and meteors, but also the micrometeors that are much more plentiful. Should we materialize where even a tiny speck is located, it may be traveling at tens of thousands of miles per hour relative to us. The outside of the ship is built to withstand such a collision, but if we should be so unfortunate as to materialize with one *inside* the TWS, well…it won't be very pretty."

Becca stared in the direction she knew her brother to be. "I'm willing," she said, "to take that risk, if it means saving my brother."

Axel nodded. With one last look at Chermal, he activated the control.

Chapter 42

Stanton glanced at his watch, now reading 11:53 a.m. He had barely over an hour to find Raheim and disarm the bomb. He picked his binoculars back up and refocused on the Gulfstream jet parked at the edge of the runway. His hand rested on a two-way radio connecting him with a dozen other agents concealed about the small airport.

A quick inspection of airport records revealed the Gulfstream was the most likely candidate for Raheim's escape. It was a corporate jet owned by THD, Inc., an automotive parts manufacturer that happened to be owned by a mid-east oil conglomerate. Doug waited. Raheim was cutting it pretty close. However, the Gulfstream's engines were running, ready to leave on a moment's notice.

Doug's patience was rewarded a short time later as a black BMW pulled up next to the plane. Doug zoomed in as a passenger got out from the back seat. It was Raheim.

"GO, GO, GO!" Doug shouted into the radio as he slammed his own car into gear. Four other cars screeched simultaneously, coming at the Gulfstream

362

from all directions. A police helicopter lurking at treetop level out of sight from the runway suddenly roared overhead. It parked itself in front of the Gulfstream, effectively cutting it off from the runway.

Raheim, to his credit, never panicked. Neither he, nor his apparent bodyguard, even drew a weapon. He merely waited for Stanton to rush up, gun drawn, and grab him.

"Where is it? Where is it?" Doug shouted at him.

Raheim merely smiled. "Make peace with your God. We are all dead men, my friend. It is too late."

"You really want to go out like this?"

"It is Allah's way."

"I can't believe Allah wants you to cremate a million innocent lives."

"They are non-believers, in the land of Satan."

Doug couldn't take it. He pressed the muzzle of his service revolver hard underneath the chin of his adversary.

"I won't give you the satisfaction of going up in a blaze of glory," Doug snarled. "You'll go out now, unless you tell me where it is!"

"It does not matter, my friend," Raheim said. "We are all walking corpses. I die knowing you will join me soon enough. It is Allah's will."

Doug started to squeeze the trigger. He stared into Raheim's cold eyes. There was no fear in them. Nor would there be any satisfaction gained in terminating his life an hour prematurely. Instead, he lowered his pistol, took Raheim roughly by the arm, and shoved him in the direction of the waiting agents, who quickly handcuffed him and whisked him off. He would be thoroughly interrogated by the Bureau's best. But could they learn anything in time?

Raheim's presence at the airport confirmed the bomb was somewhere nearby. Every law enforcement agent within a fifteen-minute radius was being called in to help with the search. Air Force planes and helicopters flew overhead, equipped with the latest military surveillance gear, hoping to find the one truck out of thousands that contained pure death. But would it be enough? Could they possibly find the weapon in time? And if they did, would there be enough time to disarm it?

The nation's best nuclear arms specialists, who had been on standby at Edwards, were now being flown here. If there was a way to disarm it, they would find a way, he told himself. If they had enough time.

Doug looked around at the airfield. He couldn't simply stand around waiting for the inevitable. He got back into the car. He would find the damn warhead himself.

Chapter 43

When Axel lowered the psionic shield, he discovered he was in the last place he wanted to be. But there was no doubt. They were on the *Druize*. He had been returned to where he had left some eight weeks ago, or was it a few moments?

The next biggest shock was who was there to greet them. Axel should not have been surprised. After all, who else could it be? But it was still surprising, and totally deflating, to see his father there standing patiently at the berth's side, awaiting his son's descent.

Axel looked over at Becca. How do you tell someone their beloved brother was doomed to die? Along with a billion or so other human beings.

"Becca, I'm so sorry…" he began.

"What's happening?" she asked, a look of fear on her face. "Where are we?"

"The Zanchee took control of the TWS. We are now on board the *Druize*, our flagship."

"My brother?"

"I'm sorry," Axel said sincerely.

"We can't just leave him!" she cried out. "We have to do something!"

365

Axel swallowed what was in his throat. "We have but one chance. I must convince my father," he said with renewed determination. Chermal purred his reassurances to them both. Axel took a deep breath. He could only imagine his father's fury. Axel opened the portal and stepped out. He was followed by his furry companion and a rather frightened, but wide-eyed young human.

****

Somewhat to Axel's surprise, he survived the descent from the TWS to the berth deck below. Nor did his father instantly kill him with his bare hands when he stepped down next to him. Instead, Axel was greeted with a strange look from his father he could not quite decipher. Nor could he get a hint of his father's feelings, as his mental screens, always tough, were now completely impenetrable.

Axel started to confront his father, but the Thermax raised his hand, signaling this was not the time for discussion. Without saying a word, his father turned and walked away. Axel, Chermal, and Becca followed. The silence was killing Axel. He would rather have the explosion over and done with. Surprising to him was his father allowing the human girl to come with them. What was happening?

Axel began trying to rehearse what he would say. The words "I'm sorry" came up but were immediately dismissed. He was not sorry. He did what he thought was right, what was *sen*, even if it might be considered wrong in his father's eyes or those of the Zanchee council. The only things Axel was sorry about were that he wasn't able to finish, and his father could not see the wrongness in letting a billion or more humans perish needlessly. Axel found himself getting more and more angry as his old feelings welled up inside. How dare his father stop him!

Axel's father stopped at a doorway leading into a small deserted lounge. He motioned the three of them inside.

\*\*\*\*

Becca was still trying to get over the shock of everything that had happened. Among the shocks was the physical presence of Axel's father. Here he was, the leader of the Zanchee, making him undoubtedly the most powerful being in the solar system. Yet Becca was as tall as he was. It was a hard fact to get used to.

Becca could not wait any more. The novelty and significance of finding herself onboard an actual alien mothership orbiting 10,000 miles above the Earth was nothing compared to her concern about her brother. "You've got to save him!" she cried out to Axel's father.

Axel's father turned to her and looked at her with an expression conveying complete authority mixed with deep sympathy. "I'm sorry, but we cannot do anything to interfere," he told her.

"At least, let me warn him! He needs to know that we cannot be there to help."

"It is against our laws for us to contact him. Besides, I'm certain he has figured that part out by now."

Becca turned to Axel. "Didn't you say that your laws only applied to, I believe the term is, 'Nescrot'?"

Axel nodded.

Becca turned again to his father. "But my brother is only seventeen! He's still a nescreet. You've got to let me telep him!"

Axel's father motioned for her to sit down. Reluctantly, she did.

"The measure of a nescrot, of being an adult, is more than simply days marked on a calendar," Axel's father began once they settled down. His "voice" was gentle and compassionate, again surprising Becca. "It is more than the physiological changes one's body goes through or when societal laws may arbitrarily accord certain privileges upon reaching a certain age. It is about maturity and how one carries oneself. It is about making the right choices," he said, looking first at Becca, then at his own son. "It is about having the courage of conviction, of pursuing your goals through adversity.

"Becca, by both human and Zanchee standards, your brother is no longer a nescreet. He is an adult. He *is* nescrot."

Becca sat stunned. A thousand emotions came to her mind—anger mixed with pride, sadness with love. She glanced over at Axel, who looked just as stunned. She could sense the turmoil welling within him. Then she recognized a truth hidden within the message Axel's father delivered. There was still hope. It was all up to Jeff.

****

Axel was shocked at his father's reaction. Where was the anger? Instead, his father radiated compassion.

He looked over at Becca, as if expecting to see her devastated at the news that they could not help her brother. Axel, himself, was extremely upset, and it showed. But when he saw Becca, he was completely amazed. "It's okay," the woman-child said. "You did your best. Have faith in your pupil."

Axel managed a half-grin at her. These human nescreets were amazing.

Chapter 44

*September 16th, D Minus 4.092 Hours*
*California Desert*

Jeff found himself in a truck's cab, sitting next to a middle easterner about thirty years old. The man, with a lengthy heavy black beard, stared out the windshield, with his mouth slightly open. A submachine gun lay on the bench between them.

Jeff quickly picked up the gun before the man realized there was someone in the cab with him. Out of the corner of his eye, Jeff saw the TWS disappear. He blocked the implications from his mind, focusing on what he had to do.

Jeff had never handled a submachine gun before. He had no idea where the safety was. No matter. He didn't plan to use the weapon. He simply needed to convince the terrorist he could and would kill him with it, if he didn't cooperate.

Jeff got the man's attention by pressing the cold steel of the barrel against the terrorist's temple, while projecting his fierceness and determination psychically. The man, already shaken by the sight of the flying saucer, nearly jumped straight out of his seat. Only the seat belt kept him grounded. The sight might have been humorous, if the situation had not been so serious.

The terrorist immediately started spewing a stream of words Jeff could only guess were Arabic. Although he could not understand a word of what he was hearing, he picked up a few images the terrorist was rather loudly, albeit unconsciously, projecting. Some of these images would not make a censor's cut for a PG-13 or even an R movie.

Jeff motioned for the man to get out of the truck, reinforcing his motions with a mental picture he broadcast. He also continued to project fear, reinforcing the terrorist's own heart-felt fright from seeing a UFO, followed by having a gun put to his head.

Fortunately, the man obeyed. He opened his door, then, with his hands raised over his head, he descended from the truck. Jeff followed, keeping the gun trained on the man. Once they were both on the ground, Jeff motioned for him to go around the truck and lay flat on the grass, keeping his hands over his head. He complied.

Keeping one eye on the terrorist, who, Jeff was confident, would not move given his current state of shock, Jeff moved to the back of the truck. Jeff's good luck held, as there was no other traffic on the road.

"Hey, guys, you in there?" Jeff yelled, as he knocked on the back door.

"*Jeff!*" came the startled cry from inside. "Is that really you?"

"It's me," Jeff declared. "I'll have you out in a moment. Stand by. Sorry I'm a few minutes late."

Jeff looked down at the rather impressive padlock keeping his friends prisoner. Grabbing it with his free hand, he formed an image of it being unlocked in his mind. He let the image float about until it became real to him. Then, with a flick of his wrist, he opened the lock.

As soon as he opened the door, Tess jumped out and wrapped herself around him tightly, like a python squeezing its prey. "Oh Jeff, Jeff," she said through sobs, "I was so scared." Then she planted a kiss on him that literally sucked the wind from his lungs.

Greg and Ashanti waited a few moments, and then hugged Jeff thoroughly. They were careful to avoid the gun Jeff still held. Steve Michaels was the last one out of the truck, his eyes like doughnuts, wide in a combination of shock, relief, and absolute amazement at the sight of his former prey. Jeff gave him a half-smile and a nod of acknowledgment. He could only imagine what Steve might be thinking. Well, he could probably find out, but that was not the way he was taught.

Greg was the first to steer the group back to reality. "So, what do we do now?" he asked.

Jeff wasn't sure. It was at this point the cavalry, in the form of Axel, Chermal, and Becca, were supposed to arrive and whisk them away. But they were nowhere in sight. Worse, despite Jeff's best efforts, he couldn't telep any of them. That likely meant they were forced to raise the psionic shield. It also meant that for the moment, he and his rescued friends were on their own.

If Axel was forced to leave, the alien teen could always "time it" so he would arrive back close to the time he had left. The fact he hadn't done so meant it must be too dangerous for him to do it now...or he couldn't. Jeff did not want to consider the second possibility for too long. But one thing was clear—right now, it was up to him and his friends to stop that warhead.

"We've got to get to San Bernardino," Jeff said. "We have to stop them."

"Stop who?" Ashanti asked.

"We have to stop the terrorists. They are planning something horrendous, and it's up to us to prevent it from happening."

"How do you plan on getting us there?" Tess asked, as she finally started to loosen her grip on him.

"We could flag down a car," Greg said, starting to head toward the freeway.

"*No!*" Jeff shouted, stopping him in his tracks. "That's too risky. They will more likely drop us off at the first police station they come to. And we could never convince the police in time."

"So, what then?" Greg said.

"We take the truck," Jeff said.

"Can you drive it?" Tess asked hopefully.

Greg headed toward the cab and peeked in the window. "It's a manual transmission. I don't know about you, but I've never driven a stick."

"Neither have I," Jeff admitted. "But we've got to try."

Sometimes help comes from the least expected places. "I'll drive," came the voice that once sent shivers of fear through Jeff's heart. "I know how to drive a stick. My Miata has manual transmission," Steve said.

Jeff looked at him with questioning eyes. There was nothing but sincerity. "You sure you can drive this thing?" Jeff asked.

Steve nodded.

Tess, meanwhile, was staring at Jeff. Something

else had changed about her boyfriend. Suddenly realizing what it was, she blurted out, "Jeff, your glasses! Where are they?"

Jeff had forgotten the last time they saw him he wore those thick glasses. "I, uh, don't need them anymore. I'll explain later."

"What about him?" asked Tess, pointing to the terrorist who was still cowering on the ground.

"We put him in the back of the truck," Jeff said. "If it was good enough for you, it must be good enough for him." And with that, he went over to collect his prisoner and herd him into the back of the truck. With a click, the padlock snapped back into place.

"Okay, you guys try to catch a ride into the next town. Steve and I will take care of the bad guys."

"Oh, no, you don't!" Tess said. "You're not going anywhere without us."

"It's too dangerous," Jeff argued. "Besides, there isn't enough room."

"You're going to abandon us in the middle of the desert?" Tess said. "I don't think so." Then she went to the cab and opened the door, motioning for Greg and Ashanti to get in.

"Where will you sit?" Jeff asked.

"On your lap," Tess replied.

Jeff smiled. He was beaten, and sometimes there were benefits to losing. He climbed in.

****

What pleasure Jeff might have had from having Tess on his lap was tempered by there being five bodies in a small cab without air-conditioning in the middle of the desert. It got worse when they discovered Steve's driving skills were not exactly perfected. Apparently, there was a big difference between driving the minuscule Miata and this large truck. As Steve eased off the clutch, the truck lurched forward about five yards, then stopped dead. It had stalled.

"I guess I'm a little rusty," Steve admitted. After another lurch and stop, Steve admitted this transmission was a lot different than what he was used to. "Maybe this isn't first gear after all…I'll try this."

On the fourth attempt, the truck continued moving forward. There was a sickening grind as Steve managed to shift the truck into second gear. As the engine revved higher, he shifted to third. With each shifting of gears, Steve gained more confidence. Gradually, they picked up speed. "Where to?" Steve asked.

"We need to get to San Bernardino," Jeff replied. "I think we stay on this highway until it intersects Interstate 15. But it's a ways up there. And don't be light of foot. I'll make sure the police don't bother us."

Steve didn't bother to ask how he could do that. He wasn't sure he wanted to know.

This stretch of the road was mostly deserted. Otherwise, they were at great risk of hitting something or someone, as the truck weaved from one side of the road to the other. Jeff hoped that Steve got the hang of it by the time they reached the Interstate.

Chapter 45

*Los Angeles Area*

Time was running out as Stanton made his way down the Interstate, staring into every truck's cab he passed. Despite all their efforts, they had nothing.

Raheim would not talk. Krenchenko and Bivardo were still at large.

He thought they may have had a lead when they found that Raheim's cellphone revealed he made a call within the past forty-five minutes. But, somehow, he managed to route the call through a foreign server. The number did not show up in the phone's registry. NSA would eventually track down the number called, which was probably another cellphone. They might even determine which cell tower the call was routed through to reach the destination cellphone. But because of the foreign server, it would take time. And time was one thing none of them had in abundance.

Doug did not know what led him to drive down I-15, other than sheer desperation, the desire to be doing *something*. He could not accept the fact that in less than twenty minutes, he would likely be no more than a memory—if there was anyone left to remember him, that is.

There was a truck stop at the next exit. It was his last hope. The warhead had to be in a truck. Why he knew, he wasn't sure. It may have been reasoning or intuition, but in any event, Doug was certain it was in a truck. It was also likely the truck would be parked, to reduce the risk of an accident or other unforeseen circumstance. To further minimize detection, it was likely parked in an open space, surrounded by several other trucks, so as not to standout or arouse suspicion. And it would have to be somewhere near the San Andreas fault. This truck stop would be a good choice.

As he pulled off the interstate onto the exit, he noted the sign over the truck stop—"It's Your Fault Gas & Grill." The actual fault line could be seen from the incline where the truck stop was located.

It was a popular truck stop. There were nearly twenty rigs parked either at the pumps or in the truck stalls surrounding the restaurant. Indeed, the trucks outnumbered the cars.

Doug looked at his watch. Eleven minutes. Where was the truck? Which one?

Doug hastily drove down through the parking area, narrowly missing a hacked-off driver making his way to lunch. Doug ignored the international gesture he received for his driving acumen.

Doug wasn't sure what he would do should he find the truck. He wasn't a bomb expert, and certainly not a nuclear expert. And there would be no time to call them in. Well, he would simply have to cross that bridge when he came to it.

Halfway down the row, one rig caught his attention. The truck and trailer appeared to be freshly painted. Yet, they were both covered with dirt and sand, as though they had just made a long trek through the desert.

Slamming the car into park, Doug jumped from his car with his pistol high in the air, grasping it firmly with both hands. This was it. He was certain.

Despite all his years of training, he was so focused on his one target he completely missed the second truck.

Chapter 46

*September 16<sup>th</sup>, D minus 0.14 Hours*
*Los Angeles*

Tom Michaels fidgeted nervously in his seat,
staring at the computer screen in front of him. The air
conditioner hummed loudly, straining to keep the
interior of the semi-trailer cool, difficult given the
presence of several heat-generating computers, not to
mention twelve well-armed and perspiring men. Even
with the extra shock absorbers added to try to smooth
out the ride, it was still rather bumpy as the truck
continued moving in a rather random pattern along the
city streets of LA.

On the screen in front of him was a map of Central
Los Angeles, showing a five-mile radius. A blinking
blue light, moving slowly across the monitor, indicated
their position. Red lights dotted the screen, showing the
location of every LA patrol car within the region. Ten
green dots revealed the location of Bivardo's men. The
size of the green dot told Tom whether it was a car, a
van, or a truck. Some of the dots were stationary, others
were moving slowly. There was enough firepower in
those ten dots to start a minor war, including one truck
with a Russian ground-to-ground missile launcher.

Sitting next to Tom were two other computer-savvy men from Bivardo's organization, who sat in front of similar consoles. Each screen showed a different part of town. Mark, who was sitting to Tom's right, had a display of the Marina del Ray area, complete with eight green dots. Calvin, to Tom's left, had an area around Beverly Hills on his screen, with six green dots. Two of the dots were within a block of 10 Damion Way, the address of one Frank Disenzio, head of the LA Mafia, and the man Bivardo believed had turned on him, providing the government with enough evidence to allow them to freeze nearly half of Bivardo's assets. He was also the same man who owned the massive yacht just arriving at Marina del Ray, supposedly full of over $100 million worth of drugs it recently picked up following an offshore rendezvous. It was Bivardo's plan to hurt Disenzio where it hurt him the most. First, they would take the drug shipment and sink his precious yacht, then blow up his home, killing him and his family.

Tom was not happy with the situation. He wanted no part in the cold-blooded murder of Disenzio's family, no matter what Bivardo's motivation might be. He hated more the attack on the Federal Reserve. Even though they might have the firepower to pull off the biggest bank heist in US history, it would cost a lot of lives. Tom did not like killing, even though he dealt with a different kind of death in his business. His victims died from choices they made. But this was different. Besides, the Government would not sit still on this one. Somehow, they would track them down. And he wasn't convinced Bivardo's goal was to take the money. He would get as much satisfaction from destroying it, which wouldn't do Tom any good. This was way out of their league.

Making it worse was that Bivardo was losing it more and more as the day progressed. He made a phone call about ten minutes after midnight. Apparently, he didn't like the news, as he shot one of his aides because he accidentally spilled some coffee on him. He then had them monitor the news on all the stations. His mood worsened as the story he was apparently expecting wasn't forthcoming...nor were his numerous phone calls being answered.

Tom looked at his watch, which now said it was nearly one p.m. The big diversion should be about to occur, whatever it was. Obviously Bivardo, who Tom last saw standing in the middle of the control center/trailer, pacing back and forth, was very concerned it would not happen. With the day's earlier incident fresh on everyone's mind, they all gave Bivardo as wide a berth as possible in the confines of the trailer.

Hearing murmurings, Tom stole a glance back to check on Bivardo, who was now consulting with Martinez and a couple other people Tom did not know. Bivardo's part in the conversation was mostly contributing expletives. Bivardo took a phone from his pocket and punched in some numbers. Whomever he was trying to call, however, apparently still wasn't answering. That did not improve Rico's mood. The phone was sent crashing down to the floor, breaking apart into several pieces.

"What do we do if nothing happens?" Martinez asked. "Without that 'distraction' you promised, things could get messy."

"We need another distraction!" Bivardo said.

"Something big." Bivardo walked over to where Tom was seated. "Let me see the map…Hmm, what's that building over there?" he asked.

"That's City of Hope Hospital," Tom said, checking the reference.

"Perfect," he said, then he turned to Martinez. "Have your boys in the missile truck drive over there and launch a few rockets into that hospital. I want lots of bodies!"

No one moved. Bivardo pulled out his pistol, "I said, call the truck."

"Okay, boss."

"God help them," Tom said softly to himself. "God help us all."

"Boss!" shouted Juan, who was in charge of monitoring police and other law enforcement. "I'm picking something on the police scanners! There's been a bomb threat at the Federal Reserve Bank."

"What!"

"They're calling for lots of back-up. They plan on evacuating an entire city block." As he spoke, the red dots all started moving toward the center of Tom's screen. Dozens more came into view.

"Rico, it will be suicide now. We won't be able to get near that building. We must wait for another day," Martinez said, trying to calm the man who looked ready to shoot everyone on the truck.

Rico Bivardo's veins popped out from his neck as he struggled to keep control. He wasn't quite ready to concede. "What of the other two operations?"

"They are awaiting your order."

"Tell them to proceed." He closed his eyes, then said tightly, "Tell the others to head to our rendezvous point. We will make new plans."

Tom heaved a big sigh of relief as he turned his attention once more to the display in front of him.

Chapter 47

*September 16<sup>th</sup>, D Minus 0.132 Hours*
*Los Angeles Area*

Jeff followed his "instinct." Axel and Chermal had not determined exactly where the epicenter of the explosion was or would be, but based on what they did know, he was very close to where it must have been, or rather where it might be.

Becca's comment flashed in his mind when the sign for "It's Your Fault Gas & Grill" appeared. This was it. The bomb was here.

Steve, to his great credit, did well driving, despite his rushed on-the-job training. Although there had been an inordinate number of police cars patrolling the interstate looking for a truck and they were clearly traveling well in excess of the speed limit, they were never stopped. Steve had wanted to slow down, but Jeff told Steve to continue no matter what. Fortunately, he *convinced* the highway patrol they were not worth stopping. They were, effectively, invisible.

When they pulled into the truck stop, Greg called out, "There it is!" as he recognized the semi that had been parked in front of the Quonset hut earlier that morning.

Jeff reached with his mind to examine the truck. It

was the one. Inside was what had to be the nuclear warhead. It was partially enclosed in a crate filled with foam, but the upper part of the bomb was fully exposed. A timing mechanism attached toward the front of the crate was ticking away. Two terrorists guarded the weapon, currently kneeling in prayer, with their foreheads touching the floor of the trailer. One of the men held a simple button, which the man kept pressed tightly. This was likely a "dead-man's switch"—if the pressure came off the button, it would instantly trigger the nuclear device. The other man held a machine gun aimed at the door of the trailer.

Then Jeff noted something else. They were not alone in their pursuit of this truck. A blue Ford Taurus had pulled into the parking lot. He perceived instantly who it was and why he was there. Jeff forced himself to calm down and think. There had to be some way of disarming that warhead!

If he somehow could get inside the truck and physically touch the device, he was confident he could figure out how to disarm it. But how to get in? And now he had another problem, as the FBI agent stopped his car a few yards away. His presence would make it extremely difficult for Jeff to simply walk over to the truck. He would never permit Jeff getting close. What's worse, the agent had no way of knowing about the dead man's switch. In his attempt to stop the terrorists, he might cause the bomb to go off prematurely.

"*If only Axel or Chermal were here!*" he lamented. Once again, he tried reaching out to them, but there was no reply. He was on his own.

He had to get into that trailer. But how? He could go into hypertime, but he couldn't maintain hypertime for very long. The effort spent getting to the truck and inside will waste precious time he will need once inside to disarm the bomb—especially since he had no idea how to accomplish that task. Teleporting was the best way into the truck, but Jeff had never teleported himself, or any living creature, for that matter. He simply wasn't powerful enough or had enough training. That was level four stuff.

As though his subconscious was trying to speak to him, Jeff became aware of the warmth of the gramirl pressing against his chest. The solution suddenly flashed in his brain. The gramirl!

He remembered when he and Becca were given the strange crystals. Axel seemingly waved his hand over them and pronounced they were now at partial strength. How could he make it full strength?

The answer must lie within the crystal itself. Reaching out with his mind, he gently caressed the surface of the crystal. The tremendous power lying within its miraculous structure tingled his fingers. Gradually, Jeff immersed himself in the ebbs and flows of energy within the crystal. He became one with it. He craved more.

The crystal pulsed. It was as though it had its own heartbeat. Jeff concentrated on that heartbeat. He made it his own. The heartbeat was slow, as though at rest. Gradually, Jeff accelerated the beat, faster and faster. He had to wake it up. It was time to move. It beat faster.

When Jeff opened his eyes, a surging flow of an energy he could not have imagined in his wildest dreams filled him. The gramirl glowed much brighter now, with the swirling pattern once again visible. It was very warm, almost hot, against his skin. He was ready.

Fifteen seconds had passed.

"Guys," Jeff said, breaking the tense silence. "I need your help."

"What do you need us to do?" Greg asked.

"There's an FBI agent, I believe his name is Doug Stanton, in that blue Ford Taurus. You cannot allow him to open that truck door. There is a booby trap he doesn't know about. He will set it off."

"What about you?" Tess asked.

"I'll be inside that truck," he said, pointing to the truck holding the nuclear weapon. "I'll signal when it's safe for you and the FBI man to come in." Before anyone could ask another question, like how they were to stop the FBI man, or how Jeff planned to get inside the truck, or what the signal would be, Jeff disappeared. Literally.

**** 

One moment, Tess was sitting on Jeff's lap in the stifling hot cramped cab of a smelly truck, the next moment, she plopped down with a thump on the seat bench. Her fleshy cushion vanished.

No one panicked. They couldn't. And Tess could still "feel" Jeff's presence. From the look on his face, so could Greg. Jeff was still there, only, somehow now inside the deadly semi-trailer.

At the same moment, the FBI man got out of the Ford, with his gun drawn. They had to act quickly. There was no time to ponder their friend's sudden disappearance.

Grabbing the door handle, Greg flung the door open so fast it banged loudly against the side of the truck. Jumping down onto the pavement, he ran toward the agent, waving his arms. Tess, Ashanti, and Steve followed close behind.

"Agent Stanton! Agent Stanton!" they shouted in unison.

Startled, the agent twirled around, leveling the pistol directly at Greg, who abruptly came to a halt, hands high in the air.

"Don't shoot!" Greg shouted. "The truck is booby-trapped!"

\*\*\*\*

Stanton stared at the teens. He looked a little foolish holding four kids at gunpoint. But this was no time to worry about appearances. The stakes were too high.

"You've got to believe me, agent! There are two terrorists inside. One of them has—" There was a slight hesitation as though the kid was being told what to say. "—a dead-man switch. He will set it off if you go in."

"How do you know this?" Stanton asked, not knowing why he bothered to ask. The only reason he hesitated was they had shouted his name. How the hell did they know who he is? But there were only a few minutes left…

"Please, you've got to believe me. My friend's inside. He says he'll tell us when it's safe."

Doug slowly lowered his gun. There was something familiar about these kids.

"Yes," the kid continued, "you do recognize us. We're the kids who have been missing from Dallas. The fifth one, his name is Jeff, is inside that truck." He waved toward the semi. Then he waved at the back of the truck they had arrived in. "Another terrorist is locked in the back of that truck."

"I don't have time for this!" Doug said, as he

turned and headed for the truck.

"Wait!" Greg shouted. "Look, I know you believe in psychic stuff. That's why they call you Mulder! My friend, he's a very powerful psychic. You've got to believe me!"

That stopped him in his tracks. How the hell did these kids know his nickname? What was going on here?

"Agent Stanton," spoke one of the girls. "Trust your instincts. You've got to trust your instincts."

He did. But it did not stop him from praying.

****

The cool air inside the refrigerated trailer was invigorating if not surprising as Jeff found himself staring at the warhead. It was hard to believe something a little larger than a coffin could mean the deaths of so many.

There were three external boxes attached to the device. This likely meant there were multiple triggers. One was obviously connected to a timer whose red letters indicated 00:04:20.25. Another was rigged to a receiver, which Jeff guessed was probably attached to the dead man's switch the terrorist lying to his right had in his hand. It might also mean it could possibly be triggered by someone outside the truck. Jeff had no idea about the third.

Jeff thought briefly about simply taking away the button from the terrorist but that would do little good. The warhead would still explode in a little over four minutes, assuming Jeff could keep the button pressed until then. Agent Stanton likely did not know how to disarm the weapon either. Nor was there time to call in an expert. No, it was up to him, and him alone.

Jeff couldn't stay indefinitely in hypertime. His physical body simply would not allow it. In real time or hypertime, he had precious few minutes to discern a solution.

As soon as he came out of hypertime the terrorists would quickly become aware of his presence. Whether they shot him, or simply released the button, the results would be the same.

Jeff turned his attention back to the warhead. OK, how to disarm it? Memories from a thousand bad flicks flashed through his mind of the hero having to pick a wire to disconnect. Pick the wrong one, and they're dead. They always managed to pick the right one. However, they usually only had two to pick from. But there were literally dozens of wires weaving about the warhead. And movies always followed a script. Jeff did not see one conveniently lying about.

Think! Think! Should he simply trust his gut and pick a wire to cut? But there were three boxes, which meant at least three trigger wires. What if it were rigged so that if any one of the devices were disabled, the others were automatically activated? Jeff had never seen that in the movies before. And he was no bomb expert. He had never previously even seen a bomb, except for in those same bad movies.

His body was beginning to give way. He would be forced to come out of hypertime momentarily.

Think! Where do the wires lead? But why does it have to be a wire? Axel told him this was a hydrogen bomb. Jeff recalled reading a hydrogen bomb worked by having a small explosion trigger the nuclear fission reaction. That meant there had to be a smaller explosion first. Maybe that's where the wires led. They set off the smaller explosion. The explosives enshrouded the container with the plutonium. But if there was nothing to explode…

The world around him started to change as motion became more apparent. The red letters glowed 00:04:20.24 then the last two decimals began to blur. Jeff had to act *now*.

\*\*\*\*

Doug held his hand on the latch to the trailer door. He did not know what signal he was supposed to get. He wasn't convinced there would be a signal. But somehow, he believed those kids. It would be like Raheim to have the bomb rigged with a dead-man's switch, complete with two soon-to-be-dead men to operate it. So, he waited.

\*\*\*\*

Tess was kept a tenuous contact with Jeff's mind. She did not want to distract him, but she had to know if he was okay. But suddenly the connection was lost. He was in trouble. He needed help. She screamed.

\*\*\*\*

Jeff could not worry about the two Arabs who were still prostrate on the floor. He had to find the explosive device, and somehow disable it. He focused all his attention on the bomb, tracing the wires down. He hoped he recognized what he was looking for when he found it.

Jeff's concentration was complete. He did not see the terrorist on his left look up. He did not hear the rush of Arabic that followed the terrorist's discovery of his presence. All he knew was he found the device.

\*\*\*\*

Doug took the scream to be his signal. Gun drawn,

he quickly lifted the latch, and flung open the door.

Immediately inside were two terrorists, one of them looking at a juvenile who had his back to them. In front of the juvenile was the bomb. One terrorist had a gun aimed directly at the kid. It fired.

Doug did not hesitate, firing a single shot and striking the terrorist on the shoulder of his shooting arm. It was enough to cause the gun to go rattling to the floor. The second terrorist, seeing what was happening, simply looked up and smiled. Then he released the button.

\*\*\*\*

On board the TWS, Becca watched the scene in horror as the Thermax had provided a 3D viewer for this purpose. On her lap, Chermal sought to give her physical warmth and psychological comfort. When the gun fired, Becca absently nearly squeezed the poor thing back into fourth dimensional space.

\*\*\*\*

Doug had faced death dozens of times in his career. He came across hundreds of fanatics. But he would never forget the expression on the terrorist's face as he released the button. The look was almost of pure joy, of one who was about to face his God. The indelible image was surpassed only by the expression of absolute shock replacing it when nothing happened.

Doug did not know how the kid survived. The gun had been aimed squarely at him, and the shooter was only a few feet away. But there he was, unharmed, grinning from ear to ear. In his hands, he held death. Death not coming today. Although he was far from being a nuclear bomb expert, the kid held what could only be the explosive trigger used to detonate the warhead. How on earth he had it in his hands, Doug could not begin to guess. Especially since there was no sign of any tools, or anything being taken apart.

The other kids rushed to the open door. One of them, the largest one, held a submachine gun. Faced with long odds, the two terrorists, who were in apparent shock over the events of the past few moments, gave Doug little resistance as he got them to roll over on their backs, with their hands behind them. Doug quickly zip-tied their hands, then frisked them to make sure they had no other surprises.

****

Tess clambered into the truck as quickly as she could and rushed over to Jeff, throwing her arms around him. She then proceeded to give him another, rather thorough kiss. Not knowing what to do, he simply stood there. He returned the kiss while still grinning, still holding the dynamite trigger in his right hand.

****

Greg was the first to notice the readout still ticking. It showed 0:24, then 0:23, then 0:22. No one breathed as the digits clicked down. Jeff tightened his hold on Tess. The clock ticked on—0:15, 0:14. No one said anything. Jeff did not need to be in hypertime for the seconds to stretch to eternity. All watched, all prayed. The two terrorists on the floor spoke in soft, reverent voices. He could only guess that they were saying their own prayers in Arabic. 0:12, 0:11. Greg looked over at the FBI agent, who still stood rigid over the two terrorists. He held his pistol with both hands, pointing at one then the other, making sure they did not move. 0:09, 0:08. What if Jeff had made a mistake? What if there were a second explosive device? 0:05, 0:04. Greg held Ashanti close to him. Both prayed they would have more time. 0:02, 0:01. The moment of truth.

The clock read 00:00:00:00.

Everyone let out their collective breaths. The display went dark.

"Well," Greg said, hoping to relieve the tremendous tension he and the others were feeling, "that was exciting." He was rewarded with nervous laughter as they all gradually regained use of their pulmonary equipment.

In the distant background, several sirens sounded. That was when Steve Michaels surprised his peers once again.

****

Doug Stanton hadn't realized he had stopped breathing, until he started breathing again. He had been holding it for quite a while as the red numerals counted down.

"Agent Stanton." Hearing his name called brought Doug out of his temporary trance. "Agent Stanton," the voice called again.

Without taking his eyes completely off the two terrorists on the floor in front of him, Doug turned his head slightly toward the source of the voice. It was the big kid, the one holding the Uzi. Christ, he had completely forgotten about the Uzi!

But before he could do anything, the kid lay the machine gun down on the ground, as though knowing what Doug must be thinking. "Agent Stanton," the kid repeated.

"Yes," Doug replied, not knowing what else to say.

"You've got to help him!"

Doug's mind was racing, still trying to make some

sense from had just happened. Who was the kid talking about? The terrorist he shot? Yeah, he was wounded, but it wasn't serious. And why would this kid care? The bum had been about to kill them all, along with a few million other innocent people.

"Promise me, you'll try to help him. You've got to do something!" The big kid was in tears. Doug was in confusion.

"My brother!" the teen cried out, apparently sensing Doug's confusion. "You must save him. He will get them all killed."

"Who, son? Tell me who." The sirens drew closer. They were responding to his last call. He noted his phone was ringing. He had no idea how long it had been doing so.

"My brother, Tom, Tom Michaels. He works for Victor Martinez, who works for Rico Bivardo."

The kid had Doug's attention now. "What do you know about Bivardo?"

"I know he's crazy! My brother is scared to death. Martinez knew my brother won't go through with it. That's why they held me hostage with them," he said, waving his hand toward the other four kids. In the back of Doug's mind, he remembered there being five missing kids from Dallas, but he would have sworn it had been three girls, not three boys.

"I overheard some of their plans. They were keeping us in the desert while Bivardo was having his men trained on all these weapons." The kid spoke in a rush. Doug wanted to stop him to ask about the weapons, but the kid wouldn't stop until he was through telling him what he had to tell.

"This Bivardo, he's insane! He killed five of his

own men, simply because they didn't say 'yes' quick enough. My brother says he's consumed with getting even…even with the government, and with the guy he said set him up.

"I know what they're planning," the kid went on without pause. "But you've got to promise me you'll save my brother, please! You've got to hurry."

"Okay, okay, calm down. I'll do my best. I think we owe you one," he added. After all, the kid had merely helped save the entire population of Los Angeles, including one particular FBI agent. "Take a deep breath and tell me what you know."

"Bivardo has an army of men, maybe 150. They're all in LA. I heard them mentioning something about the Federal Reserve Bank. They also talked about a large shipment coming in from overseas. I think they mean to get both. They also mentioned the name Disenzio. Tom said there will be a big diversion, one that will distract everyone—cops and Mafia alike. I couldn't imagine what that will be…but—" He nodded at the warhead "—now I know. I'm afraid of what Bivardo will do now, without the distraction. Tom is working some electronic gear they have in back of a large semi. They can track all the police cars."

The sirens were almost on top of them. Doug nodded at the kid. "I'll see what I can do," he said, pulling his still-beeping phone from his pocket with one hand, while keeping the gun aimed at the two on the ground with the other.

One of the Arabs shifted his weight, causing Doug to turn quickly back toward him.

When he looked back up for the kid, he was gone. They were all gone.

Chapter 48

Jeff materialized in the middle of a large room. In the center of the room was a being obviously of the same species as Axel, but was a little bigger, and much older, than Jeff's friend and mentor. Expanding his senses, Jeff found they were on board a spacecraft, heading off into space. The ship was a small one, not much bigger than the room they were in.

Jeff's friends looked more disoriented, having never experienced teleportation. One minute, they were next to an 18-wheeler, the next second, they were here—wherever here was. They would not see the alien as Jeff did, but instead would see the image of a human in military garb. Immediately, Jeff sent calming thoughts to his friends. He did not want them to panic.

"It's okay, guys," he said aloud, not fully knowing whether he was telling the truth. Seeing Steve appear uncertain as to whether or not to attack the alien, he put his hand on his shoulder.

"Steve, it's really okay. I'll explain it all to you later. For now, try and relax." Steve certainly had been exposed to some extremely unusual stuff in the past several hours, like his former victim showing up out of nowhere to rescue them from near-certain death, then that same person literally disappearing, only to reappear again inside a truck where he single-handedly disarmed a nuclear weapon. So, yeah. Steve would have every reason to be in shock. Jeff gave his shoulder a reassuring squeeze. "It will be fine, I assure you."

Steve remained quiet, eyes wide, mouth open like an alligator ready to swallow a pig.

"Your friend is correct," spoke the alien, looking up from his control panel. "You are in no danger. My name is Trallgnet. You are on board my ship, the *Marmiex*. I apologize for having to take you like this, but Thermax, our leader, has asked to speak with you. I've been told you will later be returned to your homes."

"What's this all about?" Greg asked. "Who *are* you? Where are we?"

"I'm sorry," Trallgnet said in a firm, but reassuring voice, "but I cannot answer any of your questions, mainly because I don't know the answers myself. I was only told to pick you up and bring you to Thermax.

"I assure you, however, that you are quite safe and will not be harmed. But I really can't tell you any more than that," he said sympathetically.

"But perhaps I can allow you to at least see where you are." With that, Trallgnet waved his hands over the controls. Immediately, two large view screens appeared in front of them, one showing a view of the earth falling fast beneath them, the other showing what appeared to be a star. But it soon became clear the object was not a star, but light reflected off a mammoth spacecraft.

The viewscreens were not real. But they were effective illusions. Trallgnet could just have easily made the entire ship transparent, but the result would have been extremely disquieting for his friends. However, all five of them had seen countless sci-fi flicks where the starships had viewscreens like what they were seeing now.

The viewscreens had the desired effect. For a moment, they forgot their fears as they became mesmerized with the spectacular scenery unfolding in front of them. Sure, they had all flown before, looking down at the earth from 35,000 feet, or about seven miles high. They had seen pictures from space. But this was different. For one thing, the picture was incredibly vivid, much more so than anything they had ever experienced before. Second, they knew it was real, and it was happening to them. And third, they were much more than seven miles high!

They simply stared, mouths agape, as towering mountains with rugged white peaks shrank into harmless mounds, then into specks. Wisps of white swirling around invisible poles contrasted against the blue ocean waters and the dark brown of land. Jeff was as taken in by the unfolding and spectacular scene as his friends.

They gasped as one when the horizon of earth came into view, revealing the round shape of their home planet painted against the black matte of space. The view triggered an enormous emotional reaction in the humans. There, spinning slowly beneath them, in a jumble of bright and beautiful colors, was humanity's home. Now, for the first time, they could appreciate just how small and insignificant that wonderful ball really was.

The globe shrank against the starry sky teeming

with billions of brilliant points of light. Pure joy and exhilaration mixed with fear and trepidation. Where were they heading? What would they be facing?

On the other screen, the tiny speck grew and grew. Other specks buzzed about the larger one, like bees around a hive. As they drew closer and closer, the sheer size of their destination became more and more amazing.

As they neared the giant craft, the object did not look like anything they would have imagined. It was not a solid structure, for one. That is, it wasn't completely solid. Instead, it appeared to be more of a latticework of tubes connecting thousands of nodules spiking out in all directions. Specks that were other alien craft darted to and fro amongst the maze of tubes, coming in and out of yawning holes appearing in some of the bigger nodes. The nodules themselves were of varying sizes and shapes. There was nothing identifiable to the five humans as an engine or a bridge. The massive structure simply floated there in space as though it had always been there.

"H-how big is that thing?" Greg asked.

Trallgnet surprised them by answering. "Using your American standards, the *Druize* is roughly an oblong cylinder, measuring two kilometers along the longest axis, with a radius of about three-tenths of a kilometer."

Greg and Jeff both whistled. Trallgnet continued as though he were a tour guide. "The reason for all the different sizes and shapes of nodules is the *Druize* is the Zanchee mothership for this quadrant. It is the 'home-away-from-home,' if you will, of over thirty different species making up the Zanchee." He then turned back to his panel. "We will be docking soon. The Thermax, himself, will be there to greet you."

The five of them just looked at each other.

Chapter 49

*September 16th, D Plus 2.942 Hours*
*Los Angeles Area*

Doug was a spectator as the giant Chinook helicopter lifted the entire rig as though it was Styrofoam. The trailer and nuclear warhead still within were being taken to nearby Edwards Air Force Base. From there, no one was saying where the final destination would be.

In addition to the Chinook, the air was filled with seemingly dozens of other helicopters. Doug counted no fewer than six TV news-copters, emblazoned with the logos of their stations. The media copters, normally relentless, were being kept at bay, not only by the giant Chinook, but by the three Air Force Blackhawks also circling the scene.

Only a few moments before the Chinook's arrival, an Air Force air-ambulance arrived to take away, in full view of the circling media, three body bags containing the terrorists. The reality was the three were victims only of tranquilizer darts, although one did have a shoulder wound, courtesy of Doug. They would be revived and treated upon reaching the base. To the media, though, they were dead, victims of one Doug Stanton, FBI agent and hero. The military was taking no chances on this one. They wanted the terrorists out of the public view while they learned everything they could. The stakes were very high. No attorneys invited.

Doug was extremely uncomfortable with the hero's mantle. He had always worked best in the background. He was particularly uncomfortable with the title, when he wasn't the one who deserved it. But the true heroes had mysteriously disappeared, for the second time. There was no doubt four of the kids were part of the Dallas Five, as they were being called.

\*\*\*\*

The spin doctors worked overtime trying to present enough truth to be believed and justify the Air Force's involvement yet made sure the real truth never got out. The orders came from the top. The very top. Washington made it clear it was of the highest national priority the public never learn there was a near-nuclear disaster. Washington was obviously worried, and rightfully so, of the tremendous public panic such news was bound to cause. And the most likely result of the public's reaction would be a complete deterioration of the already fragile relationship with Russia, the source of the nuclear warhead.

The spin-doctors had a very tough task ahead. At the top of their list was explaining why the US Air Force was so active in what normally was the domain of the FBI and other civilian authorities. Doug would soon be briefed on the cover, as it was inevitable he would be approached by the media. He was being made the sacrificial lamb by the FBI. But dealing with the news people would come later.

Doug produced a wry smile. Even though he was being hailed a hero, his fifteen minutes of fame had some very tough competition. What had been a slow news week turned into an overabundance of news items. In addition to stopping a terrorist threat, there was a major drug bust, netting over $100 million in booty plus the capture of two drug kingpins. That plus a bomb threat on the Federal Reserve Bank. Then you add the sighting of the Dallas Five...The spin doctors loved having the other stories to take away attention from the terrorists—but they had to work hard to make sure no one else made the connection all these stories were related...

Doug glanced over to the truck stop. The windows were full of curious eyes. All the people inside innocently now found themselves in the middle of a storm. They weren't going anywhere fast. No one had been allowed to leave or even go outside. A team of FBI agents was on its way to interview every single person in there, kids included. And once the FBI was done, the media would likely attack. Indeed, the first of what promised to be a large convoy of news trucks had already reached the scene but was currently being denied access to the grounds. Some of the restaurant's customers were bound to get their own fifteen minutes of fame.

As the Chinook roared off toward Edwards AFB, another Blackhawk came into view. It quickly landed in the field adjoining the truck stop parking area. Colonel Stankowski, who had been coordinating the truck's removal, walked over to Stanton as the Blackhawk settled down.

"Agent Stanton, I believe that's our ride," he said.

Doug nodded. Being debriefed was never fun. But being debriefed by military intelligence was something else altogether. Considering this involved a nuclear warhead plus the appearance of five kids, four of whom were supposedly kidnapped, and then disappeared by what could only be described as magic. His story was pretty unbelievable, even to himself. No doubt, he was in for a long, long day.

Chapter 50

Because the spacecraft they were in was totally inertia-less, there was no need for them to sit down or strap in for the landing. They felt no motion at all. There wasn't even a telltale bump as the craft settled down on its landing pad in one of the massive flight decks of the *Druize*. Trallgnet simply announced they arrived.

As he did so, a large red circle formed on the floor in the middle of the room. Trallgnet indicated the five of them were to join him in the center of the circle. They complied. Jeff tried to telep the others, to reassure them, but was surprised to find he was unable. Instinctively, he put his arm around Tess. He wasn't sure it was as much to reassure her as it was to help himself. For the first time since the adventure began, he was completely helpless. There must be some kind of psionic shield in place preventing him from using his newfound psychic abilities, but that knowledge was of little comfort. He tightened his hold on Tess. His newfound abilities were no match for the Zanchee.

As soon as the last of them entered the circle, the floor began to descend. That is, the floor contained within the circle began to drop.

As Jeff's head cleared the underside of the craft, he discovered they were in an enormous open area. There was a wall a mere one-hundred feet away, but the far walls were lost in the distance. The craft blocked his view of the roof, but he imagined it was very high indeed. He took in a deep breath. The air was clean and odorless. The *Marmiex* was in a dock of sorts, held about fifteen feet in the air, which was why the "elevator" was needed. There were many other ships similarly docked. The arrangement made sense as it maximized the surface area for work and moving things around as needed.

When the platform reached the ground, Trallgnet stepped off and beckoned them to follow. He led them to the near wall. Upon reaching it, he merely stood to one side. "Please go in," he said, gesturing to the wall.

As if on cue, an opening appeared in the wall next to where Trallgnet stood. On the other side of the opening, there was a small room. Taking a deep breath, Jeff led the group through.

As soon as he entered, he was hit by a blonde bullet that blazed its way toward him.

"Jeff!" screamed the platinum projectile, as she wrapped both arms and legs around her brother. "I was so worried about you!" she said, through tears of joy and relief.

"Becca!" Jeff managed to say aloud, as the air returned to his lungs. "I was so worried…"

"Excuse me."

Jeff turned to see his friend, Axel, standing patiently. He hated to admit he had overlooked his diminutive friend. "I'm sorry, Axel," he said. "Let me introduce you to my friends…Guys, this is Axel, who only just saved the world."

****

Greg studied every detail of each scene he experienced. He wanted to burn the images of his space flight, the view of earth, the insides of this giant spacecraft—in short, everything he witnessed—into his brain. The aliens, these Zanchee or whatever, would likely erase his memory of these events, and he did not want them to disappear. This was so lit.

He looked at his friends and knew they were all thinking the same thing. None of them could believe this was happening. Here they were on board an alien mothership, surrounded by beings from other worlds light-years away. They were all so caught up in the wonder of it no one had time to be frightened. He wanted to cherish these moments. Above all, he wanted to remember them.

Jeff finished introducing them to his friend, Axel. To Greg and the rest, Axel looked like a normal, human kid. Indeed, all the aliens Greg had seen so far appeared human, even though Jeff informed him it was an illusion, meant for the humans' comfort. It was a great illusion though.

Greg looked over at Steve Michaels, who stood off by himself. He felt a little sorry for the big goon. After all, he was here alone, and his world had been ripped apart perhaps more than the rest of them because he had been betrayed by his "employer." He also knew he was very concerned about his brother.

"Do you know why we are here?" Greg heard Jeff ask his alien friend.

"No. I'm as confused as you are. I only know it

was my father who had you brought here."

"Uh," Greg stuttered, "your race doesn't believe in executions, does it?"

"Not normally, no." Greg couldn't tell whether Axel was kidding or not.

He was surprised when Axel made his way over to Steve.

"You are Steve Michaels," Axel said matter-of-factly. Steve nodded. "I bear some news. Your brother has been taken into custody by the authorities. He is fine but will be in jail for quite some time."

Steve just stared at him, relieved but very curious. "How do you know...?"

Steve's question was interrupted by the arrival of a group of three Zanchee. At the sight of them, Axel immediately became somber and rigid. In the lead was a man who appeared to be six-foot-three or so tall, with dark hair and a handsome face, dressed in an immaculate dress uniform that looked distinctly military. Based on what Jeff had previously told him, the being was likely less than five feet tall. Greg cared not to speculate as to whether he really wore clothes or not. The only visible decoration he wore was a band that went halfway around his right wrist. The band glowed with a deep, dark blue hue. Greg glanced back at Axel, and he, too, wore a similar band, although his was duller and green. As he looked back at the group, he noted they all wore similar bands, although of differing hues.

The leader stopped about five feet in front of Steve, who was the closest of the humans to the doorway. As he did so, he looked over to Axel, who responded to the cue.

"May I present my father, Axelasome, Thermax of the Zanchee fleet," Axel said very formally.

Jeff bowed slightly, with his hands to his sides, and his eyes locked on the Zanchee leader. Greg recognized the gesture from having watched Jeff take his black belt test at his dojo. It was a sign of respect. Greg did his best to copy the gesture, as did the rest of the humans. He was surprised when Axelasome returned the Rae.

Axelasome looked from one human to another. Greg locked eyes with him but for the briefest of seconds, yet in that fleeting time, the Thermax's gaze penetrated him like a halogen beam of light piercing the darkest night, bearing right through to Greg's soul. Then he moved on.

He stared at Jeff the longest, before turning his attention to his son. The two locked gazes. To Greg, Axel stood defiant and unyielding, as though ready and willing to accept what punishment may come, knowing in his mind, in his heart, in his soul he had done what was *sen*. His father stood unmoving, intimidating, all-knowing, all-powerful.

Then without saying a word, Axel's father turned, stepped back, and walked away as one of the other Zanchee stepped forward. But, as the Thermax turned, something else seemed reflected in the face of the being who was leader of Zanchee—pride.

The Zanchee who stepped forward wore a crisp uniform similar to Axelasome's. Greg assumed he was second-in-command, or someone similar in rank. With a subtle motion, he gestured for Jeff and Axel to step forward, and then bade the other humans to gather behind Jeff and Axel. That's when the wall dissolved.

The moment when the wall separating them from

the flight deck disappeared was etched permanently in Greg's mind. Immediately in front of where the wall had been were eight Zanchee, half of them women, facing the Terrans. All eight were dressed in colorful robes that appeared to shimmer and glow. Behind them filling the flight deck were seemingly thousands of Zanchee of all different sizes, shapes, and colors. While they appeared human, Greg knew they were really of many different species. And they were all cheering.

When they first entered the room from the flight deck, there had been no steps. But now, the room had become like a stage, elevated several feet above the floor of the flight deck and the wildly cheering crowd. The eight Zanchee in robes were in front of the stage, with Jeff and Axel in the middle, and the rest of the humans, including Greg, at the back.

Greg turned to Ashanti, standing to his right. "You know," he whispered, "this is a whole lot better than Astroloids!" Ashanti gave him a look in reply he had thought only his mother capable of giving.

He then looked over at Axel, who still stood rigid. He appeared as shocked as Greg by the spectacle unfolding before them. Axel glanced off to his right, and a wisp of a smile appeared briefly on his face before it was quickly replaced by the more stoic expression he had been wearing. Greg looked off in the direction Axel had gazed and saw a woman and a little girl standing there. By Axel's reaction, they must be his mother and sister—and Axel was surprised, and happy, to see them there.

Axel's father ceremoniously stepped forward to the front of the stage. Immediately, the entire room became quiet. It was hard to believe so many people at such a large gathering could get so quiet so quickly. But they did.

Then he spoke. Well the "speaking" was an illusion. Jeff had told him none of the Zanchee "spoke" using sounds, but rather teleped. Besides, even if they did talk aloud, they certainly wouldn't use English. Nonetheless, that is exactly what he heard. It certainly was an effective illusion. The Zanchee spoke with a rich, deep voice reverberating throughout the room, adding to its regal quality.

"Fellow Zanchee," he began, "and honored humans." He turned to face the completely stunned humans. "I welcome you today for this truly momentous occasion." Cheers went up again in the crowd. Axelasome raised his hands and the room stilled.

"Today is of great personal significance to me." Greg could almost imagine a smile crossing the Thermax's face. "But today is important as well, not only to my family—" He glanced over to the woman and girl standing off to the side. "—or those gathered on the stage behind me, but to all the Zanchee in this system, and for the entire civilization below. For today we witness not only the passage of individuals from childhood to adulthood, but also the maturation of a race of sentient beings, forever changing our relationship with those whom we study." Thunderous applause erupted from the crowd. Thermax paused to wait for the cheering to diminish, although it seemed like forever before it did. Greg was stunned by what he heard. But so were Axel and his friends. Then Thermax continued.

"Today, as we celebrate their success, let us pay

homage to their trials. Facing adversity far beyond their wildest fears, those we honor found friendship. Through that kinship, they found the strength and courage to meet the mightiest of challenges, and from within, they found the character and will to prevail."

Cheers again welled up from the crowd. Greg looked over to Axel. The Delion appeared to have tears streaming down his face.

The Thermax then turned and faced the humans. "These young humans only a few days ago were busy playing children's games and worried about completing their homework for school." Greg and the girls chuckled. "But, today, they are heroes, saviors of their kind. Faced against overwhelming odds, dangers they could not possibly fathom, they refused to become discouraged, refused to give in. Defiant yet resilient. No matter the obstacle—terrible things from their nightmares, terrorist, nuclear bombs, sentient beings from another planet, amazing powers, and incomprehensible evil—they persevered. Because of their courage and determination, they not only conquered their fears, but won a second chance for their planet and their species… And, in so doing, they have taught us as well.

"When we gaze upon these humans standing before you, we see children, nescreet. As such, we tend to ignore them, except perhaps as objects to study or be amused by. But these children, these nescreet, have become our teachers. Let us learn from them and appreciate what the children of the earth, as well as our own—" He looked now at Axel. "—have to offer." Thunderous applause again broke out.

"Let us honor these 'children', these nescreet, by

accepting them as equals and welcoming them into the Zanchee!"

Greg was overwhelmed by his emotions and the cheering that apparently was meant, at least in part, for him. Water welled within his eyes and made its way down his face in small globules as he stared out at the crowd. Their genuine warmth, even love, embraced them. He wasn't quite sure what the implications were of the Thermax's speech. But, right now, he didn't care. He just wanted to savor the moment.

Axelasome again raised his hands and the crowd quieted. "But today I face you not only as Thermax, but as a father...a very proud, and humble, parent. For it was my job, and the job of these master teachers to my right—" Axelasome waved his hand toward the group of eight robed Zanchee. "—to teach my son the ways of the Delions and of the Zanchee. We gave him knowledge, we refined his skills, we taught him our laws, and tried to teach him right from wrong. But we have become his pupils, as he has taught us about *sen*." To Greg, Axelasome's voice trembled with emotion, his last words triggering an ovation louder than any previous.

Axel's father stepped back. The lead robed figure stepped forward. As the Zanchee moved toward the center stage, something happened to Axel. It appeared as though Axel had suddenly put on a cat collar. That is, it appeared there was a cat wrapped around his neck. There was something furry there, and it was moving!

Greg almost lost it when the head of the cat moved. He could swear it was looking right at him, with a huge grin on its face. *Cheshire*? Greg thought.

"*Chermal*" came the mental reply.

The robed figure raised his arms, and all was quiet again. As he raised his arms, there was a bracelet, like ones he had seen on Axel and his father, only his glowed a bright, deep, vibrant purple. Greg looked at the other robed figures. They also had purple bracelets upon their right wrists as well, although the shades of purple were slightly different for each, as was the intensity with which they glowed. Could the color be a way of identification, or a symbol of rank, or both?

The robed figure began to speak. "The Seckchi is a sacred and honored ceremony among the Delions," he said, his deep voice surprisingly soft and somber. "It is usually observed only by a few friends and family." He smiled. "This is obviously not the case today. But this Seckchi is unusual, as was the Nemseck preceding it.

"For those among you not entirely familiar with the Delion custom of Nemseck—" Greg felt he was addressing the humans more than the non-Delion Zanchee. "—every Delion's Nemseck is different. The Nemseck is tailored to each individual's needs and abilities.

"In Axel's case, his task was simple—do the impossible…Including defying his own father. Axel took on this task because he knew his ultimate duty was to *sen.* With only his Mentiot, Chermal…" He waved at the cat-like creature who had suddenly moved from Axel's neck to sitting high on his haunches at Axel's feet, staring at the speaker.

"…Axel set out to do what he knew must be done but do it in a way that minimized transgressing Zanchee laws and customs. Facing a near impossible situation, Axel persevered until he found a way, with no help from myself, his father, or any of the Zanchee, to save a world and a sentient species." Thunderous applause broke out in the gallery. At least, to him, it appeared to be applause. Greg and his companions joined in enthusiastically.

The speaker paused for a minute, and then bowed his head slightly. The room again quieted. "As Nescian for Axel," he said, and as he did so he raised his right arm in front of him, with the elbow bent and the hand bent at the wrist toward his face. His left hand held onto the right elbow. The curves of the robes fell from around his extended right arm, revealing his bracelet that now strongly radiated a deep purple. "I declare candidate Axelarone worthy of Seckchi."

Greg almost started to applaud again, when he realized the room was solemnly quiet. He quickly refrained from any displays. It was as though the assemblage had transformed from a rally to a church service.

The Nescian turned and faced Axel, keeping his arm and hand in the same position. Axel, in turn, raised his right arm, holding it in a similar fashion.

The Nescian and Axel bowed their heads slightly at each other, tilting their heads to the left as they did. Axel took one-step forward, the Nescian took two, until they were face to face. The Nescian raised his arm slightly so his bracelet appeared to touch Axel's, although Greg wasn't completely sure, as he was behind Axel and could no longer see Axel's arm or bracelet.

After a moment, the Nescian stepped back. The two again bowed heads as before. The Nescian then turned and walked to the edge of the stage. The second robed figure then stepped forward and basically repeated what the Nescian had done. This process was repeated seven times, with each robed figure.

After the fourth robed figure had bowed and stepped back, Greg risked leaning slightly to his right, to try to catch a glimpse of Axel's face. He couldn't see it, but he caught a brief glimpse of his arm. The bracelet had turned bright red. Then the fifth robed one stepped forward.

When the final robed figure turned away, Axel's father stepped forward. He, too, went before his son. As Greg had seen the other robed figures do before, Axel's father first raised his arm to the crowd, bending the wrist so his fingers pointed toward his face, causing the bracelet to shine brightly toward the crowd. His left hand enveloped his right wrist. The outpouring of emotion from the crowd was palatable as the Thermax turned to face his son. He seemed to move in slow motion, though it was probably Greg's own imagination adding the Hollywood effects. Still, the tremendous pride the Thermax felt as he took two steps toward his son was apparent.

Greg did not need to look at Ashanti, nor did he have to be psychic, to know she had a river of tears streaming down her face, as did Tess and Becca. He knew, because his face too was moist. It was all he could do not to openly bawl when Axel's father bowed to his son and then raised his bracelet to touch Axel's. They held that position for a moment longer than any of the others, but that moment was eternal.

When Axel's father stepped back, there was an audible gasp. Greg wasn't sure why. But then Axel raised his right arm straight over his head. An ovation that paled those before erupted from the crowd. And now he could see why. Axel's bracelet shone a bright purple.

The ovation lasted several minutes, until Axel's father turned again to face the crowd. Immediately, Axel dropped his right hand, and the giant room grew still. Greg was aware of the great joy and pride poorly concealed in Axel's father's face when he turned and faced the crowd.

"I speak now as a proud father and not as Thermax when I say my son has brought me great joy. The parents among you can understand the pride I feel at this moment, as my son went from innocent student to teacher, from rascal to leader, from my son to the son of all Zanchee. Axel has accomplished what no one before him has done, going straight from being a nescreet to becoming a master." Another long and loud ovation.

After a long moment, Axelasome raised his hand again, silencing the crowd. "We come here, however, not only to honor our own—" Axel's father motioned toward his son. "—but to expand our number." He then turned to face the humans.

"Jeffrey Daniel Miller, will you please step forward," the Thermax said to the group.

A very surprised and completely bewildered-looking Jeff stepped toward the center of the stage. And as he did, it really sank in his best friend was no longer the Jeff Miller he had grown up with or traded Astroloid cards. The Jeff Miller Greg had known only a week ago could have never been able to keep his cool in a moment such as what was happening. Even though Jeff had sung solo before sizeable audiences in school. If it had been him, Greg would have been jelly under these circumstances. Who wouldn't? It was more than the lack of glasses distinguishing this Jeff Miller from the old. This one walked with confidence, maturity, and power. His head held high, shoulders and back straight. There was no emotional betrayal in him as he stepped forward.

"Please extend your right arm," Axel's father directed.

Jeff did so. The Thermax then brought up both his hands and wrapped them around Jeff's wrist. The room was eerily quiet.

When the Thermax released his grip, there was a bracelet around Jeff's wrist, like the one worn by Axel and the other Zanchee, glowing green. "Jeffrey Daniel Miller, as Thermax of the Yonzelt Zanchee fleet, I hereby welcome you as a member-candidate to the Zanchee."

Wild applause erupted both on and off stage as Greg and his friends joined in the clapping. The humans found themselves quite embarrassed, however, for the rest of the crowd had suddenly stopped cheering, while the humans had continued applauding. Quickly realizing their faux pas, the four humans stopped. Immediately he understood why the crowd had fallen silent. The Nescian had once again moved to the center stage.

Looking directly at Axel, the cloaked figure asked of him, "*Master* Axelarone, do you deem the candidate worthy?"

The significance of the question, as well as the title, still hadn't sunk in for Greg, as Axel looked down to his cat before stepping forward and saying, "I do." It was strange Axel brought his pet to the ceremony. There was also something really weird about that cat.

"Very well," the Nescian said, then nodded to Axel and stepped back.

Axel moved forward with a gait belying his youth but reflecting his newfound status. As Greg had seen the Nescian doing, Axel stood in front of the stunned Jeff. Facing the crowd, he raised his right arm, bearing the now-brightly-glowing purple band, with his left hand holding his extended elbow. Holding the position for only a few short moments, he then slowly turned to face Jeff, arms still in the same position.

Jeff, having witnessed Axel's ceremony, did his best to echo his friend's movements. He raised his right arm, whose green band now glowed as brilliantly as Axel's, cocking his hand so it pointed toward his face and grabbing his right elbow with his left hand, left elbow facing downward. Axel bowed his head to Jeff, and Jeff returned the gesture.

Axel then stepped forward until he was only a couple feet from Jeff. He then raised his right arm slightly. Jeff, in turn, raised and extended his right arm so his bracelet touched Axel's. As he did so, Jeff's entire arm appeared to glow as his bracelet changed hues, becoming darker, more brownish color.

Axel then stepped back and bowed his head again to Jeff, which Jeff returned.

The Nescian was next to step forward. He repeated the ritual. As their bracelets touched, Jeff's became redder.

The Thermax was the next to step forward, repeating the same steps as those who had preceded. When the Thermax stepped back, Jeff's bracelet was now a brilliant red.

Jeff was lost for a second, still holding his arm in

front of him. Then, Axel gave him a slight nod, and Jeff realized what he was supposed to do. As though he were punching through a concrete ceiling, Jeff thrust his right hand forcefully upward. And with that gesture, Jeff Miller, seventeen-year-old Texas choirboy, became a nescrot and the first human Zanchee.

The applause was deafening.

Epilogue

*Edwards AFB*

Doug Stanton stared at the table in front of him. In his mind, he replayed again and again the verbal report he gave in the debriefing. He had to admit it didn't make sense. While the events of three hours ago were still firmly engraved in his mind, it all seemed like a surreal dream.

The door opened and Colonel Stankowski walked in, carrying with him a couple folders.

"I think we need to go over this again," he said, as he sat at the opposite end of the table from Doug. They were in a small interview room, much like the ones found in countless police stations across the country. The room itself was plain, except for cameras in every corner of the ceiling and a large window containing a one-way mirror. On the other side of the mirror was a panel of experts judging every movement he made and every sound he uttered. Doug himself was wired with the latest in lie-detecting technology.

"We have just received some new information that may interest you," the Colonel began. "Those kids you said you saw in the truck…"

"They were there!"

"Well, they were just reported being found in

Texas, at a convenience store in McKinney, outside of Dallas and not too far from their homes. How can you explain that? It's almost 1,200 miles from San Bernardino to McKinney, yet these kids made it in under three hours. Even if they had a private jet standing by, that would be awfully hard to pull off."

"What do the kids say?"

"They claim they don't remember how they got there. No one saw them arrive. Your buddies at the FBI are investigating."

The Colonel's face betrayed no emotion.

"Are you saying I made this whole thing up? Why?"

"You've got to admit this is awfully hard to believe."

Doug said nothing. The Colonel was right. It was hard to believe. Doug, himself, wouldn't believe it if he hadn't experienced it himself.

The Colonel sat silent for a moment, apparently waiting to see how Doug reacted. But Doug had sat too many times on the other side of the table. He knew the rule, too—"He who speaks first, loses." Doug was quiet as well. He didn't want to lose.

After a very pregnant pause, the Colonel spoke first. "Okay, let's go over how you disarmed the warhead one more time."

"I told you, I didn't. The kid did."

"Yeah, you told us how he was holding the first trigger device in his hands. We found that on the floor next to the warhead."

Doug nodded. "I don't know how he did it. I never saw him do anything. The next thing I know, he's holding the explosive in his hands. He looked almost as surprised as I was."

"Okay, okay. Let's say I give you that one. That doesn't explain how you disarmed the second trigger."

"Second trigger?" Now Doug was totally confused.

"Yes. Raheim had redundant systems for everything on that warhead, including a second explosive trigger. We found it undamaged. Our experts have no explanation as to why it failed to go off. We are hoping you can tell us."

Doug Stanton just stared at him.

\*\*\*\*

*Dallas*
*Sixteen Days Later*

The auditorium was overflowing. The Fall Festival had been moved to the 3,000 seat McFarlin Auditorium at SMU because of the sudden interest in tonight's performance. The fact two of the stars recently made national news due to their week-long kidnapping ordeal may have had something to do with it. The added intrigue came from their kidnappers being involved in a massive terrorist plot while also being part of an international drug ring made tonight's show very special indeed. No longer was this a simple show, important only to the students from a suburban high school and witnessed by parents and a few other members of the community. Now this had become an event of national importance. So great had been the interest, the festival had to be postponed two weeks to plan for a larger, then a still larger auditorium to accommodate all the requests for tickets. Even then, the college auditorium was woefully inadequate to meet the demand. And it wasn't only the local press covering it. All the national networks were represented, and one or two international ones, Doug noted.

The six teens involved were introduced at the beginning of the show, to a long and enthusiastic ovation. The fact their kidnappers had been captured and the six teens returned safely brought tremendous joy to a community who had suffered great agony with their extended disappearance. Strangely, the fact many of the kidnappers insisted there were only three kids taken and not six, did not seem to be deemed very newsworthy, as it was assumed with so many people involved, the kidnappers simply were confused, or two different teams were involved.

It also made a great human-interest story one of the teens, whose brother had been one of the kidnappers, was now living with two of the victims, Jeff and Becca Miller. Indeed, almost everything about the unusual kidnapping and rescue was fascinating to the public—and particularly to one bewildered FBI agent.

For his part, Doug was glad there were several other witnesses at It's Your Fault Gas & Grill who saw the kids come in on the truck, somewhat vindicating him. The official story was the kids were held in the second truck by the Arabs. Their role in the disarming of the weapon was never made public, for obvious reasons. Instead, the hero's mantle was given to a very reluctant FBI agent. Doug was glad his moment in the national spotlight was brief. Celebrity status was not his cup of tea. As it was, he had to disguise his appearance somewhat to avoid being recognized.

Unfortunately, his newfound celebrity status would no doubt impact his career. He might never do any more undercover or surveillance work, for example.

Because none of the teens could explain how they

got from ground zero to McKinney, Texas in three hours made the story more intriguing. Nor could, or would the teens, nor anyone else, provide information on who brought them to McKinney. Doug, for his part, felt the teens were not being exactly truthful in their explanations—but they were consistent, making it difficult to guess what the truth might be. The reigning theories were they were brought by private jet by an anonymous benefactor, whom the kids were protecting, or the government brought them, interviewing them on the trip back about their terrorist-kidnappers. The latter made the most sense, although no one he knew in the government claimed any knowledge. Doug would love to investigate the mystery further. Something told him he would, indeed, someday learn the whole story.

****

Mr. Morris was nervous as can be. But he couldn't show it, or the entire choir would fall to pieces. He was incredibly thankful his two stars, the ones the media were here to see, were as calm as a mountain lake on a windless day. Their quiet confidence was infectious and helped keep everyone else focused. He was also thankful the bright stage lights kept the kids from seeing the audience—and how many people were really there to see them. Not to mention all the TV cameras.

They had to make a few minor adjustments to the performance to accommodate the heightened interest. Thankfully, at least to his thinking, Jeff's voice was stronger than ever—no hint of the fateful squeak that once plagued him. In fact, his voice was richer and finer. What was particularly impressive to him was Jeff and Tess sounded so much better together—despite not practicing together the week they were gone. So beautiful was the new sound, Mr. Morris moved their duet to be the final one of the evening—a fitting tribute to his two talented and brave performers.

\*\*\*\*

Jeff was happy to find Axel there to see his performance. He was happier—and surprised—to find Axel's parents and sister also in the audience. He couldn't see them, as they were sitting toward the back and only the first few rows were visible through the bright glare of the spotlights. But Jeff perceived them as clearly as though they stood a few feet from him.

Tess surprised him by wanting to continue to do the Fall Festival. He was sure all the media attention would cause her to want to pull out. He certainly would have understood. As for himself, it really didn't matter that much anymore. Of course, he would perform if Tess was willing…but if she hadn't wanted to, well he really wouldn't have missed it. He had other more important things on his mind. Besides, the Festival would be good for him. It kept him "grounded" and focused on still being a seventeen-year-old teenager. A role he had to continue to play, at least for a while. After all, he may be a nescrot and may have saved the world…but he hadn't graduated from high school and still couldn't vote!

Much to their surprise, and pure delight, Jeff and Tess discovered their newfound psychic connection had a profound effect on their singing together. It was as though they were taking their harmony to a new level. The result was indescribably beautiful to hear.

\*\*\*\*

Doug wasn't completely sure why he was there. He had no "official" reason to be in the audience. After all, the case was closed. All the bad guys had been caught, save for Krenchenko and Farcie, and Doug had been given a much-needed three weeks off as his reward. So how was he spending his free time? By returning to Dallas to stand in the back of a packed, overheated auditorium to watch some high school choir perform. He wasn't related to any of the performers. And he had to pull a lot of strings just to be allowed to stand in the back.

Yet he had a connection with two of these performers no one else, outside of four other teens in the audience, could claim. These kids were special. Very special. And he wanted to learn more about them.

To his surprise, the music was good. Quite good. Doug found himself fully enjoying the concert, as did the audience.

Then it was time for the finale, which was a duet featuring his two "special" friends.

The audience sat in expectant silence, which became almost deafening when the song began. For when the two teens started singing, not a single extraneous noise could be heard. So powerful, so beautiful were the voices that everyone, including one notably tone-deaf FBI agent, simply sat in total awe.

When the last note, which was held seemingly forever, finally died out, the auditorium was eerily quiet. No one had wanted the song to end. Then the audience rose as one as all the emotion dwelling in the hearts of the parents and the rest of the audience for the past two weeks—the fear, the sadness, then the utter joy—swelled to the surface along with enthusiastic appreciation of the wonderful performance. Doug had never heard the likes of the applause that evening.

When the long ovation finally ended, the performers had all left the stage, and the lights in the auditorium were turned up, the audience still sat as though unwilling to admit the performance was over...or still recovering from the emotions it had wrought.

Finally, one by one, they got up and began filing out. Doug, too, had stood in almost a trance-like state before realizing the show was over and it was time to leave.

As he made his way toward the exit, something caught his attention. He turned as a couple with their son and daughter made their way out. There was something decidedly different about the family, but he could not figure out what it was. Then, as they got closer, Doug noted the son was holding a cat! All four also wore a bracelet identical, except for the color, as the one worn by Jeff.

Doug could not take his eyes off this strange scene. Why would anyone bring a cat to a concert? Then he looked closer at the cat and noted that it was, without a doubt, the ugliest cat he had ever seen in his life.

But the strangest thing of all to Doug was, as the pair made their way past him, he swore the boy and the weird cat both looked him straight in the eye...and winked!

### A word about the author...

John grew up in the Kansas City area before attending the University of Kansas where he received his bachelor's and master's in psychology. He left while working on his dissertation to open his first small business, meaning to return to get his PhD. But fate intervened and he went on to operate several small businesses before becoming a business consultant.

He always loved writing but could never find the time. In 2016, he was diagnosed with Stage IV cancer and given only a few months to live. The successful fight to survive caused a re-prioritizing of his life. In 2019 he decided to commit himself to his true love and become a full-time writer.

John is very happily married to Holly and has two grown children, Matthew and Elizabeth.

http://authorjohnselby.com

Thank you for purchasing
this publication of The Wild Rose Press, Inc.

For questions or more information
contact us at
info@thewildrosepress.com.

The Wild Rose Press, Inc.
www.thewildrosepress.com